D0552680

The Girl
in the
Letter

EMILY GUNNIS

REVIEW

Copyright © 2018 Emily Gunnis

The right of Emily Gunnis to be identified as the Author of
the Work has been asserted by her in accordance with the
Copyright, Designs and Patents Act 1988.

First published in Great Britain in 2018
by HEADLINE REVIEW
An imprint of HEADLINE PUBLISHING GROUP

First published in paperback in 2019
by HEADLINE REVIEW
An imprint of HEADLINE PUBLISHING GROUP

2

Apart from any use permitted under UK copyright law, this publication may
only be reproduced, stored, or transmitted, in any form, or by any means,
with prior permission in writing of the publishers or, in the case of reprographic production,
in accordance with the terms of licences issued by the Copyright Licensing Agency.

All characters in this publication are fictitious and any resemblance
to real persons, living or dead, is purely coincidental.

Cataloguing in Publication Data is available from the British Library

Edna St. Vincent Millay, 'First Fig', 1920
Mary Elizabeth Frye, 'Do Not Stand at My Grave and Weep', 1932

ISBN 978 1 4722 5510 5

Typeset in 12.5/14.75 pt Adobe Garamond by Jouve (UK), Milton Keynes

Printed and bound in Great Britain by Clays Ltd, Elcograf S.p.A.

Headline's policy is to use papers that are natural, renewable and recyclable
products and made from wood grown in well-managed forests and other
controlled sources. The logging and manufacturing processes are expected to
conform to the environmental regulations of the country of origin.

HEADLINE PUBLISHING GROUP
An Hachette UK Company
Carmelite House
50 Victoria Embankment
London EC4Y 0DZ

www.headline.co.uk
www.hachette.co.uk

For Mummy

I miss our walks, our talks, your love of life. But you
always said, don't cry, make notes.
So, I promise to try. . .

———

My candle burns at both ends;
It will not last the night;
But, ah, my foes, and, oh, my friends—
It gives a lovely light!

Edna St. Vincent Millay, 'First Fig'

Prologue

Friday 13 February 1959

My darling Elvira,

I do not know where to begin.

You are just a little girl, and it is so hard to explain in words that you will understand why I am choosing to leave this life, and you, behind. You are my daughter, if not by blood then in my heart, and it breaks to know that what I am about to do will be adding to the mountain of hurt and pain you have had to endure in the eight long years of your short life.

Ivy paused, trying to compose herself so that the pen in her hand would stop shaking enough for her to write. She looked around the large drying room where she had hidden herself. From the ceiling hung huge racks crammed with sheets and towels meticulously washed by the cracked and swollen hands of the pregnant girls in St Margaret's laundry, now ready to go down to the ironing room and out to the oblivious waiting world. She looked back down to the crumpled piece of paper on the floor in front of her.

Were it not for you, Elvira, I would have given up the fight to stay in this world much sooner. Ever since they took Rose away from me, I can find no joy in living. A mother cannot forget

1

her baby any more than a baby can forget her mother. And I can tell you that if your mother were alive, she would be thinking of you every minute of every day.

When you escape from this place — and you will, my darling — you must look for her. In the sunsets, and the flowers, and in anything that makes you smile that beautiful smile of yours. For she is in the very air you breathe, filling your lungs, giving your body what it needs to survive, to grow strong and to live life to the full. You were loved, Elvi, every minute of every day that you were growing inside your mother's tummy. You must believe that, and take it with you.

She tensed and stopped momentarily as footsteps clattered above her. She was aware that her breathing had quickened with her heart rate, and underneath her brown overalls she could feel a film of sweat forming all over her body. She knew she didn't have long before Sister Angelica returned, slamming shut the only window in her day when she wasn't being watched. She looked down at her scrawled letter, Elvira's beautiful face flashing into her mind's eye, and fought back the tears as she pictured her reading it, her dark brown eyes wide, her pale fingers trembling as she struggled to take the words in.

By now, you will have in your hands the key I enclose with this letter. It is the key to the tunnels and your freedom. I will distract Sister Faith as best I can, but you don't have long. As soon as the house alarm goes off, Sister Faith will leave the ironing room and you must go. Immediately. Unlock the door to the tunnel at the end of the room, go down the steps, turn right and out through the graveyard. Run to the outhouse and don't look back.

She underlined the words so hard that her pen pierced a hole in the paper.

I'm so sorry I couldn't tell you face to face, but I feared you would be upset and would give us away. When I came to you last night, I thought they were letting me go home, but they are not, they have other plans for me, so I am using my wings to leave St Margaret's another way, and this will be your chance to escape. You must hide until Sunday morning, the day after tomorrow, so try and take a blanket with you if you can. Stay out of sight.

Ivy bit down hard on her lip until the metallic taste of blood filled her mouth. The memory of breaking into Mother Carlin's office at dawn was still raw, the anticipation of finding her baby's file turning to shock as she discovered no trace of Rose's whereabouts. Instead, the file contained six letters. One was to a local psychiatric unit, the word 'Copy' stamped in the corner, recommending she be admitted immediately; the other five had been written by Ivy herself, begging Alistair to come to St Margaret's and fetch her and their baby. A rubber band was wrapped tightly around these letters, *Return to sender* written in Alistair's scrawl across every one.

She had walked over to the tiny window of the dark, hellish room where she had suffered so much pain and watched the sunrise, knowing it would be her last. Then she had slotted Alistair's letters into an envelope from Mother Carlin's desk, scribbled her mother's address on it and hidden it in the post tray before creeping back up the stairs to her bed.

Without any hope of freedom, or of finding Rose, I no longer have the strength to go on. But Elvira, you can. Your file told me that you have a twin sister named Kitty, who probably has no idea you exist, and that your family name is Cannon. They live in Preston, so they will attend church here every Sunday. Wait in the outhouse until you hear the bells and the villagers begin arriving for church, then hide in the graveyard until you see your twin. No doubt you will recognise her, although she will be dressed a little differently to you. Try and get her attention without anyone seeing. She will help you.

Don't be afraid to escape and live your life full of hope. Look for the good in everyone, Elvira, and be kind.

I love you and I will be watching you and holding your hand for ever. Now run, my darling. RUN.

Ivy XXX

Ivy started as the lock to the drying room where she and Elvira had spent so many hours together clicked suddenly and Sister Angelica burst through the door. She glared at Ivy, her squinting grey eyes hidden behind wire-framed glasses that were propped up by her bulbous nose. Ivy hurriedly pushed herself up and stuffed the note into the pocket of her overalls. She looked down so as not to catch the nun's eye.

'Aren't you finished yet?' Sister Angelica snapped.

'Yes, Sister,' said Ivy. 'Sister Faith said I could have some TCP.' She buried her trembling hands in her pockets.

'What for?'

She could feel Sister Angelica's eyes burning into her. 'Some of the children have bad mouth ulcers and it's making it hard for them to eat.'

4

'Those children are of no concern to you,' Sister Angelica replied angrily. 'They are lucky to have a roof over their heads.'

Ivy pictured the rows of babies lying in their cots, staring into the distance, having long since given up crying.

Sister Angelica continued. 'Fetching TCP means I have to go all the way to the storeroom, and Mother Carlin's dinner tray is due for collection. Do you not think I have enough to do?'

Ivy paused. 'I just want to help them a little, Sister. Isn't that best for everyone?'

Sister Angelica glared at her, the hairs protruding from the mole on her chin twitching slightly. 'You will find that hard where you're going.'

Ivy felt adrenaline flooding through her body as Sister Angelica turned to walk back out of the room, reaching for her keys to lock the door behind her. Lifting her shaking hands, she took a deep breath and lunged forward, grabbing the nun's tunic and pulling it as hard as she could. Sister Angelica let out a gasp, losing her balance and falling to the ground with a thud. Ivy straddled her and put one hand over her mouth, wrestling with the keys on her belt until they finally came free. Then, as Sister Angelica opened her mouth to scream, she slapped her hard across the face, stunning her into silence.

Panting heavily, with fear and adrenaline making her heart hurt, Ivy pulled herself up, ran through the door and slammed it shut. Her hands were shaking so violently, it was a struggle to find the right key, but she managed to fit it into the lock and turn it just as Sister Angelica rattled the handle, trying to force the door open.

She stood for a moment, gasping deep breaths. Then she unhooked the large brass key Elvira needed to get into the tunnels and wrapped her note around it. She heaved open the iron door to the laundry chute and kissed the note before sending it down to Elvira, pressing the buzzer to let her know it was there. She pictured the little girl waiting patiently for the dry laundry as she did at the end of every day. A wave of emotion crashed over her and she felt her legs buckling. Leaning forward, she let out a cry.

Sister Angelica began to scream and hammer on the door, and with one last look back down the corridor that led to the ironing room and Elvira, Ivy turned away, breaking into a run. She passed the heavy oak front door. She had the keys to it now, but it led only to a high brick wall topped with barbed wire that she had neither the strength nor the heart to climb over.

Memories of her arrival all those months ago came flooding back. She could see herself ringing the heavy bell at the gate, her large stomach making it awkward to lug her suitcase behind Sister Mary Francis along the driveway, hesitating before she crossed the threshold to St Margaret's for the first time. Hurrying up the creaking stairs two at a time, she turned as she reached the top and pictured herself screaming at the girl she once was, telling her to run away and never look back.

As she crept along the landing, she could hear the murmur of voices coming towards her and broke into a run, heading for the door at the foot of the dormitory steps. The house was deathly quiet, as all the other girls were at dinner, eating in silence, any talk forbidden. Only the cries of the babies in the nursery echoed through the house. Soon, though, Mother Carlin would know she was gone, and the whole building would be alerted.

She reached the door of the dormitory and ran between the rows of beds just as the piercing alarm bell began to ring. As she reached the window, Sister Faith appeared at the end of the room. Despite her fear, Ivy smiled to herself. If Sister Faith was with her, that meant she was not with Elvira. She could hear Mother Carlin shouting from the stairway.

'Stop her, Sister, quickly!'

Ivy pulled herself up onto the ledge and, using Sister Angelica's keys, opened the window. She pictured Elvira running through the tunnels and out into the freedom of the night. Then, just as Sister Faith reached her and grabbed for her overalls, she stretched out her arms and jumped.

Chapter One

Saturday 4 February 2017

'Have you cracked it yet?'

Sam pulled on the handbrake of her battered Vauxhall Nova, wishing it was a noose around her news editor's neck.

'No, not yet. I've only just arrived. I had to drive all the way from Kent, remember?'

'Who else is there?' barked Murray down the phone.

Sam craned her neck to see the usual suspects standing in the drizzling rain outside a row of pretty terraced cottages set back from the road in perfectly manicured gardens. 'Um, Jonesey, King . . . and Jim's at the door now. Why am I even here if Jim's already on the case?' She watched one of Southern News Agency's most experienced hacks trying to get his foot through the door. 'Won't he think I'm treading on his toes?'

'I thought this one might need a woman's touch,' said Murray.

Sam glanced at her watch. It was 4 p.m. – close to cut-off time for the national press going to print – and she could picture the scene in the office now. Murray on his mobile, shouting orders at everyone whilst admiring his reflection in the glass of the framed covers of Southern News scoops. Koop would be typing, pulling anxiously at his unkempt hair, surrounded by cold cups of coffee and wilted sandwiches, while Jen chewed on her Nicorette gum and

9

frantically made calls to contacts trying to fill in gaps in her copy. After he'd hung up on her, Murray would be straight on the phone to the *Mirror* or the *Sun*, lying through his teeth and telling them Sam was already on the case and to hold the press for her.

'I'm really not sure I'm the right person for this,' she said, studying her reflection in the rear-view mirror and catching sight of her grandmother's birthday flowers wilting on the back seat. She was supposed to have been at Nana's flat an hour ago to take over with Emma and cook Nana her birthday dinner.

'Well, the cream of the bunch will have already left for the Press Awards tonight. You'll have to do it.'

'Great. Good to know I'm considered the dregs of this agency,' mumbled Sam.

'Call me when you've got something.' Murray hung up.

'Wanker.' Sam threw her battered phone onto the seat next to her. She was pretty sure that the hours she'd worked that day on her tiny salary amounted to slave labour, and now she was expected to pull off a death knock.

She pressed her fingers into her eyes, massaging the sockets. She'd thought she knew what tiredness was before she became a mother. People lied to new parents, telling you to hang in there, that babies slept at six weeks, which was patently a lie. Then it became once they were weaned, then when they were a year old. Emma was four now, and it was still a miracle if she slept through. Before, Sam would complain of tiredness after getting six hours' sleep instead of eight, dragging herself into work in a haze of hangover after a night out clubbing. Now, at the grand age of twenty-five, she felt like an elderly lady; the four years of accumulated sleep deprivation had infected every muscle in her body, altering her brain and dragging her down so that some days she could barely form a sentence. On Ben's days with Emma, she could at least sleep until seven. But now that he had whittled that down to two days a week, on the pretext of needing more time to job-hunt, she had to be up at six most days to get herself and her daughter up and out of the door in time for nursery drop-off.

She sighed as she watched a dejected Jim walk back down the uneven stone pathway to join the other reporters under a golf umbrella. She knew the game, knew door-stepping was a necessary evil of her trade, but it was the worst part of being a reporter. Though she liked every one of the hapless gaggle standing at the end of this poor woman's pathway, they always looked to her like vultures circling their stricken prey.

She adjusted the mirror, pulled out her make-up bag and assessed how much of her face was salvageable. She would need a trowel of foundation to fill in the scowl-induced dent in the middle of her brow. As she dabbed at it, she closed her eyes and images of the fight she'd had with Ben the night before rushed back. It was always tense when she collected Emma from Ben's flat, the two of them trying not to snipe at each other in front of their daughter, but yesterday hadn't gone well. The fight had been a bad one, she knew that much, but as usual the exchange of insults had become a blur that had ended with them shouting so loudly they'd made Emma cry. Sam hated herself for dragging Emma into their arguments, and hated Ben for not trying harder to hide his disdain for her.

Recoiling at the sight of her frizzy hair, she reached for the portable tongs in her bag. In between getting Emma

11

dressed and pouring breakfast down them both, she had little time for pampering in the mornings. Her red corkscrew curls were usually scraped back from her face, and the five minutes she had spare were given to blow-drying her heavy fringe. Heels were her uniform, and on her wages, eBay was her best friend. Days never went right without Louboutin or Dior to prop her up in a man's world, and she often found the pack sniggering at her as she made her way across muddy fields or flooded car parks in killer heels.

'Hey, Sam!' called Fred as he turned and spotted her, breaking free from the pack and tripping on the edge of a paving stone in his rush to get to her. He laughed in embarrassment, pushing his floppy fringe back and adopting the lovesick gaze he usually reserved for her.

'Hey, yourself. How long have you been here?' Sam pulled the passenger seat forward to grab her coat, bag and Nana's flowers from the back seat.

'Not long. It's my day off and I was rock-climbing in Tunbridge Wells so I've only just got here.' Fred's waterproof waxed jacket made him look like he'd just come from a pheasant shoot, Sam thought, pulling her black mac tightly around her.

'Why has Murray called you in on your day off? That's not fair,' she said, checking her phone as she walked.

'I know, I was a bit gutted. The friction was sick,' said Fred, smiling.

'You were sick? Oh dear.' Sam moved away slightly.

'No, it was good; sick is good,' said Fred, embarrassed.

'Sick is never good when you've got a four-year-old. How long have the others been here?' Sam asked as they approached the pack, huddled in a group.

'Hours. She's a tough one; we've all tried. The *Guardian* and *Independent* have been and gone too. Don't think even you can crack this one, Samantha,' said Fred in the public-school accent that earned him merciless teasing from the troops at Southern News.

Sam smiled back at him. At twenty-three, Fred was only two years younger than her, but as a commitment-free, fresh-faced graduate full of heroic ideals, he seemed part of another generation. It was obvious to most at Southern News that he had a huge crush on Sam. Despite the fact that he was tall, good-looking and accidentally amusing, with an endless supply of blue suede shoes and rainbow-coloured glasses, she found it hard to take him seriously. He was obsessed with climbing, and as far as she could gather spent every weekend scaling mountains and then getting drunk with his friends. She had no idea why he was interested in her. She was an exhausted, joyless grump whose greatest fantasy in the bed-room was eight hours' uninterrupted sleep.

They reached the back of the press pack. 'I'm not sure why Murray's sent you,' Jim called over his shoulder at Sam. Sam smiled politely at the Southern News old-timer, who found it hard to hide the fact that he thought she should be back at the office making tea.

'Me neither, Jim! Am I passable?' she said, turning to Fred.

Fred flushed slightly. 'Yes, definitely. Look out for the old witch next door,' he added hurriedly, keen to change the subject. 'She looks like she's going to attack us all with her Zimmer frame.'

All eyes were on Sam as she walked past the pack and down the path, clutching the bouquet to her chest like a terrified bride. As she reached the front door, she caught

13

sight of an elderly lady at the window of the house next door. She had her net curtains pulled back and was staring intently. Fred was right, she did look like a witch. She was wild-eyed, her long grey hair loose around her shoulders and her bony fingers white from gripping the curtain so hard. Sam took a deep breath and pressed the bell.

It was a good two minutes before Jane Connors opened the door, ashen-faced.

'I'm so sorry to bother you at this difficult time.' Sam looked directly into the woman's reddened eyes. 'My name is Samantha, I represent Southern News. We wanted to offer our sincere condolences—'

'Can't you just leave us alone?' the woman snapped. 'As if this isn't hard enough. Why won't you all just go away?'

'I'm so sorry for your loss, Mrs Connors.'

'You're not sorry! If you were sorry, you wouldn't do this . . . at the worst time in our lives.' Her voice trembled. 'We just want to be left in peace. You should all be ashamed of yourselves.'

Sam waited for the right words to come, then hung her head. The woman was right. She should be ashamed, and she was.

'Mrs Connors, I hate this part of my job. I wish I didn't have to do it. But I've learnt from experience that sometimes people wish to pay tribute to their loved ones. They want to talk to someone who can tell the world their story. In your case, you could talk about how brave your father was trying to save your son.'

Tears sprang into the woman's eyes as she moved to close the door. 'Don't talk about them like you knew them. You don't know anything about them.'

14

'No, I don't, but unfortunately it's my job to find out. All these reporters out here, myself included, have very tough bosses who won't let us go home to our families until you speak to one of us.'

'And if I refuse?' Mrs Connors peered round the half-closed door.

'They'll talk to other members of your family, or local shopkeepers, or write features based on potentially inaccurate information from well-meaning neighbours.' Sam paused. 'That would be a lasting memory for readers that you might find even more upsetting than all this in years to come.'

The woman was looking at the ground now, her shoulders sagging. She was broken. Sam hated herself.

'These are for you.' She laid the flowers on the doorstep. 'Well, they were actually for my grandmother – it's her birthday today – but she'd want you to have them. Please accept my sincere apologies again for intruding. That white Nova is my car, and this is my card. I'll wait for half an hour and then I'll go. I won't bother you again.' She started to make her way back down the cobbled pathway, hoping she wouldn't trip in her heels in front of the bored pack.

'Would I get to check what you wrote first?' Mrs Connors' voice was faint.

Sam turned round. 'Absolutely. You can read every word before I send it off.' She smiled gently at the woman, who examined the sodden handkerchief squashed into her palm.

Sam had noticed that the elderly woman in the house next door was standing at her open door now, still staring. She must be in her nineties. What must it be like to be so old, to have lived through so much? The woman was almost bent double over her Zimmer frame, an age spot like a large bruise on her hand. Her heart-shaped face was pale apart from the dark red lipstick she wore.

'Well, I suppose you'd better come in then,' said Mrs Connors, pulling her door open wide.

Sam glanced back at the pack, then at the old lady, who had fixed her with her pale blue eyes. It wasn't uncommon for neighbours to become involved when the press were out in force, but their presence was usually accompanied by a great deal of swearing. She offered the woman a smile that wasn't returned, but as she turned to close the door behind her, she looked up and their eyes met.

Chapter Two

Saturday 4 February 2017

Kitty Cannon looked down at Kensington High Street from The Roof Gardens one hundred feet up. As she watched commuters scuttling home in the bitter February night, she leant forward over the balcony railings, took a deep breath and imagined jumping. The roar of air in her ears as she plunged forward, arms outstretched, head bowed, weightless at first, untouchable, then growing heavier as gravity sucked her down irreversibly. When she hit, the force would break every bone in her body and for several seconds she would lie twitching as the crowds gathered around her, gasping and gawping, clutching one another in disbelief.

What could be so bad, they'd say, for someone to do that to themselves? It's awful, so tragic.

Kitty imagined herself as she lay there, narrow trickles of blood making their way down her face, a small smile frozen on her lips, formed at the moment of her last breath, knowing that at last she would be free.

'Kitty?'

She stepped back and turned round to face her young assistant. Rachel stood two feet away, her neat blond bob framing the look of slight alarm in her green eyes. She was dressed from head to toe in black, apart from neon-pink heels and a skinny belt to match. Her pencil skirt and jacket fitted so closely around her narrow frame that they didn't move when she did. She had a clipboard in her hands, which her long fingers were clutching so tightly they had lost their colour.

'They're ready for you,' she said, turning towards the stairs to a function room Kitty knew to contain her production team and many of the stars of stage and screen she had interviewed over the twenty-year run of her talk show. She imagined the acoustics of the room, voices straining to be heard above the clashing cutlery and clinking glasses. Voices that would all fall silent as she walked in.

'Kitty, we should go,' said Rachel slightly nervously, standing at the top of the stairs. 'They'll be serving dinner soon and you wanted to say a few words.'

'I don't *want* to say a few words; I *have* to,' Kitty said, shifting from one leg to the other in an attempt to ease her already throbbing feet.

'Kitty, you look ravishing as always,' said a male voice from behind them, and both women turned to see Max Heston, the executive producer of every one of Kitty's shows. Tall and slim, he was dressed in a perfectly fitting blue suit and pink shirt; his clean-shaven face was as handsome as ever. The man didn't age, thought Kitty as he smiled broadly at her; he looked the same now as he had when they had first met over thirty years ago – better, in fact. She watched Rachel as Max walked towards them; the younger woman's cheeks flushed red, her head tilted slightly, and as he reached them, she lifted her hand and played with her blunt fringe to check it was perfectly straight. Max always had the effect of turning Rachel into a schoolgirl, and it annoyed Kitty intensely.

'Everything all right?' he said, in the tone he used to use

18

when Kitty was due on set. Knowing she was in need of propping up, he would dole out compliments and praise, easing her out of her awkwardness by making her laugh, knowing exactly how to settle her.

Except this evening he wasn't settling her; he was enraging her with his lack of attention. Since the last show of her previous series, his loyalty had unquestionably faltered. He had cancelled lunches with her at the last minute, ignored several phone calls, and not sent flowers or even a card when news of her retirement broke. She had sensed that the BBC executives were losing interest in her: there was no talk of a start date for the new series despite her agent putting in several calls to the commissioners. She had imagined that she would soon be called to a lunch to tell her that the next series would be her last, and it had been this suspicion that had prompted her to retire. She, not Max, would decide when it was time to go and make way for the younger, prettier broadcasters snapping at her heels. She had half expected him not to turn up to this dinner, but at the last minute he had called to accept, probably when he discovered the number of heavyweights attending.

'I think I'm getting one of my migraines. Where am I sitting again?' said Kitty, clutching the railing tightly as she walked carefully down the steps in her white Dior heels, the label from her new pink chiffon dress scratching at her neck. She caught sight of herself in the huge mirror hanging on the stairs and recoiled. She had been talked into the pink by a pushy young sales assistant in Jenny Packham. She had known instinctively it was too young for her, but had let the girl's much-needed flattery go to her head. Rachel, in contrast, looked effortlessly stunning, and walking next to her made Kitty feel like the spinster aunt at a wedding.

'Table One. As you requested, you're next to Jon Peters from BBC Publicity, and Sarah Wheeldon, head of development at Warner Brothers,' said Rachel, scuttling after her.

'I don't remember asking to sit next to Jon. He's a crashing bore,' Kitty snapped as Rachel nervously checked her paperwork.

The room was warmly lit with fairy lights and candles, and the white linen tablecloths acted as a backdrop to the huge arrangements of Kitty's favourite flowers: pink peonies.

'Where are you sitting, Rachel?' said Max, turning to her.

Rachel's cheeks flushed again as she looked up from the table plan. 'Oh, I'm not sure I'm eating. I think I'll be needed on standby,' she said, tearing her gaze away from Max and smiling at Kitty, who didn't catch her eye.

'Oh nonsense, I'm sure we can find you a seat on our table. I could introduce you to some people,' said Max.

As Rachel toyed with her fringe again, the first claps echoed around the room and slowly built to a thunder. The room was full of everyone who had helped Kitty get to the top: actors, editors, producers, agents, journalists, sports personalities. All here this evening, but soon they'd be gone: like Max, bored of her now she was no use to them. People who had crossed rooms to talk to her would look over her shoulder at events, cut short their conversation and make their escape to talk to the new, younger Kitty – whoever she was – congratulating themselves quietly as they walked away for making the effort with the old has-been.

Kitty smiled and glanced at Rachel. 'Will you go to my

apartment and get me my navy Jaeger dress and heels? I'm going to change after dinner.'

Rachel looked over at Max, her shoulders drooping, then turned and began to make her way through the tables towards the exit, her cheeks flushing with self-consciousness. As the applause finally died down, Kitty cleared her throat.

'Thank you all so much for coming. And thank you particularly to my long-suffering team for putting up with me for the past fifteen series: my beautiful assistant Rachel, who I could not cope without, and of course my executive producer Max Heston, who has been there since day one.'

Max smiled broadly at her. 'Careful what you say, Kit. I can still remember those *Dynasty*-inspired shoulder pads!'

Kitty laughed. 'Thank you for reminding us, and for throwing such a wonderful and undeserved dinner for me. As many of you know, I am not keen on being in the spotlight and prefer to be the one asking the questions. But I will say this. From the moment I saw John Freeman interviewing Gilbert Harding on *Face to Face* in 1960, I was hooked. Here was this larger-than-life personality – one of the few people who could make my father howl with laughter on *What's My Line?* – being reduced to tears as the man behind the mask came out. I was only ten years old but already acutely aware of the expectation piled upon me to play a part, and as I sat glued to the black-and-white television in my parents' lounge, it was an epiphany to realise I wasn't the only one.'

She looked around the room at the eyes fixed on her. 'People fascinate me. What you see is very rarely what is going on inside. And I have always tried to use television as a platform for the truth. Few of us have won an Oscar or

21

an Olympic gold medal, but most can relate to the struggles, on some level, our idols have been through. Struggles so profound and loneliness-inducing that they lit a fire in them that propelled them to success.'

She took a glass of champagne from a waiter standing next to her and smiled at him graciously.

'I would like to raise a glass to anyone brave enough to remove their mask and share their pain. I am immensely proud of those of my guests who made a difference and touched people's hearts – some of you achieved the best ratings in BBC history. I am of course sad to be climbing down from this wonderful platform, but I figured better that than to be pushed.'

'Never!' shouted a voice from the back, and Kitty smiled briefly.

'As a policeman's daughter growing up near Brighton, I certainly never dreamed I would be keeping company such as this. Thank you all so much for coming. Now please, eat, drink and behave appallingly.'

As the applause died down, Kitty turned to walk to her table, but paused when she heard the chink of a knife on a glass. Max stood up and smiled warmly around the room.

'I first met Kitty when I was a relative newbie, a recently promoted producer at the BBC, and a young, handsome buck if I recall.'

'And didn't you know it!' said Kitty, causing Max to frown.

'Now as all those who know Kitty will attest to, she has a disarming ability to convince you that what she wants is what you need. A colleague of mine in Light Entertainment back in 1985 asked if I could take on an intern who had written a letter every day for a year and was driving him insane.'

A ripple of laughter ran through the room before Max continued. 'I needed a researcher on *Parkinson*, so I agreed. The following day, this dark-haired, dark-eyed, stunningly intelligent girl turned up and took over.' He smiled over at Kitty, who raised her glass to him.

'Over the next few years, she came up rather fast on the inside lane, eventually pitching the idea of her own show, and "The Cannonball" was born. For those of you who aren't familiar with this term, it is Kitty's skill at relaxing her interviewee and then throwing in her own unique brand of grenade. I thought I knew research until I met Kitty. She knows things about her guests not even their spouses know. Overnight she became a national treasure and I am incredibly proud to have been part of this wonderful roller-coaster ride for over thirty years. Kitty, you are kind and generous and will never be forgotten. I am proud to call you a friend.'

As dinner was served, Kitty made her way through the tables, greeting guests as she went, flattering them with compliments on their appearance and with talk of their lesser-known achievements, as was her speciality.

As she reached her seat, she felt her phone buzz in her jacket pocket. Rachel was texting her to let her know she was five minutes away with her dress. Kitty swiftly tapped out a reply.

Don't worry about the dress, darling, I'm fine now. You must be shattered. Head home. Night night. Xx

Chapter Three

Saturday 4 February 2017

The lift was broken again. Sam climbed the steps of the White-hawk Estate stairwell two at a time and let herself into Nana's flat where she and Emma were staying after storming out during a particularly bad row with Ben two months before.

'Nana?' she whispered, catching her breath from the climb.

No reply. She crept along the brown swirly carpet into the lounge, where the gas fire was ablaze. Nana was asleep in the rocking chair with Emma curled up on the sofa under a blanket. The lighting was dim and the familiar smell of baking made Sam feel instantly at home. Pictures covered every inch of wall and windowsill: of Nana and Grandad on their camping adventures, Emma naked and building sandcastles with her grandad, but most were embarrassing photographs of a much younger Sam, in which she resembled a knobbly-kneed, toothless Mick Hucknall.

As she trod carefully over piles of crossword puzzle books and newspapers, abandoned cups of cold tea, colouring pencils and half-eaten rice cakes, her eye fell on a hand-written letter on the floor next to where Nana's arm hung, as if she had fallen asleep while she was reading it.

Something about the faded sloping writing and the aged cream paper immediately caught her attention, but as she leant in closer to read it, Nana opened her eyes and smiled. Sam smiled back at her, amused that Nana was wearing both pairs of glasses; one on the end of her nose and a second pair tucked neatly into her shoulder length hair – which, over the years, had faded from deep red to copper.

'Hello, darling, how are you?' Nana asked sleepily, her soft blue eyes creasing at the corners.

Sam felt a wave of comfort at the sight of her two favourite girls. Nana looked beautiful in jeans, a white shirt and a pink cashmere jumper that was a present from Grandad. She had, as usual, fallen asleep in front of her beloved Planet Earth box set. Though it was a cold February day, her softly lined face was flushed with colour. Nana had suffered with early onset arthritis since her early 50s, but her beaming smile disguised the fact that she had dragged her painful hip out in the freezing rain. Sam couldn't help thinking that, despite soldiering on and doing everything she could to be a wonderful grandmother to Emma, and substitute mother to her, the grief of losing Christine, her only daughter and Sam's mother, had taken a huge physical toll on her. Sam suddenly felt a rush of irritation at Ben.

'Oh Nana, you should have told me the lift was out of order again. I could have got some food in at least and brought it home.' She kissed them both on their foreheads.

'It's fine, darling, we had a lovely time. Emma helped me up the steps. She's such a good girl, Sammy; she's a credit to you and Ben, she really is.'

'Well, I'm sorry Ben offloaded her on to you. I'm not happy with him.'

'He had an interview,' said Nana, looking fondly at Emma.

'On a Saturday?' said Sam frowning.

Nana shrugged, 'He said something about it being for a restaurant chain. You should be excited for him.'

Sam shook her head. 'I just don't know what's going on with us any more . . . Is there a pot of tea on the go?' Nana nodded and Sam headed into the kitchen. 'Did she go off okay?' she called.

'Eventually, though it was quite a late one, I'm afraid. She wanted to wait up for you. I tried to persuade her to get into bed, but she fell asleep here. You must be exhausted, darling.'

Sam returned with two mugs, which she placed on the coffee table. 'I got an exclusive for one of the nationals, so I guess it was worth it.' She sank back onto the sofa next to Emma, resting her hand on the child's back as it rose and fell to the rhythm of her contented breathing.

'Well done, darling. Does that mean you'll finally get your name up in lights?' Nana shifted in her chair.

'No, the staff on the nationals get the bylines, but it all helps to build up my portfolio. I don't think you've ever missed a word I've written, have you?' Sam eyed the piles of newspapers around her.

'Of course not,' said Nana. 'I'm incredibly proud of you, my darling.'

'I'm glad someone is. Ben resents me so much he can barely look at me at the moment.' Sam took a gulp of tea.

'You'll be fine. It's difficult for you young girls, trying to juggle everything. It looked like your generation were being handed it all. I think you were just being handed a big pile of steaming shit.'

Sam let out the bellowing laugh Ben used to love, covering her mouth so as not to wake Emma.

'Anyway . . .' she said, reaching into her bag and handing Nana a small parcel and a huge box of chocolates. 'Happy birthday, Nana.'

'Oh, you naughty girl, what have you gone and done?' laughed Nana playfully, lifting out a silver charm bracelet with the number 60 and the initials S, A and E hanging from it along with a little silver teapot and a butterfly. Her eyes welled up. 'All my favourite things,' she said, blowing her granddaughter a kiss. 'That's beautiful, my darling, thank you.'

'I'm so sorry I wasn't here for your first birthday without Grandad. I'll take you out to dinner next week, I promise.'

'Don't be silly. You're here now, and I had Emma. Anyway, Grandad was here in spirit. Do you know what I found today?'

'What?' Sam reached for a slice of malt loaf.

'Emma dropped a toy down the side of our bed, and when I was retrieving it, I found a big dent in the wall.'

Sam frowned. 'Do I want to know about a big dent in the wall by yours and Grandad's bed?'

Nana let out a giggle. 'It was there because Grandad used to listen to the radio in the next room. He'd have it on so loud that I used to bang my walking stick against the bedroom wall.' She took a moment to compose herself before continuing. 'After he died, I used to put it on full volume just so I could pretend he was still there. You think you'd only miss the good bits about a person, but you miss everything.'

Sam smiled at Nana and blew her a kiss. Aged seventy-five when he died, Grandad was fifteen years older than Nana and when she had wandered into his antique shop one fateful, rainy Sunday afternoon in the autumn of 1980 it had been love at first sight. He had swept her off her feet and they had soon become inseparable, marrying at Brighton Registry Office only a year later. Grandad had proved to be Nana's rock throughout her life, not least when they received a phone call from Social Services to notify them that Christina, Nana's only child, from whom she was estranged, had died and that she had a twelve-year-old granddaughter they had never met. Grandad had embraced Sam as if she were his own, and the three of them had existed in their happy bubble until it had burst thirteen years later with the news that Grandad had inoperable lung cancer.

Nana wiped her eyes with Grandad's handkerchief.

'What's that?' said Sam, pointing to the letter on the floor. 'It looks like you were reading it before I came home.'

Nana glanced down. She seemed to pause for a moment before picking the pages up. 'It's a letter, darling.'

'Who is it from?'

'I'm not sure. I found it in Grandad's paperwork.' She eased herself out of her chair.

'It looks interesting. Can I see it?' said Sam.

Nana hesitated, glancing down at the pages in her hand, then passed them across.

'Are you okay, Nana?' said Sam.

'Fine darling, just tired,' replied Nana, walking away. 'Nature calls. Back in a min.'

Sam carefully smoothed out the two thin pieces of yellowing paper. They were both covered with perfectly spaced lines of neat and purposeful handwriting in black ink; the date at the top read *12 September 1956*.

My love,

I am fearful that I have not heard from you. All my anxieties have been confirmed. I am three months pregnant. It is too late for anything to be done; it is God's will that our baby be born.

'I think I'm going to have to go to bed, darling,' said Nana, returning to the room and snapping Sam back into the present. 'Emma looks so peaceful on the sofa; shall we leave her there?'

Sam glanced at her sleeping daughter and then back at the letter. 'It's from a young girl to her lover, telling him she's pregnant. She sounds really frightened.' Nana began tidying up around her. 'Why would Grandad have a letter like this?'

'I don't know, Sam. It was probably in one of the bits of antique furniture from his shop.'

Sam turned carefully to the second page and read the signature at the end. 'Are there any more letters from this girl Ivy, do you know?' she asked.

Nana paused for a minute, then turned away. 'I'm not sure, possibly.' She went out to the kitchen, and Sam heard the clatter of plates in the sink.

She continued to read. 'This poor girl, it sounds like her family are furious. They're planning to send her away to a place called St Margaret's to have her baby. I didn't know that happened here, did you? I thought it was just in Ireland. She sounds heartbroken. She's pleading for this person, whoever he is, to come back and marry her.'

'The fifties wasn't a good time to be an unmarried mother,' said Nana, sighing heavily. 'I must go to bed now, darling, sorry.'

'You don't think it was a letter to Grandad? I mean, obviously from before he met you?'

Nana glared at her. 'No, Samantha, I don't. Could I please not be interrogated about this now?'

Sam felt her cheeks flush red, 'Of course. I'm so sorry, I didn't mean to say that. I've got my work head on. I'm really sorry, Nana.'

'It's okay, darling, I'm just shattered. Grandad owned that antique shop for most of his life, you know, and he was always finding trinkets and letters from other people's lives stuffed in the drawers of desks and dressing tables; they were insights into people's lives that we pored over for hours sometimes. I was just missing him a lot today, so I buried myself in his paraphernalia.'

'Of course. I'm sorry again for working late and you having to look after Emma, and missing your birthday and having to stay with you . . . I'm just sorry for being born, basically.'

'Well, I'm not, I'd be lost without you.' Nana kissed both Sam and Emma, then disappeared down the corridor.

Sam picked Emma up and carried her into her room. She lowered her into the little bed and switched on the night light. 'I love you,' she whispered, before creeping out as quietly as possible.

Back in the living room, she fired up her laptop and brought up Google, typing in 'St Margaret's baby home Sussex'. A black-and-white picture of a Victorian Gothic mansion appeared on the screen. She examined the image for a while, noting two nuns in full habit in the grounds. The caption under the photograph read: *St Margaret's Convent for unmarried mothers, Preston, January 1969.*

As she read the history of the mother-and-baby home, and stories of women who over the years had tried to trace babies they were forced to give up for adoption, she found herself shocked to the core. Infertile couples, it seemed, had had nowhere to turn before IVF and were willing to pay a lot of money for a baby right up until the mid seventies, when St Margaret's closed its doors.

She thought of Emma curled up peacefully in the next room. The idea of anyone taking her by force seemed impossible. But as she pored over Ivy's letter and the accounts of dozens of women, it became clear to her that if she herself had fallen pregnant in 1956, as an unmarried woman she would have been thrown out on the street by her family, and St Margaret's would have been her only option.

She carried on scrolling through the results, and realised that the same headline kept reappearing. In the end, she gave it her full attention. MISSING PRIEST'S REMAINS FOUND ON BUILDING SITE OF FORMER MOTHER-AND-BABY HOME. She scanned the article, which had appeared in *The Times* just the previous week. *Court finds on Father Benjamin's death in derelict Victorian manor.*

Intrigued, she went back to the letter.

Dr Jacobson is going to speak to Father Benjamin at church on Sunday about sending me away soon. I think it will be a matter of days before it is decided. I do not know what to think or do. Please, my darling, I beg of you, I will make you happy and we will be a family. Please come for me quickly. I'm frightened for the future.

'Father Benjamin,' Sam said out loud, glancing back up to the article on her screen. She checked the byline and picked up her mobile.

'Hey, Carl, it's Sam. You on lates this week?' She could hear the late-shifters at work down the line, and the vague sound of Murray shouting in the background. No one could rest until the nationals were finally put to bed or Murray lost his voice – whichever happened first.

'Do you know who covered the inquest last week of a priest from Preston in Sussex called Father Benjamin? Went missing in 2000 and his remains were found in 2016 on a building site.' She poured herself more tea and curled her legs underneath her.

Carl was shouting to be heard over the clatter of night cleaners in the office. 'Give me a minute and I'll bring it up. Father Benjamin . . . rings a bell . . . Okay, here we go. Kevin covered it, it made all the nationals. Priest died at the site of a disused convent, St Margaret's. Verdict: accidental death. Slade Homes are pulling the place down and turning it into a posh development, but the inquest held it all up. Slade must have been pissed because I saw a local news feature saying it's already taken well over a decade to get the graveyard moved and planning through.'

'I wonder what Father Benjamin was doing there. What happened to him?' said Sam.

'No idea. I remember Kevin was more interested in the fact that Kitty Cannon was at the inquest.'

'Who?' Sam could barely hear him over the sound of the vacuum cleaner.

'You know, Kitty Cannon, the talk show host.'

'You're kidding me.' Sam sat up.

'Yeah. Upset, apparently; she snuck out before the verdict.'

'Why the hell was Kitty Cannon at the inquest of an elderly priest from Preston?' Sam walked over to the window to get better reception on her phone, her heart beating faster. If she could get an exclusive with someone as high-profile as Kitty Cannon, it might be enough to get her through the door at one of the nationals. She'd been treading the carpets at Southern News for too long. Since Emma had been born, she hadn't been able to put in the sort of hours she had in the past, and Murray seemed determined to keep her down. She still pulled blinders on nearly every story she was given, just as she had done with Jane Connors that day, but she was constantly overlooked for promotion. She needed to start earning some decent money; much as she loved Nana, she and Emma desperately needed to find a place of their own. She knew Murray had a day of dull stories lined up for her tomorrow, but her shift didn't start until ten, and she was pretty sure she could have a dig into Kitty Cannon and St Margaret's in her own time.

'Not a clue. Kevin spoke to Murray about it – he thought there might be a story there – but he didn't get any pictures, and Cannon's office said it wasn't her. That was the end of that.'

'So he just dropped it? That's weird. Did she know this Father Benjamin?' Sam pulled her notebook from her bag and began scribbling.

'I've no idea. It's not really in the public interest, Sam. She wasn't doing anything illegal, so there were no grounds to pursue it.'

'But . . . Is Kevin there? Can I talk to him?'

'Nope, he was on earlies. Look, sorry, Murray's shouting at me. Gotta go.'

'Okay, thanks,' said Sam to the silent phone.

She glanced over to the article on her laptop screen, then turned to a fresh page in her notebook and wrote *Father Benjamin* on the first line.

Then she picked up the letter in her lap and started reading again.

Chapter Four

Wednesday 12 September 1956

Ivy Jenkins sat on the edge of her bed, her fingernails digging deep into her knees, as Uncle Frank's voice travelled
up through the floorboards. She'd heard Dr Jacobson
arrive, the doorbell sending a bolt of fear through her body,
and had opened her bedroom door just enough to watch
her mother rush along the faded brown hall carpet to greet
him. She had strained to hear the exchange, her mother's
voice flustered and breathless as she fluttered around Dr
Jacobson nervously.

'Good evening, Doctor, thank you so much for coming.'

Ivy had barely heard her mother speak since they had
visited Dr Jacobson earlier in the week. She had sat staring
at the doctor, watching his lips move as the words came out
and sped across the room towards her like bullets from a
gun. Wanting to stop that split second she had left of her
eighteen years of innocence before the world as she knew it
changed for ever.

'Well, Ivy,' he had said after he'd examined her and she'd
been told to sit on the chair next to his desk, 'the reason you've
been feeling unwell is because you're going to have a baby.'

Mother had gasped, and held a gloved hand up to her
mouth. In that moment of pure shock, Ivy had reached for
her other hand, but her mother had pulled it away.

After that, Mother had spoken only to Dr Jacobson, asking him what they were to do. What would the neighbours say? Did he know that Ivy wasn't married? Dr Jacobson had replied that if the father of Ivy's baby wasn't prepared to marry her, there was one other option. He said he would need to talk it through with them, and that he would come over to their house on Wednesday evening. After that, during the long bus ride home, and for the three days since, Mother had barely said a word.

Uncle Frank hadn't noticed her mother's silence. He had continued to rant, as usual, about the inadequacy of his dinner, the draught from the back door, the neighbours' noisy children. But Ivy had noticed; she had watched her mother's shoulders sink even lower than normal, and her eyes glaze over, with no emotion in them at all.

Since that first moment when she had found out that she had Alistair's baby growing inside her, Ivy had been desperate to see him. She had told him about missing her period, and although he had smiled at her and told her not to worry, his voice had turned cold.

He had failed to arrive for their weekly Saturday drive in the country, for which she had waited excitedly all morning. She had sat in the sitting room, dressed in her new pale blue cotton skirt and white blouse, as Uncle Frank shouted at the horse racing on the wireless, and eventually she had conceded that her love was not coming for her.

In desperation she had snuck out the following night to the Preston Arms, a pub she knew Alistair drank at. She had walked through the smoky bar, tugging at her dress self-consciously, until she spotted the girlfriend of one of the other players from his football team and plucked up the

36

courage to ask her to get a message to Alistair that she needed to see him urgently. The girl had smiled and promised that she would. But as Ivy had turned away, she had heard the girl's friend laughing.

'Al's got another lovesick puppy pining for him, I see.'

'Don't,' the girl had said. 'We've all been there.' Ivy had turned back to see them sniggering as she stepped out from the bustle of the pub onto the silent street.

Now she heard Uncle Frank's voice bellowing through the floorboards, bringing her back to the present. 'Wait till I get my hands on that girl!'

'No, Frank!' Ivy heard her mother trying to calm him, then Dr Jacobson's low tones.

In a desperate effort to distract herself, she walked over to her desk, pulled a piece of paper from the drawer and began to write.

12 September 1956

My love,

I am fearful that I have not heard from you. All my anxieties have been confirmed. I am three months pregnant. It is too late for anything to be done; it is God's will that our baby be born.

Ever since Dr Jacobson confirmed the news, I hear Mother crying in her bedroom. I took her some flowers in a vase and put them next to her bed, but she just turned away. How can you stop loving your own flesh and blood in an instant? We have been everything to each other since Daddy died. Uncle Frank thinks Mother loves him, but I know she doesn't. I watched my parents dancing in the lounge when they thought I'd gone to bed; the way Mummy smiled at him when he spun her round, well, she never has that smile for Uncle Frank. In fact I've never seen her smile at him. She just takes things on a tray for him from the kitchen into the sitting room. He never thanks her.

We aren't allowed to speak of Daddy now that we are living with Uncle Frank, but I know she hides a picture of him that Uncle Frank doesn't know about in a box in a cupboard under the stairs. I hide in there sometimes when he's angry, to stay out of his way, and I take my torch so that when it's gone quiet I can get the picture out and look at it. It's of Daddy in his uniform, and he is so handsome. His hair is slicked back under his hat and he is looking away into the distance, as if someone terribly important is standing on the horizon.

Daddy used to pull me onto his lap when he was going back to war and I was begging him not to leave. He would hold me close and tell me that whenever I was missing him, to look up at the sky and find the biggest, brightest star, and that he would look for it too every night. Then we would both know that we were wishing on the same star that he would be home soon, and that way, it would come true. But it didn't come true and I felt dead inside after Daddy died – until I met you.

Oh why do I feel so wretched and scared? Where are you? Do you not love me any more?

'Ivy! Get down here now.' Uncle Frank's voice bellowed up the stairs.

Ivy slowly returned the paper to the drawer, put her pen down on the desk and swallowed the sickness in her stomach. Her body trembling, she walked across the bedroom, down the stairs and towards the lounge.

'Where is she? Ivy!' Uncle Frank shouted again as she hovered at the door.

'She's here,' said her mother quietly as Ivy forced herself over the threshold into the room where they all sat staring at her. The air was thick with smoke. Uncle Frank and Dr Jacobson sat on the faded brown sofa holding cigarettes, while Mother perched awkwardly on a chair in the corner.

'Yes, Uncle,' said Ivy.

'Don't you "yes Uncle" me, you little whore.'

'Frank! Please, we have a visitor.' Ivy's mother wrung her hands anxiously.

'Don't protect her, Maude. You clearly can't discipline the girl, so I'm going to have to do it myself. Well, what have you got to say for yourself?'

Ivy stood in silence, her head bowed. Tears stung her eyes and she felt so dizzy that the circles on the orange and brown carpet below her began to move and she thought she might faint.

'Has the baby's father any intention of marrying you?' Uncle Frank spat.

'I don't know, Uncle,' she whispered.

'Well, have you spoken to him?'

She blinked, and tears began to streak down her cheeks. She reached up and brushed them away.

'Speak up, girl, or you'll feel the back of my hand.'

'I can't get hold of him,' Ivy said.

The room fell silent before it erupted with the sound of Uncle Frank's bellowing laugh. 'I bet you can't.'

He stood and walked over to the drinks cabinet, where he poured himself a large whisky.

'I don't know what made you believe a boy like that would

39

be interested in you, other than to get into your knickers. Mark my words, you'll never hear from him again.'

'Frank, don't!' said Ivy's mother again.

Frank walked across to Ivy and paused for a moment. She didn't dare move as he circled her, his cheeks flushed with rage. She tensed every muscle in her body, waiting for him to strike her.

'Lord knows I've tried to step into your father's shoes and do a good job of raising you, but I have clearly failed. You were just waiting to disgrace yourself and bring shame on this family.'

Ivy looked over at her mother, who let out a sob.

Frank went on, 'If it weren't for Dr Jacobson, who has kindly offered to speak to Father Benjamin about a place at St Margaret's for you and the baby, you'd be out on the streets. I'm disgusted with you, Ivy. I've never felt such disappointment in my life. I only hope they can take you soon, before you start to show.'

'There will be a cost involved, I'm afraid, Frank,' Dr Jacobson said. 'They won't take her for nothing.'

'How much?' said Frank.

'I'd have to confirm with Father Benjamin on Sunday, but it's about a hundred pounds.'

'We don't have that kind of money!' Frank shouted.

'Then she'll have to stay after the baby's been adopted and work to repay the debt.'

'For how long?' Ivy looked to her mother, who was as white as a sheet.

'Three years, I believe,' said Dr Jacobson calmly, as if he were discussing the weather rather than handing out a prison sentence.

Ivy gasped and rushed over to her mother, clutching at her hand, in which she held a sodden handkerchief. 'Mummy, please don't make me go.'

Uncle Frank strode over and pulled her away. 'Don't put this on your poor mother; don't you think she's been through enough already?'

'You're glad about it because it means you're getting rid of me.' Ivy wrenched herself out of Uncle Frank's grip.

'Ivy, that's enough!' said her mother, her eyes red from crying.

Ivy stood with her head bowed, watching the ripples move across Uncle Frank's whisky as he clutched it tightly. Suddenly he threw the glass against the wall, shattering it into fragments.

'Get out of my sight!' he shouted. 'Your father must be turning in his grave.'

Ivy ran to her room, frantically wiping tears away as she pulled the sheet of paper out from her desk drawer and began to write again.

Uncle Frank says the only way out of this terrible shame I have brought on the family is for me to be sent away swiftly, before I begin to show, so that the neighbours won't know. There's a place called St Margaret's in Preston where girls like me go to have their babies.

I know Mother won't want me to go, but she'll tell me that it's Uncle Frank's house and we are lucky to have somewhere to live as Daddy left us with nothing. I hate it when she says that about Daddy; it's not his fault he was sent away to die in the war.

Dr Jacobson says I will have to be away for some time to pay for my keep at the home, up to three years, as we don't have the

£100 to cover the cost. From our dinners and the gifts you have so kindly bought me, I don't think £100 is a lot of money for you. I understand that you may not want a scandal in the newspapers at the start of your first season at Brighton, but if you were to pay the £100 and promise Uncle Frank that we would be married some day, then I could bear this pain knowing we were to be reunited once the baby, our baby, is born.

These last few months, and that precious night we spent together at the Rose Hotel, have been the happiest of my life. I miss you terribly. I cannot eat or sleep; I am fearful of what will happen to me and to the baby growing inside me. I lie in bed at night stroking my stomach and wondering whether it is a boy who will grow up to be strong and handsome like his daddy.

Uncle Frank thinks that I am naive to presume that you ever loved a girl like me. He says that now you have got what you wanted, I will never hear from you again.

Please, my darling, prove him wrong. I will post this by hand now through your letter box, to make sure it reaches you.

Dr Jacobson is going to speak to Father Benjamin at church on Sunday about sending me away soon. I think it will be a matter of days before it is decided. I do not know what to think or do. Please, my darling, I beg of you, I will make you happy and we will be a family. Please come for me quickly. I'm frightened for the future.

With all my love for ever,
Your Ivy xx

She carefully folded the letter, pushed it into an envelope and sealed it. She would wait until Mother and Uncle Frank were asleep and then creep out and deliver it.

She knew the place they were thinking of sending her: St Margaret's in Preston. For as long as she could remember, the huge mansion had haunted her as they passed it on the drive to church on Sundays. From a distance it looked like a burnt gingerbread house; tall and stretched, with jagged iced turrets, twisted candy cane for pillars, and stained-glass windows. The heavy crosses on every section of the house dominated the skyline, while ivy clambered up towards the slate roof, taking over like an uninvited guest.

There had been hushed gossip about a couple of girls from school going there to have babies. One had returned months later a shadow of her former self. The other girl had not been seen since. Ivy would persuade Alistair to marry her and do everything in her power not to be sent away. Once she stepped over the threshold of St Margaret's, her fight to keep her baby would be as good as lost.

Chapter Five

After two hours of reading harrowing accounts of babies being taken away from their mothers, an experience it seemed the women never recovered from, Sam could bear no more. The girls were made to work in laundries, often handling heavy machinery right up until they went into labour. Their babies were then taken at birth, the mothers forced to sign away any right to try to find them.

The thought of it made Sam cry as she lay cuddling Emma in her white-framed bed, the little girl's small, soft body melting into hers. It was such an overwhelming instinct to protect your child; how did the nuns have such a hold over the women? To persuade them not only to give up their babies, but also to sign contracts that made it illegal for them to try and find the children at any point in the future. It was barbaric.

She looked down at the letter and traced the sloping handwriting with her finger. Ivy had been born one generation too soon. As a recent single mother herself, it shocked Sam that St Margaret's was on her doorstep and had been taking babies away from their mothers until the mid seventies.

She had to go there to see how they had lived, where the babies slept, where the girls worked to pay for their keep. Kitty Cannon's potential link to the place intrigued her, but for some reason she could imagine herself in Ivy's shoes, and felt compelled to see St Margaret's through her eyes.

Her online searches had indicated that the old convent was going to be torn down on Tuesday, which gave her only two days to get to it before it was gone. She'd only just started her five-day shift, so she didn't have any time off until after the house was due to be demolished. She would have to get up at dawn tomorrow if she was going to see the place for herself and still be at work at ten.

As she fell into a fitful sleep, her mind wandered again to the letter on her bedside table – a letter that had somehow found its way into her grandfather's things – and to the terrified young woman who had written it.

Chapter Six

Sunday 5 February 2017

Kitty stood on the doorstep of Richard Stone's central London mews house as he undid the double lock and then opened the front door, gesturing for her to come in.

The burglar alarm beeped its thirty-second warning as she stood in the hallway watching Richard punch in the numbers on the keypad. His hands, gnarled and covered in age spots, shook slightly as he did so.

'Sorry about that. Since my wife passed away, I always forget to turn off the alarm when I get up.'

Kitty smiled. 'I really appreciate you giving me this emergency appointment. I didn't know where else to turn.'

'Of course, that's what I'm here for. I'm just sorry it's so early. I've had this lunch with my son in the diary for weeks.'

Richard returned his keys to the hook on the wall, then led the way down the soft-carpeted hall lined with black-and-white photographs of his two sons on various holidays.

'Would you mind if I used your bathroom quickly?' said Kitty.

'Of course not, you know where to go, don't you? I'll wait for you in here,' said Richard.

When Kitty returned he gestured towards the brown leather chair in the corner.

'Please take a seat.'

Kitty looked around the room, which by now was almost as familiar to her as her own sitting room, and let out an irritable sigh. The low table with the obligatory box of tissues, the innocuous print on the wall, the cream blind letting in just enough daylight to stave off claustrophobia. She had been coming to see Richard for weeks, pussyfooting around, talking about her insomnia, her career. She was sick of this room, sick of waiting for him to press her about her past, to have the breakthrough all psychiatrists harped on about – and to see his reaction.

'Can I take your coat?' Richard said, smiling at her warmly as he hovered next to her.

'No thank you, I'm still frozen through,' said Kitty, tugging at the fingers of her grey cashmere gloves one by one before lowering herself into the chair.

Richard sat too, crossing his legs and leaning back. Kitty avoided looking at him until she had finished putting her gloves in the handbag on her lap, which she then dropped by her chair with a soft thud. Finally she glanced up, checking that his blue eyes were fixed on her, then immediately looked away again.

'How are you, Kitty?'

She shifted twice before eventually sitting back in her seat, her shoulders hunched. She listened to the sound of her own heavy breathing. A horn went off in the traffic outside, making her jump. 'I don't know how you can bear living in the centre of town,' she said.

Richard smiled gently. 'It keeps me young.'

'I'm surprised that listening to people's moaning pays well enough for you to afford it.'

47

Richard took a sip of water. 'I wouldn't call it moaning. Are you sure you're comfortable with your coat on?'

'Yes. Please stop fussing. I come here to get away from all that insincerity.'

'Do you think that if people are checking you are all right, they're being insincere?' asked Richard.

Kitty looked away again, examining his shoes to avoid his stare. They were worn brown leather brogues, but they had a shine to them that showed they were well taken care of.

Like Richard himself, Kitty thought.

He was over eighty, his head nearly bald, his eye bags heavy, but his faded jeans were pressed and his woollen jumper was soft and freshly washed. Everything in the room suggested that despite his wife's recent death, some-one was looking after him – a housekeeper perhaps, and of course his loving sons.

Kitty always felt Richard had the air of someone who had everything planned out, who had spent his life with a wife who wasted nothing and lived frugally: 'Don't throw that chair away, darling, I could varnish it and use it as a stool in the boys' room.' She could see them now, enjoying hearty camping holidays instead of expensive trips abroad. Enab-ling them to save enough money to buy a house in central London when they were young. A decision that meant that, apart from the odd very lucrative client, they had retired into a comfortable existence.

'You look well,' she snapped, as if she were dealing out an insult. 'Have you been away?'

'Yes,' said Richard, 'just for a couple of days with my son.'

He absent-mindedly twisted the ring on his wedding finger with his left thumb, and Kitty pictured him and his devoted offspring sitting in a picturesque town square, smiling occasionally at one another as they watched the world go by. Richard would have done such a good job raising the boy that there was an understanding between them and they wouldn't have the need for constant conversation. Maybe the odd reference to how much his wife would have loved the place in which they sat.

'Do you want to talk about what's bothering you, Kitty?'

Kitty tugged at a piece of fluff on her coat. The radiator behind her was belting out heat and making her skin throb. She felt her cheeks flush red as she undid her buttons and pulled the coat open.

Richard rested his hand on his knee. 'How did your dinner go?'

Kitty shifted in her seat and sighed. 'Fine. Aside from the fact that I felt invisible.'

'I'm sorry to hear that. Why did you feel invisible?'

She started to pick at the skin around her nails. 'Because of all those people I respect looking past me and not at me. They used to watch me, stop conversations to listen to me. I don't know when it started happening, but last night, they didn't do that. They looked at people younger than me, more attractive, with their whole lives ahead of them. I felt as if a light in me was going out and they no longer saw me as I was.'

She traced a circle on the leg of her trousers with the tip of her finger, round and round.

Richard paused for a moment, waiting for her to go on. 'Perhaps that's just how you saw it; perhaps they very much still see the light in you, as you put it.'

Kitty looked up at the clock, its hands seemingly

slowing to a stop. 'When I left, alone, I felt as if I was leaving my own funeral. I knew none of them would really miss me. It's different for you, Richard. What you have, you've got it right. You have experienced true love, you've pursued the right things in life, you treasure your family. Your work comes second.'

'It is dangerous to compare yourself to others, Kitty. We can only truly know what is going on in our own lives.'

'Come, come, don't do yourself a disservice. I'm in your home, I can feel the happiness, the contentment. I'm merely speaking the truth and I mean it as a compliment. I am jealous of what you have. My work is all I've got, and now that is fading to black.'

Richard cleared his throat. 'You say your work is all you've got, but you went to a party full of people wanting to show their love and admiration for you.'

Kitty glared at him, shaking her head. 'They were there for themselves.'

'I think you are being very hard on yourself. Could it be the other way around: that they no longer hold your interest or love? That you are angry at them for not being what you want them to be?'

'Because they don't love me for who I really am? It's a bit of a cliché, isn't it?' She looked away and stood up, pulling off her coat as she walked over to the balcony doors which overlooked a small, beautifully kept garden.

'No, it's not a cliché to want to feel loved for who you really are. But if you don't show them the real you, how can they love you? Perhaps this work of yours provides you with a mask that you are scared to take off for fear of rejection. Perhaps you are tired of pretending. Do you have someone you can really talk to, Kitty? Other than me, I mean. A friend? A soulmate?'

'I did once,' said Kitty, crossing her arms and looking away.

'What happened?' said Richard.

'I lost her,' Kitty said quietly.

'What do you mean by "lost"?' He shifted slowly in his chair, wincing as he did so, his back or joints clearly hurting him.

Kitty fell silent. Eventually she walked back to her own chair, folded her coat and threw it on the floor next to her bag. Then she sat down, sighing.

'You're right, I am tired. It would help if I could get some bloody sleep. The temazepam you prescribed knocks me out, but then I'm awake two or three hours later. It's enough to make anyone crazy.'

'And what is waking you?' said Richard.

Kitty watched a black cat chase a squirrel across the lawn and up a large sycamore.

Richard pressed her. 'Is it a recurring dream? Or a nightmare perhaps?'

Kitty examined the bracelet on her wrist, twisting and turning each charm between her fingers. 'I'm running through the tunnel she escaped through, but I can never reach the light at the end. I keep on going, but it never gets any closer.'

'This is your sister? The tunnel your sister escaped through?' said Richard.

Kitty nodded.

'Dreams are unresolved issues trying to process themselves in your brain while you sleep. They will keep recurring

51

until you can work out what they are trying to tell you.' He watched Kitty carefully.

'I never asked my father why my sister died. She was alive when I went to get help,' Kitty said quietly. She could feel her mouth becoming dry. 'I knew he had been lied to, and so did he.' She began to pick again at the skin around her nails, drawing blood and flinching with the pain.

'Lied to by whom? What do you think happened to her?' said Richard.

'I think they found her and punished her for escaping,' said Kitty, staring into his eyes for the first time.

'Escaping from where?' Richard slowly uncrossed his legs and leant towards her. 'Was she in some kind of institution, do you know?'

Kitty felt every muscle in her body tighten. 'She was living in a place called St Margaret's; it was a mother-and-baby home in Sussex.'

Richard was staring at her intently. All the colour had drained from his face and the hand resting on his knee was now white from gripping it.

'They made a mistake,' continued Kitty. 'They didn't know she'd found me after I came out of church – I was on my own, you see, without my parents. She signalled to me from the graveyard. They knew she was missing, but they didn't know she'd found me and that I went to get help.' She paused and looked up at Richard, who was breathing very slowly and deeply.

'How old were you when all this happened, Kitty?' he said finally.

'Eight. I was only eight years old.' She looked at Richard's hands, which were shaking.

'Will you excuse me?' he said, before slowly easing himself out of the chair, letting out a dull groan as he did so. He staggered slightly as he walked towards the door.

'Are you all right, Richard?' said Kitty.

'Yes, I'm just tired from the trip. I'll only be a second.'

Kitty looked up at the clock: thirty minutes to go.

After two minutes had ticked by, Richard came back into the room with a glass of water in his hand. 'Please excuse me for leaving you like that. I would never normally walk out on a patient. It's been rather a difficult time of late. Let's get back to what we were talking about. Why did you go to church on your own that day?'

Kitty stood and walked over to the bookcase, picking up a snow globe that sat on one of the shelves and shaking it. Snow started falling over the tiny village inside.

'My father had been at the hospital all day. I knew my mother was seriously ill. I'd gone to church every Sunday my whole life – if Father was working, Mother and I would catch the bus. I knew which bus to get, I knew what to do. I had been at home on my own all day, pacing, thinking about Mother in the hospital, desperate to get out, to do something, anything to help. I'd missed the morning service, but I knew there was also an afternoon service because Mother sometimes went to it on her own.'

She walked back to her chair and sat down with the globe on her lap. The snow had settled now, and she pictured her eight-year-old self inside it, in her best red coat, standing outside the church.

'I so nearly didn't go that day. That decision changed the whole course of my life. I just wanted to pray to God to save my mother. I'll never forget how cold it was. The ice

53

crunching under my feet was louder than the church bells.'
Kitty looked over at Richard as her mind darted back to
the bus that had trundled through the ice-covered country
lanes of East Sussex, bringing her sister and her together for
the first time in their lives.

Chapter Seven

Sunday 15 February 1959

Kitty tugged at the toggles on her new red duffel coat as the bus made its way through the winding lanes towards the village of Preston. Ice-glazed hedges lined the road before opening up into snow-dappled fields. She had climbed onto the bus alone, handed over the change she had taken from her father's bedside table, and sat down next to the window before being joined by an elderly lady she recognised from church. Her breath had made a circle of fog on the window, which she periodically wiped away with her black woollen gloves. As she gazed out, she could see nuns scattered in the fields, peering behind hedges and bent over ditches, their breath condensing in the freezing air.

She glanced at the woman next to her. She was dressed smartly, her hair scraped back in a bun that Kitty imagined took several attempts to get right. She wore a black glass brooch on her thick brown coat, which looked to Kitty as if it were made of carpet. The lady jolted as the bus struggled on the icy road, but her eyes stayed fixed ahead and she clutched the handbag in her lap. Kitty longed to ask her what she thought the nuns were searching for in the fields, but the woman hadn't looked at her once since they'd boarded the bus together, and her jaw was clenched tight as if she had no wish to talk.

Kitty bit down hard on her lip as they stopped at a junction. She fixed her eyes on the road sign ahead, which read *Preston Lane*. They turned into the lane, passing the deep shadow of Preston Manor and heading out towards the South Downs, where a Victorian mansion came into view on the horizon. For as long as she could remember, the four-storey double-fronted building had captivated her. From a distance, it looked to her like a neglected doll's house sitting empty and unused in a dusty loft. Ten dull-looking windows across each of the four floors, with never any light in them; a beige facade with ivy creeping up it. As they drew nearer, its bland colour appeared to drain away entirely and turn a shade of grey as its angles hardened. Large crosses rose from every section of the house, and there were turrets that reminded Kitty of the story of the imprisoned Rapunzel that her father sometimes read to her.

The gravel drive up to the house was surrounded by woodland, and as they slowly bumped along it, they reached a clearing where the bus stopped. The doors hissed open and a young woman struggled down the aisle with a suitcase in her hand. Her large, rounded stomach was pressing against the suitcase, and as she heaved it down the steps of the bus, Kitty heard the old lady next to her tut in disapproval.

In the shadow of the trees, dressed in black from head to toe save for the white band around his neck, stood Father Benjamin, who Kitty recognised as the priest from Preston church. She looked around to see several girls walking up and down in a ditch that ran around the perimeter of the woods. They were wearing brown overalls and two nuns in full habits were standing over them. Kitty examined the girl nearest to her intently. Her hair was as short as a boy's and her skin as grey as the snow-covered ground beside her.

One of the nuns signalled the girl over, and Kitty watched as she pulled herself up out of the ditch. She wobbled for a moment, then managed to steady herself before slowly straightening up and pressing her hand into the small of her back, revealing a huge stomach.

As the bus pulled away, the girl looked up and stared directly at Kitty, her piercing eyes as black as coal. Kitty pushed herself back into her seat, but she was unable to peel her gaze away, until the nun snapped at the girl in the snow to move on.

Kitty huddled into her seat, biting frantically at the skin around her nails. At home she had felt she had to get out, to do something, but now that she was here on the bus, alone for the first time without her parents, she began to panic. Though the engine was running and the heater was on, she felt the cold seeping under the concertina door and rectangular windows, trying to get to her. Her breathing grew erratic as they pulled up outside the church and everyone started to get off.

It was only three in the afternoon, but as the icy February wind blew, the winter light was beginning to fade. Being careful not to slip in her best patent shoes, Kitty started to climb off the bus.

'Are you all right, miss?' said the driver as he wrenched the vehicle into gear, ready to move off.

'Yes, I'm meeting my father at the church,' said Kitty, reciting the lie she had prepared in her head whilst getting ready earlier.

'Right you are. Well, be careful on the ice.'

The doors clunked shut behind her and she stood alone, watching the congregation bustling into the small church. She wished her father really was there beside her, his large hand wrapped around hers. As she moved forward, feet crunching on the ice, she could picture his shoes next to hers; imagined herself taking two or three steps to keep up with his long stride.

As she walked through the gate, past the snow-speckled gravestones and towards the entrance to the church, she paused briefly and looked around. The chatter of the group ahead of her had disappeared into the building, and the only noise left was the cawing crows, two of which stared at her from the bare branches overhanging the path.

Slowly they too fell silent and she became acutely aware that someone was watching her.

As she stood staring at the rows of headstones, something moved in the distance. The crows launched themselves into the sky, unsettling the snow from the branches on which they'd perched, causing a flurry to fall onto Kitty's hair and down the back of her new red coat.

She gasped, brushing away the flakes of ice, just as a man in a long black coat began closing the church doors.

'Wait!' she called out as she scuttled towards the shelter of the building, trying not to slip on the ice. She glanced back once at the graveyard, a trickle of goose bumps crawling up her arm, then stepped inside, the doors closing behind her.

Chapter Eight

Sunday 5 February 2017

It was still early when Sam pulled up outside St Margaret's. Leaving Nana and Emma warm in their beds, she'd crept out into the freezing dawn, where her Vauxhall Nova waited to take her through the winding lanes of Preston and out into the foggy Sussex countryside.

The Gothic mansion stabbing the skyline ahead of her was much bigger than she'd anticipated, with rows of narrow arched windows beneath a steeply pitched roof dominated by crucifixes. Nature had already reclaimed the place, with thick damp climbing up its walls and ivy covering the exterior so profusely that it was hard to make out where the house ended and the ground began. It stood completely alone in a huge expanse of land, and the preparations to tear it down were clearly under way. Diggers and great heaps of builders' sand dotted the foreground, and a hundred-foot crane leant into the house, the wrecking ball poised as if counting down to its imminent task.

Pulling her coat tightly around her, Sam stood at the steel fence that surrounded the site, imagining the girls who must have stood here all those years ago, one hand on their kicking bump, the other clutching a small bag of belongings; abandoned by everyone they loved, with no inkling of what lay ahead.

She checked out the two heavy padlocks keeping the site entrance steadfastly shut, then stepped back to take in all the signage:

Notice of Intended Demolition
Warning Construction Site: Keep Out
Unauthorised Entry Strictly Forbidden

A large architect's impression of seven detached family homes stood on stilts by her side:

Award-winning luxury new homes: Slade Homes blends
the traditional elegance of classical architecture with
21st-century interior design, situated close to the secluded
village of Preston in the heart of the Sussex countryside.

In huge blood-red letters, the words *ALL SOLD* dominated the blurb.

Sam turned and began walking around the perimeter of the site, running her gloved hand along the fencing. There were no signs of life, but she could hear a dog barking in the distance, and as she got closer, she noticed a Portakabin with a light on. She made her way towards it, stumbling twice on the frozen mud under her heeled boots, and as she passed in front of the house, a German Shepherd tethered to the ground reared up, barking frantically. Sam instinctively stopped, despite the fact that it was on a leash and there was a steel fence between them her heart was hammering in her chest.

'Max!' a male voice shouted. 'Shut up.' The light from inside the cabin showed the outline of a ponytailed man moving towards the door. 'What is it?'

Sam could see that he was tall, with a thick neck and broad shoulders. He was wearing only a wrinkled grey T-shirt despite the freezing temperature. His black biker boots were unlaced and he had a sovereign ring on his left hand, in which he clutched a tin cup with steam rising from it. After pausing to look around, he came down the steps to see what was bothering the dog who was still snapping and snarling at Sam.

She had run through all the scenarios of what she'd find at St Margaret's: best case would have been loose fencing around the site, no one around and a broken window in the old Victorian house that she could climb through. Failing that, bored secretaries were usually a safe bet, and she figured that if there was a marketing office for the posh new development, she might be able to convince them she was interested in one of the properties, then wangle a tour before making her excuses. Even a security guard she could probably have charmed or slipped past, but she hadn't anticipated a burly site manager living on the premises, with a werewolf for a pet.

'Hi!' she sang, waving merrily. 'So sorry, I didn't mean to startle your dog.'

He turned towards her, squinting in the sunshine, his thick goatee catching the light as the smoke from the cigarette in his mouth drifted up into his eyes. Sam registered the slogan on his T-shirt – *Blow me, it's my birthday* – and attempted a smile, which he didn't return. He stared at her for an uncomfortably long time. The dog started to bark again and the man finally dropped his eyes, kicking the dog so hard it yelped.

'What you doin' creeping round 'ere, love?' he asked in a thick Cockney accent.

'I wasn't creeping. I came over because I saw a light on and wanted to see if there was anyone about.'

'Why's that then?' He took a deep drag on his cigarette and blew the smoke in her direction as he walked towards her. Despite the steel fence between them, she felt a wave of panic, but smiled again and leant in.

'Because I want to see inside that house before it's torn down. Can I bum a smoke?'

'There's a lot of people been interested in that house lately, since them priest's remains were found.' He handed her a cigarette and lit it with a lighter through a break in the fence.

'Thanks. Yeah, I saw it in the paper. It's the reason I'm here.'

The key to lying, Sam always found, was to keep it simple and as close to the truth as possible. She reached into her bag and pulled out Ivy's letter, holding it up so he could see the faded pages and dated handwriting.

'My grandad died very recently and I found this in his belongings. I think it was written by his mother and I believe he was born here. When I read last night that they were tearing the house down, I just wanted to come and see the place where he spent the first weeks of his life. If any of the nuns who looked after him are still alive, it would be nice to thank them.' Her voice wobbled. It hadn't been her intention to talk about the man who'd been like a father to her.

The man sniggered. 'Thank them? That's a first.'

'What do you mean?' said Sam, squinting up at him in the low winter sun.

'You're not from the press, are you?' he said, taking a drag on his cigarette.

'What makes you say that?'

'They were millin' round 'ere for a while, but they've had the inquest now. The demolition order's finally through.

This house is comin' down in two days and there ain't nothing anyone can do to stop it.'

'But they still need you to sleep here every night? That must be rough, it's freezing.'

'Yep, the new houses are a million apiece, so they're not taking any chances. Can't wait to get the hell out of here.'

'I bet. I'm Sam, by the way. It's nice to meet you.' She reached her hand through the fence, and the man paused before taking it.

'Andy. So, Sam, if I show you around, you gonna have a drink with me tonight?' He took a drag on his cigarette, his stare not leaving her face.

Sam forced a smile. 'Are you celebrating your birthday?'

Andy glanced down at his T-shirt. 'I am if you are.' He hesitated, then cocked his head towards the building. 'Come on in then, can't do any harm.'

As the heavy oak door of St Margaret's slammed behind them, Sam paused in the grand entrance hall, which was dominated by a sweeping staircase. The trapped dust danced in the early spring sunlight that was now pouring through the faded stained-glass windows at the top of the staircase. She noticed a broken sign lying on the chipped black and white tiles. Squatting down, she brushed the dust away.

Dear Lord, may the fallen find their way back to you
through the strength of their prayers and hard work.
St Margaret's, Preston, Sisters of Mercy

She pictured the staircase gleaming, the heavily pregnant girls polishing frantically while the nuns stood over them. Nuns who were infamously the face of the mother-and-baby homes, providing a service to Catholic families who wanted to turn a blind eye to what went on, whole communities relieved to wash their hands of it. It felt to Sam like an image from centuries past, not just one generation.

'Look in 'ere, love.'

She was so deep in thought, she'd almost forgotten her guide. Broken glass from one of the windows crunched under her feet as she walked to a doorway and looked in at a huge room flooded with light from two vaulted windows. Oversized ceramic sinks lined the walls, and a large mangle lay on its side in the middle of the blackened floor. She stood in the doorway and imagined the ghosts of decades past drowning in thick steam, wiping their hair from their faces with the backs of their hands, washing stained sheets at the sinks and guiding tablecloths through the mangle.

A crucifix dominated the back wall and a moth-eaten tapestry hung above the sinks. Goose bumps rose on her arms as she read the intricately stitched words.

O MOST MERCIFUL JESUS, lover of Souls,
I beseech Thee, by the agony of Thy most Sacred Heart,
and by the sorrows of Thine Immaculate Mother,
wash clean in Thy Blood the sinners of the whole world
who are to die this day.
If it should please Thy Majesty to send me a suffering this day
in exchange for the grace I ask for this soul, then it too
shall please me very much, and I thank Thee,
Most Sweet Jesus,
Shepherd and Lover of Souls; I thank Thee for this
opportunity to give mercy in thanksgiving for all the mercies
Thou hast shown me. Amen.

'This place is nuts,' said Sam. 'It feels like the girls are still trapped in here.'

'You've got no idea, love.' Andy leant in so close she could smell the cigarette smoke on his breath.

'So do you know if any of the nuns are still alive?' She turned away.

'You ain't answered my question yet.'

'Which question is that?' She was unsure if the rising nausea she felt was due to Andy or the haunting room.

'About having a drink with me tonight.'

She smiled and peered down the hallway. 'What's down here?'

'A dining hall, nothin' in it now.' He looked at his watch. 'To be honest, they cleared everything out for the demolition. I doubt you're gonna find nothin'.'

'And what's in there?' Sam nodded to a dark wooden door.

Andy remained silent, so she crossed the hall to open it, brushing past him to enter when he didn't move. In stark contrast to the laundry, the small room felt claustrophobic, the dark wooden panels absorbing the scant light a small window let in. A mahogany desk was pushed up to the wall in the corner and there was a large gilded portrait of a nun in full habit resting on it. The woman's long face was expressionless, her lips narrow, and when Sam propped the picture up, her emotionless eyes appeared to follow her around the room. A plaque at the base of the frame told her the woman was 'Mother Carlin, Mother Superior, 1945–1965.'

'Do you know if she's still alive?' Sam gestured to the portrait. 'Mother Carlin?'

'I know there's a couple of the nuns from here living in an old people's home down the road. But I couldn't tell you their names. Listen, we can't be too long, love. The build manager's due in soon.'

'Sure, sorry. Let's go.' She scanned the room one last time, then turned towards the door. As she did so, her heel caught on a small catch slightly raised from the floor. She stopped abruptly. 'What's that?'

Andy shrugged, pulling a cigarette from his pocket and lighting it. Sam crouched down, slid her finger through the catch and pulled. It was stiff, but after a couple of goes a trapdoor started to lift, letting out a loud creak that echoed through the empty room. She stepped back to examine the opening.

'What do you think it's for?' She glanced up at Andy.

'What's it look like?' He blew smoke across the damp room.

Sam felt a wave of nausea as she realised the space was just big enough for a person, a young girl perhaps. Roughly five foot by three, it resembled a coffin. She suddenly felt paralysed, picturing herself locked in the darkness for hours, in a space so small she couldn't move, where she would have time to reflect and learn her lesson thoroughly. And as Andy gestured for her to leave, she heard the faint sound of a girl crying. It was a moment before she realised that it was her.

Her chest felt constricted as he pulled her by the arm along the corridor, back past the laundry, where she imagined she saw the girls motionless at their sinks, watching her. When they reached the front door, she staggered out into the fresh air, gasping for breath.

'You all right, love?' Andy let go of her arm.

'I'm sorry, I just need a minute. That place is too much.' She waved away the cigarette he offered her.

66

'Like I said, you've got no idea. The sooner they raze the place to the ground, the better. Probably best if you get out of here now.'

Sam took deep breaths, nodding. She had no idea why she was having such an emotional reaction to Ivy's plight, but in the stifling atmosphere of the house, she had felt the suffering of all the girls incarcerated there. Coupled with Father Benjamin's death and Kitty Cannon's potential link to him, her instincts were screaming out to her that this was a story she needed to run with.

If Mother Carlin was still alive, she had to find her. But first she needed to know exactly why Kitty Cannon had attended Father Benjamin's inquest. She would put in a call to Cannon's press office just to test the water. If she got any reaction at all at the mention of St Margaret's, she'd know she was onto something. Then it was just a case of getting one of the nuns to spill the beans on Cannon's link to St Margaret's and she'd have her way in.

She looked at her watch: 7.30 a.m. Still two and a half hours before she needed to be at her desk. If she hurried, she might even be able to track down Mother Carlin now. She looked at Andy. 'I'd like to buy you a drink tonight to say thank you for your trouble. And if you can remember the name of that old people's home, I'll make it two.'

Chapter Nine

Sunday 5 February 2017

Richard looked up at the clock, which told him they were only halfway through their session, then back at Kitty. His hands were clammy as he clasped them together and hooked them round his crossed leg. 'What happened when you came out of the church?'

'I stood for a little while by myself while the adults around me chatted. I was just about to walk to the bus stop. And then I saw her.' Kitty's voice broke and she paused.

Richard took a deep breath. 'It's okay, Kitty, take your time.'

She cleared her throat, and bit her lip. 'She was hiding behind one of the gravestones, signalling to me.' Kitty stood and replaced the snow globe on the bookshelf from where she had picked it up.

'Did you realise straight away it was your sister?' He didn't look at her when he spoke, keeping his eyes fixed on her empty chair as if in a daze.

'No. I could tell she was my age but I didn't know who she was. On any other day I might have thought she wanted to play a game with me, but I was very upset about my mother so it troubled me straight away. Somehow I knew something was very wrong.' She paused again. 'I looked around to check it was me whose attention she was trying to get. I thought I was imagining her; that maybe she was a ghost. Then she put her finger up to her lips so I would know to be quiet and beckoned me over.'

'And you went?' said Richard quietly.

'Yes. Nobody was looking at me. People ignored children much more then, and of course my parents weren't there.' Kitty walked back over to the balcony doors and glanced over at Richard. He was hunched over, looking uncomfortable. She turned her attention to the garden again.

'And what did she say when you got to her?' said Richard.

Kitty could still see her sister's face as she approached. Despite the smudges of dirt, the knots in her hair and the oversized brown overalls, it was like looking in the mirror. She had glanced down at the girl's open-toed sandals and her bare arms and had instinctively taken off her own coat and wrapped it round her. Her sister was shaking as she reached out her hand, and Kitty had taken it.

'She didn't say anything when I first got to her. We ran to the outhouse. We stayed there all night; she was too scared to move. She told me her name was Elvira and that she'd escaped from St Margaret's. She been out in the snow for hours, waiting in the graveyard for me since the morning service. I knew my father would be desperately worried, but she wouldn't let me leave and get help. She just kept saying, "They'll kill me if they find me. They'll kill me."' Kitty's voice wavered again and she crossed her arms, hugging herself as she looked out of the window. 'She was so tired and hungry. I just wanted to help her, but she wouldn't let me go.'

'But you did go for help in the end?' said Richard, finally looking up.

'Yes, eventually she let me go, on one condition. She made me promise not to call out. She said that if I did, they'd find us. Then she showed me the key that she'd used to escape. She pulled out a loose brick in the wall of the outhouse and slotted the key behind it. She said if I came back and she was gone, my father and I should use it to open the trapdoor in the graveyard because it would be the only way to find her.'

'And did you use it?' said Richard quietly.

Kitty turned and looked at him. He glanced away and reached out with a shaking hand for his water. 'No. Father Benjamin said she was dead. But what if she wasn't, what if he was lying? I should have gone back. I could have saved her.'

'Have you ever been back to St Margaret's, Kitty?' said Richard, his shoulders hunched, his jaw clenched.

She shook her head slowly.

'Do you think the key could still be there? Is that what you think your dream is telling you?'

Kitty could still feel the enormity of the night as she ventured out into it. The black hole that lay ahead of her, full of the sound of owls in the trees and rustling creatures in the undergrowth. As she ran, tripping and falling in the dark, she felt as if the cold was a person, pulling her back, slowing her down, trying to take her prisoner. She began to lose sensation in her face and hands, and thoughts of her father came vividly to her: wrapping her up in the coat that Elvira was wearing now; doing up her toggles; smiling at her as he pulled on her bobble hat.

'I thought I knew the way, back to the church, to the road. I thought my father would be out looking for me. But it was so dark, I couldn't see anything. I was terrified. I looked for

70

the road for a long time, but I was starting to get dizzy. I'd fallen, I was cold and wet and so frightened. I was only eight, I tried to go back to Elvira, but I couldn't find her either. So I did what she'd begged me not to do. I shouted for help.'

Kitty looked down at her hands as the tiny tear next to her fingernail turned to a small stream of blood. As she dragged the red trail around the tip of her finger, she could hear the clink of cutlery on her plate as her father paced in front of the kitchen window of their tiny unheated house. She had watched him intently as he pulled back the net curtain every few seconds to glance down the narrow overgrown path. She could taste the cheap, gristly meat from the stew some well-meaning neighbour had made to feed them both while her mother was in hospital. She had only been home from hospital herself for a few days, after they had found her near to death in the ditch into which she had fallen trying to get help for her sister. The twin sister who less than a fortnight ago she hadn't even known existed.

'Eat up, Kitty, it's late,' her father had said, pulling her plate away and scraping the remains into the bin.

Kitty had looked up at the clock: ten to seven, nearly an hour before her bedtime.

'What's the matter, Daddy?' she had asked quietly.

'Enough questions, Kitty,' he had snapped. 'It's time for bed.' He had rushed her up the stairs and into her nightie, turning out the light and disappearing without asking if she needed taking out to the toilet in the yard. She could hear him tidying up, the clattering of plates, the crashing of cutlery into the drawer. Then finally a knock at the door.

She had sat up in bed, lowered her feet onto the cold floorboards and crept across the creaking floor of her bedroom.

Slowly and carefully she had pulled the door open as far as she dared, to reveal Father Benjamin standing on the faded blue rug in the hallway.

'Come through, Father.' Kitty had watched the two men walk towards the lounge and disappear inside, a loud click echoing up the stairs as the door was shut firmly behind them.

'Do you know how your sister came to be at St Margaret's?' said Richard, pulling Kitty back to the present.

'My mother was ill for most of her life with kidney failure, and I think my father sought solace in another woman. I suspect we were both born at St Margaret's and that our mother probably died in childbirth.' Kitty closed her eyes and rubbed them. 'Then for some reason, my father took only me home with him.'

Richard cleared his throat. 'You weren't angry that he chose to leave Elvira behind?'

Kitty looked at him, 'I doubt my mother gave him a choice.'

Richard paused before speaking. 'Okay, but I need to make sure you've thought through your feelings towards your father in all this. You've told me that he had an affair, and that this woman, your birth mother, probably died in childbirth. And that your father chose to take just one of you home, but that you harbour no ill will towards him for what happened to Elvira.'

Kitty glared at him. 'My mother was a very ill woman; there's no way my father could have coped with twins. He thought Elvira would be adopted, that she would be happy.'

'But why do you think he chose you?' said Richard. 'Obviously it was life-changing and tragic for Elvira, but in many ways it was as hard for you. What a burden to carry through your whole life. You are not to blame for any of this, Kitty.'

'But my father is, is that what you're saying?' Her reflection in the glass stared back at her, and she reached out and touched it gently with the tips of her fingers. She could still hear her father's voice through the lounge door all those years ago.

'She was my child, Father, I had a right to know she had been returned to St Margaret's.'

Kitty's hand shook as it ran down the banister. She had tiptoed down each step trying desperately not to wake the sleeping floorboards. When she reached the bottom, her heart was throbbing so much it hurt. The two men's voices were as clear as if she were in the room with them.

'With all due respect, George, you gave up your rights to Elvira at birth.' Father Benjamin's voice was calm and reasoning, as if he were giving a sermon in church.

'I thought she had been adopted, I thought she had gone to a loving home.' Her father sounded strained and breathless; Kitty could picture him pacing as the priest sat watching.

'She had; she was there for the first six years of her life,' said Father Benjamin.

'And what happened?' George's voice rose slightly.

'I don't know exactly, but they struggled with her; said she was troubled.' Kitty heard Father Benjamin cough, and imagined him relaxed, his legs crossed, sipping at a drink.

'Even so, you don't return a child as though she's a gift you don't like.' George was pacing again; Kitty could hear it in his voice, feel the floor shaking gently.

'It often happens that a couple who think they can't have children fall pregnant after they adopt. Elvira found it very

73

hard to adjust to the new baby and they said there were a couple of occasions when she tried to harm him.' The room fell silent then; Kitty panicked they were about to appear and turned to dart back up the stairs.

'So did you try and find her another family?' said George, his voice more resigned now.

'We did, but young couples don't want difficult six-year-olds, they want babies,' said Father Benjamin.

'Why didn't you at least tell me?' Kitty could hear the resignation in her father's voice.

'Helena was so ill, George, you could barely cope with Kitty. I didn't want to burden you. I have to say, I find these accusations quite testing. May I remind you that you came to us, begging for our help, I might add, to make this problem of yours disappear.' The priest's voice was harder now.

'I know, Father, and I am grateful. It's just so shocking for Kitty, and hard for me. To try to explain to her what happened, and why we never told her she had a sister. Dr Jacobson said I would need to give her time, but she has nightmares every night; she hasn't been herself since this dreadful episode. And now you tell me the poor girl is dead. I can't help but feel responsible. Where is she buried?'

Kitty held her breath.

'In the graveyard next to St Margaret's. We blessed her and gave her a proper burial.' Father Benjamin's voice was softer again now.

'Why didn't she go to the hospital? You can't just bury a child without going through the proper channels.' George's voice was breaking.

'Dr Jacobson wrote her death certificate. It's all by the book, George. It was unfortunate, but it was her choice to run away on one of the coldest nights of the year. Now, you mustn't upset yourself any more. You need to concentrate on getting Helena well, and helping Kitty through this difficult time. I think I'd better go. I'll see myself out.'

Kitty had shot up the stairs before Father Benjamin appeared. All night she had sobbed into her pillow at the thought of the sister she had never known, and who she longed for so desperately, lying alone in her grave, cold and scared.

'She's not buried at St Margaret's, you know.' She looked up at the clock now, knowing their session was coming to a close.

Richard sat back in his chair, his body sunken now, his hands clinging to the armrests as if they were keeping him upright. He looked exhausted.

'They're tearing the house down to make way for a new development and they excavated the graveyard,' she continued. 'I got hold of a copy of the excavation report.'

'And did it give details of what was found in the graves?' said Richard slowly.

'Some of the women were buried with their newborn babies. But none of the graves contained older children.'

'So they buried her elsewhere?'

'Or she's still alive,' said Kitty, watching him carefully.

'How can she be alive?' Richard's eyes were wide.

Kitty shrugged. 'Maybe she escaped and someone took her in. If they lied about what happened to her, maybe they lied about burying her. Or maybe she's been hiding out at St Margaret's all this time.'

Richard hesitated before speaking. 'It seems quite unlikely. Do you not think she would have tried to find you again?'

'Not if she blamed me for abandoning her,' Kitty said simply. 'I've been thinking a lot lately about the night my father died. The police woke me up at two a.m. I was ten years old and all alone. My mother was in hospital; my father had been visiting her and crashed on his way home.'

'I'm sorry, Kitty,' said Richard, shaking his head.

'I just remember telling them he was a good driver. That he wouldn't have crashed. I wanted to ask them why they were so sure it was an accident. My father told me once that if there was no motive, you could easily get away with murder. A neighbour came round and I sat in my room until the sun came up, thinking about it over and over: maybe there *was* a motive, maybe someone had wanted to hurt him.'

She paused and looked at Richard, expecting him to encourage her to go on, but instead he stared through her, not meeting her eye, then slowly looked up at the clock.

Chapter Ten

Monday 23 January 1961

George Cannon sat on the hard wooden chair by his wife's hospital bed, watching tubes of blood snaking from her pale forearm into the churning machine. He'd sat there a hundred times before, holding her hand, talking the hours away as the dialysis did what her kidneys could not. Yet tonight, as he watched her wasted body and listened to her strained breathing, everything felt wrong. Minutes seemed to drag like hours and the night felt like an endless black hole ahead of him.

He looked up at the ticking clock: 10 p.m. He couldn't leave her before she was back on the ward; she was covered in bruises from the prodding of endless needles and, he was convinced, from being lifted too roughly from bed to bed. The bruises covered her entire body and never seemed to heal – some green, some dark purple, the cluster of five over her hip almost black, as if the devil himself had left his handprint while trying to pull her down.

Matron had insisted that he leave at the end of visiting hours; he had insisted on staying. In the end, his position as Chief Superintendent of Sussex Police had won through and he'd been permitted to stay. Not that her consent, or lack of it, would have made any difference to his resolve. He was losing control over every other aspect of his life, and nothing

Matron or anyone else did would make him leave his wife tonight. Not when every waking and sleeping minute that he was not with her felt like utter failure on his part. For soon, too soon, she would be gone and he would hate himself for ever for leaving her side when she was still alive.

Tap, tap, tap. Matron's heels grew louder as she made her way down the silent corridor towards them. George looked at his wife's face and followed the line of her hollow cheekbones down to her mouth, where her lips were so cracked and dry they were bleeding at the edges.

'She's thirsty, she needs more water,' he snapped as Matron entered the room.

'Mr Cannon,' she sighed. 'She's still on five fluid ounces, I'm not permitted to give her any more.'

'Well, can you check again? She's been begging me for water. Does it really make that much difference? She's dying, for God's sake . . .' His voice faltered as he glared into Matron's tired eyes.

'I know it's hard,' she said, checking that the dialysis machine and all its workings were in order. 'But there is still hope that we will find her a donor. If we do, it will help her chances. Why don't you go home and get some sleep, Mr Cannon? We'll take good care of her.'

'I'm not going home.' George stood up.

'As you wish,' said Matron stiffly, turning to leave the room. She turned back to him at the door, the faint whiskers on her chin catching the light. 'Her treatment should be finished soon. Please come and find me when the machine stops and I'll see to her.'

He was reliving it all again, the desperation, the helplessness. Helena's body was rejecting the kidney she had been given two years ago after he had gone to Father Benjamin and asked for his prayers. Prayers that had been answered the day their lives changed for ever.

With only hours to spare, a kidney had been found for Helena. But on the day they should have been celebrating her new chance at life, their daughter Kitty had disappeared. For two days and nights they had searched, desperate, until finally her filthy, broken body was found in a ditch two miles from Preston church. With his wife having transplant surgery in one part of the hospital and his daughter in a coma in the other, George had made a deal with God that if he had to sacrifice one of them, it should be Helena rather than Kitty. And it seemed two years later that his prayers were being remembered.

He stood glaring at his reflection in the window as the icy rain battered full pelt at the glass. He felt as if the throbbing pressure in his head was going to crush his skull from the inside. He turned and looked back at Helena. He couldn't leave, but he couldn't bear to stay. There was no comfort for him anywhere, no escape from himself, and it was pushing him to the brink of madness.

The grinding noise of the dialysis machine and the ticking clock were eating through his eardrums. It took every ounce of strength not to smash them both to pieces. He sat back down and closed his stinging eyes again, his whole body throbbing, begging him for sleep. He tried to control his breathing and calm himself, but as soon as he relaxed, he felt himself falling, down and down like sand through an hourglass. He jerked himself awake, barely able to breathe through the tightness in his chest. His eyes strained to focus as they wandered up Helena's motionless body.

Her legs were so swollen she could no longer lift them, and he ached as he recalled a time when she had been free of all this pain. Images flashed into his mind of when they had first met – her hand outstretched, her wavy blond hair falling forward as she'd removed her glasses and smiled. He hadn't been able to take his eyes off her.

Before long, he lived to be with her; he had never met anyone like her. She was so strong and fearless, no one could ever have guessed what was going on inside her perfect body. When she had started getting dizzy and tired less than a year after their wedding, they'd presumed it was the baby they longed for, but within a week they were sitting in disbelief in Dr Jacobson's office, grief-stricken and unable even to look at each other. There was no baby, nor would there ever be, and their married life – their future as they had envisaged it – was gone.

George made his way out into the tiled corridor and crept past beds of sleeping patients towards Matron's mottled glass door. He knocked quietly, then slowly turned the handle. A wireless crackled in the corner of a pristine space furnished with a coat stand, a filing cabinet and a wooden desk, upon which sat a china cup half filled with tea. The room was empty.

'Hello?' he whispered.

'George?'

The voice from behind him startled George so badly that he stumbled into the desk, sending the teacup and its contents crashing to the floor. He looked up to see the familiar face of Dr Jacobson, his family doctor of twenty years, who was peeling a snow-sodden coat from his arms and shaking the flakes from his greying hair.

'Are you all right?' He peered with concern at George over his half-moon glasses. George could feel the freezing night radiating from the doctor's face; could see the burst blood vessels on his nose glowing purple against his pale skin.

'Yes, I'm fine. Have you seen Matron anywhere, Edward? Helena's treatment is finished and I need to get back to Kitty.'

'Not yet. She's probably doing her rounds.'

George lifted the telephone from its cradle.

'You're wasting your time,' Dr Jacobson said. 'All the lines are down from the storm. Are you sure you're all right?' He hung his coat up on the stand. 'I can see to Helena if you need to leave.'

'Can you? Will you stay with her until I get back?'

'Of course,' said Dr Jacobson, crossing his arms and lowering his voice. 'George, how is Kitty doing?'

'Despite what you said, she doesn't seem to be getting back to her old self,' George replied curtly. 'She's terribly worried and upset about her mother. She didn't want me to leave her tonight.'

He knew it wasn't hard for Kitty to sense his anxiety, and that nothing he did alleviated it. Not the whisky he drank before he finally fell asleep at dawn, nor the assurances from Dr Jacobson that they would find Helena another kidney. His daughter had been troubled since coming so close to death two years previously. She spoke often of meeting her twin the day she went missing, something he thought was impossible when she first told him about it in the hospital, but which to his horror had turned out to be true. Elvira had been returned to St Margaret's by her adoptive family and had then escaped. And now she was dead and he would always blame himself.

81

He had never even met the child, but he would never forget Father Benjamin walking into Mother Carlin's office at St Margaret's. 'You have a beautiful daughter, George, though I'm sorry to tell you that her mother didn't survive.'

George had sat down heavily. 'That's terrible. Did she suffer?'

'No, she delivered them both and then she had a bleed. It was very quick; there was nothing we could do.' Mother Carlin had rested her hand on his shoulder.

'Both?' he had said. 'There was more than one child?'

'She had twins, George, but the other child got a little stuck, so she took a while to breathe. She's alive, but we need to keep her here and care for her. When she's well enough, we'll find her a lovely home.'

'Can I see her?' he had asked.

'No, she's in the infirmary. Please don't worry, George, you have a beautiful daughter to cherish, and one is quite enough for you to manage.'

At that moment, the door to the dark office opened, and as the light came into the room, so did Kitty. She was in a Moses basket, and so quiet, George wasn't sure there was even a baby in it until he peered over the top. She had looked up at him with her huge brown eyes and instinctively he had put his hand on her cheek. She had reached up and clutched his finger, her fist was so tiny but her grip was so strong and she wouldn't let go; it was the start of their unbreakable bond.

He missed the way Kitty used to be before she went missing, his carefree, happy Kitty. He should never have left her alone. He suddenly felt a desperate need to get away.

'I'm sorry, but I really think I should go, I don't want to

82

leave Helena, but I'm very worried about Kitty. She was terribly upset when I left; her nerves since she went missing are only getting worse.'

Dr Jacobson patted his shoulder as Matron reappeared. 'Yes, George, of course. You go.'

'Thank you.' He turned, making his way hurriedly through the entrance and down the icy steps of the hospital into the falling snow.

His car was barely distinguishable as he trudged across the car park in the dark, but eventually he found it and fumbled at the lock with freezing fingers. The door creaked open and he climbed in, pushing the key into the ignition and turning it several times before it caught.

The engine groaned in protest, the wipers batting ineffectually at the thick layer of snow on the windscreen. He forced the freezing gears into reverse and pumped on the accelerator, but the car stood still, rocking against the snow pressed up against its tyres. Losing patience, he slammed his foot to the floor, and it skidded backwards over the ice and into a vehicle parked in the next row. He had no time to assess the damage; he had no time even to think – he just had an overwhelming need to get to Kitty. Frantically he righted the wheel and rubbed at the windscreen with his arm before inching slowly across the car park and out onto the pitch-black road.

He had hoped that the road would prove less treacherous, but the snow and sleet had turned other cars' tracks to black ice. As he slid around a sharp bend, a clump of snow fell with a great thud from the trees above onto his windscreen. The wipers continued to jerk and drag at the snow so that for some time he could see nothing at all. When it finally cleared, he was startled to see a crow pecking at the guts of a dead rabbit in the middle of the road. It launched itself skyward just as the car was upon it, its long black wings beating frantically as it flew over the bonnet to safety.

George felt his heart racing in his chest and tried to steady his breathing as the road ahead of him became a white carpet once more. Devoid of life, so innocent-looking, he thought, yet utterly deadly. He pumped his foot on the accelerator, his pulse throbbing in his ears. Slow down, slow down. You'll skid, you'll crash. Speed up, she needs you. Get home.

His frantic breathing seemed to suck up the oxygen in the car, the heater making no impression in the frozen air. His foot shook as it hovered over the accelerator. Just get home and you can put this right. She'll be fine. She's ten years old, she's exhausted, she'll have fallen asleep. Calm down.

He hit another sharp bend and looked down at the speed-ometer. The needle was hovering at 45: much too fast even on a clear summer's night. He was no use to Kitty dead; he needed to slow down. Another bend and the wheels tugged at the steering wheel as he fought to keep control. Why was this taking so long? Where was the main road?

'Damn it!' he yelled out in frustration. He had done this drive a thousand times before with Kitty beside him, smiling, chatting, laughing, easing the stress of their visits to Helena, reading his mind, saying what he needed to hear. 'She'll be fine, Daddy. She looked better, don't you think? I read in the newspaper that there are more people than ever signing up as donors.'

Why had he left his daughter when he knew she was so anxious? He should have taken her with him. What if she did something stupid, took it upon herself to venture out into the blizzard and try and make her way to the hospital. The image of her walking through the snow flashed into his mind's eye, torturing him on his painfully slow journey back to her.

Where was the bloody main road? The car slid again and he hit the brakes, but nothing happened. The car was turning sideways. If something comes the other way now, he thought, I'm dead. He was in a nightmare, a bottomless pit from which he would never escape. He had let her down. Again. He didn't deserve her. He never had.

When Helena had agreed that he could bring Kitty home, he thought his heart would explode. She would always be devastated at his betrayal, but she had found it in her to understand. With his wife in hospital, he had needed companionship, and Kitty's mother had provided it. He had desperately wanted a child and Helena had found a way to give him one when she never could.

As the car finally righted itself, he could at last see the lights of the main road in the distance. But as he turned the final bend, he saw her. Although he had pictured her battling through the snow to get to him, he found it nearly impossible to take in the image before him. He frantically tried to shake the hallucination from his head, but she was still there, wearing her red duffel coat, walking towards him, her small body bent forward, her head buried into her hood, trying to shield herself from the pelting snow. How could she have done it? How was she here? It couldn't be her, it couldn't. No, Kitty. NO!

He knew immediately that he was going to hit her. He pressed his palm on the horn and slammed on the brakes, wrenching the steering wheel as hard as he could in the opposite direction to where she stood. As the car roared towards her, the headlights fell into her path and she looked up, blinking in their glare. For a moment their eyes locked, and as the car spun past, George reached out to her. For a second she was in his arms again, as she had been the first day he held her, her life in his hands.

A rushing, scraping sound filled the car as the tyres tried to grip what they could not, and as he spun round and round, over and over, he began to scream her name. Run to me, Kitty, he thought frantically, get to me, hold my hand before I die.

The snow-covered world rushed past his window, and he spun uncontrollably for one last time, then suddenly plummeted downwards, his head forced against the windscreen so hard he felt as if somebody had cut his skull open with an axe. Pain like he had never felt before radiated down his back, as if each vertebra was being twisted loose. Screaming, grinding metal began to crush his body as he felt the cabin closing in around him tighter and tighter, until finally everything stopped and he could not move at all.

For a second there was silence as fluid began to pour from his head and mouth into his eyes and down his neck. He tried to turn his head and shout Kitty's name, but only liquid came out. He coughed and spluttered, blood and mucus filling the footwell below him.

He lay helpless, crying out in agony, tears and vomit mingling with his blood as he waited desperately for his daughter to get to him. Help me, Kitty, help me! Don't let me die alone.

Chapter Eleven

Sunday 5 February 2017

Gracewell Retirement Home was a modest two-storey red-brick building at the end of a quiet cul-de-sac on the far side of Preston village. Sam walked up the path to the front door and pressed the bell, glancing at her watch. She had called the office on her way over, and Fred had looked up Mother Carlin's cuttings, which revealed that she had died at Gracewell in August 2006. As she was en route, Sam had decided it was still worth the trip. Andy had told her that a couple of the nuns were living there, so there was a chance Mother Carlin wasn't the only staff member from St Margaret's who had retired to Gracewell.

'Shit,' she mumbled under her breath, painfully aware that she needed to be back at her desk in less than two hours. When no reply came, she cupped her hand over one of the glass panes on either side of the door, peering down the empty hallway.

'Come on!' she urged, ringing the bell again before the sound of heels tapping on tiles finally began to echo towards her. After a quick glance through the peephole, a heavily made-up girl in her mid twenties opened the door, her large bosom straining against her nurse's uniform.

'Yes?' she said, returning a stray hair to her scraped-back ponytail.

'Oh, hi,' said Sam, realising that she hadn't prepared a speech. 'I was wondering if you could help me. I'm looking for someone called Mother Carlin,' she said, pretending she didn't know about Mother Carlin's death. 'She was Mother Superior at St Margaret's down the road in Preston and I believe she may be living here at Gracewell.'

'I'm sorry, Mother Carlin died many years ago I believe, any queries regarding St Margaret's need to be referred to the council,' said the girl.

'Oh right. It's not really a question about St Margaret's,' said Sam. 'My grandfather worked there as a caretaker, and he was very fond of Mother Carlin. He recently died and I found some letters and documents of hers amongst his things. They seem important and I was hoping to trace any family members or friends in case they might want them.'

'Um, this isn't a great time. We're actually in the middle of doing breakfast.' The girl looked over her shoulder.

Sam stamped her feet and rubbed her hands. 'Blimey, it's freezing out here. I'm happy to wait.'

'Well, I suppose you'd better come in, but you could be waiting a while.'

'Of course, no problem.'

The girl let Sam in, closing the door behind them, then led her down a corridor lined with staff photographs and faded prints of the Sussex Downs and into a lounge containing threadbare chairs and a few pieces of tired-looking furniture.

'I'll tell my manager you're here. Hopefully she won't be long. What was your name?'

'Thank you, it's Samantha Harper,' said Sam, seeing no reason to lie.

The girl left her alone in the room presumably reserved for afternoon dozing and *Columbo* reruns. The smell of bleach and yesterday's food hung in the air. Sam felt nauseous as she paced, scanning the bookcases and windowsills for any records or photographs of the residents of Gracewell.

'Miss Harper?' The girl popped her head round the door. 'I'm afraid our manager is rather tied up at the moment. She's suggested you write to Sister Mary Francis, who knew Mother Carlin well.'

'Oh, right, is Sister Mary Francis living here?' Sam forced a smile as the girl nodded at her whilst backing out of the room. 'Is there no chance of seeing her today?'

'I'm afraid not. She's in her nineties now and sleeps most mornings because of her heart medication. She wouldn't cope with a surprise visitor; she'd be unsettled for the rest of the day.'

'I understand.' Sam nodded. 'Would it help if you told her it was related to St Margaret's?'

'I don't think so. We get the occasional visitor looking for information about babies born at St Margaret's that they're trying to trace. They are often very distressed and Sister Mary Francis finds it upsetting. She won't meet with them at all any more, so we refer them to the council.'

'Yes, yes. I'm sure it must be very upsetting,' said Sam, as the girl checked her watch. 'But as I said, this documentation looks quite important to me and relates to Mother Carlin's affairs. I think, as a friend of hers, Sister Mary Francis might want to see it. It isn't anything to do with tracing babies.'

'Still, we'd have to go through the proper channels. I'm sure you understand.'

'Sure. Thanks for trying.' Sam took out her phone, then

glanced at the girl's name badge. 'Would I be able to just make a call in here before I go, Gemma? My grandmother is waiting to hear if I've managed to track down Mother Carlin or anyone who knew her. It's very important to her, as my grandfather only just passed away.'

'I can't leave you in here, and I really need to get on or I'll be late finishing my shift.'

'You pulled the short straw this week then? You must be wrecked!'

'Yup, night shift all this week, been on my feet since eleven last night.' The girl smiled faintly.

'Look, I'll be two minutes,' said Sam. 'I'm fine to let myself out if you're busy. I'll stick my head into the dining room to let you know I'm going.' She smiled and started to make the call as if it was a done deal, giving Gemma little choice but to leave her there.

Once the girl had gone, Sam dropped her phone into her bag and, making one more sweep of the room for any useful information, went out into the corridor. It was obvious where the dining room was from the clatter of cutlery and aroma of burnt toast. As she reached the entrance, Gemma came flying past with a trolley of dirty plates.

'Bye then, thank you!' called Sam. Gemma waved distractedly, not looking up, before charging through the double doors into the kitchen.

Knowing her window was a small one, Sam slammed the front door, yelling out another 'Bye!' for good measure, then darted towards the brown-carpeted stairway, bolting up two steps at a time. The bustle of the floor below gave way to an eerily quiet landing, and as she looked down the long corridor of numbered bedrooms, her heart sank at the impossibility of her task. Even if she were somehow to discover which room Sister Mary Francis was sleeping in, if she bounded in unannounced, she would possibly cause the old lady's heart to give out. But now that she was here, she couldn't give up. In two days the ghosts of St Margaret's would be gone, and whatever tied Kitty Cannon to the place would be severed for ever. Sister Mary Francis was here somewhere, and Sam felt compelled to try and talk to her.

She checked the stairs again for signs of life, then started to make her way down the long corridor, scanning each room as she went for any clue as to who its occupant might be. By the time she'd reached the fire escape at the end, she was none the wiser, and when she heard the sound of doors slamming and staff chatting in the hallway below, her nerve started to fail her completely. She glanced at her watch – 8.15. If she left now, she could still escape Gracewell unscathed and make it back to the office in time for her shift.

Just as she was turning to go, she saw it: a blue file resting on a shelf next to the fire extinguisher. Quickly she walked over and flicked it open to find that its back page contained a map of the building, with a list underneath of every resident. She ran her finger down until she found who she was looking for: Sister Mary Francis – Room 15.

'Gotcha!' she muttered, returning the file and setting off back along the corridor.

It felt like the most daunting doorstep of her career to date, but without giving herself a moment to change her mind, she lifted her fist to the door of Room 15 and knocked. Silence. As her heart hammered in her ears, she knocked again. 'Sister Mary Francis? It's Gemma. There's a visitor here to see you, can we come in?' Slowly she pushed the door handle down, then, checking the corridor one last time, she entered the darkened room and closed the door quickly behind her, locking it shut.

The curtains were drawn and it took Sam's eyes a moment to adjust and decipher the layout of the room. It was divided into two parts: she was standing in a lounge area containing a large armchair, a television and a small table; beyond that she could make out the outline of a person lying in the bed by the window. The blinds were down and the slats closed, but as Sam approached, she could see the sunlight trying to get in, illuminating Sister Mary Francis's face.

'Sister? Are you awake?' The woman didn't stir, and after a second or two Sam moved closer.

Despite her age, the nun's skin was smooth of wrinkles, as if she'd never expressed an emotion in her life, and her grey hair had spread itself out obediently across her pillow like a fan. She was very thin, and her arms lay straight alongside her body, her arthritic fingers reaching out stiffly over the sides of the bed. Her covers were perfectly intact, as though she hadn't moved all night, and she was so deathly white that if the blankets hadn't been gently rising and falling with her breathing, Sam might have assumed she was dead.

'Sister? Are you awake?' she said as loudly as she dared.

Sister Mary Francis began to stir, turning her head from left to right and then finally opening her dark blue eyes. Sam froze, terrified that she would scream at the sight of a complete stranger in her room. But the woman just looked at her briefly, then closed her eyes again.

'Where is Gemma?' she said croakily, beginning to cough slightly.

'She's just making your breakfast.'

Sister Mary Francis was coughing harder now. Sam listened to the phlegm bubbling in her lungs, waiting for the coughing to subside. Finally the old woman managed to whisper, 'Who are you?'

'My name is Samantha. I asked Gemma if I could have a quick word with you.'

'Gemma knows I don't like visitors,' said the nun, wiping the spit away from around her mouth.

'I'm sorry. I only need to ask you a couple of questions, then I'll leave you in peace.'

Sister Mary opened her eyes and looked at Sam intently. 'Questions about what, child?'

'I recently attended the inquest of someone called Father Benjamin. I believe you worked at St Margaret's with him.'

'Any questions about St Margaret's need to be directed to the council,' said Sister Mary Francis, her dozy state evaporating suddenly.

'I don't need to speak to the council,' said Sam, 'I'm just trying to find out if you ever knew someone by the name of Kitty Cannon during your time at St Margaret's.'

Sister Mary looked at her as if she were a fly in her soup, then sat up slowly and swung her legs out of the bed. She pulled a cord to open the blinds and sunshine flooded in. Sam blinked, looking away momentarily.

'Who are you again?' said Sister Mary. The door handle began to rattle, making Sam jump.

'I'm a friend of Kitty Cannon's. We were at Father

Benjamin's inquest together, and she was looking for you. I mean, she hoped to see you again.'

Sister Mary glared at her. 'I'm certain I've never met any-one by that name.'

'Sister? Are you okay?' Gemma called out urgently. The nun looked to the door and then at Sam. 'I thought I heard voices in there. Sister, why is the door locked?'

'Could you get the key, Gemma? I've locked myself in and I can't get out of bed,' said Sister Mary Francis, her eyes fixed on Sam.

'Okay, Sister, I'll be right back,' called Gemma. 'Just hold on!'

'You'd better go, child. They'll call the police if they catch you in here.' Sister Mary sat on the end of her bed and wound her rosary beads through her fingers.

Sam stared at her, her heart pounding. 'Well, maybe we should speak to the police about St Margaret's. I'd hate to bring the name of the Sisters of Mercy into disrepute and for you to spend your remaining time here having to answer awkward questions about what went on in that hellhole. Times are different now, Sister. I've seen the makeshift coffin in Mother Carlin's office floor and I think you'd find the protection you enjoyed all those years ago might have fallen away.'

Sister Mary stood slowly and walked over to the Bible by her bedside table, running her fingers over the gold cross embedded in the front. 'Why is it that all these years later, everyone is looking for someone to blame?'

'Maybe because they can't get over what you did to them,' said Sam.

Sister Mary Francis smiled. 'Be careful, child. Satan disguises himself as an angel of light.'

'Who do you think Kitty Cannon should blame, then?' said Sam.

'She could start by accepting that her father was a philanderer,' she hissed, 'we gave those girls a roof over their heads when they would otherwise have been on the streets. I know what some of the staff here say about us, how they talked about Mother Carlin. I heard her shouting out when she died and nobody came to help. Nobody cared about what happened to her that night.'

'What do you mean what happened to her?'

But Sister Mary Francis didn't answer her. The old woman turned her back and Sam knew her time was up. She unlocked the door and darted along the corridor back towards the fire escape. Pushing it open, she ran down the steel staircase, frantically dialling Fred's mobile number.

'Fred, it's Sam. I'm gonna be a bit late. Can you cover for me?' She jumped into her car. 'And can you look up any cuttings on Kitty Cannon's father. Yes, the chat show host. I'll fill you in when I get in.'

As soon as she hung up, she rang Nana to check she and Emma were okay.

'We're fine, darling, are you all right? You left very early.' Nana's voice was deep, as if she had just woken up.

'I'm good, Nana. I was wondering, could you possibly look in Grandad's paperwork and see if there are any other letters from that girl Ivy. You know, like the one you were reading last night.' The line went quiet. 'Nana? Can you hear me?'

'Yes, I can hear you,' said Nana, as Sam heard Emma calling out to her in the background.

'Sorry to ask, Nana. I know you're busy, but could you possibly check now? It's pretty important.'

'All right,' Nana sighed. 'Hold on.'

Sam felt a surge of guilt at the thought of Nana having to run around after her as well as Emma. But she had two days before St Margaret's was torn down, and if this was the story that was going to get her noticed, then she was doing it for all of them. Nana needed her flat back, and Sam needed to earn some proper money so that she could provide for her and Emma.

As she looked at her watch, panicking about getting back to the office before Murray noticed she was late, she heard Nana pick up the phone and let out another heavy sigh as she sat back down.

'Why are you so interested in these letters?' Nana said.

'Who wouldn't be? That poor girl.'

'You're not using them for your work, are you?'

Sam hesitated. She'd never lied to Nana before, but then again, she wasn't strictly using them for work; she was doing some digging for her own purposes. 'No, I just think she's fascinating.'

'Who?' said Nana.

'The girl in the letter,' replied Sam, as Nana cleared her throat and began to read.

Chapter Twelve

Sunday 16 December 1956

Ivy waited until she was sure everyone was asleep, then reached under her pillow for the ballpoint pen and folded sheets of paper that she had smuggled out of letter-writing that evening.

The writing pad she had brought with her was in the suitcase that Mother Carlin had confiscated on her arrival, but on a Sunday they were allowed a few minutes before prayers to write home. Their correspondence was strictly supervised and double-checked by Mother Carlin before the letters were handed to Patricia to give to the laundry delivery driver. Patricia, the mousy-haired girl with freckles who sat next to Ivy at dinner, had whispered to Ivy that only tales of the nuns' kindness and the girls' deep appreciation were permitted. But after much pleading on Ivy's part, Patricia had agreed that if Ivy wrote a second letter, she would slip it in with the others. Ivy had smiled at her, gripping Patricia's hand tightly under the table until Sister Faith had barked at them to file out from the dining hall, their stomachs still rumbling with hunger.

Now she looked up to the locked window next to her bed. She guessed it was nearing midnight, but the moonlight cast just enough light for her to see. As her pen hovered over the page, Alistair's face flashed into her mind. It had been months since his smiling brown eyes had watched her every move but she could still smell him, feel his hands on her back, slowly pulling her into him. She missed him so much her whole body ached. She didn't know how to begin to describe how desperate she felt. As she lay on the coarse blanket of her dormitory bed, she could still reach out and touch the crisp white sheets of their hotel room, recall her cheeks flushing as he smiled over at her from the open balcony doors, the goose bumps forming on her skin as the sea breeze danced over it. She had to find the words to make him act. It was her only hope of escape from this terrible place.

My love,

I have found myself in a place where I have never felt so wretched and alone.

Things at home got unbearable. Uncle Frank was so angry that he raised his hand to me most nights. He would drink, then come into my room and shout that the neighbours knew I was a slut and a whore, and as I curled into a ball and waited for the pain, I dreamed of you walking in behind him and knocking him to the ground. Mother did her best to pull him off me, but the one time she couldn't get between us, he punched me so hard that I feared for our baby's life. Things at home had become so wretched that when Dr Jacobson told us Father Benjamin had got me a place at St Margaret's, I was relieved to have somewhere to go, away from the tension and the shouting and Mother's pain.

But now that I am here, I am so utterly miserable and homesick I would do anything to be back home. Uncle Frank refused to drive me, so I had to get the bus. Mother was too upset to say goodbye. St Margaret's is way out in the country-side, beyond the church at Preston. 'This is your stop, love,' said the driver, without me even asking him. How many other girls must he have dropped here, I thought, their bumps making them carry their cases awkwardly. And as he drove off and left me all alone, there it was: a huge Victorian house alone on the horizon. It was surrounded by a brick wall and in its centre a wrought-iron gate adorned with a heavy pad-lock. As I approached, I saw a steel bell hanging from it. I hesitated for a moment, then reached out my hand and pulled the string from side to side, so that the bell let out a high-pitched ding that unsettled the crows in the trees overhead.

I stood there for a while and was about to ring it again when a nun in full-length black habit appeared at the door of the house and began to walk down the long stone pathway towards me. She looked very solemn and her hands were clasped in front of her, and as she walked silently towards me, the keys hanging from her belt jingled noisily like those of a jailer.

Eventually she reached me, and we stood for a moment star-ing at one another until eventually I said, 'I'm Ivy Jenkins, Dr Jacobson sent me.' I held out the piece of paper in my hand, but she just looked at it as if she might catch something from it. Even-tually she undid the padlock and said, 'I'm Sister Mary Francis, follow me.' The hostility in her voice was like a speech bubble that hung in the air between us.

I dragged myself and my case through the gate, then she closed it behind me with a slam and secured the padlock once more. She was no taller than me, but her frame was narrow and she moved fast, her starched skirt hovering along the path as if she had no feet, while I staggered awkwardly behind her, stopping to set my case down several times. The ash trees looking down on me *rustled, as if whispering their disapproval to one another. Finally we reached the dark wooden front door, criss-crossed with black iron, which brought to my mind a dungeon. Sister Mary Francis had her back to me, and as I finally caught up with her I could hear her keys jingling before one rattled in the lock and turned with a heavy click. Slowly the front door opened.*

One of the younger girls let out a cry in her sleep, and Ivy startled. She pulled back the covers and tiptoed over to her. If Sister heard her, they would all suffer.

'Shh.' She held the girl tight as she sobbed, rocking her to calm her down. 'Shh, go back to sleep, you need your sleep.' She stroked her tear-drenched cheek, then crept back across the floor, her heart hammering in her ears. She waited for her own breathing to calm before picking up her pen again.

As Sister Mary Francis disappeared down the long, gleaming tiled corridor, I looked up briefly at the vaulted ceiling and the vast staircase, at the top of which hung a huge sign: 'Dear Lord, may the fallen find their way back to you through the strength of their prayers and hard work.' I hurried to catch Sister Mary Francis, and passed three or maybe four girls in brown overalls – some with large stomachs, some not – all on their hands and knees scrubbing the spotless floor. No one stopped their tasks to look up at me; no one spoke.

A bellow of steam hit me then as I passed a huge doorway and briefly looked in to see a laundry. Dozens of girls stood at sinks, pulling sheets from mangles and hanging them from drying rails. It was all too much to take in in such a short time, but what struck me again was the deafening silence. It was broken only by Sister Mary Francis, already waiting for me at the end of the hallway with a scowl on her face. 'Mother Carlin doesn't have all day, hurry up. You can leave your suitcase there.' I rested it on the ground next to the door and nervously entered the Mother Superior's office.

It was a dark, miserable room that contained only a small window and a fierce-looking woman in full habit behind a large mahogany desk. I stood in silence while she continued to write in a little black book. I knew better than to speak. Finally she looked up at me, and with her pointed chin, white complexion and hooked nose, I knew her immediately to be a witch. A portrait of her hung on the wall behind her. It was a great deal more flattering than the real-life version.

She cleared her throat, then spoke. 'What is your name?' I told her, and she said I would no longer be called Ivy; that I would be known here as Mary instead as our own names are forbidden. I felt a rush of panic, and a sting of tears to my eyes that I managed to swallow down. 'All the girls who come here have duties assigned to them, and you will be working in the laundry. You will be expected to work just as hard as we do, to rise early and use the day productively, to attend mass and ask the Lord's forgiveness. Do you understand?' It was hard to stay composed but I managed it and said I understood. She told me that Sister Mary Francis would show me to my dormitory.

When I came out of her office, my case was gone and Sister Mary Francis said I wouldn't be needing it again. I was hysterical. It had my only picture of Father in it and a blanket I had knitted for my baby. A pink one, as I am so sure it is a girl. I begged them to give it back to me, until Mother Carlin appeared and started to thrash me with a belt right then and there in the corridor. She told me that I should be ashamed, carrying on like that.

Ivy bit her lip at the memory of the moment she realised they had taken her father's photograph. It was like they had stolen his final touch, his final moment with her, when he had blown her a kiss from the bottom of the stairs as she stood in her nightie staring down at him. It was as if Sister Mary Francis had gone back in time and taken it away. But she knew she shouldn't keep mentioning her father. She needed Alistair to feel that she saw him as her saviour, that there was no hope other than him.

Her eyes stung; she desperately needed to sleep. Her arms throbbed from propping herself up to write, and her whole body ached. But she needed to leave the letter under her pillow before morning or it wouldn't be ready for Patricia to give to the laundry delivery boy.

Afterwards I followed Sister Mary Francis up the stairs to my dormitory. More girls were on the stairs, but no one looked at me, no one smiled, no one said a word. She left me in the dormitory and told me to change into my overalls. The room was cold and grey, with hospital-style beds, a chipped wash-basin under a sash window, faded curtains and a bell on the wall. Then they showed me the laundry. We are expected to work the huge machinery, and all the girls' hands are red raw from scrubbing in the cold water. After six hours in the laundry we had dinner – watery soup and hard bread. We are not allowed to talk at dinner; we are never allowed to talk.

The nuns are beyond cruel. They beat us with canes or anything they can get their hands on if we so much as talk. A girl burnt herself so badly on the red-hot steel sheets that she developed a blister up her arm that is now infected. Sister Mary Francis just came over and scolded her for wasting time.

The only time we are allowed to speak is to say our prayers, or to say 'Yes, Sister.' There are prayers before breakfast, mass after breakfast, prayers before bed. And then black emptiness before the bell at the end of the dormitory wakes us again at 6 a.m. We live by the bell; there are no clocks, no calendars, no mirrors, no sense of time. No one talks to me about what will happen when my baby comes, but I know there are babies here because I hear them crying at night.

She winced as a little foot inside her suddenly kicked her hard. Her bladder throbbed; she needed the bathroom desperately, but they weren't allowed to get up in the night. She thought of her baby, warm and safe inside her. She had no idea how it would come out. She had heard a girl at school saying that they came out of your belly button, but she couldn't see how. All she knew was that God would decide when it was the right time and take care of both of them.

She shifted onto her other side to try and get comfortable. The covers rippled as her baby wriggled happily inside her, oblivious to what lay in store. Ivy had watched the girls without bumps, who sat at a separate table at dinner. They carried a sadness she had yet to know. She had to get out of St Margaret's before her baby came. She had to make him understand.

I miss you so much, my love. I miss our drives down to the seafront, I miss the feel of the grass on my skin as we lay looking up at the sky. We are not allowed outside. I feel so cut off, from nature, from home, from you, from myself. I dream about running away, but the only time the nuns aren't watching is at night, and the dormitories are so high up you would break your neck trying to get down. Even if I did get out, where would I run to? Uncle Frank would bring me straight back; Mother wouldn't be able to stop him. I would run to you, but I do not know if you want me, and I couldn't bear it if you turned me away in the street. I have nothing left of who I am, who I used to be. Not even my name. At night I feel my bump in the darkness, our baby moving around inside me. I have let my child down. I have let everyone down. I cry myself to sleep every night.

I don't know if you are reading these letters, but I cannot bear to let you go. Please, if you still love me, come and get me. Nobody needs to know that this baby is yours; perhaps you could pay for me to stay in a boarding house. I would be happy to work to pay you back as soon as the baby is old enough for me to leave it. I don't care what I do or where I go, I would never be an embarrassment to you.

Please, I'm begging you, come quickly, or I shall go mad in this place before long.

With all my love for ever,
Your Ivy

A tear dripped onto the page and Ivy wiped it away, before folding the letter neatly, kissing it and placing it under her pillow. Then she turned onto her side, buried her face in the covers and began to cry.

Chapter Thirteen

Sunday 5 February 2017

Preston Lane was a narrow road full of twists and turns that Sam needed to take at a snail's pace. According to the cutting that Fred had dug up for her, after driving past Preston church, George Cannon had made the fateful turning into the road that she couldn't help noticing led to St Margaret's. Then, according to the inquest written up in the *Sussex Argus* on 12 March 1961, he had skidded on black ice and landed in a ditch, dying instantly.

After pulling into a lay-by, Sam stood by the busy road taking in her surroundings. From the paper's description of the crash site, nothing much had changed in fifty years. It was still a single-lane road with high hedges on either side and ditches lining it. It was a cold day, as it must have been in January 1961, and Sam could see black ice in the road ahead of where she stood. She reached into her bag and pulled out her notepad. *Chief Superintendent of Sussex Police killed in horror crash*, the *Sussex Argus* headline from 24 January had stated. The road curved dramatically just ahead of where the accident had happened, and Sam made her way towards the bend, noting a large Georgian house on the corner. There were no other houses as far as the eye could see, so she decided she might as well knock on the door and ask if they knew who'd been living there at the time of the accident. It would be her last stop of the morning. After that, she had to get to work.

She walked up to the front door, where a stone plaque read *Preston Manor*, and reached for the lion's-head knocker. She could hear loud classical music coming from some-where inside, but after a minute or so no one had answered. She tried again and finally heard someone coughing on the other side of the door. It was opened by a man in his fifties with a round face, red cheeks and thinning grey hair. His large belly was covered with an apron bearing Michelan-gelo's David, and it was obvious from the amount of food on it that she'd interrupted a culinary session.

'Hello. I was wondering if you could help me,' she smiled. 'I'm a student, and I'm trying to find out about a car acci-dent that happened on the corner here.'

'We get a lot of accidents happening here,' said the man, cutting her off. 'It's a nasty bend. I wouldn't be able to remember any individual cases.'

'Okay,' said Sam. 'The one I'm interested in happened in 1961, so some time ago.'

'No, I really wouldn't have a clue, I'm afraid.'

'Were you living here at the time?' said Sam, trying to prolong the conversation.

'Yes, my family has lived here for generations.' The man wiped his hands on a tea towel.

'It's a beautiful house, I can see why you wouldn't want to leave.'

'Thank you. I'm sorry, but I must rescue my soufflés,' he said, reaching out to close the door.

'Of course. Would there be anyone else around who was living here at the time, your mother or father perhaps?' The man sighed openly, then pointed to a gate across the drive-way. 'Try my mother, she's in the granny flat next door. But be warned, she likes to talk,' he added before slamming the door.

'Thank you,' said Sam to the door knocker, then walked down the cobbled path that led to a small bungalow adorned with hanging baskets and window boxes. She pressed the buzzer and waited until a short elderly woman with curly white hair and rosy cheeks appeared at the door.

'Can I help you?' The woman was clutching a pair of secateurs in one hand and a large bunch of calla lilies in the other.

'Hello, I was just talking to your son. My name's Sam. I'm doing some research on the area and was interested in a car accident that happened on the bend next to your house in January 1961.'

'I see. Nice of him to send a complete stranger to his eld-erly mother's door.' The woman winked.

'Yes, he was mid-creation in the kitchen,' smiled Sam.

'He usually is. Why don't you tell me what you want to know, and I'll see if I can remember anything.' She set her flowers down on the hall table.

'That would be great, thank you so much, Mrs . . . ?'

'I'm Rosalind,' said the woman, putting on her glasses and pulling the door to as she stepped outside.

'Nice to meet you, Rosalind.'

'So do you know who the accident involved?' She placed a heavy woollen blanket on the bench by the back door and carefully lowered herself onto it. 'It's a terrible corner that; so many people come off the road, especially in this icy weather.'

'I can imagine,' said Sam, pulling her notebook from her bag. 'The accident I'm interested in involved a local policeman, a Chief Superintendent George Cannon.'

'And was it a bad accident?'

'Yes, he was killed instantly, I believe. I don't think anyone else was involved; he just took the corner too fast and lost control. Ended up in the ditch.'

The woman stared at the ground for a moment while Sam rubbed her gloved hands together.

'Cannon, that name does ring a bell.'

'He was the father of Kitty Cannon, I believe, the chat show host. She was a local girl; I don't know if you've heard of her.'

'Oh, right,' said the woman, frowning.

Sam looked up at the stunning Georgian building with clematis creeping up the side towards the windows. 'I just thought one of you might have seen something from the house.'

Rosalind shook her head. 'No, I'm sorry, I can't help you.'

'Well, thank you for your time. If I leave you my number, would you call me if you think of anything?'

'Of course, dear,' said Rosalind, before waving her off cheerfully.

It wasn't until Sam got back to her office and settled down with a strong coffee that she had a chance to digest the morning's events.

'So what's going on?' asked Fred, looking over his glasses at her.

Sam pulled the letter from her bag. 'My nana found this amongst my grandad's paperwork. It's a letter written by a young girl called Ivy in 1956. She's pregnant by her footballer boyfriend, who doesn't want to know by the sound of things.' She pulled her laptop from her bag and fired it up. A picture of Emma filled the screen as it loaded.

'Nice pic,' said Fred. 'She's beautiful.'

'Thanks, she would be – she's mine,' said Sam, smiling as she clicked on Google and typed in Father Benjamin's name.

'So who is this Ivy?' said Fred, glancing at the letter.

'No idea, but the letter mentions Father Benjamin, who is the priest whose remains were found at that derelict mansion. Kevin covered it last week,' said Sam, turning the screen towards him. 'And Kitty Cannon, as in the chat show host . . .'

'Cannonball?' said Fred.

'That's the one,' said Sam. 'She was at Father Benjamin's inquest, apparently.'

'Why?' said Fred, leaning over towards her.

'Not sure yet. I went to the house this morning,' added Sam, tapping at a picture of St Margaret's on the screen.

'What? When?'

'Before I came to work.' She took another glug of coffee.

'You're a maniac. I haven't even had breakfast yet,' said Fred, laughing.

'Well, they're pulling it down on Tuesday, it's a building site,' said Sam, taking a flapjack from her top drawer and ripping it open with her teeth. 'Anyway, in one of the rooms was a portrait of Mother Carlin, who was mentioned in Ivy's second letter. The site manager who showed me round St Margaret's sent me to an old people's home down the road where he thought she might be. As you kindly found out for me, Mother Carlin died many years ago, but I managed to blag my way into the room of another nun who used to work there. She made a strange comment about Mother Carlin, saying no one cared about what had happened to her on the night she died. Want one?' She pulled out another flapjack and threw it at him.

Fred picked up the squashed snack and put it to one side.

'Also, this nun, Sister Mary Francis,' Sam continued, 'she definitely knew of Kitty, and her father, George Cannon. She called him a philanderer.'

'Maybe Kitty was the product of an affair and was born at this mother-and-baby home, St Margaret's,' said Fred, taking his glasses off to clean them, then looking over at Sam. 'Jesus, if that's the case, it'd get picked up by all the nationals. You could write your own ticket.'

'Maybe. You look nice without your glasses,' said Sam, smiling at him.

Fred turned seven shades of red and stammered for something to say. 'Well, I wear contacts for climbing; it's just my eyes are a bit sore as I was out at Harrison's Rocks all night.' He went to put his glasses on again, then hesitated.

'You climb in the dark?' said Sam, flicking to her emails and scrolling through them.

'Sure, I've got my head torch. I'm stuck here most of the time, so I don't really have a choice.' He shrugged.

'Would you climb every day if you could?' asked Sam, finishing off the last of her breakfast.

'Definitely. It's vertical Zen. When I'm soloing a hard route, I don't care about all the shit with my family and what a disappointment I am to everyone. It's just me and the rock.

When you free solo you can't make mistakes. You get one chance at doing it right.'

'So climbing up a huge rock with nothing but the ground to catch you relaxes you?' said Sam, laughing.

'Harper!' yelled Murray from across the room. 'Get over here.'

Fred pretended to wrap a rope around his neck and hang himself as Sam stood up and walked over to her boss.

'Why has Kitty Cannon's press officer just called wanting the low-down on you?'

'Um, I read that her talk show is finished and she's retiring. She grew up in Sussex, so I just put in a request for an interview.'

'What's that got to do with St Margaret's mother-and-baby home?' said Murray irritably.

'Kevin mentioned he'd seen her at Father Benjamin's inquest, so I did some digging. I think she might have some connections to it.'

'What kind of connections?' Murray coughed loudly, clearing phlegm from his lungs.

'Well, I'm not sure yet, but I'm working on it.'

'That's Features' job; aren't I giving you enough to do?' Murray snapped.

'Yes, I was going to pass it over. It was just an idea,' said Sam, trying not to stare at Murray's monobrow, which looked like a large slug.

'Well, did you get a result?' barked Murray. Sam shook her head. 'Fine, well let's focus on news, shall we? I don't want to piss off a press office as powerful as that without good reason.'

'I'm obviously rattling some cages if Kitty Cannon's

office are bothering to find out about me,' said Sam, returning to her seat.

'What did you say to them?' said Fred.

'That I had some information about Kitty's association
to St Margaret's mother-and-baby home.'

'And look what just came in on the wire,' said Fred,
turning his screen towards her.

Sam rubbed her throbbing eyes. She had got up at 5 a.m.
to be at the St Margaret's building site before sunrise, so she
thought her caffeine-soaked brain was hallucinating as she
read the news on Fred's screen.

'Jesus. There's going to be a funeral service for Father
Benjamin today.'

Fred nodded. Sam felt a surge of adrenaline as she read on.

Born Benjamin Cook in Brighton in 1926 and raised in
Preston, Father Benjamin was the son of Dr Frank A. Cook,
a surgeon, and Helen Elizabeth Cook, a housewife.

He attended All Saints' School and was a 1944 graduate of
Brighton High School. He also attended classes at the Brighton
College of Art and played the piano.

Father Benjamin was the highly regarded vicar of Preston
church for over thirty years, before retiring at the age of sixty-
five to Gracewell Retirement Home in Preston village. He
went missing on 31 December 1999, and his friends received
the shocking news in September 2016 that his remains had
been discovered in the foundations of St Margaret's in Preston. He has no surviving relatives.

'Fred, you've got to cover for me, I have to go to this.'
Sam turned to her long-suffering colleague.

'What? You'll be out for hours. I've got the afternoon off for the British Bouldering Championships,' Fred whispered.

'Look, if I'm right about this Kitty Cannon stuff, it's gonna be huge. I'll be back by half one at the latest. What time do you need to be there?'

'Three,' said Fred, 'but I can't be late.'

'You won't be. Please?' Sam started whimpering like a lost puppy.

'Fine,' said Fred, looking over at Murray's office. 'I'm doing an interview later with the daughter of one of the original Suffragettes for the centenary. I'll say my car won't start and you've gone in my place. But file it before you go to the service, will you? He's on the warpath for me too at the moment because he thinks we're in cahoots.'

'Sure. Oh, and one more favour,' said Sam, throwing her belongings back into her bag.

'One of my kidneys perhaps?'

'I really need to find out who Ivy was writing these letters to. He was a professional footballer, she mentions his first season at Brighton in her letter dated 12 September 1956 and talks about him being handsome and not wanting a scandal. Maybe see if you can pull up any names in the cuttings around that time, he must have been a bit of a star. It's a long shot but if any footballers around that time died unexpectedly, we could be onto something. It certainly looks like everyone else mentioned in these letters met a rather sudden demise.'

Fred saluted her.

'I love you,' said Sam as she grabbed her laptop and notepad and charged out of the newsroom.

As she started up her trusty Nova in the car park, Sam's

mobile began to ring. She pulled it out of her bag, not recognising the local number. 'Hello?'

'Is that Samantha?'

She pressed her finger into her other ear to make sure she could hear.

'Yes, who is speaking, please?'

'This is Rosalind. You came to my house this morning, do you remember? My son was cooking.'

'Oh yes,' Sam replied hastily.

'I'm calling because I rang my cousin after we spoke and he remembered the accident you were asking about. It was talked about a lot in his local pub at the time. Chief Superintendent George Cannon, you said?'

'That's right.' Sam waited patiently for her to go on.

'He was a very well-liked local policeman, so it was quite a shock when it happened. My cousin couldn't remember anything about the accident other than the fact that his little girl was in the car with him.'

'His little girl? There's nothing about that in the cuttings,' Sam said, pulling her notebook out.

'Yes, she survived, I believe. Well, according to a local lad who drank in the Sussex Arms and who was walking home that night. He came along just after the crash had happened, and said there was a young girl in the road.'

'In the road?' repeated Sam.

'He was a known drunk, this lad, so I don't think the police took much notice of his statement. She was wearing a bright red coat, apparently. The car was in the ditch but she was standing in the headlights, and she ran off as soon as she saw him. He tried to chase her to check she was okay, but she was gone.'

'Thank you, Rosalind, that's really helpful,' said Sam, scribbling in her notebook. 'I really appreciate you calling.'

She ended the call and threw her mobile into her bag, then flipped to the page with Father Benjamin's name and wrote *George Cannon* underneath.

Chapter Fourteen

Sunday 5 February 2017

Kitty sat in the black cab on her way home from her session with Richard Stone and switched on her mobile to check the messages. Two from Rachel asking her to call back. She sighed, leaning back in her seat. She felt utterly drained.

As the cab turned onto Victoria Embankment, the phone rang and 'Rachel Ford' sprang up on the screen.

'Yes?' said Kitty, answering it, 'I was just about to call you back.'

'Hi, Kitty, sorry to call you on a Sunday. Can you talk for a second?' said Rachel, her tone slightly anxious.

'Yes, what is it?' Kitty snapped, pressing the phone harder to her ear.

'I wanted to run something by you. Does the name Samantha Harper mean anything to you? She's a journalist at Southern News who wants to speak with you.'

'Never heard of her, what's it about?'

'She's asking about your connection to a mother-and-baby home. St Margaret's in Preston, Sussex.'

Kitty felt a rush of blood to her head. A bike pulled out in front of them and the taxi swerved to avoid it, honking his horn and shouting as they went past.

'Kitty? Hello?' said Rachel.

'I've no idea what she's talking about. What else did she say?'

'Nothing as far as I'm aware. She just put in a request for an interview. I called a guy called Murray White who runs Southern News but he didn't seem to know anything about it and said he'd ask her,' said Rachel.

'Who is this Samantha Harper? Email her biog over straight away.'

'Okay. I thought you'd want it, so it's ready – sending it now.'

'Good, hold on while I look at it,' said Kitty, opening the email and clicking on it impatiently. Slowly a picture of Sam came up on the screen.

Instantly she knew who she was. Her hands began to shake as she stared at the picture of the red-headed girl with the blue eyes looking back at her.

'Are you still there, Rachel? I need you to find an address for me. I want you to focus solely on this all day, nothing else. Do you understand?'

'Yes, okay, what's the name?'

'Annabel Rose Creed, age sixty, born and raised in Sussex. She's six years younger than me but we went to the same school; Brighton Grammar. I haven't seen her for many years, find her.'

'Okay,' said Rachel. 'I'll do my best.'

Kitty carefully placed her phone back in her bag as they pulled up outside her riverside apartment on Embankment. She thanked the driver, gave him a hefty tip, and then disappeared inside.

Chapter Fifteen

Sunday 5 February 2017

The Black Lion pub, with its thatched roof, oak beams and roaring fire, was the centrepiece of what appeared to Sam to be the perfect chocolate-box village. After tearing herself away from an interview with Clara Bancroft, whose mother was one of the first Suffragettes, she had driven at high speed over to Preston. Making her way through the meandering high street, where hanging baskets adorned the street lights and pavements were lined with perfectly manicured hedges, she had spotted the pub and rushed out of the rain into the busy bar – which seemed to be harbouring all the men of the village – to ask for directions to the church.

'Straight up the road, love, top of the hill. You can't miss it,' said a bearded gentleman with a bulbous nose and bloodshot eyes.

'You going to the memorial service?' asked a man at the bar.

'Yes, I am,' said Sam.

'Know him, did you?' asked another, peering at her over his pint.

'No, but I believe he was involved with St Margaret's and I'm doing some research on mother-and-baby homes in the UK.' She scanned the pub quickly as she chatted, and noticed an elderly lady in a scarlet woollen coat watching her from across the room.

'What do you wanna do that for? Miserable business. You should be writing about something happy, nice pretty girl like you.'

'Er, okay. I'll bear that in mind,' said Sam, slightly taken aback. 'Well, thank you for your help.'

As she turned to go, she saw that the elderly woman was being helped across the room on her Zimmer frame. As she reached the pub entrance, she stopped and turned back as if looking for someone. Sam recognised her but couldn't place where from. She was in her nineties she reckoned, painfully thin, with no colour in her sharp cheekbones and her white hair scraped back in a bun. As she watched, the woman scanned the room and then suddenly stopped as she locked eyes with Sam. Her hollow cheeks flushed red as she stared, her eyes glistening. Feeling uncomfortable, Sam turned away, and when she looked back, the woman's companion was helping her over the threshold and out of the door.

Sam thanked the men hurriedly and ventured out into the cold just as the elderly lady was being helped into a minicab. The church bells began to chime as the cab drove off, the woman staring at Sam as they passed her. After jumping back into her car, Sam followed them up the steep hill. By the time they reached the church, the front pews were full and the service was starting. Sam waited as the elderly woman was helped to her seat, then perched herself at the end of the opposite aisle. As the vicar stood at his lectern and began to speak, she switched her phone to silent.

'We are gathered here today to celebrate the life and work of Father Benjamin, who touched endless hearts in his life as parish priest for thirty years, and to pay tribute to his devotion to those who needed help.' Sam looked from the vicar to the old woman, who was staring ahead and clutching her handbag tightly. 'The discovery of Father Benjamin's body at St Margaret's has been a difficult time for many people here. None of us could rest easy in our beds while he was missing, but the news of his death was a tragic fulfilment of our worst fears. Now, given strength from our beloved Lord Jesus Christ, we can lay him to rest, and pray for his soul to live in peace for all eternity.'

Sam looked around at the small congregation. Most were elderly; she spotted Sister Mary Francis amongst them, her head bowed. Next to her was Gemma, the carer who had let her into Gracewell, who was staring up at the vicar intently.

'Father Benjamin, who also founded and over-saw the running of St Margaret's mother-and-baby home in Preston, went on to volunteer with the Community Care Trust well into his retirement, going out into the community, sometimes in the harshest winter months, and giving out food and blankets to those most in need. He was a wonderful influence on the younger members of our congregation, teaching at Sunday school and helping to strengthen Christian values throughout our village, where modern-day life can sometimes distract from what is fundamental to us as human beings – the teachings of Jesus Christ our Saviour. In light of this, we have a reading from Hannah Crane, who remembers Father Benjamin fondly from her Sunday school days at the church.'

A woman with long blond hair made her way up to the lectern and unfolded her piece of paper. At first she wasn't able to be heard, and a chuckle of laughter ran through the church as the priest fumbled with the microphone. Eventually she began to speak, her voice wobbly.

> Do not stand at my grave and weep,
> I am not there, I do not sleep.
> I am a thousand winds that blow.
> I am the diamond glint on snow.
> I am the sunlight on ripened grain.
> I am the gentle autumn rain.
> When you wake in the morning hush,
> I am the swift, uplifting rush
> Of quiet birds in circling flight.
> I am the soft starlight at night.
> Do not stand at my grave and weep.
> I am not there, I do not sleep.
> Do not stand at my grave and cry.
> I am not there, I did not die!

Sam glanced over at the elderly lady, who was staring down at the floor now, wiping tears away with a handkerchief she clutched in her shaking hands. Slowly she opened her handbag and pulled something out, holding it between her narrow fingers.

'Thank you, Hannah.' The vicar returned to his perch as the woman walked back to her seat and an approving smile from her husband. 'Father Benjamin would have been very proud. And so to one of his favourite pieces of music, to be sung by Sister Clara Gale.'

The congregation looked up to the choir stalls as a nun in a blue-and-white habit began to sing 'Ave Maria'. Silence fell and nobody appeared to move or breathe, utterly spellbound by the angelic voice. Goose bumps prickled Sam's arms as she listened, so transfixed and overcome that when she suddenly felt a presence next to her and turned her head to see the old lady standing in the aisle beside her, she couldn't help gasping.

The woman was bent over her frame, but in her left hand she was clutching what Sam could now see was a photograph, her eyes fixed on the coffin in front of her. No one else had noticed her yet, their attention utterly absorbed by Sister Clara's voice. She had almost reached her destination before anyone even looked up. Tap, tap, went her frame over the grey stone floor of the church.

Suddenly everyone turned to stare as she slowly reached out and laid the picture on top of the coffin. As the music ended, she bowed her head, blessed herself in silence, and spoke.

'May God forgive the unforgivable sins of this man, and save the souls of all those whose lives he destroyed. Amen.' Despite her bent posture, her voice was strong.

As she straightened up, she stared up at the silenced vicar. Then, before anyone could react, she turned and slowly made her way back along the aisle. No one moved or made a sound as she reached the entrance and moved her frame across the threshold and out of the door.

The vicar seemed momentarily paralysed. Eventually he walked back to the lectern. 'Please, don't be upset by what you just witnessed. A parish priests' life is sometimes one without thanks or gratitude. Those whom we try to help cannot always be helped. Let us now pray for all those helpless souls. Our Father, Who art in Heaven, hallowed be Thy name; Thy Kingdom come, Thy will be done on earth as it is in Heaven . . .'

As everyone joined in the prayer, one of the younger nuns darted forward and swept the picture to the floor. Sam was on her feet before she knew it to pick it up. When she glanced up at the congregation, she met the red-rimmed eyes of Gemma the carer, who clutched at a tissue and dabbed her nose.

Anxious to catch the old lady before she disappeared, she sidled to the entrance as fast as she could, while the others returned their attention to the vicar. As she burst from the dark church, the sunlight made it impossible to see for a second. She looked around desperately and eventually saw the lady disappearing into her minicab, which drove off down the hill. She called out after her, running down the steep road in the hope she would see her waving and stop – but she was gone. As she slowed to a walk, she realised her phone was vibrating in her bag.

'Sam, where the hell are you?' asked Murray as soon as she answered.

'I've just finished interviewing Clara Bancroft and I'm on my way back,' Sam hastily replied, as a van driver honked his horn at her.

'Don't lie to me. The photographer called and said you'd left nearly an hour ago,' Murray barked. Sam could visualise the veins in his neck bulging, as they always did when he was in a rage.

'I'm just on my way back now, Murray. I had some problems with my car.'

'Yeah, well, your grandmother called the office. She's been trying to get hold of you – your kid's sick. I want your copy in by two. After that, you and me need to have a talk.' The line went dead.

123

Feeling utterly overwhelmed, Sam sank onto a bench and tried to calm herself down.

The old woman's sadness was so tangible, it still hung in the air where she'd stood moments before. Sam looked down at the photograph she had picked up from the floor of the church. It was a black-and-white picture of a little girl, no more than ten, smiling at the camera. She had corkscrew curls and wore a beautiful white dress with flowers around the waist. She turned the photograph over and read the faded writing on the back. *Ivy, summer 1947.*

She caught her breath. Ivy. No doubt there was more than one Ivy in Preston, but if she was nine or ten in 1947, she would have been a young woman of childbearing age by 1956 when the letters were written. Could this be the same girl?

She picked up her phone and dialled Ben's number: no answer. She tried again and let it go to voicemail, leaving him an angry message asking him to call Nana. Then she called her grandmother.

'Hi, Nana, it's me. I'm so sorry, my phone was on silent. Is Emma okay?'

Nana assured her she was fine; that she had been sick but had since perked up.

'I've left a message for Ben, so he should be with you soon,' said Sam, 'Sorry. Are you sure you're okay? You sound a bit down.'

Nana wasn't okay. It took Sam a while to get it out of her. There was a third letter from Ivy, she eventually explained. It was even worse than the first two.

'I'll call you back once I've written this piece. Murray needs it yesterday.'

She was as good as her word. Once she had filed her interview for the Suffragette centenary and received a dressing-down from Murray, she called Nana back, and as her grandmother read out Ivy's third letter, neither of them could stop the tears from coming.

Chapter Sixteen

Monday 11 February 1957

My love,

She's here, our baby is here.

I have barely been allowed to see her, but she is certainly the most beautiful baby I have ever laid eyes on. She has little tufts of hair, which is copper like mine, and bright blue eyes like yours that sparkle. She was so peaceful, she didn't cry at all, not like her mummy, who hasn't stopped. They let me hold her for a few minutes before they started to stitch me up, and she gripped my finger so tight in her little fist that I know she knew I was her mummy. I'm sure she smiled at me. Sister said it was nonsense and that newborn babies don't smile. But I know she did – it was her way of trying to tell me that everything was going to be all right. I don't remember anything after that. I think I must have fainted, as when I woke up, I was in the infirmary and Rose, as I've called her, was gone.

Ivy heard a key in the door at the end of the infirmary, then a bang as it opened and bumped into the wall. She pushed her pen and paper under the covers and looked up to see Sister Faith and Sister Mary Francis bustling towards her, their long starched tunics rustling as they walked. She

126

dropped her eyes, so as not to be chastised for staring, and put her hands in her lap.

'Well, child, there's work to be done in the laundry. You've been here for a week; you can't be lying here forever,' said Sister Mary Francis before she'd even reached her.

'I think she'll be ready to go back in a couple of days, Sister,' said Sister Faith. 'She can still barely stand.'

Sister Mary Francis turned and scowled at the younger nun. 'You'd be tucking them all in with eiderdown quilts and hot chocolate every night, Sister Faith, so I think I'll judge for myself. Get up, child, and be quick about it.'

Panic trickled through Ivy as she nodded and reached for the covers, slowly pulling them back and praying that her pen and paper remained hidden. The sheet beneath her was clean, but her legs and back were caked in dried blood. She was unsure what had happened to her in the blurred days and nights that followed the birth, though she had deciphered from various mumbled conversations that she had started bleeding and wouldn't stop. She had lain in the infirmary ever since, unable to move due to the pain between her legs.

Patricia had appeared that morning before breakfast, look-ing tired and pale. It was her job to change the sheets in the infirmary, and as she did so, she put a pen and paper under Ivy's pillow. Sister Faith had left the room momentarily to fetch something from the store cupboard, and Patricia had gushed that she had seen Ivy's baby, that she was absolutely beautiful and quite content, hardly crying at all between feeds. Ivy had cried and kissed her friend on her freckled nose, telling her to pass it on to Rose. 'It's not long for you now, is it, Pat?' she had said, stroking Patricia's bump.

'Is it terrible? The pain? I heard you all night,' said Patricia, staring down at Ivy then back at the door.

'It's not so bad,' Ivy had reassured her. 'I was making a terrible fuss. You'll be fine.'

'Look at the terrible mess you've made,' snapped Sister Mary Francis now when she saw the bloodstained bedding that Patricia had left in the corner of the room. 'Do you not think we've enough to do without having to clear up after you? You can wash those sheets as soon as you're up.'

'Yes, Sister,' said Ivy, wincing with the pain as she forced herself off the bed and slowly stood up. She felt sure that her legs would give way, and looked at Sister Faith with tears in her eyes.

'Walk up and down, girl. You need to get moving or you'll never get out of here,' said Sister Mary Francis, tight-lipped with disapproval.

Ivy didn't dare argue. Ignoring the burning in her groin, she took a step. Immediately her trembling legs folded beneath her and she came crashing down onto her knees.

'Get up,' said Sister Mary Francis grimly. Ivy stared at the floor, clutching her midriff. 'Get up now or you'll be taking a visit to Mother Carlin's office.'

Sister Faith stepped forward and reached out a hand, but Sister Mary Francis put out her arm to stop her. Ivy slowly struggled to her feet, then pulled herself onto the bed.

'Stand up,' Sister Mary Francis barked.

'I can't, Sister. I'm sorry, my legs don't work. I'm trying, I really am.' Ivy's whole body was shaking.

'Stand up,' said Sister Mary Francis again.

Slowly Ivy got to her feet, using the bed for support. She daren't cry, though the pain tearing through her abdomen was making her feel as if she would throw up any moment. As she straightened her legs, she looked down to see drops of blood appearing on the floor by her feet.

She took a step, then caught the end of the bed as her legs went again. She came crashing down onto the floor, landing on her side, and let out a cry of pain.

'I want her out of bed by the end of tomorrow, Sister, and she's to wash those sheets herself,' said Sister Mary Francis.

Ivy lay on the floor, watching Sister's black shoes click away from her on the cold ceramic tiles.

As soon as the older nun was gone, Sister Faith helped Ivy up and back into bed. 'She means it, you know,' she said quietly. 'You can't stay in here any longer than tomorrow.'

'Yes, Sister, I understand. I'm sorry about the mess,' said Ivy as Sister Faith ran a cloth over the streaks of blood on the floor.

The bell on the wall began to ring out around the infirmary and Sister Faith looked at her watch. 'I'm going to dinner. I'll bring you back some soup.'

'Thank you, Sister.'

Once Sister Faith had left the infirmary and locked the door behind her, Ivy eased herself up and reached for the pen and paper that were still safely under the covers. She winced as she sat up on the hard iron bed and continued to write.

I am writing this from my bed in the infirmary. The labour was terrible. I didn't know what to expect, but I'm glad I didn't. If the room they left me in alone all night had had windows, I would have jumped out of them. I have never known pain like it, not for a minute, and I had to endure hour after hour of it. With no one to comfort me, and no idea if it would ever end.

I knew the room they left me in already. The memories it held will stay with me for ever. Mother Carlin makes the heavily pregnant girls clean up after births that have just happened. Nothing fills you with fear more than a floor covered in blood. It was so hard to shift with cold water and very little soap; I was on my hands and knees for a whole day scrubbing once. One time, I had to clear up around a tiny baby who had died. He had been left wrapped in a bloody blanket in the bin. I took him out and held him and cried and told him he was loved, until Mother Carlin snatched him away to put him in the tank where the dead babies go. She told me not to waste my tears on the devil's spawn and hit me so hard that her ring made a gash in my cheek.

My labour started at the end of a long day in the laundry. They wouldn't let us use the lighter machinery, but my bump was so large I couldn't keep up.

Ivy paused at the memory of the last day she had had Rose all to herself. The last time she had known exactly where her daughter was, and that she was safe.

The equipment in the laundry had felt even heavier than usual, and the aches and pains in her body unfamiliar. Her stomach had started cramping soon after lunch, cramps that got worse and worse until she was doubled over with the strength of them. She had walked slowly over to Sister Edith, trying not to cry out from the pain.

'What on earth do you think you're doing? Get back to work,' Sister Edith had snapped.

'Sister, could I possibly work in the kitchen this afternoon? I'm having bad cramps.'

'No you cannot. You're not in labour; you're not due yet. Get back to work!'

Ivy had shuffled back to her post, all eyes on her but no one daring to say a word. By dinner time, she could no longer stand. The other girls had filed out, and Mother Carlin and Sister Edith had stood over her as she crouched in the corner clutching her bump and crying out in pain.

'Stop your fuss. You'd better get to the infirmary, child. Go on,' Mother Carlin had said.

Ivy had waited for the last wave of cramps to finish and then staggered along the hall. She had felt such relief at talk of the infirmary. Maybe she would experience some kindness at last, some comfort. How wrong she was.

Now she composed herself and picked up her pen again. Sister Faith would be back soon and she wouldn't have another chance to write.

When I reached the infirmary, they shut me in there all alone. The room that I had cleared of blood only a week before; a room I suspected would soon be filled with blood again.

I thought so much about that tiny dead baby when I was alone that night. I thought that the pain I was in meant our baby was going to die. Various sisters came and went, telling me to be quiet, to stop making a fuss, that it was punishment for my sins of the flesh. I tried to be brave but the pain made it impossible. I cried out for my mother, for my father, for you. But nobody came.

She stopped and put the pen and paper down next to her, then sank her head into her hands. It was too painful to remember: lying on the floor, alone in the dark, the house deathly quiet. She had begun to lose her mind with each wave of pain, and she remembered her father's shoes appearing on the floor in front of her. They were so highly polished that she could see her face in them. She had looked up at him smiling down at her.

'Daddy, help me.'

'Darling, you are doing so well. I'm so proud of you.' He had taken off his hat and crouched down next to her.

'I'm going to die. I can't take the pain.'

'Yes, you can. And think what you will have when it's over.'

Another wave of pain had hit and she had reached up for him. 'Please look after my baby if anything happens.'

He had taken her hand. 'Be brave, Ivy. I will always look after you, both of you.'

She shook the memory away and pinched the pen in her fingers. She had to focus on finishing the letter before Sister Faith returned.

I think I was close to death when Dr Jacobson came. I begged him to save my baby and so he cut me, so much I thought he had sawn me in two. Then I heard her cry and there she was. Our baby. I asked Dr Jacobson if he had seen my mother. I begged him to take me home. But he wouldn't talk to me and just left me there with Rose. Hopefully he will tell Mother about her.

After Dr Jacobson left, they stitched me up. This was even more painful than the birth itself. The nun stitching me was clumsy and old and kept dropping her reading glasses. I have been unable to walk for days, but Sister tells me I need to go back to work soon to earn my keep. I have written to Mother and Uncle Frank asking if they can pay the £100 I owe for my

stay here, but they have not replied. I am told that the stand-
ard stay is three years. I will go mad if I have to stay that long.

They put the nursery next to the infirmary, and I can hear
the babies crying all day and night. Apparently it's another
part of the punishment. I am losing my mind thinking I can
hear Rose cry and not being able to go to her.

My milk has come in, but we are not allowed to feed our
babies as nature intended. They are given formula milk
instead. Maybe this is to break the bond between mother and
baby. I have been given tablets to make my milk dry up, but
they're not working fast enough. I leak at night and am ter-
ribly sore. Sister gets furious when my sheets are wet. She is
tired of me being in the infirmary, tired of my tears. Tired of
my fuss.

I miss my baby so much. I cannot bear that someone else is
going to take her away from here. She belongs with me, with us.

Please, my love, come and get us, so that we may be a fam-
ily at last. Please, come quickly, before Rose is adopted and
lost to us for ever.

With all my love,
Your Ivy

As she wrote the last word, Ivy heard the key in the lock
and quickly pushed the letter into the envelope Patricia had
brought. Sister Faith was carrying a bowl of clear soup, a
bread roll in her other hand. 'Here you are.'

'Thank you, Sister.' Ivy took the warm bowl gratefully.

'We'll need to put those sheets in to soak or they'll never
come clean,' Sister Faith said, not unkindly.

'Sorry for the trouble, Sister,' said Ivy. 'I'll do it now.' She
went to put the bowl down.

'I'll do it; you need to rest. Mother Carlin is coming for you in the morning and you'll have to get back to work.'

'Thank you,' said Ivy, and began to eat her meagre dinner hungrily.

Chapter Seventeen

Sunday 5 February 2017

Sam pulled up outside Ben's flat with a heavy heart. She still remembered the day they had found it, traipsing round countless dives while she was heavily pregnant until they had been shown this place and fallen in love with it. It had needed a lick of paint and some TLC, but it had a small patio garden and the lounge had a woodburner. They had moved in the day after the wedding and Ben had tried to carry her over the threshold, but as she was eight months pregnant, he had put his back out.

So he had lain on the sofa while she, Grandad and her bump did most of the decorating. With Nana making cushions and Grandad donating bits from his antique shop, it had slowly become their home. She had loved that flat, and the memories they had built there: the three of them in the bath, Emma's first steps in the lounge. Fast-forward four years and – in the heat of a row – she had suggested she and Emma move out for a bit to give them some space. She had been shocked when he'd agreed.

She could see him through the window now, pacing up and down, picking up Emma's toys with a tea towel over his shoulder. As she watched, his shoulders hunched and his jaw clenched; he had caught sight of her and pounded his fore-finger at the watch on his wrist. It wasn't his weekend to have

Emma, but he'd had to as she was working and Emma was poorly and he was clearly furious about it.

Sam locked her car and headed for the front door. She had already taken an earful from Murray, and it would take everything she had to stay reasonable if Ben started on her. As she walked up the path, her conversation with Murray came back to her in waves. He had been punishing her ever since Emma was born.

She had returned to work as soon as humanly possible, but she couldn't pull the all-nighters she used to, or drop everything and chase up a lead over a weekend off, and as payback, he'd been giving her the dregs of the story barrel. Which was why she was keeping the Cannon story to herself for now. Murray didn't pay her enough and he didn't deserve a story as good as this one. She was going to jump ship as soon as she got a better offer, and that would be revenge in itself.

She reached out and pressed the buzzer to the flat.

'Hi, how you doing?' she said when Ben finally answered the door.

'Hi,' he muttered through gritted teeth, not meeting her eyes. 'You're late.'

'Sorry, I tried really hard to get away. How's Emma?' She was speaking to the back of Ben's head as he charged back down the hall. She missed the Ben of old so much, the one who poured her a glass of wine and ran her a bubble bath after a hard day. Not this Ben, who would most probably drown her in it.

'Okay. She seems fine in herself, but she hasn't eaten anything, so I'm trying to get her to have something now.' He began tidying away Sam's coat and bag from where she'd dropped them on the sofa. Clearing up had never been one of his strong points, but since she'd moved out, he made a point of highlighting any fault of hers, as if to show her how much better off he was without her.

'Maybe I can help,' she said.

'I doubt it, she plays up for you.' He settled back down at the table, and Emma immediately started reaching out for her mother. Ben tried to force some broccoli into her mouth. Emma promptly picked it up, screaming, and hurled it across the room.

'Emma, that is very naughty,' he shouted.

Sam walked over to Emma's chair and crouched down beside it. 'Hi, darling.' Emma leant over and wrapped her arms around her mother, falling off the chair into her lap and descending into giggles.

'Thanks!' snapped Ben.

'What?'

'She needs to eat something. She needs a proper meal. And she's not getting down from there until she's had some vegetables.'

'Sorry, I was just saying hello to my daughter.'

'Well, she won't sit up again now. I'm trying to get some sort of routine going and you're undermining me.'

'Okay, well do you want us to just go?' Sam started picking up bits of broccoli from the carpet.

'Go? She's in the middle of her meal. Oh, forget it,' said Ben irritably.

Sam straightened up. 'Okay, I can see you're gunning for a fight. We'd better leave.'

'That's right, just walk away and leave me to clear up the mess. How poetic.'

'Ben! I'm sorry you had to have Emma, but I don't have a choice. Nana's exhausted and I can't just take a day off.'

'Here we go. Poor me, I've got no control over how my roller-coaster life has turned out. Everyone hold on tight, sorry, not my fault.' He tried to force another spoonful of food into Emma's mouth. Sam bristled: Emma was old enough to feed herself.

'That is so unfair,' she hissed. 'It was your idea for me to work, for you to stay at home with Emma. I told you it would be hard.'

'Yes, well, I thought you'd grow a heart once she was born. Most mothers can't bear to leave their child for a day, let alone five days a week, six sometimes.' Ben winced as Emma pushed his hand away.

Tears stung Sam's eyes. 'I see her a hell of a lot more than you do now, because of your supposed job-hunting days.'

'Yes, well, I do have two job interviews lined up for tomorrow, which I needed to prepare for, but since I had to look after Emma, no doubt I've blown any chance there!'

'We can't keep relying on Nana. I've been hoping for a promotion so we can afford a childminder, but it's hard when your boss is an asshole.'

'If I get a job, then we can afford a childminder!'

'That would be great,' said Sam, trying to calm the situation, 'but I know you've been struggling with it. I didn't know about these interviews; what are they for?'

Ben let out a sarcastic scoff. 'What do you care?'

'I care quite a lot actually. I think it's great that things are happening for you but if you're going to be working long hours, then we need to maybe think about a plan.'

'A plan to keep me in my place, you mean.'

'I need a wee!' Emma shouted.

Ben sighed heavily and reached down to where she was sitting on the floor next to Sam.

'Mummy take me!' Emma cried. 'I don't want Daddy, Daddy's a wanker.'

Ben glared at Sam. 'I can see you're being very complimentary about me behind my back.'

'I did not use that word around her. I would never say that about you. She probably got it from the language you use when you're driving her around. And what the hell did you mean by saying I want to keep you in your place?'

Ben fetched some wipes to mop up Emma's face. 'I mean that Nana won't always be around and one of us still needs to be able to have Emma if the childminder's poorly or if you have to work late and won't be home on time. I might get a job, but I'll never have a career. You're completely oblivious to how much slack I have to pick up. The power that job has over you, it's weird.'

'I need a wee!' Emma shouted.

'That just isn't true. I can't believe you said that!' Sam's eyes welled up, just as Ben picked Emma up and she weed all down his leg.

'Great!' he shouted. 'You're four years old, Emma, you're starting school soon. You can't keep having accidents!'

As he pulled at Emma's wet clothes, fat tears poured down the little girl's cheeks and she stared up at Sam, reaching out her hands. She would remember this moment, thought Sam. She would remember this as the moment they'd hit rock bottom.

She walked over to her daughter and stroked her hair,

shushing her gently until she calmed down. Once Emma was changed, Ben picked her up and handed her to Sam.

'There you go, you can have her now. I need a beer.' He strode out of the room before calling back to her. 'And Nana or you will have to have her tomorrow if she's sick, because I'm not cancelling those interviews. You can let yourself out.'

As Emma nuzzled into her, Sam stood staring at the sofa where she and Ben had spent so many nights curled up together with their daughter asleep in the Moses basket at their feet.

Then, as the front door slammed so hard that the lounge walls shook, for the first time since she and Ben had met, she felt nothing at all.

Chapter Eighteen

Sunday 5 February 2017

Despite her racing heart, Kitty was overwhelmed with exhaustion. Her eyes stung, but closing them did nothing to stop the avalanche of thoughts in her head. She had wanted to get to bed early because of the sleepless night following her party, but after her session with Richard that morning, every tiny sound was jerking her awake. When she did nod off her ticking carriage clock was a constant reminder of how much sleep she wasn't getting. She let out a heavy sigh and resigned herself to another sleepless night, propping herself up in bed instead and turning on her bedside lamp.

She looked round the bedroom, her eyes darting between the dark oak floorboards, vintage furniture and carefully selected prints from galleries all over the world. Despite spending months working with an interior designer, she could never settle on what she liked, and as soon as she did, she hated whatever it was and wished she'd chosen something different. The result was an impersonal show home, and she felt as if she might as well be in one of the many hotel rooms she had stayed in throughout her life.

She had moved house so many times, desperately trying to find somewhere that felt like home, and it seemed to her now, staring round the room, that it was something that would always evade her.

She pulled back the covers, pushed her feet into her slippers and walked across the polished floor, opening the heavy curtains to reveal the River Thames below. As she watched the water reflect the lights from passing cars, her body grew tired, and after a while, she sank into the velvet armchair that sat by the window.

With the light behind her, her reflection glowed back at her against the dark night sky and soon her eyes grew heavy. As she began to drop off, she heard noises, panting. Someone running.

A black tunnel. She was running towards a splinter of light at the end of it, her feet splashing in the dripping water below. Gasping in the darkness, she felt overwhelmed with the need to escape. As she ran, she looked down at her hands, which were covered in dirt. She was clutching something. She opened her palm and a key tinkled onto the ground in front of her. *Come back here!* The voice behind her was loud, her fear overwhelming. She picked up the key and followed the light. There were running footsteps behind her now, splashing faster and faster. *Stop, child!* She could feel the woman gaining on her. She reached some steps, with a door at the top of them, and fumbled with her cold hands, pushing the key into the lock and trying desperately to turn it. Using both hands she twisted it and, pushing with all her might, finally prised it open, running up the last few steps into the night. Turning round, she slammed the door back down and locked it behind her.

Open this door! The woman was shouting; she was banging on the door so hard it shook.

The cold winter night surrounded her, paralysing her with its enormity. Terror spurred her to move, and she ran towards a stone building in the distance, lit up in the moonlight. Her legs were like lead, and the ground was uneven and frozen. She bashed into headstones, tripping on a stone cross, which made her lose her balance and come crashing down. She pulled herself up, the woman's voice still shouting faintly behind her.

Her breath was her only companion in the freezing night as finally she reached the safety of the outhouse. The wooden door at its entrance was hanging from its hinges, and she pushed it aside carefully. Bent double trying to catch her breath, she looked around for somewhere to hide. There were holes in the wall where the moonlight came through, and her eyes fell on an old plough in the corner, propped up by a pile of bricks. She ran over to it, pushing it with all her strength until it began to tip. As it came crashing down on its side, she heard angry voices shouting in the distance, coming towards her. *Elvira! Elvira!*

Kitty woke suddenly, gasping for breath. It took a moment for her to realise where she was. That it was the dream again. Richard's words ran round her head: 'Dreams are unresolved issues trying to process themselves in your brain while you sleep . . . Do you think the key could still be there? Is that what you think your dream is telling you?'

One more day, thought Kitty, one more day and St Margaret's would be gone for ever. Then she would never know for sure if she could have discovered the truth.

She stood up and rushed over to the wardrobe, frantically pulling out clothes.

The journey to the front door seemed a long one, but with every step her strength grew, a tiny flicker of hope igniting in the pit of her stomach. She found a torch and pulled on her boots and waterproof mac, then left the apartment and took the lift down to the ground floor.

As she stepped out into the street, the freezing air stung her face and she smiled slightly. The night was dark and cold, but as she set off in the shadows of the plane trees lining Victoria Embankment, the eight-year-old Elvira she remembered skipped ahead of her, cheering her on with every step.

She flagged down a black taxi as she walked.

'Would you take me to Preston village, north of Brighton, please?'

'Blimey, love, that'll set you back about two hundred quid,' said the driver, leaning over to the window.

'Fine. I'll need to stop for some cash then.' She opened the door and settled herself into the seat.

Chapter Nineteen

Sunday 5 February 2017

'I'm just so tired of taking shit, Nana, from Murray, from Ben.'

'Then don't take it.' Nana put her crossword down and looked over at Sam.

'What choice do I have? If I tell Ben to take a jump, Emma loses her dad, and if I tell Murray to sod off, I'm out of a job.'

'Ben would never disappear from Emma's life, he loves you both too much. And as for Murray, well, would that be such a bad thing?'

Sam was sitting in her grandmother's rocking chair, with Emma cuddled up to her. 'Nana, she's really hot, do you think she's okay?' She felt tears springing to her eyes.

Nana eased herself out of her own chair and felt Emma's back. 'She is a bit hot, darling, but I took her temperature and she's fine. She's just fighting a virus. Couple of days and she'll be right as rain.'

'Nursery won't have her tomorrow if she's poorly, and Ben's got these interviews.'

'I can have her, I don't mind.' Nana smiled fondly.

'No, Nana, it's not fair. I'll ask him to come and get her after his interviews. I just don't have the strength for another argument tonight. I feel like everything has completely unravelled since I moved out, and I don't know if there's a way back.' Sam started to cry, angrily wiping away tears as Emma stirred and snuggled in tighter.

'You can't go back, but you can move forward if you're both prepared to work at it,' said Nana. 'I know Ben's struggling, but he's not really sticking to his side of the bargain. It's not entirely fair to make you feel so guilty.'

'I don't know, I think he might be depressed. I miss the old Ben, but he makes it so hard for us to be nice to one another. I feel like I'm the one breaking up our family, but he's the one who's determined for it to be that way.'

'You'll pull through. A few years down the line, you'll be established and can call the shots a bit more with work. You're just at the hardest part, carving out a career with a small child to care for.'

'That's just it. By then I'll have missed her being little. I can never get this time back.' Sam twisted Emma's curls gently between her fingers and kissed her warm cheek until the little girl pushed her away.

'You'd be miserable if you were at home all day with her. She has Ben, she has me, she loves nursery. She'll be going to school soon. You're with her as much as you can be at the moment. She's a very lucky little girl who is well cared for. She'll need you a lot more when she's older, and if you've given up a job you love and are utterly miserable, what kind of example is that to set for her?'

'But I work such long hours. I don't see Emma, Ben hates me, and my boss doesn't respect me. I'm so tired of killing myself every day and yet still being a disappointment to everyone.'

'I don't think your boss doesn't respect you. I think you don't respect him. And neither would I. He sounds like a nincompoop.'

Sam looked across at her grandmother. She loved every part of her, every inch of her skin, which smelt of rose water, every smile when she knew her hip was hurting her. She knew Ivy's letters were getting to her too, that her grandmother would have loved to have known her own mother.

'I'm sorry the letters have been so upsetting for you, Nana. They've made you think about your mother, haven't they? Did you ever try and find her?' she asked softly.

'Don't you worry about me, sweetheart,' said Nana, concentrating on counting stitches.

'But you didn't always see eye to eye with your adoptive parents, did you? I mean, they weren't very happy when you got pregnant with my mum, were they?'

'They found it hard, yes, but they always did what they thought was best. I doubt I was the easiest child.'

'But don't you think about her? Your real mum?' Sam watched her, waiting for her to look up.

'Sometimes, but she's probably long dead by now,' Nana said quietly.

'You don't know that. You're only sixty, she could be alive. I could help you look for her.'

Nana focused on her crossword, humming gently as she always did, to aid her concentration. It was such a familiar sound, one Sam had fallen asleep to so many times.

'Sammy, there's something you don't know,' she said eventually, 'something I need to talk to you about.'

'Of course, Nana, what is it?' said Sam, leaning forward. As she did so, Emma let out a cry. 'Let me just try and put Emma down, then we can talk, okay?'

Nana nodded and rested her newspaper on her lap, her eyes full of tears. Sam suddenly felt ashamed of herself for pushing her so hard.

She walked into the bedroom she shared with Emma and placed her in the little bed. As soon as she put her down, Emma started to cry again. 'Shh,' said Sam, feeling her forehead. 'It's okay, honey.'

She went back into the lounge. 'I'm sorry, Nana, have we got any Calpol left? I think I need to try and get her temperature down.'

'I'll have a look,' said Nana, easing herself out of her chair.

Sam watched her walk towards the kitchen. 'I'm sorry about what I said about finding your mum,' she said. 'It's up to you what you do. It's just that I can't get those letters out of my head. Something really bad happened in that place. I know it, I felt it.'

Nana paused in the doorway. 'Then you have a responsibility to find out what it was.'

'How?' said Sam, sighing heavily.

'By proving it. I didn't spend all that money on your education for you to be a quitter.' She disappeared into the kitchen, and Sam heard the clatter of cupboard doors.

'Nana, I went to a state school,' she laughed.

'Well, I worked three jobs and paid my taxes! Remember what Grandad always said: "If you think you're too small to make a difference, try sleeping with a mosquito in the room."' Nana came back into the room with the Calpol, smiling as she passed it to Sam.

148

'Thanks, Nana. I'll just give her some of this and then we can talk.'

'It's okay, darling, you focus on Emma.'

'It's fine, it won't take long to settle her. I want to know what's upsetting you.'

'I just wanted to talk to you about Grandad, but it can wait. I'm being silly.' Nana turned towards her room. 'I think I might go to bed, if you two will be okay. Come and wake me if you need me. There's one final letter from Ivy, I'll slot it in your notebook along with the others.'

'Okay, thank you, Nana, I'll look at it as soon as I can.' As soon as Emma was dosed up with Calpol and asleep in her little bed, Sam quickly put her laptop and notebook in her handbag and snuck out into the dimly lit street. Her cold Nova took three goes to start before the engine eventually turned over and coughed into life, but it wasn't until she finally pulled up in front of Gracewell Retirement Home that some warmth started dribbling out of the vents.

She looked at her watch: 10.45, fifteen minutes until Gemma started her shift. She turned her headlights off so as not to draw attention to herself, leaving the engine and the very ineffectual heater on. Of course, doorstepping was not new to her, but she felt very uneasy loitering outside a property without her boss's consent. Her meeting with Murray had unnerved her at a time when her confidence was already at a low ebb from the constant fighting with Ben and her guilt over Emma. Despite all the yelling, she had always thought Murray had her back, that there was an understanding between them, a mutual respect. Clearly not. She wanted not to care, to rant and rave about his shortcomings, but it still hurt.

149

She was so lost in thought that it wasn't until Gemma was actually passing the car that she looked up and spotted her. Her stomach lurched in panic. She needed to get hold of Gemma before she went inside, but if she pounced on her, she'd give the poor girl a heart attack. She frantically wound down the window and waved as if they were long-lost friends. 'Gemma! Gemma, it's me, Sam. From the other day.'

The girl stopped and turned in Sam's direction, unable at first to make out who was hollering at her through the darkness. Sam stepped out of the car. 'Sorry, I didn't mean to startle you. How are you? I just wondered if I could have a quick word?'

'Not really. My shift starts in ten minutes and I need to get changed.' Gemma looked pale and tired, thought Sam, and lacking the cheery demeanour she'd had before. She kept pulling irritably at stray hairs from her ponytail and tucking them behind her ears.

'I saw you at Father Benjamin's funeral,' Sam said gently. 'You looked very upset. I didn't realise you knew him.'

'Please, you have to leave. I can't be seen talking to you. I got in a lot of trouble because of you sneaking into Sister Mary Francis's room. I nearly lost my job.' Gemma glared at her, 'My manager wanted to call the police but Sister Mary Francis convinced her not to.'

'I'm sorry, really I am, but I had to talk to her.' Sam was surprised at Gemma's outburst.

'Well, she was very upset!' Gemma snapped. 'She has a bad heart. She finds it difficult talking about Mother Carlin; she still misses her.' She shoved her hand into her bag for her phone, which had started to ring. 'That's my colleague wondering where I am. I've got to go.'

'Do you know who that woman was who stood up in the middle of the service?' said Sam.

'No, I don't. Who are you really? What the hell do you want?' Gemma snapped.

'I'm a reporter,' admitted Sam. 'Sister Mary Francis implied something might have happened to Mother Carlin and I'm trying to find out what.'

'Oh God. Just leave me alone.' Gemma turned and began walking up the path.

'Gemma, I think there's something you're not telling me. It would be a shame to take my suspicions to the police.'

The girl stopped in her tracks. Sam's heart hammered in her chest, as if everything in her life hinged on this moment.

'If you tell me what's upsetting you, I promise it will go no further,' she said quietly, feeling awash with guilt and relief when Gemma turned back, tears in her eyes.

'I can't talk to you now, I'll be late for my shift. My colleague is waiting for me to take over.'

'Can't you just give me five minutes?' implored Sam, anxious that Gemma would change her mind if she let her out of her sight. 'Text and say your bus was late or something. If you speak to me now, I will never bother you again.'

'Do you promise?' Gemma wiped away a tear.

'Yes,' smiled Sam. 'Do you want to sit in my car? It's freezing out here.'

As soon as Gemma slammed the door of the passenger seat, she started to cry in earnest. Sam waited patiently, watching precious seconds tick away as the girl sobbed into her mobile phone while she texted, wiping snot away with her sleeve when she'd finished.

'Take your time,' said Sam, handing her a tissue.

Gemma sniffed loudly. 'I've been in so much trouble since your visit. I've had two meetings with the manager about it.'

'I'm really sorry, Gemma. I would never have snuck in if it wasn't important.'

'Well, whatever you said upset Sister Mary Francis a great deal. She's been talking about Mother Carlin non-stop ever since. There's always been a lot of talk about Mother Carlin. I feel like I know the woman even though I never met her.'

'What do you mean?'

'I really shouldn't be telling you this.' Gemma crushed the tissue in her grip.

'You won't get into any trouble. I never reveal my sources – it's more than my job's worth.'

Gemma stared at Sam for a moment, then took a deep breath.

'Mother Carlin was here before my time, but apparently she was a bit of a handful. Very underhand and manipulative. Got one member of staff fired and was generally a bit of a miserable bitch as far as I can gather.'

'Go on,' said Sam, turning up the heater.

'My mum's friend Amy, who got me the job here, told me that the staff were always taking the piss about doing something to cheer her up. One morning Amy went into Mother Carlin's room and found she'd had a heart attack in the night and died. It's not unusual for that to happen at Gracewell, but Amy also found half a hash cake on a plate by the bed. She recognised it immediately because she'd made them herself. The thing was, lots of people knew about them because the manager overheard Amy saying

152

they were in her bag and confiscated them. Apparently there was this big staff meeting about having drugs at work and she almost lost her job. There was even a memo about it up in the staff room. The hash cakes would have been in the manager's office and someone must have taken one and given it to Mother Carlin. The problem was, apparently they had acid in them, so they were seriously strong.'

'What?' said Sam, open-mouthed.

'Amy swears she didn't give it to her, and I'm sure who-ever did thought it was harmless fun, but Mother Carlin had a weak heart, which gave out. Luckily it was Amy who discovered her, so she was able to grab the other half of the hash cake before the ambulance arrived. She was waiting for this huge fallout, but nothing ever happened. I guess coroners don't test seventy-five-year-old nuns for hash. Amy never told another soul except me. This was over ten years ago, and I think she just needed to get it off her chest.' Gemma started crying again. 'Sister Mary Francis told me she heard Mother Carlin crying out to Satan that night but that Mother Carlin suffered from nightmares so she didn't call the night manager. She says she will never forgive her-self. It had nothing to do with me, but even I feel guilty that this thing happened and no one knows. Why would anyone want to hurt Mother Carlin?'

'That's what I'm trying to work out,' said Sam. 'And you're sure you don't know anything about the woman at Father Benjamin's funeral?'

'Only that a couple of the nuns seemed very agitated about it. We had drinks at Gracewell after the service and I overheard them talking.'

'What were they saying?' said Sam, leaning forward.

'I think I've said enough.' Gemma opened the car door. 'You said you'd leave me alone now; you promised.'

'And I will. Please, Gemma, just tell me what they said. It's really important.'

'They said that it was good all the records had been destroyed, because it was time to move on.' Gemma climbed out, then paused, looking back into the car, one hand on the roof. 'And maybe you should take their advice.'

Sam watched Gemma walk off down the frozen path and into Gracewell. Then she pulled out her notebook and wrote Mother Carlin's name under those of Father Benjamin and George Cannon.

Chapter Twenty

Mother Carlin sat at the end of her bed, her stiff, inflamed hands clasped together in prayer over her Bible. As was usual in her increasingly frail state, she felt physically exhausted despite the fact that it had been a long day of doing nothing at all. There was little good about getting old, she reflected, as she blessed herself and set her rosary beads and Bible on her bedside table. All you had to look forward to were chronic ailments and endless illnesses, accompanied by the upset of losing every one of your contemporaries. She couldn't remember the last time she had woken up feeling free from discomfort and optimistic about the day ahead.

She reached for her walking frame and eased her frail body round to face it. She was still shaky from her trip to the hospital the previous day. The conclusion of the brusque young consultant poking and prodding had been that her heart was giving up and she needed a pacemaker fitted as soon as she'd recovered from her current bout of bronchitis. As her coughing fits were still so violent that she sometimes felt her ribs would burst out of her chest, she didn't think that would be any time soon. Indeed, as she had been peeled out of her wheelchair and into her bed the previous evening, she had felt so tired she couldn't imagine ever having the energy to wake again.

The heat from outside was stifling but a light breeze gave some momentary relief. The Bible lay open on the bedside table, its faded pages flapping like the wings of a trapped butterfly. They settled eventually on the front page, where the St Margaret's stamp was still visible. Closing her eyes, she felt herself being pulled back in time.

Standing in her office, she could smell the varnish on the mahogany floor and hear rain tapping on the tiny window as she spoke to the new arrivals. They would stand in a line in their uniform of brown overalls, their stomachs protruding in front of them. 'Mass is at six a.m.,' she told them, 'followed by breakfast, then you will work in the laundry until eight. Talking is not tolerated; the devil works on idle tongues.' The girls always stood with their heads bowed as she ran her rosary beads through her fingers, pacing before them. 'It is a grievous sin you have committed, but sinners can find their way back to the Lord Jesus Christ through the strength of prayer and hard work.'

She looked at the clock on her bedside table and sighed. The night manager was hard-working enough by modern standards, but she did tend to get distracted. Mother Carlin had asked for hot milk some time ago, and, due to not eating her supper, her stomach was rumbling painfully. She had called out twice to no avail, and the buzzer had brought no response either.

With a flutter of irritation, she lifted her walking frame and began making her way over to her slippers at the end of her bed. Living at Gracewell was comfortable, but the attention to detail in the running of the house wasn't what it had been when she was at the helm of St Margaret's. It would have been inconceivable for herself or Father Benjamin to be ignored, particularly at such a late hour. If it was something they required every night, it would have been brought to their door punctually, and if it was out of their ordinary routine, a ring of the bell through to the kitchen would have seen the arrival of the night-duty sister within minutes to attend to them.

The youth of today were chaotic and irresponsible because there were no consequences for their actions. She came from a different world, Mother Carlin reflected, where punishment – and the threat of it – was part of everyday life. At home, disobedience was met with a beating and you prayed every night for the Lord to forgive you for your sins. Even if your parents didn't know you'd been bad, God was always watching; indeed, the very hairs on your head were all numbered. It made her seethe that the Church, once revered above all else, was no more now than a picturesque venue for Christmas carol services, christenings and weddings. She'd read the articles in the paper about the mother-and-baby homes, heard the carers here whispering when the visitors came trying to trace their relatives. She knew what people thought of her and she paid them no attention.

The Lord had chosen her to cleanse lost souls so they could present themselves to the all-merciful Father at the gates of heaven and be allowed in. She'd had a job to do, and when she met the Lord at the hour of her death, she knew he would show mercy on her soul.

'Amy?' she called as she opened her bedroom door and stepped out into the corridor. The strain caused her to cough repeatedly and she stood for a minute or two, so short of breath that she thought her legs might give way. But hunger drove her on, and when she peered down the corridor, she saw that there was a light on in the kitchen. Her slippers stubbed against the carpet underfoot as she struggled to raise them high enough to move forward.

'Can I get you anything, Mother?' a gentle female voice enquired, and Mother Carlin looked up to see the silhouette of a woman standing over a hoover at the end of the hall.

'I wanted some hot milk, but as usual Amy has vanished.' The lights were dim and she couldn't make out the woman's face.

'Of course. You go back to your room. I'll heat your milk and bring it straight to you,' said the woman as she squatted down, winding up the hoover cord.

'Thank you. Do you know which room is mine?'

'Yes, Mother, I know.'

She was in the bathroom five minutes later when her door opened and a tray set with hot milk and a home-made biscuit was placed on the table across her bed. She called out to thank the woman, but got no reply – a refreshing change from all the chatter and empty promises she had become accustomed to. She pulled her aching limbs into bed, where she drank the milk and ate half the biscuit hungrily, saving the rest for later. It was nice to want to eat something for once; her belly often rumbled and groaned but the desire for food was always absent.

Her eyes soon felt heavy, stinging from the inside as her head began to jerk in and out of sleep. She clicked off her bedside light and began to doze. Before long, the ticking of the clock stirred her, like a fly in the room buzzing too close to her ear. It grew so noisy that it soon became unbearable. Before long, the ticks stretched out until eventually they morphed into one long, deep drone. She tried to turn away from it, but her torso felt heavy and her arms like lead. She couldn't even lift them to scratch an itch on the end of her nose.

Worry began to rise in her as she slowly moved her head to check the time. She felt as if hours had gone by, but it had only been minutes. As she stared at the clock, its hands began to melt before her, turning to thick clots of blood dripping slowly into a small tube, which she followed down to her arm. She blinked repeatedly as she looked at it. The tube led into a thick needle, which had been inserted in her forearm and stuck down with tape.

'That should get things going,' said Sister Mary Francis, who was now standing over her bed.

'Sister, what on earth are you doing?' said Mother Carlin.

'I beg your pardon?' snapped Sister Mary Francis.

'Get this thing out of my arm, now,' said Mother Carlin.

'That baby needs to come out, child, and it's clearly not going to do it on its own. This will get the contractions going.'

'What baby?' said Mother Carlin.

'Oh dear, we are in denial, aren't we? Did you not flirt with the boy and let him put his hands all over you? Did you not commit sins of the flesh?' said Sister Mary Francis.

Mother Carlin looked from Sister Mary Francis down to her own stomach, which was now so large that she couldn't see her feet. She was dressed in brown overalls, and when she tried to pull herself off the bed, she was paralysed from the neck down.

'Sister, it's me, Mother Carlin. I can't move. Help me!' A wave of pain shot through her stomach, and she clutched it, screaming out in agony.

'Good, it's working. I'll be back in a couple of hours to see how you're getting on.'

'Don't leave me on my own, Sister.'

Another wave of intense pain shot through her as she watched Sister Mary Francis leave the room. She looked over to the drip. Tiny black snake-like insects were thrashing around in the liquid, and she cried out as she watched them travel down towards her arm.

She glanced down at her stomach, where the baby was thrashing around so violently inside her that she could see its limbs protruding through her overalls. Another wave of pain was followed by a gush of liquid splashing on the floor. She looked down to see blood surrounding the bed.

'You're doing really well. It looks like the baby is coming.'

Mother Carlin looked to the end of the bed, where two girls in brown overalls were standing. 'Where is Sister Mary Francis?' she asked.

'She's busy, she told us to help you,' said one of the girls, placing the nun's legs in stirrups.

Mother Carlin let out a cry of pain as another wave hit.

'Stop your screaming.' The second girl, with pale dirty skin and hair cut away from her head in clumps, walked over to her. 'Do you think everyone wants to be woken by your crying? If you suffer, it is because you deserve it, because it is the Lord's choice that you do so and you must accept it.'

'Get away from me,' said Mother Carlin, as she let out another scream of agony.

'I can see the head!' said the first girl, appearing from between her legs and smiling brightly. 'Push, push now.'

Mother Carlin pushed hard, panting and groaning

loudly. After a few seconds, a baby's cry echoed through the room.

'It's a boy!' said the girl brightly. Mother Carlin watched, horrified, as the two of them cooed over the baby, then wrapped it in a blanket and brought it over to her.

'He's beautiful, look,' said the first girl.

The baby was covered in blood. Its skin was completely translucent, so that Mother Carlin could see every vein in its face and its heart beating in its chest. It had horns growing out of the sides of its forehead and it was crying loudly, showing razor-sharp teeth. 'Get it away from me,' she screamed.

'Oh dear,' said one of the girls. 'She's still bleeding. Should we call the doctor?'

Mother Carlin looked down at the floor. The pool of blood was spreading now and covered most of the carpet.

'No, I'll give her a few stitches. That should stop it.'

The girl rummaged in her pocket, pulling a dirty needle and thread away from some sticky sweets and a tissue, then dragged a chair up in between Mother Carlin's legs.

'Don't touch me with that needle,' Mother Carlin cried as the girl began to stitch. She sobbed, clinging to the pillow as she writhed around in pain. 'Please, stop, I can't bear it.'

'What a fuss you're making,' said the girl. She whistled as she worked. Mother Carlin watched, gasping in pain as the needle stabbed in and out.

'Are you ready for us to take him now?' The other girl picked up the baby and opened the bathroom door, where a well-dressed young couple were standing waiting anxiously.

'Oh Geoffrey, he's beautiful,' said the woman to her husband. The girl handed the baby over as Mother Carlin watched, her legs still in stirrups, her tears flowing.

161

The blood on the floor had turned into a sea of red lava now. She could feel the heat from it, and hear it hissing and popping. Fragments flew up, setting the covers alight. Gradually the lava thickened: she was surrounded by it now, and her bed began to sink lower and lower as it incinerated beneath her. She pulled her legs from the stirrups, rolled onto her side and began to pray as flames danced around her.

'Though I walk through the valley of the shadow of death, I will fear no evil, for you are with me; your rod and your staff, they comfort me.'

As she looked over towards the door in desperation, it seemed to move further and further away, so that it became like a mouse hole in the distance. She was at sea now, a sea of burning flames from which children's hands reached up to claw at her and pull her down with them.

The bed sank deeper, until it became a raft that she clung to for dear life. Laughing, the children began tipping it up, as if it were a harmless game. She tried to pull their fingers off, but there were too many of them and eventually she could cling on no longer. She held her breath as she plunged into the molten lava, kicking frantically to get to the surface as the intense heat engulfed her.

A streak of indescribable pain shot up her arm, making it impossible for her to cling on to what was left of the bed. She tried to scream, but the children's hands covered her face and mouth and pulled her under.

Chapter Twenty-One

Sunday 5 February 2017

Kitty clutched her front door keys as the taxi sped down the motorway. The sharp teeth of the keys digging into the palm of her hand provided focus as anxiety overwhelmed her. She had no idea what would be waiting for her when they arrived. She had not been back to the outhouse since that night; the coward in her had stopped her, and there had seemed to be no point. Father Benjamin had told her father that her sister was dead and buried. But now she wasn't so sure.

As they reached Brighton, fear and doubt grew within her so that her body felt paralysed. Memories came flooding back at the thought of that night. Of searching for the outhouse in the pitch black. The house was being torn down the day after tomorrow; it would be fenced off and no doubt there would be a security guard on patrol. The chances of being able to get near the outhouse suddenly seemed impossible, but still she watched the road, not stopping the driver, not telling him to turn back. This was her one and only chance; she had to try.

As she breathed steadily, her resolve returned. She wished they could go faster so it would be over. She looked at her watch, it was just past eleven. She could see the cab driver glancing at her a couple of times in the rear-view mirror, knew he recognised her, that he would probably speak to his friends about this strange outing with the woman off the telly. But suddenly she didn't care. Samantha Harper appeared to be gaining on her, and soon her connection to St Margaret's would be out. She had hidden the truth for so long, but why? Who was she protecting? Perhaps she *wanted* it all to come out; why else would she have attended something as public as Father Benjamin's inquest? All she needed to find out now, before they tore the place down, was whether she had made a mistake in not going back to the outhouse. If there was any sign of her sister at St Margaret's, she had to know.

As they curled their way through the country lanes, the driver spoke to her. 'Any idea where we're headed in Preston, love?'

'Just the other side of the village,' said Kitty, moving her head from side to side to loosen her stiff neck. 'It's a large Victorian house, St Margaret's. It's due for demolition so I suppose you need to look out for a building site.'

'Is that it?'

Kitty's eyes followed the direction of the car's headlights as the driver pointed to the horizon. It was drizzling, and the wipers swished from side to side as the black outline of St Margaret's came into view. As he pulled up at the gates, the grey clouds parted and the moon cast its light on the imposing Gothic mansion that had dominated her memories for so long. Now that she was here, it felt very different to the overbearing image in her mind's eye; like a grown-up child visiting a strict grandparent in their dying days.

'What do I owe you?' She reached into her handbag, glancing at the meter.

'Are you sure this is the right place?' The taxi driver looked doubtful.

Kitty looked down at her wallet, pulling out a wad of twenty-pound notes. 'Yes, this is fine.'

'Are you meeting someone?' he said, frowning up at the house.

'Yes,' said Kitty quietly. 'I'm meeting someone in the outhouse at the back.'

'Do you want me to drive round?'

'Okay. That's very kind of you.'

Kitty sat back again as they headed down the bumpy track next to the house. The car jolted up and down, throwing her around. The broken windows of the house looked down at her as they passed. Soon the taxi would be gone, and she would be alone in the middle of nowhere in the freezing rain, utterly vulnerable. She closed her eyes and tried to calm her breathing, reaching out her hand to feel her sister's fingers on the seat next to hers.

'How about through there?' asked the driver, stopping the car, the sound of the brakes cutting through the night. 'Looks like there's an opening in the fence. And look, some lights the other side of the cemetery.'

Kitty opened her eyes. In the beam of the headlights she could see a huge fence surrounding the perimeter of St Margaret's, and a small hole peeled back, probably by kids. Just beyond it were row upon row of ivy-covered head-stones. 'I'll find it, I've been here before.'

'I'm happy to take you back. Doesn't feel right leaving you out here,' said the driver. 'I'll have to go and grab some food, but I'll be back after that to pick you up.'

'Thank you,' said Kitty, relief flooding her that he had thought of it for her. 'I'd really appreciate that.'

The driver clicked the button to unlock the door, and

Kitty stepped out into the night. She pulled her jumper around her and tied her mac tight before making her way over to the fence and pushing her way through. She fumbled with the buttons on her torch until a faint beam sprang from it. Then, trying to calm her nerves, she closed her eyes and pictured her sister's face, the memory hazy after all these years.

As the taxi rattled off down the drive she ventured on, ignoring the anxious stabbing pain in her guts. The foggy graveyard seemed to come alive, the sounds of the night filling the black gaps beyond the torchlight. The ground rustled below her feet as wildlife scattered, and leaves crackled above her as squirrels and birds darted to safety. Kitty directed her torch at the gravestones; polished marble adorned with loving messages for the Sisters of Mercy who had died during their service at St Margaret's. A comforting view of death: gone but not forgotten. She pressed on as fast as she could, the frozen ground of the graveyard uneven, a maze of gravestones in her path.

Every grave had been dug out, the bodies within them taken for reburial elsewhere and the pits left behind filled with sand and stone. Kitty walked amongst them, wondering how far from where she now stood her sister had been buried. If they had killed her, the excavation report told her that they hadn't given her a proper burial, so where, in this freezing hell, were her remains hidden? And if they hadn't killed her, if she was alive, was Kitty insane for thinking she could still be living here after all these years?

She pressed on, stumbling several times as the ground became increasingly uneven. The gravestones grew smaller as she moved further into the graveyard, shrinking to mere stumps of stone engraved with only names and dates. *Sarah Johnson, January 1928–April 1950*. Only twenty-two when she died, thought Kitty, as her foot caught in a tangle of thorns. She put down the torch to free herself. *Emma Lockwood, July 1942–December 1961* read the inscription on the broken cross lying on the ground. Nineteen. Still a child. Many of the mounds of earth had no official headstone at all, just tiny wooden crosses, their sharp corners worn down by the passing of time. *Clara Lockwood, infant, December 1961* read a small slab of grey stone just ahead of her. *Catherine Henderson, February 1942–July 1957*. Kitty tried to stay focused on her destination, but her head started to throb as she thought about this young girl, just fifteen, her body not ready to give birth, most probably dying in agony in the infirmary of St Margaret's.

As she made her way towards the light at the edge of the cemetery, a dog barked and she jumped, struggling to steady herself as the night spun around her. Sinking down onto a large rock, she took in huge gulps of freezing air, tucking her hands in her pockets to stop them going numb. The torch lay on the ground where it had fallen. *Clara Jones, Penny Frost, Nancy Webb*. No epitaph or poetry to accompany these poor souls.

The noises around her grew louder, like voices whispering among the trees. Burying her head in her hands, Kitty heard a thud. An image flashed into her mind of a young mother and her baby being thrown into a cheap coffin and lowered roughly into the ground. She covered her ears, yet she could still hear the grunts and groans of a tired gravedigger shovelling the earth back into the hole. This was a part of the cemetery nobody visited. She felt sick at the thought of all these poor souls lying in makeshift graves, trampled on, unacknowledged by the families who had dumped them at the gates.

She snapped back to the present as the dog barked again, and looked up to see shadows moving between the trees. Increasingly she felt as if she was being watched. If Elvira were here, she would be waiting for Kitty to get closer so she could reach out to her without anyone else knowing. She needed to get up, to keep moving. The more ground she covered, the more chance she had of finding her sister.

With a groan, she picked up her torch and pushed herself off the stone, picking her way forward as the dog barked yet again. She tried to shake off the thought of it appearing in front of her suddenly, knocking her down, attacking her, tearing her ice-cold skin.

She staggered and grabbed at the steel fence at the perimeter for support, the impact making it rattle through the silence. She walked alongside it, using it as her guide, running her numb fingers over the wire until her legs became too tired to hold her up any longer. The dog was now silent, and the light in the distance had faded completely. If she followed the fence back, it would take her to the graveyard and back to the safety of the taxi. Then what? Home? More despair? She would rather keep going and die out here than go back having failed her sister again.

'Hello?' she called, her voice shaking from the cold. Still using the fence as a support, she walked on, so frozen she could no longer feel the bruises and cuts on her body from the countless thorns encircling her.

Suddenly she stumbled in a dip in the ground and crashed down, hot pokers of intense pain shooting through her legs. She screamed out and rolled onto her back, then lay still, unable to move, and looked up at the moon, waiting for the pain to pass.

Through the throbbing in her ears, she heard footsteps coming towards her, quiet at first, then louder as they crunched on the icy ground and came to a halt beside her. Elvira squatted down next to her, reaching out and stroking her hair.

'Look,' she said, stretching out her tiny arm in its brown overalls. 'Over there.'

Twenty feet away was an outbuilding that Kitty immediately recognised from her dreams. She pushed herself up onto all fours, then stood and slowly began making her way towards it.

Chapter Twenty-Two

Sunday 5 February 2017

'Are you coming, or what?' said a male voice down the phone.

Sam was still sitting in the car outside Gracewell, overwhelmed with the temptation to let St Margaret's go for ever. It was just too hard. Her body and mind ached from being pulled in so many different directions.

'Who is this?' She fished a bottle of water from her bag.

'That's charming. It's Andy.'

Andy. Who the hell was Andy?

'From the building site.'

'Oh, shit! Andy! I'm so sorry,' said Sam, looking at her watch. 'We were supposed to meet at ten, weren't we? It's been a hell of a day.' She glanced at her reflection in the rear-view mirror and sighed.

'You'll be needing that drink then.'

When she arrived, Andy was sitting in the corner of the brightly lit Wetherspoon's he'd chosen as their venue. Though she'd felt a migraine coming on as soon as she stepped onto the swirly blue carpet, at least there was no chance of bumping into any of Ben's painfully trendy friends in there. The last thing she needed was Ben thinking she was having an affair.

'All right?' Andy asked, not standing as she approached his table.

'Yeah, good, thanks. You?' Sam perched awkwardly on a stool next to his.

'S'pose so.' He downed the rest of his pint.

'Drink?' She dug into her bag for her purse.

'Go on then, I'll have a pint of Stella.'

As she stood at the bar, Sam suddenly missed Ben so much she felt like she'd been punched in the stomach. Walking into the pub had made her recall their first date, which they'd spent in a cocktail bar on Clapham High Street, making their way through every drink on the menu until the manager had physically thrown them out. Ben had bought a new shirt, which still had the label on, and he'd sprung out of his seat so fast when she'd walked in that he hit his head on the beam above him, almost knocking himself out. Sam had scuttled to the bar for an ice pack, after which they had spent the next four hours swapping life stories and pawing at each other until all the other customers were put off their nachos and left. From that moment on, she'd never wanted anyone else. She loved Ben more than she had ever loved anyone, but they were so bloody miserable at the moment and hurled such bile and vitriol at one another that there just didn't seem to be any hope for them. That was why people broke up, she thought, handing over her cash. It was why they walked away. Staying with someone who had seen you at your worst, and thrown it back at you, was soul-destroying.

'Sam!' shouted a familiar voice from behind her, and for a second her heart lurched, terrified that it was Ben. Then she turned and before her stood Fred, clutching a pint of beer and beaming at her.

'Oh, hi, Fred, how's it going?' Sam looked over at a

171

group of people behind him, all clutching pints of beer and heckling.

'Yeah, good, I'm celebrating,' said Fred, turning back to his friends and signalling for them to pipe down.

'Oh yeah?' said Sam, glancing over at Andy. 'What are you celebrating?'

'I just came third in the British Bouldering Championships,' Fred said proudly, his voice slurring.

'That's fantastic, Fred, well done.'

'Fancy joining us?' he said, gazing at her.

'Thanks, but I'd better not. I'm here with a contact. I'll see you later.' As she turned to make her way back to Andy, she was aware of Fred's eyes on her.

'Cheers,' said Andy as she put down his pint and sat opposite him, smiling awkwardly. He was huge, the sort of bloke you saw on a Harley-Davidson on the motorway. His hands were wrapped around his pint as if it were a shot glass, and the leather jacket on the back of his chair nearly reached the floor. He smelt of body odour and cigarettes, and when he spoke, he leant in a bit too close.

'So, how was the rest of your day?' Sam sipped her Diet Coke.

'Same old shit. What about you?'

'Yeah, same here,' said Sam, thinking the opposite. That was why she did this job: she loved it. She'd done jobs where she'd watched the clock all day, feeling as if her soul was being sucked out through her fingernails. She'd never go back there again.

'What do you do, then?' asked Andy, raising his voice to be heard over the blaring house music.

'Not a lot at the moment. I've got a young daughter, and

172

we're living at my nana's at the moment, just keeping her company.'

'Oh yeah, your grandad died, didn't he.'

'He did.' An awkward silence fell between them. Andy took a huge gulp of his lager. Sam always took the piss out of Ben for taking an hour to drink a pint. She suddenly felt like crying. What was she doing here? She needed to go home, now.

'So did you find that nun you were looking for?'

Sam put down her drink. 'Yes, I did. Thank you for your help.'

'No worries. I'll be glad when they tear that place down and I can finally get out of there. I'm sick of everyone breathing down my neck.'

His mobile started to ring and he picked it up, looked at the number then cut off the call.

'Fuck it,' he said.

'What?' said Sam.

'There'll be a bollocking waiting for me on the answer-phone when I get back.' He took out a Zippo lighter and began flicking it open and closed. 'You wanna rollie?'

'I'm okay, thanks. So when was St Margaret's meant to be demolished?'

'Four months ago. The hold-up has cost them nearly a million quid.' He pulled a packet of tobacco from his pocket.

'Jesus! What, because of the inquest?'

'Yeah, it took a while because that priest was down in the sewers when he died.' Andy began pinching tobacco from the packet and pressing it into a paper.

'What was he doing down there?' said Sam, noticing that Fred was still watching her from the other side of the room.

Andy paused, then shrugged. 'It's a rabbit warren, that house, gives me the creeps, and a magnet for waifs and strays. You just can't keep them all away. There's a tramp been living in the outhouse for months. I keep kicking him out, but he comes back.' He drained his glass.

'Another pint? I think I owe you two, if I remember rightly,' said Sam.

'Go on then. Only got that shitty Portakabin to go back to.' He eyed her in a way that made her feel uncomfortable.

She returned from the bar with a pint and a whisky chaser. She was beginning to think her drink with Andy might be getting her somewhere. 'There you go.'

'Cheers.' He knocked back the whisky, not dropping his stare.

'So you've felt the ghosts walking round that place too?' said Sam.

Andy laughed emptily. 'Put it this way, it's a relief to get out into the graveyard when you've been in that house.'

'So why do you think he was down in the sewers?' said Sam, pulling her long red hair back and wrapping it into a knot.

'It doesn't make any odds come Tuesday,' said Andy, picking up his pint. 'Sooner that place is buried under concrete, the better.' He eyed her glass. 'Aren't you gonna have a proper drink?'

'Sure,' said Sam, glancing at his keys on the table. 'I'll have a white wine, please.'

He picked up his wallet and headed off to the bar. As soon as his back was turned, she grabbed the keys and started fumbling through them under the table. There were only three: one was a car key, another looked like it was for a padlock, so

174

the third had to be for the Portakabin. Quickly she peeled it off. She'd leave it on the floor of the cabin once she was done; with any luck he'd think it had just fallen off. She looked up to see him on his way back from the bar, and slid the keys under her bag.

'There you go,' he said, slopping half the contents of her wine onto the table. 'Oops, sorry.'

'No worries.' Sam took a glug of the battery acid. She would need it for Dutch courage. Hopefully the dog would be tied up, otherwise she was screwed.

'So don't your boyfriend mind you going out with strangers?' Andy put his hand over hers.

It took Sam all her willpower not to tug it away. 'What he doesn't know won't hurt him.'

'You gonna give me a kiss then?' He drained his pint and turned to her.

'Sure. I just need to go and do something first. Can I meet you in half an hour?' She forced a smile.

'What? Why?' snapped Andy.

'I need to pop home and get some stuff for tomorrow. I don't know where tonight is going to take us, but if I've got my stuff, I can go straight to work in the morning.' She clutched the key in her fist as she stood up.

'Oh, right, sure!' His mood instantly lifted again. 'Meet you by the pier?'

'Perfect,' said Sam.

Chapter Twenty-Three

Kitty tripped and stumbled as her numb feet struggled to respond to her demands. When she finally reached the red-brick outhouse, she barely had the strength to pull back the splintered stable door, which was swinging from its hinges. After three attempts, she finally opened it wide enough to squeeze through and fell inside, collapsing on a pile of leaves by the entrance.

She sat motionless, her eyes scanning the space around her as the moonlight came through the holes in the brick-work. The walls had split and crumbled and most of the roof had collapsed, leaving wood splintered over the stone floor.

It was exactly as she remembered, with the old plough turned on its side in the corner.

Another door at the back of the building stood slightly ajar, revealing a room with green paint peeling from the walls. Kitty stood up and shuffled across towards it. As she put out her hand to push it open, a large brown rat ran out from under the rubble and into the room ahead of her. She watched as it scuttled around the edge of the toilet, then disappeared under the bed. The room was filthy, with black mould climbing the walls and the stench of sewage filling the air.

There were cans of food on the floor and an open packet of biscuits. Someone had been here. Someone was living in this room and had been here very recently. She approached the bed, running her fingers over the blanket before picking it up and inhaling its smell. Then she walked over to the basin and turned one of the taps, letting out a gasp as water came spluttering out.

'Hello?' she whispered. 'Is anybody here?'

She had been right. Her sister had been here at St Margaret's all along, and this was where she was going to find her. It was too much to take in. The room was starting to spin, and she leant over the basin, put her hands under the water and splashed it on her face.

When she stood up, there in the mirror behind her was Elvira, old now, like Kitty, her grey hair scraped back from her thin, pale face.

'Have you forgotten what I told you?' she asked, her eyes black.

She walked over to the wall and pulled a loose brick away. Behind it was a heavy iron key. She held it out to Kitty.

'Burn the house and set them free.'

As Kitty reached out to her sister, a crash came from the other side of the room, and she looked round to see a man with a long beard and torn clothes standing with a pile of kindling at his feet.

'Who the hell are you? Get out!' he shouted.

Kitty looked around for Elvira, but she was gone. 'Come back!' she called. Tears stung her eyes. 'My sister, where has my sister gone?'

'Get out! This is my place. Get out!' As the vagrant came charging towards her, Kitty let out a scream and ran.

Chapter Twenty-Four

Monday 6 February 2017

After searching the entire perimeter of the house and finally finding a hole in the fence by the graveyard, Sam stumbled over the freezing pitch-black grounds feeling as if every ghost in St Margaret's was watching her. As she approached the Portakabin, Sam was relieved to find Andy and his dog were nowhere to be seen and despite the fact that it was stifling, with the windows firmly shut and a pungent smell of damp in the air, she was nonetheless glad to be safely inside. Sam fumbled in the dark for the light switch, her chest tightening as the lack of oxygen ignited her nerves. Finally she located the plastic switch and pressed it down, flooding the pitiful room with light.

The sight that met her was unpleasant but not a surprise. At one end, a single bed lay unmade, with a sea of porn magazines and empty beer cans scattered over the floor. A filthy sink sat in the corner, a tube of toothpaste oozing its contents, and various bottles of aftershave and deodorant on a dirty shelf above it. At the other end of the cabin was a small grey leather sofa and a TV. An array of pizza and takeaway boxes covered a small coffee table at its centre.

Dirty net curtains hung at the window. Sam pulled them aside to check for any sign of car headlights, then turned on the lamp by the sofa and clicked off the glaring overhead lights before scanning the room.

Eventually her eyes fell on what she was looking for: a filing cabinet. The top drawer appeared to be crammed mostly with marketing material, brochures for the soon-to-be-built mansions in all their glossy beauty, as well as notebooks, Post-it notes and pens embossed with *Slade Homes*. The second drawer similarly held little of interest: a Yellow Pages, two copies of *Top Gear* magazine, and several empty cigarette packets. As Sam reached for the final drawer, she began to feel slightly panicked. It had been nearly an hour since she'd left Wetherspoon's, and Andy would soon start to lose patience. If there was nothing in this room of any use, she needed to get out of here before he came back and realised his key was missing.

She knew that somewhere there must be some reference to Father Benjamin and what had happened to him. She needed some records, a file with paperwork in it. When she pulled open the bottom drawer, she knew she had found it and her heart leapt. Hanging files filled the entire drawer. The first two thirds were mostly bills, pay slips and a contract. She slid open the 'S' file, and pulled out a wedge of paperwork with the heading 'Slade Homes'. Quickly checking the window to make sure the coast was clear, she perched on the end of the sofa and began to read.

The file began with several written warnings from the Slade site manager to Andy about his timekeeping. Under the terms of his contract, they stated, he was to be on site every night, from 9 p.m. until 9 a.m., when the first workmen arrived. He was clearly not the most diligent of employees, as two of the JCB diggers had been broken into, and when the police had arrived, Andy was nowhere to be found. On another occasion, several sacks of cement had been stolen, the cost of which had been docked from his wages. There was also a reference to the tramp he had mentioned; clearly a nuisance but one who, according to Andy's copied reply, stayed in the outhouse and never came near St Margaret's.

The final letter in the file concerned Father Benjamin.

While Father Benjamin's death occurred many years ago, on 31 December 1999, the underground sewers and adjacent tunnels remain accessible at this time and we must be extremely vigilant in order to avoid any such tragic accident occurring again before the final date of demolition: Tuesday 7 February 2017. If anyone is found in the vicinity or on the property itself, you are instructed to detain them and call 999 immediately.

Underground sewers and tunnels. Sam's conversation with Andy in the pub sprang back into her mind. What had he said? 'It's a rabbit warren that house, gives me the creeps.'

She looked back down to the file. The article from *The Times* that had first pricked her interest was scrunched up in between the letters.

The remains of an elderly man, 74, who was overcome by fumes while trapped in an underground sewer were discovered at a condemned mansion in East Sussex. The man, a retired priest from Preston in East Sussex, had become trapped after gaining unauthorised access to the property, an inquest has found.

Born Benjamin Cook in Brighton in 1926, Father Benjamin was parish priest for thirty years.

Father Benjamin went missing on New Year's Eve 1999, but his remains were not discovered until 30 September 2016. He died as a result of hypoxia, secondary to exposure to toxic concentrations of hydrogen sulphide, Sussex Coroner's Court heard on Tuesday.

The inquest into the retired priest's death was opened and adjourned before Coroner Dr Brian Farrell. Detectives said there was no third party involvement. Slade Homes extended its deepest condolences

There were no other files of interest, and just as she was thinking she ought to leave before Andy came back, Sam noticed that there was a landline phone on top of the cabinet and that the red answerphone attached to it was flashing. She checked the coast was clear again, then walked over and pressed the button.

'Andy, it's Phil, pick up your mobile! Where the fuck are you? You don't seem to be getting what's at stake here. We've got one day to go. We've navigated a full-blown inquest and I don't want this deal falling through because someone else manages to get locked in those tunnels.'

Locked in? There was no mention of that in the article. Sam's ears suddenly pricked up at the faint sound of an engine in the distance, and to her horror, she saw headlights slowly making their way towards the cabin. She jumped up, pushed the file back into the drawer and turned off the lamp, then ducked down, watching breathlessly as a blue truck approached. As she looked around desperately for a way out, she heard the vehicle pull up outside and the engine judder before being turned off, along with the headlights. The cabin was plunged into darkness.

There was no second door, nowhere to hide in the tiny room. He had a vicious dog that would attack her if she made a run for it, then he'd no doubt call the police. She would lose her job. She would lose everything. As she heard footsteps coming closer, she knew she had only one choice. Pulling off her top, she jumped onto the stinking bed in just her bra.

The door opened and the overhead light came on.

'Hi, gorgeous,' she said, trying to hide the panic in her voice.

'What the hell are you doing in here?' said Andy.

'I wanted to surprise you.' Sam's whole body was shaking.

'Did you take my key?'

'Yes. You don't mind, do you?' She attempted a smile.

'Yes, I do fucking mind.' He strode over and glared down at her.

'I'm sorry. I thought you'd like us to be alone.' She gave a rueful smile. 'Let's have a drink and relax, shall we?'

She climbed out of the bed and went to the fridge as Andy watched in silence. It was empty apart from some mouldy cheese and the dregs of a bottle of milk.

'You're all out. Why don't I go and get us something to drink?' she said, reaching for her top.

'Why don't you tell me what the hell you're playing at?'

'I wanted to surprise you. I thought you'd like it. I clearly made a mistake.' She hurriedly put her top on. Her hands were visibly trembling as she reached for the door.

'I don't like people breaking into my property.' He stepped in front of her to stop her leaving.

'I didn't break in. Please let me past.' Her heart was hammering so hard in her ears that her head was pounding. All she could think of was Emma, lying safe in her bed while she was here trying to commit suicide. You stupid bloody idiot, she thought.

'You're lucky I'm a gentleman.' He slowly moved aside and Sam darted to the door. As she stumbled down the steps, Andy's dog, who had arrived back with him, began to bark at her. She felt sure, as she headed off into the darkness, that Andy was watching her, waiting for any excuse to let the vicious animal off the leash. She glanced back, and could see him standing at the Portakabin door, holding onto the dog's collar while it strained to chase after her.

With every step that she couldn't find the hole in the fence, her panic increased. She could feel the lactic acid in her legs burning as she ran backwards and forwards along the perimeter. Shaking the wire fencing and swearing under her breath, she tried desperately to hold back the tears. She needed to retrace her steps: that was the only way back to the car. She had to try and stay calm, but the barking dog in the distance was making her nauseous with anxiety.

She turned round and launched herself back alongside the fence, but tripped on something sticking out from the ground and came crashing down hard. She lay for a moment clutching her knee, gasping with pain. She could feel it was wet with blood, but it was too dark to see her hand in front of her face. She assumed she had tripped on a tree root, but when she pulled her phone from her bag to examine the damage, the light from her screen caught the reflection of something on the ground behind her. Ignoring the pain in her knee, she leant over to look at it. It was a brass catch, like the one on the floor of the Mother Superior's office, jutting out from the weeds and thorns.

She started to pull at the undergrowth around it, gasping as thorns tore at her fingers in the dark. After clearing what she could, she found that the brass ring was connected to a cast-iron plate. She pushed herself up, yelping at the pain in her knee, and tried to pull it open, but it wouldn't budge. It had a keyhole and it was locked.

Moonlight spilt through the clouds and she stared up at the house, its empty windows appearing like hundreds of eyes watching her. The same eyes that must have watched Father Benjamin that night. What had the man on the answerphone said? It sounded as if the priest had been trapped deliberately in the tunnels under the house. Did this trapdoor lead to them?

Suddenly she heard the dog barking again, much nearer now, and gaining. Sam began to run. The pain from her knee was excruciating, but she blanked it out. Any second now, the animal would appear and sink its teeth into her leg or arm. Andy would have had time to think; maybe realise that she had been through the filing cabinet and listened to the message on the machine. He would probably call the police and it would all be over.

She picked up her pace, trying to control her terror. Please, please, she pleaded to the freezing, unrelenting night.

Suddenly she spotted a light on the other side of the fence and began to run towards it. As she got closer, she saw it was the headlights of a car coming down the track. To her relief, the lights illuminated the break in the fence and she forced herself through it. The dog let out another bark; it could be no more than twenty feet away now. She realised that the car was a black cab and as it pulled to a stop, Sam hammered on the passenger window. The man inside looked up at her in shock, then slowly opened the window.

'You all right, love?'

'No, there's a dog chasing me. Please can you let me in! Quickly.'

He unlocked the doors, and she pulled at the handle and leapt inside. As she slammed the door closed, the dog ran round the car barking furiously.

'Jesus Christ, you gave me the fright of my life,' said the man.

'Thank God you were here.' Sam was trying to catch her breath.

As the two of them sat staring at one another, Andy appeared at the fence and started shouting at the dog to come back.

'Blimey, this place is like Piccadilly Circus,' said the driver as the dog retreated and Andy put him on a lead before walking off into the darkness.

'What are you doing here?' said Sam, as her breathing calmed.

'I've come to collect my fare,' the cabbie said, looking at his watch. 'She's been gone nearly an hour. I brought her down from London, didn't feel right leaving her out here alone.' He pulled a polystyrene cup from a take away bag. 'Speak of the devil . . .'

Sam looked up to see Kitty Cannon staggering towards the fence. Before she could reach it, her legs went from underneath her and she collapsed.

Sam opened the door and jumped out, pushing herself back through the hole in the fence and running over to where Kitty lay. She knelt by her side and listened to her breathing, then took her coat off and laid it over her.

'Ivy?' said Kitty faintly.

'We need an ambulance!' Sam shouted to the driver.

'No, please, just take me home,' said Kitty, before she started to cry.

Chapter Twenty-Five

Friday 31 December 1999

Father Benjamin paused momentarily as he stood in the entrance hall, catching his breath from hurrying through the grounds of St Margaret's in the darkness. Unable to turn on his torch for fear of being seen by a nosy passer-by, he had tripped twice, only just managing to avoid a fall.

It had been early evening by the time he had seen the note posted under his door at Gracewell. There had been a New Year's Eve tea in the dining room, after which he made his way into the lift and along the corridor to his room. He had spotted it as soon as he walked in. Curious, but not remotely concerned, he had picked it up and walked over to the chair by the window to open it.

As soon as he slid the single sheet of white paper out of the envelope, worry had set in. Two lines, unsigned, in handwriting he did not recognise.

Meet me in the ironing room at St Margaret's at midnight tonight to discuss the records you destroyed. If you don't turn up, I will go to the police. Come alone.

He had sat for most of the evening looking at the television in his room, his mind far away. He tried to tell Amy about the note when she came to check on him, but the words wouldn't come. Where would he start?

By eleven o'clock, he knew he was too anxious to sleep. It would be better to go and meet whoever it was and see what they wanted, rather than lie in his bed worrying. It wasn't far, just along Preston Lane. He still had his keys to the old house. No one would even notice he was gone. And so he had dressed in his warmest woollen jumper, tucked the note into the pocket of his corduroy trousers and snuck out at twenty minutes to midnight.

Now, in the safety of the house, he clicked the torch on. It was unnerving to be back after so many years. The place felt familiar yet alien at the same time. The sweeping staircase in the entrance hall was just as he remembered it. But instead of shining with polish, it was dull and covered in broken glass and fallen debris from the high ceiling above it. Dirt and grime coated the black and white tiles that had sparkled and shone in the days of Mother Carlin. The windows he passed as he walked along the corridor towards the laundry were mostly smashed, their frames cracked and split, with paint curling off like claws. The whole building smelt of rotting wood. As he reached the door of the laundry, he shone his torch inside. Once a vast, steam-filled room crammed with girls and their bumps, it was now an empty shell strewn with debris and broken mangles.

As he walked down the corridor, the light from his torch lit up his reflection in the only window that wasn't broken. His round face was pale, covered in stubble, and tufts of grey hair stuck out of his head in a wiry mess. He was curled forward in a permanent bow because of a constant ache in his back. From the side he looked as if he had no

188

neck at all, he thought, as his grey eyes stared back at him through his cheap spectacles. Whereas once he would have been freshly shaved every morning, his perfectly pressed vestments laid out for him on his bed, now an oversized grey woollen jumper and baggy cords were his uniform. He was a ruin, he thought as he turned away from the window; just as this mansion had become.

He let out a heavy sigh at the memory of St Margaret's in its heyday. With kind donations from the congregation and a hefty loan from the bank, they had managed to buy the former boarding school at auction and open its doors less than six months later. For three decades they had made enough money to keep a roof over their heads, and put something aside for the future.

But not enough, it seemed, to ensure that he and the Sisters of Mercy were comfortable in their retirement. In the end, the offer from Slade Homes had come just at the right moment. The house had been condemned, and pressure from the council over the whereabouts of records from the home had reached a peak. There was an undercurrent of finger-pointing that made him very uneasy; it troubled him that he and the sisters were not treated with the respect they deserved.

He stopped and listened to see if he could hear anyone moving about below him. Silence. Perhaps whoever it was had not arrived yet; perhaps their only motive had been to upset him and they wouldn't come. Only a handful of people knew about the records, and he had no idea why they had asked to meet here rather than discussing the issue with him at Gracewell. He felt a great deal more uncomfortable than he thought he would being back at the house. It had been a tortuous decision to agree to the sale, but at the same time he would be glad when it was gone – as long as Slade stuck to the contract, building inside the agreed perimeters and sealing off the tunnels, which he had insisted be done on signature.

As he reached the end of the last of the long corridors, he found himself faced with a locked door. He took out a brass key, a tag attached to it saying *Back Stairs*, and, using the torch to guide him, turned it in the lock. Then he opened the door and flashed the light down the dark stairway below him.

'Hello? Is anyone there?' he called out. No reply.

He sighed to himself at the thought of the pain his back was about to give him. His heels clicked on the cold stone steps as his tired hands gripped the rail. Through the silence of the empty house, he thought he could hear the sound of Mother Carlin's heels as she carried a stillborn baby down the stairs, through the ironing room and out into the tunnels. There had been so many deaths. The births were frequent and often went wrong. It was impossible to give every stillborn child a proper burial; they just didn't have the money or time.

At the bottom of the stairs, Father Benjamin was faced with another heavy oak door and reached for his keys again, shining his torch at them until he found the label saying *Ironing Room*. As he did so, he dropped the torch; its back came off and the batteries fell out onto the dusty floor.

Without his torch, in the bowels of the house in the middle of the night, it was impossible to see his hand in front of his face. He knelt down and patted the floor, puffing and panting, growing dizzy and disoriented. Mice scuttled around him as he tried to remain composed. Eventually he found one battery, then the other.

'Blasted thing,' he muttered, turning the batteries this way and that before eventually clicking them into place and turning the torch back on. At the same moment, the door at the top of the stairs banged shut.

He was sure he had closed it. He flashed the torch up the stairs into the blackness but could see nothing. 'Hello,' he mumbled to the dark. 'Who's there?'

Focusing on his task again, he used the door handle to pull himself up, letting out a loud groan that echoed up the stone stairs behind him. Shaking with exertion, he paused to gather his strength and inserted the key into the lock. It took several tries before it eventually turned.

It was clear the room hadn't yet been cleared of all the ironing presses. It was smaller than he remembered, and as he walked through, his feet crackled over broken glass from the two barred windows. The low ceiling was claustrophobic, and down here the damp permeated the walls and the smell of mould was overwhelming. Twice he bumped into the sharp edges of the presses. The floor was black from the build-up of grime and dirt, which stuck to his feet as he shuffled through it. His legs ached from his journey, and he let out heavy breaths that echoed round the room, gripped by an anxiety he was not familiar with. In the dim light, he almost felt he could see the girls watching him through clouds of steam as they worked, wiping away the perspiration on their foreheads with the sleeves of their overalls.

He looked at his watch: midnight. He trailed his torch beam around the room, but nobody was here waiting for him. It was a hoax, a sick joke by someone who was probably at home now, safe and warm by the fire, toasting the start of a new millennium.

'Where are you?' he called out one last time. Silence.

As he turned to go, he heard a noise. It was faint, like the crashing of metal against metal some distance away. He moved forward slowly and shone his torch in the direction it had come from.

Then he stopped dead. The door that led down to the tunnels was open. He moved closer: he could definitely hear someone down there. It sounded like they were hitting metal with a hammer. But the only thing that could be was the door to the septic tank, and that was impossible. Slade had assured him that the tunnels beyond the perimeter would be blocked off and filled in as soon as he signed the contract.

Panic surged through him as he shuffled towards the open door. If they had broken their word, he needed to know. The tank had been filled in with rubble and sand by a contractor he had paid himself years ago, but the tunnel leading up to it should have been cemented in by now.

Father Benjamin stood at the top of the stone steps that led to the tunnel and the septic tank. Once cleaned regularly, and lit with lamps, the walls were now dark green and covered in foul-smelling gunge. Water dripped from the ceiling, its echoes ringing out like bells. He tried to ignore his rising panic at being in such a dark, confined space. The smell hanging in the air – a pungent mix of mould and rotten eggs – was making him nauseous. Using the wall to guide him, he eased his foot to the edge of the top step and began to make his way carefully downwards, knowing that if he fell, no one would find him before morning, if at all. He counted to himself as he moved – one, two, three – as if warning anything below that he was coming.

The rotting smell began to act like an acid, burning the lining of his nose. The dead air around him was impossibly hard to breathe, and as he reached the bottom of the steps and began to walk down the tunnel towards the tank, he soon became disoriented in the darkness.

The dripping water had turned the tunnel into a trench. The burning pain in his nose began to travel to his throat and eyes. One more minute, he told himself, one more minute and he would have the proof he needed and could go home to bed. He forced his heavy legs forward, the burning sensations now accompanied by pressure on his chest. As he tried to keep the torch steady in his trembling hand, he heard something behind him, like a brown paper bag rustling in the wind. He stopped and turned, pointing the torch in the direction the noise had come from, but saw only empty space. As he continued, desperate now to reach the tank, the rustling turned into a whisper. First one voice, then two, incomprehensible hushed exchanges. Several times he stopped and turned, listening to his own laboured breathing when no response to his calls came.

'What is he doing?' whispered a clear voice right next to his ear. Father Benjamin startled and flashed his torch in its direction, but again saw only the black tunnel surrounding him.

A feeling of suffocation pressed down on him. He must be nearly there. 'Where is it, where is it?' he mumbled, feeling in front of him for the stone wall at the end of the tunnel. His head throbbed; the tunnel seemed to narrow, closing in around him as the cold, stinking water dripped onto his head.

'He's looking for the tank, I think,' said another voice, deeper this time. Father Benjamin paused, then moved on again. It was the smells and the fumes affecting him, he told himself, as he began to cough violently. He bent over, retching. Stop, please stop, he pleaded to his body. He couldn't take enough air into his lungs in the stagnant tunnel to stop the dizziness that was overwhelming him.

Finally his coughing fit ended, but his legs had no strength and he had to lean against the wall to hold himself up.

'It's the fumes from the tank,' said the first voice. Father Benjamin looked up to see two girls in brown overalls standing over him. One had a nasty black eye; both had shaved heads and were white as ghosts.

'They are bad,' said the other girl. 'I was locked down here all night once. I was sick so many times that my nose bled. It wouldn't stop, do you remember? Mother Carlin was so angry.'

'I do, I remember it well. Poor Martha, you were very brave,' said the first girl. They hugged each other.

Father Benjamin stood up as straight as his back would allow, staggering forward until he finally reached the end of the tunnel. He stopped and sank to the floor, feeling the wall with his hands as if it were an old friend's face. He had made it. He gasped for breath and felt a wave of nausea rising in his stomach. Leaning forward, he began to vomit. Over and over he retched, unable to catch his breath in between. Finally the sickness abated and he leant his head against the wall, gasping.

Why were there still fumes coming from the tank? It had been filled in months ago.

As he struggled to his feet, a loud bang echoed through the tunnel.

'What was that?' asked one of the girls.

When Father Benjamin looked up, he saw that the original pair had now become a group of eight or ten. They were standing in a semicircle around him.

'I think it was the door to the tunnel,' said another. 'I hope he has a key.'

Father Benjamin reached down to his pocket: it was empty; the keys were gone. He must have dropped them when he was sick. Slowly squatting down, he felt the ground around him, his hand landing in a pile of warm vomit.

'Oh dear, I think he might have lost them,' said a third girl, suppressing a smile.

Father Benjamin was finding it painful to breathe as the crushing feeling in his chest intensified. He began to cough again, his eyes streaming. His lips were parched and his tongue was covered with a thick dry fur. A sudden stabbing pain in his head sent him crashing to the ground, gasping for breath again.

'Ring a ring o' roses, a pocket full of posies. A-tishoo! A-tishoo! We all fall down.'

As they laughed and skipped around him, the priest lay on the damp ground, his skin growing cold, his pulse racing. He tried to move, but any effort made him gasp in jerky, shallow breaths as his chest grew tighter and tighter. The coughing started again, so painful it was like shards of glass.

'Oh my Jesus, forget and forgive what I have been,' he mumbled over and over. Every time he tried to move, the girls pushed him down and continued to chant:

'Ring a ring o' roses, a pocket full of posies. A-tishoo! A-tishoo! We all fall down.'

'Help me!' Father Benjamin said, as a sensation of falling

began to take hold. He could barely see now, his vision failing and the light from his torch fading.

'Pray for your sins, Father,' one of the girls said, then they all turned and walked away.

Father Benjamin crawled along the foul-smelling corridor on his knees. Everything had stopped: the coughing, the sickness, the pain in his head. Finally he reached the door back through to the ironing room, heaving himself up and onto his knees. His eyes stung so much he could barely see, but he felt for the handle and turned it. The door was locked.

He let out a cry as he twisted and rattled the handle with all his failing strength.

His eyes grew heavy; eventually he lay down and closed them. He couldn't move any more now. All he wanted to do was sleep. Sleep until it was over and he was standing at the gates of heaven with the Lord. Just as the girl had told him to, he began to pray.

Forgive me my sins, O Lord, forgive me my sins; the sins of my youth, the sins of my age, the sins of my soul, the sins of my body; my idle sins, my voluntary sins; the sins I know, the sins I do not know; the sins I have concealed for so long, and which are now hidden from my memory.

I am truly sorry for every sin, mortal and venal, for all the sins of my childhood up to the present hour. I know my sins have wounded Thy tender heart, O my Saviour; let me be freed from the bonds of evil through the most bitter passion of my Redeemer.

O my Jesus, forget and forgive what I have been.

Amen.

Chapter Twenty-Six

Monday 6 February 2017

As the taxi wove in and out of traffic back to London, Kitty slept, slumped against Sam's shoulder. Sam looked at her watch: 5 a.m. Nana and Emma would still be fast asleep; she would ring at six and check all was well. She felt anxious at being so far away from Emma, but she could not just let the taxi driver take Kitty Cannon away after she had discovered her in the grounds of St Margaret's. A buzz of excitement swept through her as she looked down at the face that had been a weekly guest in almost every lounge in the country for two decades. She had been right: Kitty Cannon was connected to St Margaret's and she was determined to find out how.

'Are you sure we shouldn't take her to hospital?' said the driver.

Sam felt for Kitty's pulse, which was strong, and then took her frozen hand in hers. 'No, I think she's okay. Her pulse is fine but she's cold. Can you turn up the heater, please?'

She pulled Kitty's coat up around her, causing the mobile phone in the pocket to fall onto the floor of the taxi. 'Damn,' said Sam, trying and failing to reach it without waking her.

Kitty's long, unkempt grey hair reminded Sam of a white

witch. She had beautiful fine features, a narrow mouth and a button nose. Her skin was porcelain white. She looked completely different to her onscreen persona: younger, more vulnerable, with an almost childlike air about her.

Kitty's phone flashed up a reminder. Sam looked down at it: *Richard Stone midday*. She knocked the phone towards her with her foot, then picked it up and returned it to Kitty's pocket.

'Do you know where she lives?' she asked the driver.

'No, she flagged me down on Embankment, so I'm just heading back that way.'

Sam could hear the faint sound of her own mobile phone beeping in her pocket. It was a text from Nana asking where she was and telling her that Emma was on the mend. Sam quickly replied, asking Nana to take Emma to Ben's after breakfast and saying she would call her as soon as she could. She stroked Kitty's hair as they drove along by the river. It was torture to be so close to her and not be able to talk. But one thing she was sure of: Kitty had called her Ivy. Somehow, she had known the poor girl.

'This is where I picked her up,' said the driver, pulling over to the side of the road.

'Kitty?' said Sam gently. 'We need to know where your house is so we can get you home.'

Slowly Kitty opened her eyes and looked up at her. Then she pushed herself up and pulled away, straightening her coat and twisting her hair into a knot as if trying to save face.

'We're back in London?' she asked.

'Yes, you wanted us to take you home, but we don't know where that is.'

'Thank you for bringing me back. I'm sorry about what happened,' said Kitty.

'It's fine,' Sam replied, smiling, 'I think you're going to have quite a taxi bill, though.'

Kitty stared at her, not returning the smile. 'Who are you?'

Sam hesitated for a second. 'My name is Samantha, I'm a reporter with Southern News.'

'Oh no,' said Kitty. 'What is it with you people? Do you follow me night and day?'

'Kitty, please, if you can give me one minute to explain—' began Sam.

'No, I can't.' Kitty turned to the driver, raising her voice to be heard through the glass partition. 'Can you please get this girl out of my taxi!'

'Blimey, I'm starting to feel like Jeremy Kyle here,' he said, opening his door.

'I know about your links with St Margaret's. I believe you may have been born there,' said Sam.

Tears sprang to Kitty's eyes and she waited to compose herself before speaking. 'That is my private business and of no concern to you. If you try to print anything about it, I will sue you.'

Sam frantically raked through her bag as the driver opened the door on her side.

'Out you get, love.'

'Please, look, I've been reading letters written by someone called Ivy about her time at St Margaret's. I think you must have known her: you called me Ivy when I found you there.' Sam held out the letters which Nana had tied in a red velvet ribbon, but Kitty didn't take them.

'Stay away from me,' she said coldly.

'The people mentioned in these letters, they were all involved with St Margaret's, Mother Carlin, Father Benjamin, and they're all dead. And I'm pretty sure their deaths weren't accidental,' Sam pleaded.

The taxi driver pulled at her arm, 'Come on, I don't want to have to get the police involved.'

'Get your hands off me!' said Sam, pulling away.

'Get out!' Kitty shouted.

'Okay,' said Sam, 'I'm going. I know you were there when your father died. It must have been horrific for you as a child to see something like that. It was never my intention to upset you, and I'm very sorry. I just wanted to get to the truth and I thought you would too.'

'Wait? What did you say?' said Kitty as Sam climbed out of the cab.

'That I'm sorry,' said Sam quietly, 'and I am. It's just these letters, they've done something to me.'

'No, before that, about me being there when my father died.' Kitty leant across to the door.

'Someone I spoke to who lived on the road where your father died said a witness saw a young girl in a red coat. They thought you were in the car with your father when he crashed.'

'What's happening now? Are we going or not?' said the driver, throwing his hands up.

'That wasn't me,' Kitty said. 'The first I knew of the accident was when the police woke me up.'

'Well, who was it, then?' said Sam.

Kitty put her hand over her mouth. 'Oh dear God.'

'What is it?' said Sam, leaning towards her.

Kitty pulled out a wad of notes from her wallet and handed them to the driver, then climbed out of the taxi and took Sam's arm. 'You had better come back to my apartment,' she said. 'We need to talk.'

Chapter Twenty-Seven

Tuesday 5 March 1957

Ivy lay in the dark, staring up at the beamed ceiling, listening to the young girl in the next bed crying quietly. The dormitory was bitterly cold. Every girl lay on her side, curled up in a ball, trying to stay warm. The locked window next to Ivy's bed had no curtains, and the moon cast a beam on the poor girl beside her. She was so young, she looked like she still belonged in school. She'd had puppy fat when she had first arrived, and a colour to her cheeks, but now her collarbone jutted out from under her overalls and her pale skin pulled at her haunted eyes, from which tears were now falling.

Ivy guessed she was about fourteen. Whispered rumour had it that her pregnancy was the result of abuse at home by her father. Ivy thought she had heard Patricia wrong when she first told her: the child's own father had got her pregnant and then left her to rot in this hell on earth? At least Rose had been conceived in love, albeit only on Ivy's side, as she was beginning to fear. The girl had only gone into labour two days before, and yet here she was, back in her scratchy cold bed, all alone in the world, her baby taken from her. At dawn the bell would go and she would be expected to do a long, hard day in the laundry.

Ivy listened for the sound of footsteps in the corridor;

when she heard none, she pulled back her covers and got out of bed. The girl looked up as Ivy knelt down next to her.

'It hurts,' she whispered, her face stained from crying.

'I know, but it won't last,' Ivy said softly. 'Your milk's come in. You have to take the pain for a few days, and then it will go, I promise.'

The girl was shivering uncontrollably. Ivy slipped her hand under the covers. The sheet was drenched through, the girl undoubtedly had a fever. She looked to the door again, then pulled her overalls over her head. 'Here, take this and give me yours.'

The girl sat up slowly, wincing as she tried to take her own overalls off. 'I can't lift my arms.'

'Come here,' said Ivy, leaning in to help her. As she eased the scratchy material up the girl's back, a vivid image came to her mind's eye: her as a little girl, the light in her warm, cosy bedroom faint as evening drew in. Her mother pulling her nightie over her head and then suddenly stopping with Ivy's hands still raised, her face covered, so she could tickle her. She bit down hard on her lip as she fought back tears and pushed the memory away.

'You'll be all right,' she said, reaching over and pulling the blanket from her own bed and swapping it for the girl's before lying her back down.

'Thank you. Why did they shave your head?' said the girl, trying to get comfortable.

'Because I fought back. They won't do it to you. I'll look out for you tomorrow; we can swap if Sister puts you on any of the heavy machinery. I'll try and get you in the kitchen if I can.' She knew she couldn't arrange anything of the sort, but she wanted to put the girl's mind at ease so she could rest.

'Where is my baby girl?' said the girl quietly as Ivy turned back to her own bed.

Ivy stopped and thought of Rose, probably crying at that very moment with no one to comfort her. She looked at the girl. 'She's safe in the nursery. Now you need to rest. The bell will go before you know it.'

Ivy lay in the dark with the girl's sweat-soaked blanket over her feet and hugged herself to try and keep warm. Thoughts of Rose alone in the nursery made it impossible to sleep. Every day since she had begun working in the laundry again, the walk past the nursery was torture. The noise of the babies' crying was deafening. She would occasionally see Patricia rushing from cot to cot, where the babies lay on their backs, swaddled tightly. There were about forty cots in total in the huge whitewashed room. The nursery was cold and colourless, nothing like the room she had imagined her baby would spend her first months in. One filled with soft blankets and a comfy chair in the corner for her to nurse her in. It took all her strength whenever she passed not to hammer on the door and scream for Patricia to hand Rose over to her. She knew there was no point; she would only receive a beating, and they would probably find a way to punish Rose too, by skipping one of her feeds perhaps. Still, she had begged Patricia to tell her which cot Rose was in.

'I can't, they'll kill me,' her friend had whispered as one of the sisters shot them a glance.

Eventually, hidden briefly by the din of the ironing presses, Patricia had told her that Rose's cot was at the far end of the room, next to the kitchen. She had told her of the intense cold in the nursery. How ice formed inside the windows and the babies screamed constantly as she struggled to change their nappies with her freezing fingers. Once they were fed, they had to be put back down in their cots. If they didn't finish their bottles in time, they were put back anyway, even if they were still hungry. Most of them cried non-stop until their next feed, but some had given up crying because they knew already in their little hearts that no one was coming.

Ivy curled up tighter into a ball. Her back and thighs were still all shades of purple from Mother Carlin's beating, but it was the pain of being apart from Rose that made it impossible to breathe sometimes. She sat at dinner pushing the cabbage around her plate. The nights were longer than the days, hearing Rose's cries in her head in the silence of the dormitory. The only thing keeping her from losing her mind was the thought that Alistair might still come for them, though even there doubt was beginning to creep in and her daydreams starting to fade. She thought of him continuing his life as it had been before, while she and Rose experienced nothing but pain and suffering. Was he getting her letters; did he not care at all? Why would he have gone to so much trouble to convince her of his love just to abandon her now?

The events of the past two days had changed her for ever. If he knew what had happened, he would surely come. Shaking from the cold, she reached under her pillow and wrapped her trembling hand around the pen. As long as she could still hear Rose's cry when she passed the laundry in the morning, she knew she was here still at St Margaret's.

Whilst there was still hope, she had to fight, but time was running out.

My love,

I am frantic.

I was summoned from the laundry to Mother Carlin's office today, and Father Benjamin was there. Mother Carlin stood in the corner, a fixed smile on her face, while Father Benjamin sat behind the desk. A woman I didn't recognise was there too. Father Benjamin asked me to sit down, and I felt an overwhelming fear like I have never known before. He told me that the woman was Mrs Cannon, that she worked for St Margaret's Adoption Society. I sat looking at the floor so he didn't see my tears while he said the words he must have said to so many: 'I have spoken with your parents, and we feel it would be better for the child if you put her up for adoption. The child's father does not want her and as such she would be subject to ridicule all her life. Would you have her go through life rejected by society and her peers, paying for the sins of the flesh you have committed? You have no means to support her; you would both end up on the street.'

Through my tears I tried to tell him I was sorry, and pleaded with him not to take my baby. Mother Carlin spat at me not to interrupt. Father Benjamin asked me again if I wanted my child to pay for my sins. He wore me down, my spirit fading; he told me that I had nothing to offer her, that my parents would not have me back, and she would have a much better chance of life without me. She would grow up in a good Catholic home, with a loving mother and father. I told them I wanted to keep her, that she was my daughter. I begged them.

206

As Father Benjamin stood over me, the lady came and sat next to me. She took my hand, and told me to call her Helena. She said I must sign the adoption papers for Rose, that she was a beautiful baby and they would have no trouble finding her a loving family. I begged her to contact you, I gave her your name, but Mother Carlin told me that you had been contacted and told about the baby and that you weren't interested. She smiled when she said it: a smile I will never forget. Mrs Cannon placed the pen in my hand and said I was doing the best thing for Rose.

I told them I would never sign. Mother Carlin hit me so hard that a rage I had never experienced before came over me and I told her to go to hell. Then Father Benjamin and Mrs Cannon left. For the next hour, Mother Carlin set upon me with her scissors. She cut away the last part of me that I had any pride in, my long red hair, and with every clump, she made sure that the blade was too close to my skull so that streams of blood poured down my face. As she stood over me, she said that if it was up to her, I would never set foot outside St Margaret's again. That little sluts like me only ended up getting themselves in trouble again, and that if I didn't sign the papers, she would recommend to my parents that I be committed to an asylum.

After she had finished, she beat me with a belt, then opened a door in the floor and pushed me into the hole beneath it. I screamed and begged her to let me go, but she closed the door on top of me and locked it. As I lay there in the pitch black, I heard the tapping of her shoes across the floor before she turned out the light and locked her office door.

She left me there for fourteen hours, with no food or water, in a space so small I couldn't lift my hand to my nose to scratch it. I had never stopped to imagine what it would be like to be buried alive, but the first thing that happened to me was that I had an attack of sheer panic. I started to scream and kick, pushing frantically at the floor above me, until I realised it was sealed tight. My breathing became very fast and shallow, until I was sucking air in and out so fast that I became dizzy, my mind spinning inside a space in which I couldn't move. The more I panicked, the less air there was for me to breathe. Hot, stagnant air that smelt of floor polish and damp earth. It was only when I forced myself to think of Rose that I managed to gain some sort of composure. As I remembered her tiny fingers, her button nose, her blue eyes, her red hair, I was able to calm myself. Breathing slowly in and out until somehow the hours passed.

It was the longest night of my life and I have no idea how I got through it. Something inside me died that night, and for the first time since she was born, I couldn't hear Rose's cry.

In the morning, when Mother Carlin came back, she asked me if I'd like to sign the papers or stay where I was for another day. I told her I wouldn't sign, and without a second thought she closed the door on me again.

By the time she came back that night, I couldn't breathe. My thirst was overwhelming and my hunger all-consuming. My fingernails were bleeding from scratching at the lid of my coffin for hours on end.

When she opened the door, she told me that if I didn't sign, they would stop feeding Rose and it would be my fault. I signed the papers and made a silent promise to Rose that one day I would find her. One day I would find a way to escape and let her know how much I love her.

I can't go on living in this hell if they take Rose away from me. I don't know what the reason for you ignoring me — ignoring us — can be, and I no longer care what you think of

208

me. But you have a duty to come and get us out of this prison, for it is you – in part – who has put us here. And you are our only way out.

With all my love for ever,
Your Ivy

Ivy pushed the pen and paper back under her pillow and listened to the sound of the girl next to her breathing heavily. She was finally asleep.

She thought of the tiny dark-eyed girl who had come into the laundry that day. She had been horrified at the sight of her. She had seen girls as young as thirteen arriving, but this girl, with her overalls nearly reaching the floor, couldn't have been more than six or seven.

There and then, she made a decision: if she had to be here, powerless to help herself or Rose, she would do everything she could to protect that little girl. She would defy the sisters by doing what they detested most: making someone heartbroken feel loved.

As the sun came up, Ivy finally fell asleep. She dreamed she was sitting on her father's shoulders, his hands clasped round her feet as she stared down at his long stride. She was happy; smiling down at everyone who passed them from high up in her invincible tower, as the sea breeze blew through her long red hair.

Chapter Twenty-Eight

Wednesday 3 April 1957

Ivy looked up from the sheet press. The little girl she had seen several weeks before was standing in the doorway. Ivy had observed her at the time, standing on the footstool at the sinks, barely able to reach. She couldn't have been more than seven years old, thought Ivy, with small, fragile features, matted black hair, and yellowy skin that looked like it had never seen the sun. Then after a few days, she had disappeared completely. Ivy had no idea where she had gone, to a happy home, she prayed most nights, until the little girl reappeared weeks later looking even more pale than she had before.

She was staring around the room now, wide-eyed, her small hands clasped tight in front of her. The brown overalls she wore hung from her bony limbs like a tent, and only her tiny ankles and narrow sandal-covered feet were visible beneath them.

Ivy watched as Sister Faith and Mother Carlin spoke to each other, dropping her eyes as soon as they pointed in her direction. She kept herself busy, pulling the heavy red-hot sheets from the press with Patricia; stretching them out and folding them ready to be taken to the drying room. She felt her body tense as Mother Carlin appeared next to her, conscious that she was being watched critically, her fingers beginning to fumble over her task as the presses hissed and snapped at her like snakes.

'Mary.' She felt Mother Carlin's breath on her neck.

'Yes, Sister,' she said, stopping what she was doing.

'Put this child to work. She can take the sheets to the drying room so you and the girls don't have to stop your work here. And she can go down to the ironing room at the end of each day and divide up the laundry. Ask Sister Andrews to take you.'

'Yes, Sister,' said Ivy again, noticing that the little girl was instinctively moving away from Mother Carlin and towards her.

'She has the devil in her,' Mother Carlin said, with a look on her face as if she were chewing on something bitter. 'If you cannot manage her, I will find someone else who can. Now get on with your work,' she snapped at the little girl, who nodded fearfully.

Ivy was painfully aware of how much Patricia would be struggling on her own. As Mother Carlin walked away, she turned to catch the huge sheet before it could drop to the floor, for which they would both receive a beating. She gasped as the boiled cotton sank onto her skin, burning it and causing her to yelp.

The little girl looked up at her, reaching out to help her lift the sheet away from her arm. Ivy nodded her thanks, and a tiny smile formed at the corner of the child's mouth.

She watched intently as Ivy and Patricia folded the damp sheets and added them to the pile on the trestle tables in front of them. Ivy looked at Sister Faith, who was sitting darning, and then over at the little girl. Despite the obvious neglect she was suffering from, she was beautiful, with long eyelashes and dark brown eyes holding a stare that seemed to take her away for minutes at a time. She had an air of intensity about her and stood tall, her back straight, her head high, watching every move Ivy was making as if her life depended on it.

As Ivy tried to concentrate, questions troubled her about why the girl was here. Was she another child of a pregnant mother, or had she wandered in off the street? Her skin was filthy, with ingrained dirt under her fingernails and grime pleated into the creases of her elbows. Her scrawny arms were covered in bruises, and at the top of them yellow bandages poked out from under her brown overalls, stained with little speckles of dried blood. They reminded Ivy of the sparrow eggshells her father sometimes found in a nest in their oak tree.

Ivy's head spun with the responsibility that had just been handed to her. Work in the laundry was hard enough for a twenty-year-old woman, let alone a small child. The day started at six and ended at eight, with only two short breaks in between for meals so meagre they left your belly rumbling more than when you first sat down to eat. The youngest girl she knew to be working there was fourteen, and most days she would struggle with the heavy lifting, the intense heat, the relentless repetition of the backbreaking work. She couldn't fathom how this fragile creature would cope.

She reached up and pressed the button to shut off the press, and she and Patricia began loading the sheets onto the trolley next to them. She was trying to figure out a way to make the task manageable for the little girl. It would be nearly impossible for her to steer the trolley through the laundry and along the corridor to the drying room without banging into anything or tipping it over. The trolley was old, and heavy with the weight of the sheets, the wheels awkward and clunky and the handle rough and splintered. At the end of the long corridor, each soaking sheet needed to be laid out carefully on the drying rails and then the whole platform had to be hoisted up to the ceiling. Ivy looked down at the thin creature, knowing it would be hard, but figuring that if she was precise enough, it just might work.

She began pulling the trolley, signalling to the girl to follow her, which she did eagerly. As it rumbled and groaned its way past the wall of sinks that lined the room, dozens of girls standing at them in silence, the little girl watched intently, taking mental note of everything Ivy was doing to constantly correct it and keep it moving straight. As they reached the door, Sister Faith turned to Sister Andrews and handed her a bunch of keys. 'Hurry up!' Sister Andrews barked, as Ivy turned the handle and eased the heavy trolley out into the corridor.

She repeated the movement to ensure the little girl understood. There was a knack to it. They both knew she'd have only one chance to get it right, or she'd be punished. The child seemed to be reading Ivy's mind. Watch carefully, Ivy's eyes pleaded, and the girl did, nodding to let her know she understood.

Sister Andrews marched ahead of them down the corridor in the direction of the drying room, opening it with a heavy iron key and standing at the entrance. The rickety trolley trundled and clunked over the black and white tiles, its rusty wheels groaning loudly under the strain. They walked in silence, Ivy moving quickly but carefully to make sure it didn't hit the wall. As they reached the drying room, once again she pointed to the way the trolley turned, reaching out and giving the little girl the handle so she could have a go. It had taken Ivy several attempts to get the hang of it at first, but the little girl got it in two and, using both arms, finished the job on her own, heaving it over the threshold and into the dry, humid room. As soon as they were inside, Sister Andrews went back out into the corridor and pulled the door shut, locking them both inside.

Ivy looked up. Hundreds of sheets hung from the twelve ceiling racks hovering above them like ghosts on broomsticks, and she walked quickly to the corner of the room, where the last rack hung empty. She unhooked the cord that lowered it and let the rope down hand over hand as quickly as she could, then pulled a sheet from the top of the pile on the trolley. Without an audience for the first time, she crouched down and spoke to the little girl.

'They must be laid on straight, or they'll get creases that even the ironing presses can't get out. And you must work quickly,' she said, laying the sheet out on the hanging rack. 'We fold enough sheets to fill a trolley in no time, and we need you back by then to bring them in here.'

The little girl nodded, saying nothing, but helping Ivy as they began to take the rest of the damp sheets off the trolley one by one, throwing them over the wooden rods and pulling them out straight. Ivy watched her as she worked. The child's hands moved fast, and she studied Ivy closely to make sure she was doing it right. Several times Ivy opened her mouth to ask one of the many questions troubling her, but she would always stop herself, not wanting to cause any upset. In the end, she settled on a harmless one.

'What's your name?' she said, smiling gently.

'Elvira,' the little girl replied quietly.

'It's nice to meet you, Elvira. I'm Ivy, but you'd better call me Mary, which is the name Mother Carlin gave me. Now, at the end of each day, I'll come back to this room with you and we'll take all the dry sheets down from the racks, then bag them up and send them down the chute to the ironing room.' Ivy pointed to a small hatch in the wall.

Again the little girl nodded, and Ivy began to drag the rickety trolley towards the narrow doorway that led out into the hall.

'How old are you, Elvira?' she said.

Before Elvira could reply, there was a click as the lock turned and the door suddenly opened. The faint colour Elvira had had in her cheeks drained away.

'What in God's name do you think you're doing?' said Sister Andrews, her round cheeks flushed with anger. 'Will I tell Mother Carlin you were talking idly while the other girls are having to do your work?'

'No, Sister, sorry, Sister,' said Ivy, heaving the trolley along as Elvira scuttled behind her like a frightened mouse. 'Mother Carlin wants the girl to see the ironing room,' she added, 'so she knows where to go at the end of the day.'

Sister Andrews let out a sigh and glared at them both, then turned on her heel and began marching towards the end of the corridor, where a dark staircase awaited them. She snapped on the dim light and began her descent, the heels of her boots clicking on the steps as she went.

Ivy looked back, signalling to Elvira to hold tight to the banister. As they neared the bottom of the steps, Sister Andrews took out her bunch of keys and opened a heavy oak door. Ivy instinctively took Elvira's hand to guide her through the ironing presses in the fearsomely hot and airless room. At every press, the size of a dining table, stood a girl in brown overalls. Each was scarlet in the face, moving as deftly as she could with an enormous bump, pulling the poker-hot ironing presses up and down over the sheets beneath. Sister Andrews stopped beside a large steel chute and turned to the child.

'This chute leads down here from the drying room. At the end of each day when the bell goes, you will come down here and stand at the chute to catch the dry sheets in the basket.' She pointed to the huge wheeled wicker basket sitting at the back of the room. 'Divide the sheets up equally between the girls ready for the morning. I don't need to tell you what will happen if the job isn't done properly, do I, child?'

'No, Sister,' whispered Elvira, her voice barely audible over the din.

'Then leave the trolley by the door,' said Ivy.

'Which one?' said Elvira, looking at a small door at the far end of the room and then to another larger door at the opposite end.

'You'll speak only when you're spoken to,' snapped Sister Andrews, slapping the little girl around the side of her head. 'The black door over there. Don't you be worrying your ignorant head about any other door. We're not wrong putting you in a dormitory with the mongoloids, are we? Well, speak up, child.' She came closer, and Elvira cowered away.

'No, Sister,' she said, twisting her fingers so hard that the colour left them completely.

Ivy glanced at the small door, which rumour had it led to the tunnels under the house. She had never seen anyone come in or go out of that door, and Patricia said she should avoid finding out what was beyond it at all costs. She said she'd heard there was a tunnel that led to the septic tank and the graveyard, and that it smelt of death.

For the rest of the day, Elvira worked diligently and methodically, carrying out her tasks exactly as Ivy had shown her. Ivy kept expecting the little girl to become tired, to start to lag, to complain of blisters on her hands or aches in her shoulders. But the complaints never came, and by the end of the first week, she seemed to be managing to get the insurmountable job done. When the sisters weren't looking, Ivy helped her, and far from feeling resentful, it gave her hope to focus on something other than herself.

The child was quiet and cautious with her answers, but by gently coaxing information out of her in their precious minutes in the drying room at the end of each day, Ivy slowly gathered that Elvira was six years old, soon to turn seven, and slept in a room in the attic of the house. That she had been adopted for the first six years of her life, but had then returned to St Margaret's because 'I did something bad.' She wouldn't say what it was she had done, and Ivy trod carefully, rehearsing in her head the questions she so desperately wanted to ask before speaking them out loud. There was an invisible line that Elvira was clearly fearful to cross. When Ivy asked about the bloodstained bandages on her arms, whether there were any other children in the attic with her, or whether she had enough to eat, Elvira's hands would begin to shake and she would go quiet.

After several attempts to get to the truth, with Elvira try-ing to hold back tears, Ivy gave up and they began to speak of other things. Things that took them out of St Margaret's and back into the world they both missed so desperately.

How they longed to go out into a large open field in mid-summer, lay out a picnic rug on the soft grass and sit in the sun eating all their favourite food. Bread with cheese, thick pastry pork pies, scones with jam, and crisp red apples.

Then one morning, Elvira didn't appear at the laundry door.

Ivy spent the day in a state of panic, praying it was because she had been sent to a lovely new home, but fearing it was for a reason much more sinister. She begged Patricia to find out if Elvira was in the infirmary, but she wasn't.

As before, Elvira was gone for a month and Ivy thought of little else. It was as if, in her grief for Rose, she had imagined the little girl, and now she too had disappeared from her life.

Then, as suddenly as she had disappeared, she was back again.

She had been very poorly, she told Ivy quietly in the drying room; she always was after the doctors came and gave them their injections. 'We all have to look after each other,' she added.

'What do you mean, all?' said Ivy, stroking Elvira's hair.

'All the children in the attic.'

Chapter Twenty-Nine

Monday 6 February 2017

As soon as they reached Kitty's apartment, Sam called Nana to check in on Emma, who was still poorly but seemingly on the mend.

'Is anything wrong, Nana? You sound upset,' she said.

'I'm fine, darling, just tired.' Nana's voice was quiet.

'I'm going to call in sick today, so I'll be with you soon, okay?' said Sam gently.

'I don't want you to do that, darling,' said Nana. 'You could get into trouble. Ben said he'd be here about lunchtime.'

'It's fine, Nana. You sound wrecked; I'm worried about you. I've got a bit of a journey ahead of me on the train, and then I've got to pick up my car, but I'll be back as soon as I can, hopefully by eleven. Emma's ill, and I need to be there.'

'Okay, I love you, sweetheart, and don't you worry about us.'

'I love you too, Nana, see you soon.'

'Have you had a chance to read Ivy's last letter?' added Nana as Sam went to end the call. Nana's voice had faltered as she'd asked her, it seemed Ivy's story was affecting Nana as much as it was her. So much had happened since Nana had given it to her the evening before that she hadn't had a chance to read it.

219

After finishing the call, Sam had reached into her bag and pulled out the small parcel of Ivy's letters, untied the red velvet ribbon and peeled open the final one. She had read it quickly, conscious that Kitty was about to reappear. It was as heartbreaking as all the others and mentioned a lady called Mrs Helena Cannon, who had dealt with the adoptions at St Margaret's. Sam's heart had stopped as she had read the name. Cannon. Could this be Kitty's mother? A quick search in Google told her that Kitty's mother had indeed been called Helena, and that she had died suddenly and unexpectedly whilst receiving dialysis treatment in hospital.

'Everything all right?' said Kitty, appearing behind her and handing her a mug of tea. Sam smiled up at her as she placed her mobile and the letters back in her bag.

'Yes, thank you. Thanks for the tea,' said Sam, her eyes wandering around the room. It was a large modern apartment, with floor-to-ceiling windows overlooking the River Thames. The room was softened with heavy curtains, oversized rugs and warm lamps scattered everywhere. A framed tapestry hung on the wall above a desk in the corner. It read: *Indeed, the very hairs of your head are all numbered. Don't be afraid.*

Sam suddenly felt slightly faint. She couldn't remember the last time she'd eaten, and her eyes were heavy. She looked around for something to perch on. Everything in the apartment was so pristine and neat, she felt as if she was part of a window display, scared to sit on any of the immaculate furniture in case she made a mark on it.

'Have a seat, Samantha,' said Kitty, gesturing to the space on the sofa next to her. 'You look a bit pale. Relax and make yourself at home.'

'Thank you,' said Sam. They sat for a moment in silence, Sam trying to calm down. She couldn't work out why she felt so ill at ease. *Make yourself at home.* But a home was full of paraphernalia, pictures and souvenirs. She had sat in hundreds of lounges, interviewing people, listening to their stories, and nowhere had ever felt like this. Although everything matched perfectly, there was nothing personal in the space. She looked around for a photograph of Kitty with family or friends, but couldn't see any. Everything was beautiful, including Kitty herself, but nothing in the room gave anything away. There would be no use looking for evidence of Helena Cannon here.

'Was that your grandmother on the phone?' Kitty watched Sam intently.

'Yes,' said Sam, sipping her tea. No wonder she felt strange, she thought: she was sitting in Kitty Cannon's apartment, having been up all night chasing leads on a story she had been told not to pursue by her boss. 'My daughter and I, we live with her. She's very good to us. I'd be lost without her.'

'You sound like you're close. Does your mother live with you too?' Sam looked down, not sure how to respond. 'Sorry, I didn't mean to pry,' said Kitty.

'No, it's fine,' replied Sam, feeling the opposite. She didn't want to talk about Nana, or think about Emma and how far away she was from them. From Nana's cosy, happy, cluttered, messy home. 'It's only fair that you want to know about me; I've certainly been doing a lot of prying into *your* life the last couple of days.'

Kitty smiled. Her teeth were perfectly white and straight. Sam tried not to stare, but there was something impossibly perfect about her. She knew Kitty had to be in her sixties, slightly older than Nana in fact, but in contrast to her grandmother she barely had a wrinkle, and her skin looked like it belonged on Emma's bottom. Her fingernails were neat and her pretty face freshly made up. Sam felt the urge to reach out and touch her, just to check she wasn't a hologram.

She clutched her mug in her hands for warmth. 'My mum died when I was twelve. She was an alcoholic. I didn't know my grandmother existed before that; they weren't in touch. My family history is quite colourful, to say the least. I think these letters have affected us both deeply.'

'May I see them? The letters?' said Kitty.

For reasons she was unsure of, Sam suddenly felt protective of them and hesitated before reaching into her bag and pulling them out.

'They're written by a woman called Ivy, who had a baby at St Margaret's and was forced to give her up. They would be thought-provoking for anyone, but Nana was adopted and never met her mother, so I guess more so for her.'

'I think a baby being taken from its mother can affect families for generations,' said Kitty, reaching out for the letters in Sam's hands. 'These look very old; where did you get them?'

'My grandfather was an antiques dealer, and Nana found them in his paperwork after he died – presumably they were in an old desk he bought.' Sam paused. 'I think I may have run into a relative of Ivy's, but I don't know where to find her.'

'Oh?' Kitty looked up from the letter in her hand.

'Yes, I went to Father Benjamin's funeral service and there

was a very elderly lady there. I'm sure I've seen her some-where before. She put this picture on Father Benjamin's coffin.' Sam reached into her bag and pulled out the photo-graph of Ivy, handing it to Kitty.

As Kitty looked at the picture, her hands began to shake. She stared, transfixed.

'Are you okay?' said Sam, taken aback by Kitty's reac-tion. Sam looked down at the black-and-white image of Ivy, then back up at Kitty. 'Do you recognise her?'

Kitty shook her head slowly, 'No, not at all. I just, I think last night is catching up with me.' Kitty went to put her coffee cup down and misjudged it, sending it toppling, its contents spilling all over a cushion.

'Shit,' said Sam, as she looked around for something to mop it up with.

'Would you excuse me for a moment?' said Kitty, putting the photograph down and walking out with the cushion.

'Of course. Are you okay?' Sam called after her. There was no reply.

Sam pulled her mobile from her bag and dialled. After a few rings, Fred picked up. 'Fred, it's me, how you doing?'

'Fine. I forgot to tell you yesterday, someone called Jane Connors called, asking for your address; said she wanted to write to you.'

'Jane Connors? As in the Jane Connors I got an exclusive with on Saturday?'

'Yeah, the one who lives next door to a witch. How's it going anyway?' said Fred, as Sam scribbled Mrs Connors' name in her notebook.

'It's okay, though I haven't slept a wink and it's D-Day today. St Margaret's is coming down tomorrow morning

223

and there's still a mountain to climb. Think I'm going to have to call in sick later, which Murray will love.'

Sam flicked through her notebook. Since reading the last letter, another name had been haunting her, one that had been mentioned several times by Ivy; Dr Jacobson. He had referred her to Father Benjamin when she first fell pregnant and been at the birth of Ivy's baby at St Margaret's. She lowered her voice. 'Fred, could you do me a favour and see if you can dig up anything about a Dr Jacobson, and also Helena Cannon. They're local to Preston, I think.' Sam glanced up as Kitty returned to the room.

'Sure,' said Fred. 'Oh, and you know that footballer you asked me to find out about? The only person who played for Brighton and died suddenly was a guy called Alistair Henderson. But it was an asthma attack, so I don't know if that counts as suspicious?' Sam could hear his keys tapping in the background.

'Interesting, thanks,' she said, scribbling *Alistair Henderson* on her pad.

'There's more,' said Fred. 'Kitty Cannon was engaged to him when he died.'

'What?' Sam looked up at Kitty, who was moving around the room, opening the curtains, turning on lamps, glancing over at Sam occasionally. Something about the way she was acting jarred with Sam. She didn't come across as a sixty-something woman who had been up all night finding her way round a derelict building site. She seemed calm, composed and totally unrattled.

'Yeah, March 1969, so she was what, eighteen or nineteen? Maybe explains why she never married or had kids.

You can ask her about it when you see her next,' said Fred, chuckling to himself.

'Will do,' said Sam. 'Thanks, Fred, call me if you find out anything about those names I gave you.' She ended the call, then looked at Kitty, who had sat back down on the sofa. 'Can I ask you something, Kitty?'

'Of course.'

'Do you know if your mother ever, um, worked for St Margaret's?' she said nervously.

Kitty looked away and began playing with the tassels of a blanket lying next to her. 'Yes, she did, but Helena Cannon was not my birth mother.'

It took every ounce of self-control Sam had not to react to Kitty's statement. Instead, she stayed deathly still, scared to speak or move in case she put her off continuing. Kitty was so composed, she thought: she moved so gracefully, sat up straight and thought hard about what she wanted to say before she said it. The result was that when she spoke, you felt compelled to listen.

'I have a twin,' Kitty said. 'She is called Elvira. I think my father had an affair, and the woman, whoever she was, had us at St Margaret's and probably died in childbirth, though there are no records to prove it. They told my father Elvira was brain-damaged, but she wasn't. She was adopted by a family, but after six years they returned her to St Margaret's, where she lived a very miserable existence as far as I can tell.'

Kitty sat still, perched on the edge of the sofa. Sam reminded herself to breathe.

'Of course I knew nothing of all this. I grew up an only child in Sussex, mostly happily, mainly with my father caring for me, as Helena, the woman I thought was my mother, was very sick in hospital with kidney disease.'

Sam looked over at her notebook, desperate to grab it but terrified that any movement might tip Kitty into silence.

'Then one Sunday in February 1959, when I was eight years old, I went to church in Preston, which is half a mile from St Margaret's. I was on my own because my father was with Helena in hospital. I was standing outside the church, alone, when I saw a little girl hiding behind a gravestone, signalling to me. I looked around, not sure what to do, and eventually I went over to her.' Kitty paused. 'It was me, thinner and dirtier but we were identical; it was like looking in a mirror.'

'My God,' said Sam, unable to stop herself. 'That's unbelievable. What did you do?'

Kitty shook her head. 'She was freezing and had been waiting outside all day for me. She was clearly terrified, whispering that we had to hide and taking me by the hand to an outhouse. She was dressed in dirty brown overalls and open-toed sandals, and it had been snowing. I gave her my coat and begged her to come with me to find my father, but she refused. It's hard to describe the state she was in, she had escaped from St Margaret's and was paralysed with fear.'

Kitty stopped for a moment. 'I stayed in the outhouse with her for two hours or so until it got dark. I told her I would find my father, our father, and that he would take her home with us, but she just became hysterical about who else was out there looking for her. She said that if they found her, they'd take her back to St Margaret's, and that they'd kill her.'

'That poor little girl,' said Sam. 'Is it really possible to return a child you've adopted?'

Kitty paused, her face blank, unreadable. 'In those days, certainly. I remember when I came home from hospital after all this had happened, Father Benjamin came to the house to talk to my father. I sat on the stairs, straining to listen and overheard him saying that the couple who adopted Elvira had gone on to have a baby and that Elvira had tried to harm him.'

'So they just gave up on her? Nice people.' Sam shook her head.

'I asked Elvira about it,' Kitty continued, 'I think she said they sent her back because she did something bad. But I was eight; you can imagine it was all totally overwhelming and too much to take in. In the end I said that I would have to go and get help, then come back for her. She begged me not to go, tried to pull me back, but I told her it would be all right. And then I ran out into the dark.' Kitty stood and walked over to the window, crossed her arms and looked out.

'And did you find your father?' Sam shifted slightly, her legs stiff from not moving them for so long.

Kitty shook her head. 'I just remember running, my breath a freezing fog, my heart thundering. It's hard to describe how cold it was, late at night, in February. And I had no coat because I'd given it to my sister. I was in the middle of the countryside. I didn't know what pitch black meant until that night: I couldn't see a thing. She'd made me promise not to call out, but I was desperate. I could hear animals scuttling in the undergrowth. The moon was covered in cloud. I got very cold very quickly. I ran across a few fields hoping to find a road, but I know now I was just getting deeper onto the Sussex Downs. All I could think was that I had to get back to Elvira or she'd die.'

'Poor you, and poor Elvira.' Sam shook her head. 'It's so sad.'

'I don't remember what happened exactly, but there was a ditch and I fell and broke my ankle. I was in agony, unable to move, unable to get out. For that whole night I lay there alone, crying, and by the time the sun came up, I had hypothermia. I don't remember thinking about myself, though; I just remember seeing my sister's face and feeling as if I'd let her down.'

'But you didn't let her down; you did everything you could.' Sam walked over to Kitty and went to put her hand on her back, then stopped herself.

Kitty turned and looked at her. 'Three days later, I woke up in hospital. I'd nearly died. I was very upset, of course, asking for Elvira. Father told me she was dead. He said he'd had no idea she was back at St Margaret's, that he thought she'd been adopted. He never admitted that Helena wasn't my birth mother.'

'Is there no record of Elvira? I heard from one of the sisters at St Margaret's that their records had been destroyed, but I didn't know which records they meant,' said Sam as Kitty walked back to the sofa and sat back down.

Kitty shook her head. 'They were referring to birth and death records, which St Margaret's should have handed over to the council. There was no record of Elvira at all. Most of the records from around that time were destroyed in a flood, or so they claimed. I tried to find her, but there was no trace. She had disappeared. I've never cried for her,

228

Samantha, not once. It's as if I never really believed she died, and now it seems I might be right.'

Sam's eyes widened and she leant in towards her. 'Sorry, you think your sister is alive?'

'Yes, the girl at the crash site where my father died. I think that was Elvira.'

'But what makes you think she didn't die?' said Sam.

'Father Benjamin told my father that she was buried in the graveyard at St Margaret's, but there was no trace of her body in the graveyard excavation report,' said Kitty, straightening the cushion behind Sam. 'I hadn't been back to St Margaret's since that day. I thought it might help me see what could have happened to her. To feel closer to her. It's stupid, I know, but I left her alive; maybe somebody found her.'

'Who?' said Sam.

'I don't know; the person who wrote these letters perhaps,' said Kitty, looking down at them. 'You said yourself that the people Ivy wrote about, who were involved with St Margaret's, died in suspicious circumstances. And I'm pretty sure that people like Mother Carlin and Father Benjamin were the ones responsible for Elvira being in the state she was in.'

Sam watched Kitty's face. It was the picture of serenity, despite the harrowing nature of the conversation they were having. She felt herself torn between wanting to go on and feeling uncomfortable at the lack of emotion Kitty was showing. The words she was saying made sense, but something was amiss. They felt rehearsed somehow, as if she was in a bad play in a village hall.

'Can I ask you a personal question?' said Sam.

'Of course,' said Kitty.

229

'Your fiancé, Alistair Henderson, do you know how he died?'

'Yes, he had an asthma attack.' Kitty frowned.

'And was there anything strange about the circumstances?' Sam watched Kitty's face. As usual, it gave away nothing.

'What do you mean?' said Kitty, an edge to her voice suddenly.

'Ivy's letters are written to the father of her child, who was a footballer with Brighton football club. He might be another piece of the puzzle that relates to you,' Sam replied.

Kitty paused. She was suddenly elsewhere, her shoulders and jaw clenched as she took herself back to what must have been a painful time. She had never married, or had children, so there was no doubt that Alistair had been the love of her life.

'Yes, in answer to your question, something strange did happen,' she said eventually. 'I told the police, but they never followed it up. I was due to collect him after a match on the day he died, but I received a phone call to say he had left with another woman. So I never went, and he died waiting for me. I'll never forgive myself,' she added, her voice quieter now.

'Who was it who called you that day?' Sam eyed her notebook again.

'They wouldn't say, but it was a woman.' Kitty looked at her. 'It has never occurred to me before now, but I suppose it could have been Elvira.'

'You said you met Elvira in 1959. These letters are dated around the time Elvira would have been at St Margaret's. Maybe Ivy knew her. God, I wish I could remember where I've seen that woman before,' said Sam quietly.

'The woman at Father Benjamin's funeral?' said Kitty.

'What did she look like? Was there anything about her that stuck in your mind? You said she was very elderly; did she have trouble walking?'

'Yes, she had a Zimmer frame.' Sam thought back to her conversation with Fred, and suddenly it all began to make sense. The one who lived next door to a witch, he'd said. The woman who had stared at her as she had walked down the path to Mrs Connors' house: she was the one who had put the picture of Ivy on Father Benjamin's coffin.

'That's it! I remember now.' She sprang to her feet. 'I need to talk to her.'

'Are you going there now?' said Kitty, standing up too.

'Oh God, I can't, I need to get home to Nana and Emma,' said Sam, gathering her things.

'Does this lady live in Sussex?' Kitty followed her out into the hall.

'Yes.' Sam pulled her boots on as Kitty stood over her.

'Well, you could go on your way home, leave her a note. It needn't hold you up too much. We don't have long before they tear St Margaret's down, and if she knows something, we need to know today.' Kitty stood in front of the door; her face was hard suddenly, and Sam looked down at her hands, which were tapping her legs anxiously.

'Did you want to come with me? It would make the journey much quicker if you could drive us,' said Sam hopefully.

'I'm sorry, Samantha, it wouldn't be safe for me to drive. I've been up all night and I really need to get some sleep. I'd be a danger to us both.'

'Okay. I'll call you as soon as I've spoken to her. She may know if Elvira is alive!'

*

231

Kitty smiled and waved from the window as Sam's cab disappeared down the road. Then she picked up a holdall lying on the floor in the hall, stepped outside and closed the front door behind her.

Chapter Thirty

Saturday 1 March 1969

Alistair Henderson staggered off the pitch just as the spring light began to fade.

It had been a close call as Brighton football club found themselves 0–0 in the last ten minutes of the friendly away match against Fulham. As the seconds ticked by at an alarming rate, Alistair had finally slowed for a moment and watched Fulham's defence closely. He was breathless, but his Ventolin inhaler had remained firmly in his bag in the changing room for fear of drawing attention to himself.

His manager had been expressing concern over his performance of late, and Alistair was not going to hand him an excuse to bench him because his asthma was playing up. Having been selected for Brighton FC when he was twenty, he had now been on the team for thirteen years and was in no doubt that his golden days were over. The season had been a particularly bad one for him, and if he didn't get a result soon, he was in serious danger of being replaced.

Two minutes from the final whistle, he had attacked the fleeting moment when Fulham's guard was down and scored. As his team-mates clambered all over him, his breathing became so strained that his legs began to feel weak. He looked up to the stands, where hundreds of supporters were waving their blue scarves and shouting his name, the cheers ringing in his ears. He scanned the faces at the front; he couldn't see her, but it was a comfort knowing Kitty was there.

As the referee ended the match and the players dispersed, he punched his closed fist on his chest. It was cold, and the stands were emptying fast, everyone keen to get to the warmth of the pub. He stood on the edge of the pitch, looking around for any sign of Kitty. She would normally have appeared by now, leaning against the doors to the players' tunnel, her arms crossed, her long black hair framing her beautiful face.

'There's something I need to talk to you about,' she had said the last time he'd seen her. She'd taken his hand, curled her fingers around his. 'I'll meet you after the match at Fulham and treat us to a hotel in town.'

'You coming?' said Stan, snapping him back into the moment.

'No, thanks, Kitty's on her way,' said Alistair breathlessly.

'You all right, Al?'

Alistair nodded. The last thing he wanted was to get on the players' bus and have a full-blown attack in front of the team. To have everyone fuss around him, gawping as he fought for air, full of sympathy to his face then swapping fears for his future place on the team behind his back. He'd scored, he was the hero of the match, and he desperately needed it to stay that way.

As the final supporters headed off chanting into the fog-filled night, the coach doors hissed closed behind the Brighton players and Alistair hurriedly made his way into the changing room, anxious to inhale his much-needed salbutamol and relieve the tightening in his chest. The room was full of steam as the Fulham players showered away their disappointment at losing, their mood quiet and subdued. Towel-covered bodies traipsed back and forth, and the heat of the room in contrast to the freezing dusk outside intensified his disorientation as he searched for his bag.

'Has anyone seen a blue bag? It was hanging here,' he asked as loudly as his breath would allow. A couple of the players looked round but said nothing. Having scored the winning goal for the other team, he knew he wasn't going to be the most popular man in the room. He needed to get outside before he passed out in the heat. It was all beginning to feel like a bad dream.

He had felt overwhelming uneasiness all afternoon, looking out at the freezing mist forming over the South Downs. Nothing was worse for his asthma than the cold, and talk on the radio of Fulham's pitch being frozen and unplayable had given him fleeting hope of the match being cancelled. Hope that on his arrival at the ground had proved false. By the time he was in the changing room, a pre-match atmosphere was building and he had resigned himself. He had phoned Kitty just to make sure she was coming, and her flatmate said she'd already left. He had taken several puffs from his inhaler in a cubicle in the toilets, then hung his bag near the entrance.

The temperature had been plummeting all afternoon, so that by the time the teams ran out, the grass was crunching under his feet, his warm breath hanging over him like a black cloud. He had known half an hour in that it was getting worse. The creeping scratchy awareness of his body telling him to stop, his inability to catch his breath, the prickling feeling of his neck muscles tightening like a noose.

Giving up hadn't been an option. Two reserves stood on the sidelines, watching and waiting, biding their time, their warmed-up limbs aching to run, tackle, shine and be chosen; to prop up the bar at the busiest pub in town, pretty girls vying for their attention. 'It's a shame,' his team-mates would say. 'Alistair's good but he hasn't been on top of his game for a while.' 'It's his asthma,' another would pipe up. 'He can play all right, but what use is that if you can't breathe?'

And what would be waiting for him if he lost his place on the team? A pile of bad debts, a house he couldn't afford to keep up the mortgage payments on, a car that would be taken away by the bailiffs along with anything else of value. He would be declared bankrupt, probably go to prison, and no doubt lose the love of his life.

No. He had no choice but to keep playing, to fight and to score, which he had. Two minutes before the end, after pushing himself to the point of throwing up from the exertion of it. And from that moment, as his team-mates rushed at him and his coach yelled his approval, he had sucked the needles of air through his nose into his contracting lungs and begun counting down the seconds until he could get to the tiny pressurised canister at the bottom of his bag. The bag he had left by the hooks by the entrance. The bag that was now gone.

'Damn it,' he exclaimed to the fast-emptying room, coughing relentlessly in the hot air as he checked each hook and cubicle. His wallet was also in the bag; he had no cash, no way of getting out of there. Kitty needed to turn up soon.

Someone turned out a light, then another. If he didn't ask for help soon, he would be in trouble, but he knew that if he did, Kitty would turn up and he would wish he hadn't exposed his weakness. Trying and failing to keep calm, he began to make his way out to the car park, taking shallow breaths and attempting to think straight. The last of the players were leaving, climbing into their cars, their tyres rattling the gravel beneath his feet.

'Good game, Alistair,' said one of them. 'Hopefully your bad run is over.'

Alistair half smiled at the insult disguised as a compliment. He watched the car heading out to the main road, its headlights joining the stream of traffic in the distance. Kitty had just been held up, he decided. She was on her way; there had been no message to say otherwise. He would head out to the gates and wait for her. He could always flag down another car if he got really bad; a stranger was a better prospect than a Fulham player for keeping this whole episode a secret.

'Stay calm, stay calm,' he mumbled to himself as he pushed back the panic overwhelming him.

As he trekked past the floodlit pitch towards the road, the lights began to go out one by one. With each step, he was plunged further into darkness. Memories of his first attack came flooding back. He could see his fourteen-year-old self on the pitch, pushing himself to his limit at try-outs for the Brighton youth team. Halfway in, he had started to realise that he couldn't catch his breath. As his legs grew as weak as his breathing, he'd collapsed in the grass, the other boys standing over him until he'd eventually lost consciousness.

Dr Jacobson had told his father it was unlikely he would be able to play professional football. He would never forget the look on his father's face, the colour visibly draining from his cheeks at history repeating itself. It was the first moment he knew how much it mattered to him to make it, that if it came to it, he would rather die pursuing his dream than live a half life, a life of drudgery, like his father had resigned himself to.

As he staggered on through the bitter cold, feeling as if he were trying to breathe underwater, the headlights on the road beyond the gates started to become interconnected. There weren't many cars, but when one did come, the light seemed to linger after it, so that when the next vehicle arrived, it was as if it were taking the baton of light from the last one.

'Please help me,' Alistair wheezed under his breath as he trudged on. With every second that passed, he prayed that he would hear the crunch of a car pulling up, feel Kitty's arms around him, helping him into the car, rushing him to the hospital. Comforting him, saving him, as she had from the moment they met.

She was the only one he had ever told about Ivy. Thirteen years had passed since she had got pregnant, and in all that time, he hadn't told another soul, apart from Father Benjamin. It was 1956 and he was on the cusp of signing with Brighton FC. He had loved Ivy, but he was young and on the crest of the biggest wave of his life. His father had warned him repeatedly that beautiful smiling girls turned into miserable nagging wives who made you give up your dreams. So when he had confessed his sins at church and Father Benjamin had offered him a solution, he had taken it.

But Ivy wouldn't let him go. They had shared some great times and he had been fond of her, but he hadn't promised her anything. She wrote to him for months after she'd had the baby, letters full of such fabrication he stopped opening them. It made him angry that she was putting such pressure on him; she had clearly lost her mind and he'd had a lucky escape. She wasn't the kind of girl he wanted to marry, and he soon realised he'd been right to feel that way. She had no class, no composure or restraint. The pregnancy had been a mistake; why couldn't she just accept it and move on, like all the other girls at St Margaret's? The letters became so disturbed that he began to fear what would happen if she ever got out, and he decided to speak to Father Benjamin about his concerns. He couldn't have a young girl bad-mouthing him to his manager and the press. He and Father Benjamin had agreed: for a generous contribution, St Margaret's would find a way to hang on to Ivy for a while.

Alistair could see the road now, only feet away. A series of hacking coughs tore at his throat; he couldn't stop, couldn't gather his breath. Breathe hard. *Breathe.* He sank down onto a bench by the entrance, pushed his head between his knees and managed to gasp a few shallow breaths. He needed to get out of this freezing-cold fog; it felt like fire in his lungs.

Disorientation began to take hold. As he tried to stand, his legs buckled under him and he collapsed, hitting his head on the bench and knocking out any air he had left in his body. He lay on his back on the ground, helpless, like a beetle unable to flip over, clawing at the gallons of air surrounding him, unable to take in a single breath.

'Get up, Al! We'll be late!'

He slowly opened his eyes and looked up. Standing over him was Ivy, her red curls tied up with dead flowers, a huge beam across her pale face, which was covered in streaks of grime.

'Ivy?' He strained to speak.

'The service starts in a minute; everyone is waiting. What are you doing on the ground, silly? You'll get your suit mucky!' As she leant forward to take his hand, he saw her stomach straining her white silk dress at the seams so that in places it had torn. Her fingernails were full of dirt, and she had no shoes on her blackened feet.

'I can't move,' he whispered.

'What do you mean?' said Ivy, her eyes filling with tears, 'Father Benjamin is waiting to marry us. We need to go!'

Another girl appeared from behind them. She was wearing a light blue bridesmaid's dress covered in mud and grease and holding a tiny crying baby dressed only in a soiled nappy.

'What's wrong, Ivy?' she said.

'Alistair said he won't come with me,' said Ivy, wiping her tears away with the back of her grubby hand.

The baby started to cry more loudly and determinedly.

'Get up!' the girl shouted. 'You'll break Ivy's heart.'

Alistair looked over towards the phone box further down the road. If he kept pushing on, he might be able to make it.

'Where are you going?' asked the girl.

His head snapped back: she was standing over him now, angry and intent. He had no more strength to move, no more air to breathe, no way out. Tears began to pour from his eyes.

'Shame on you.' She was straddling him now, covering his nose and mouth with her hands. He struggled at first, clawing at her arms, trying to push her off, but he was no match for her.

'You never cared about Ivy. You don't care about anybody but yourself,' said the girl, slapping him hard around the face.

No air, no strength, no fight. He looked at Ivy cuddling the baby she had taken from her friend, singing a song and making it laugh. 'Round and round the garden, like a teddy bear, one step, two step, tickle you under there.'

Get her off me. Help me. HELP ME. Alistair struggled, trying to kick his legs, but they lay motionless, as if trapped under a fallen tree. The girl stayed focused, pressing harder and harder on his nose and mouth until a searing pain began to radiate through his chest, up his neck and into his brain, where it exploded over and over like a firecracker. Darkness slowly started to creep in as a tunnel formed around his vision, narrower and narrower. Round and round the garden, like a teddy bear . . .

The baby's laughter grew muffled, and Alistair's efforts to breathe became futile, as if he were underwater. He felt as though he was weightless, sinking further and further down, and tipped his head back to suck in the last few pitiful bubbles of air before he disappeared for ever.

It was then that Kitty's face swam into his vision.

His eyes fixed on her face as he floated down, further and further, until a bright light suddenly pierced the blackness and filled the tunnel.

Her voice, crying his name.

'Alistair. *ALISTAIR!*'

Kitty, is that you?

He tried to open his eyes, but he had sunk too deep, it was too late. He was tired, so very, very tired.

Just let me sleep now. Please, let me sleep.

Chapter Thirty-One

Monday 6 February 2017

After a two-hour train journey back to Sussex, Sam collected her car and drove to Jane Connors' house, as she had done less than forty-eight hours earlier, when the world had felt like a very different place.

She pulled her notebook out and the page fell open at the list of names: Father Benjamin, George Cannon, Mother Carlin, Alistair Henderson.

She felt her stomach knot as she took a deep breath and drew Ivy's letters from her bag, clutching them as if they were the key to a secret world she was both terrified and desperate to enter. Then she stepped out of the car and walked up to the gate of the house next door, the house where the old lady had stared at her so intently it had made her uncomfortable. The wooden plaque on the gate said *Rose Cottage*, but the pergolas over her head were bare. She walked slowly, wary of the icy paving stones, her legs unsteady from lack of sleep.

As she reached out and pressed the bell, her whole body was trembling. She waited, tying her coat tighter round her waist. And waited. Her nerve began to slowly ebb away and she suddenly felt ill equipped to deal with whoever was on the other side of the door. She rang the doorbell again, then stepped back, looking up at the house, and down again just as the curtain in the front room twitched.

She turned to a fresh page in her notebook.

To the lady who left the picture of Ivy on Father Benjamin's coffin.

We have never met, but I feel I know you. I have in my possession some letters that I believe were written by the same Ivy as is in that picture, but I am desperate to meet you to find out.

I'm sure you believe, as I do, that pain and injustice on the scale that Ivy lived through should not be ignored and forgotten.

I would love to talk to you. I am a reporter and think the world needs to know about St Margaret's, but I respect your need for privacy. As your neighbour Mrs Connors will testify, I will take this at your pace and share nothing that you feel uncomfortable with.

Ivy would be very proud that you have reached out; she would have wanted others to know what happened, and I believe that you do too.

Please call me today, for Ivy's sake. As I think you may already know, we don't have much time before her story will be buried for ever when St Margaret's is pulled down tomorrow.

Samantha Harper

She scribbled her number at the bottom, then folded the page and posted it through the letter box. She walked back down the path knowing she was being watched, aware that as she climbed back into her car, the elderly lady was reaching down to her doormat and picking up the note.

She started the engine and stared at her phone, willing it

to ring. In the eerie quiet, the events of the past two days thundered round her head. Despite time galloping past at an alarming rate, she felt unsure about her next move. The conversation with Kitty Cannon felt like a dream. If Elvira had existed, Ivy would know.

She looked back down at the letters, longing to pull Ivy from their pages. Was the grey-haired lady in the cottages Ivy herself? Her head spun with tiredness, with thoughts of Emma and Nana. And Ben – she missed him so much. She would do better; they'd been through a rough patch, but they had to try harder for Emma's sake.

She knew she was running away from it all, but she didn't know how to stop herself. If she could just speak to the old lady, unravel this mess, she might find some peace in her own life.

She was startled by the sound of her phone ringing. She looked at the display.

'Hi, Fred.' She couldn't keep the disappointment from her voice.

'Listen, Murray's on the warpath, wanting to know where you are.'

'I told you to tell him I was sick,' Sam said, panicked.

'No, you said you'd call in sick later.'

'Shit. Can you tell him I've got a migraine and won't be in, I don't have the strength to talk to him.' She looked in the mirror and began running her fingers through her hair in an effort to tidy it.

'You sound terrible. Are you okay?' said Fred quietly.

'Not really,' said Sam, rubbing the mascara away from under her eyes.

'Well, I've done some digging like you asked and

according to the *Sussex Times*' report on the inquest, Helena Cannon was on a prolonged stay on the renal ward at Brighton Hospital due to acute kidney failure. At some point in the early hours of 3 July 1968, the needle of her fistula became dislodged and she bled to death.'

'How did that happen? Who was on duty that night?'

Sam heard Fred tapping his keyboard. 'A nurse by the name of Carol Allen. She gave evidence at the inquest saying that Helena Cannon was having her dialysis through the night at the time. Apparently she was on the machine for long periods, as she was in the late stages of kidney failure. Nurse Allen stated that the last time she checked on Helena, she was sleeping peacefully and all was well.'

'What about Dr Jacobson?'

'He died in 1976; drowned in the pool at his house. It wouldn't be hard to track him down – he was a GP in Preston for years – but I can't really do any more on this, Sam. I'm one cutting away from my P45.'

Sam sighed. 'Please, Fred, is there no way you could maybe pop into Dr Jacobson's house this afternoon and speak to his wife? I really need to get home to Emma.'

'I'll see what I can do, I'm not promising anything, though,' said Fred.

'Thank you, thank you. I'll make it up to you.'

Sam threw her phone on the seat, where Ivy's letters lay in a heap, then looked up again at the house. She flipped back to the page of names and added two more: Helena Cannon and Dr Jacobson. Six people dying unexpected deaths, and apart from George Cannon, all mentioned in Ivy's letters.

Sensing someone was watching her, Sam looked up. There in the doorway was the elderly lady she had seen at Father Benjamin's funeral the day before. And she was signalling for her to come in.

Chapter Thirty-Two

Monday 20 May 1957

Ivy lay still in her bed in the dormitory while the bell for prayers rang out. Girls rushed back and forth around her to the bathroom, pulling their overalls over their nighties, straightening their beds and standing to attention at the end of them in anticipation of Sister Mary Francis's entrance.

'Mary, you need to get up. Sister will be in any second,' said the girl who slept in the bed next to her, shaking her gently.

Ivy had not slept all night, drenched in sweat with her eyes wide open. She didn't even think she had drawn breath since she had seen, with her own eyes, a young couple taking Rose away two days before.

It had been a particularly hard day in the laundry; she had been pulling sheets through the mangle for hours and had burnt herself badly. Elvira had vanished again, and she had no idea where to. Without her one solace, her only escape, she was in despair. She had been finding it hard to keep any food down for weeks now, and although there were no mirrors at St Margaret's, running her hands over her collarbone and ribs in her bed at night told her everything she needed to know about her emaciated body.

Sister Mary Francis had been watching her intently all morning, and although she wasn't sure why, she knew something was amiss. After lunch, Sister Faith had come in and the two nuns had begun conversing, glancing at Ivy in turn as they spoke. As she tried to read their lips, the steam from the mangle had fired out and she hadn't moved in time.

She had cried out: she couldn't help herself. The intense heat had landed exactly where she'd burnt herself only hours before. She looked at the sisters nervously, waiting for one of them to charge over and make a fuss about her outburst. But neither of them had even looked up, until their conversation eventually ended and Sister Faith had nodded at Sister Mary Francis, looked at Ivy one final time and left.

On her walk past the dining room to the nursery, it had hit her. Through the cacophony of babies' cries, Rose's was absent. She had felt a surge of sheer panic and stopped dead at the nursery, the girls in the long line behind her bumping into her.

'What on earth do you think you are doing, Mary?' Sister Mary Francis had hissed at her.

'Where is she? Where's Rose? I can't see her.' Ivy was peering frantically through the glass of the nursery door.

'She's going to a much better home than you can ever provide for her. Now stop with your insolence immediately.'

She had broken free then, and run up the stairs two at a time to the dormitory, as Sister Mary Francis's cries for her to come back echoed below her. Terror soaring through her, she had sprinted to the dormitory window and looked out.

A smart black car sat on the front drive, and next to its open door stood Mother Carlin, holding a baby in a pink blanket. Rose's blanket, that Ivy had knitted herself. A woman in a cream summer dress and black shoes was lowering herself into the passenger seat, helped by a man in a grey suit.

Ivy began hammering at the glass, screaming at the top of her lungs as Mother Carlin handed Rose to the woman. The man closed the car door and shook Mother Carlin's hand, then looked up to the window where Ivy stood just as Sister Mary Francis pulled her away. She hadn't been able to remember much after that, other than that she had felt she was losing her mind with grief. Patricia had told her later that with the help of Sister Mary Francis, Mother Carlin had physically dragged her down the stairs and into her office.

'Get up, Mary.' Sister Faith stood over her now as she lay in bed, staring at the ceiling.

She knew that if she didn't move, she would be taken to Mother Carlin's office again. And if whatever punishment she was given didn't bring her to her senses, she had been told that Mother Carlin wouldn't hesitate in sending her to the Lunatic Asylum.

'Get out of bed this moment, or you'll wish you'd never been born.'

As Sister Faith's shoes tapped to the door and her voice called for help, Ivy closed her eyes and thought about the letter she had written to her love the night before.

Alistair,

Rose is gone.
I saw her leave with her adoptive parents and I feel sadness to the depths of my soul.

I cannot stop crying, despite my fears of being sent to an asylum if I do not pull myself together. I cannot eat, so I have no strength in my limbs and burn myself often on the machinery in the laundry. I am almost glad of the physical pain, because it is a momentary relief from my mental anguish.

Before now I have always thought of myself as strong. Nothing got the better of me, and even after Father died, I would find a way to dig myself out of my sadness – because I had my freedom. I could take a walk, or gaze at the stars and imagine him looking down on me. But I haven't been allowed out of these walls since I arrived, and every day I feel the air here is suffocating me a little bit more.

Since that night in Mother Carlin's office, I have fits of being unable to breathe and have to curl up in a ball until it passes. Sleep is impossible. I lie awake all night, my mind racing with thoughts of Rose and where she is now, where they have taken her and whether she is safe and happy. I can still smell her skin, I can still remember her moving around inside me. I feel an emptiness where she used to be, like a black hole sucking the life out of me one day at a time.

If I fall asleep momentarily, I dream of you and of Rose. Of you carrying Rose on your shoulders while she eats ice cream and we walk along the pier. I can feel the salty air on my face, the pure happiness in my stomach. Then I wake and realise where I am and lose my mind all over again. I can no longer conjure any feelings of joy, as though there is an invisible wall between the me I am now and the me I knew before. Every day I tell myself I am Ivy, I had long red hair, I was loved, but every day the voice inside my head becomes fainter and fainter. I miss school, I miss my friends and my life. I miss

250

you, Alistair; why do you not come for me? Soon there will be nothing left of the Ivy you used to know. They have my baby; why must they take everything else – my future, my dreams, my love? Why do they not let me go? Have I not suffered enough?

The other girls watch me crying and do nothing to try and comfort me, because talk is forbidden and they will be punished mercilessly. Sometimes I look at the faces of the nuns, twisted with hate as they beat a skinny, broken girl, and I think how desperately unhappy they must be to behave this way. But really I feel sorry for them. They are the victims as much as us; what misery they must tolerate. The nuns are the faces of this institution, but they are not the people who have put us here. It is our lovers, parents, doctors, vicars, everyone who is supposed to care for us, who have abandoned us. Had they not turned their backs on us, the beds in St Margaret's would be empty.

I no longer care if I am sent to a madhouse. What could be worse than this living hell? Working in the laundry from the moment they rip me from my sleep until I am dead on my feet. I have years of this yet to endure to pay off my debt.

I dream of running away, but everywhere we go we are watched. The only time they are not watching us is in our dormitory at night, but the window is forty feet off the ground. If it were not for Rose, for the thought that one day we will be reunited, I would break it open and jump.

I cannot die without telling her that I loved her and wanted desperately to keep her. Please, if you ever meet her one day, show her these letters. I want her to know how much I loved her, that every minute I craved to hold her. Tell her I had no choice to give her up. Tell her I fought for her.

I know now that you do not love me. How can you when you have read these letters and still leave me here to rot? I hate you for what you have done to us. One day you will live to regret it.

    Ivy

Chapter Thirty-Three

Monday 6 February 2017

Sam calmed her breathing, and made her way down the cobbled pathway of Rose Cottage for the second time. She tried to relax and focus on making the elderly lady feel at ease. Sam had not taken her in properly when she'd first laid eyes on her in the rain two days before. Now in the harsh light of day she could clearly tell her age; it showed in her skin, her frame and the way she held herself, hunched over, clinging to her frame, as if terrified to fall. Sam had done the calculations in her head, if Ivy had given birth to Rose in 1957, then Ivy's mother *must* be nearly a hundred.

'Hello, you got my note?' Sam said smiling.

'Yes,' said the woman, a faint smile forming at the corners of her mouth. 'You must be Samantha.'

'I am,' said Sam brightly. 'It's very nice to meet you.'

The woman was resting her thin arms on her Zimmer frame, and a pair of glasses dangled on a chain round her neck. 'I'm Mrs Jenkins. Would you like to come in?'

'Very much, yes please,' said Sam.

Mrs Jenkins shuffled her frame to make room for Sam to come inside. Sam reached out to help. 'I can manage,' the old lady said. 'Could you close the door, please, dear? And if you wouldn't mind taking off your shoes I'd be grateful. I struggle to keep the place clean.'

'No problem,' said Sam, sliding her heels off and putting them by the front door.

'Would you like a cup of tea?' asked Mrs Jenkins, leading the way down the hall.

'Yes please.' Sam looked around at the fairy lights strung between paintings of the Downs, black-and-white photographs and a driftwood mirror in which she caught her reflection and baulked.

'Please have a seat,' said Mrs Jenkins as they walked into a cosy country kitchen with a wooden table at its centre.

Sam pulled out a chair and sat down. 'Thank you, Mrs Jenkins. Everyone calls me Sam.'

'Then you must call me Maude.' The old lady switched on the kettle. 'So, you're a reporter?'

'Yes, for my sins,' said Sam, reassured to see that when she looked over at Maude, her smile was returned.

'I got your note,' said Maude. 'Do you have the letters with you?'

Sam took them from her bag. 'If these are anything to go by, Ivy sounds like she was an extremely special person.'

Maude eased herself into a chair next to her. 'She was. Not one day goes by when I don't think about her.' She looked down at the letters and slowly turned the pages. 'I miss her so much.' She reached out and stroked Sam's hair. Sam startled slightly, but managed a smile.

'So Ivy was your daughter?' she asked gently.

'Of course,' said Maude.

'Maude, can I ask you something? Obviously the letters touch on it, but from your point of view, can I ask how Ivy came to be at St Margaret's?'

Maude let out a sigh. 'She got pregnant by a local boy,

whom she loved very much. Ivy's father died in the war and I think he would have let her keep the baby with us, but I had married his brother, Ivy's Uncle Frank, and he was a very strict man. Dr Jacobson, our local doctor, suggested St Margaret's as a safe place for her to have the baby, and for it to be adopted, which the father of Ivy's baby saw as an agreeable solution.'

'And this was Alistair Henderson?' said Sam, referring to her notebook.

'That was his name. Eventually they wore me down. I'll never forgive myself for not fighting harder; it destroyed our lives.' Maude's eyes drifted to the window. 'Soon after she had the baby, I think Ivy got terribly depressed. Father Benjamin persuaded me that she needed to stay and be treated at St Margaret's. I used to write to her and take the letters to the gates, but however much I begged, the sisters would never let me see her and in the end I had to accept it.'

'Treated at St Margaret's? For what?' asked Sam, scribbling in her notebook.

'They told us that Ivy was suffering from psychotic episodes. I went back week after week asking if I could see her, but Mother Carlin said she didn't feel it would be appropriate and that it might upset Ivy more. I felt like it was my fault, you see, that she was there in the first place.'

Maude paused for a moment, then looked up at Sam. 'You can't imagine it now, but the Catholic Church still had quite a hold over the community then. I was a grown woman and it didn't occur to me to argue with a nun. I think if my husband had encouraged me, I would have gone down there and forced my way in, but for Frank . . .' Her voice wobbled. 'From the start he found the whole episode extremely tiresome. It was all very unsettling and St Margaret's seemed a good option at the time, and one we had no reason to distrust.'

Sam looked up from her notes. 'Why would you? I don't see what more you could have done.'

Maude shook her head at the memory. 'Ivy was at St Margaret's for over two years. I always hated myself for it. In the end, I had a terrible bout of depression and the situation with Ivy seemed to be at the heart of it. I told Frank that I was going to seek legal advice about getting her back, and that if he wouldn't help me, I would leave him. He was coming round to the idea when we got the letter.'

'The letter?' Maude looked so tired, thought Sam, like every movement was a huge effort that required all of her strength.

'Look in the bottom of the cupboard over there, child. Save me getting up. There's a box inside.' Sam looked to where the old lady was pointing. She opened the cupboard door and took out a shoebox, putting it down on the table in front of Maude, who started to root through its contents.

'Ah, here it is.' She passed Sam an envelope. It had faded to a dark cream in the fifty years since the date on the postmark. Sam carefully pulled out a typed letter on St Margaret's headed paper and started to read.

20 February 1959

Dear Mr and Mrs Jenkins,

I am writing on behalf of all at St Margaret's Mother-and-Baby Home, Preston. We are sorry to notify you that your daughter,

Ivy Jenkins, took her own life on Friday 13 February. As you are aware, Miss Jenkins had been suffering for some time from psychotic episodes, and in an effort to help her, we had recommended her for referral to Brighton Psychiatric Hospital. Unfortunately she died before we were able to have her admitted.

We will make arrangements for Ivy to be buried here at St Margaret's on Friday. If you wish to pay your last respects, you will be allowed admission to the cemetery on that day.

With deepest sympathy,
Mother Carlin
Mother Superior, St Margaret's

'I tried so hard to see her,' said Maude, her pink-rimmed eyes filling with tears. 'She was my only child, Samantha. I was supposed to protect her, and I let strangers stop me from doing that. Why? Where are all those strangers now? They lived happy lives while my baby died.'

Sam looked down at the list in her notebook. She wanted to tell Maude that she was wrong, that the reason she was here was that far from living happy lives, they had all died horrible, premature deaths.

Maude took another letter out of the box with shaking hands and handed it to Sam. It looked to Sam as if it had been torn up for some reason and then taped back together. Sam began to read; it had been typed on an old-fashioned typewriter and was addressed to the admissions department at Brighton Psychiatric Hospital.

I am writing to refer Miss Ivy Jenkins for immediate admission under the Mental Health Act. I met with Miss Jenkins on the recommendation of Mother Carlin and Father Benjamin at St Margaret's on 12 February 1959, as they were concerned for her safety and the safety of the other girls at St Margaret's.

Miss Jenkins' appearance was ungroomed and she is very underweight, as she has been refusing to eat. She has also been encouraging the other girls to do the same. She presented as manic and was experiencing self-abusive and suicidal behaviours. Her thought patterns were psychotic, and severe psychopathology was observed. Miss Jenkins admitted to some anxiety and depression, which may have been triggered by the adoption of her baby but has since become much more serious.

It is my opinion that Miss Jenkins should be referred to Brighton Psychiatric Hospital within forty-eight hours, where she should remain for the foreseeable future so she can rest and recuperate, so as not to be of harm to herself or others.

Yours sincerely,

Richard Stone

Maude picked up a Bible from the box and toyed with it in her hands. 'I asked if it would be possible to know where Ivy's baby was, and Mother Carlin just smiled at me. I'll never forget it. She said Ivy had signed a contract saying she would never try to trace the baby, and gave me this.'

She handed Sam a piece of paper, Sam took it and scanned it, reading one of the lines aloud: 'I hereby relinquish full claim for ever to my said child, Rose Jenkins.' Ivy's signature was at the bottom, and next to it Helena Cannon's, of St Margaret's Adoption Society.

Sam's eyes fell on a ballpoint pen with a faded logo lying in the box.

'What's this?' she said, pulling it out. 'Mercer Pharmaceuticals.'

'It was in the spine of Ivy's Bible,' explained Maude.

Sam picked up her phone. 'Could I use your bathroom, please, Maude?'

'Of course, dear, it's along the hall on the left.'

She locked the loo door and immediately typed *Mercer Pharmaceuticals* into Google. Nothing obvious came up, so she continued to dig, traipsing through lists in Wikipedia until she came to a reference to Mercer. It had been taken over in the seventies and was now called Cranium. When she typed that in, a webpage came up: *Cranium Pharmaceuticals, seeking solutions in the pharmaceutical industry for nearly 100 years.*

It was hard for her to make any sense of the medical blurb. Unsure what she was looking for, she scrolled through the various sections. Just as she was about to give up, the 'Founders' tab caught her eye. She clicked on it.

Cranium, formerly known as Mercer Pharmaceuticals, was founded by cousins Charles James and Philip Stone in 1919. Their purpose: to find a medical solution to the widespread problem of post-traumatic stress disorder – then known as shell shock – for hundreds of thousands of soldiers returning from World War I. Their advances in the world of psychological medicines were industry-changing. Most notably James and Stone discovered trimethaline, a sedative that helped to relieve many of the debilitating symptoms experienced by those in the trenches.

Through their pioneering research in the mid 1950s, James and Stone discovered the more widespread demand for tranquillisers, particularly amongst housewives. In 1959, Mercer brought cocynaranol to the market. Reducing symptoms of chronic anxiety, depression and episodes of mania, the drug gained Philip

259

Stone a Nobel prize for medicine shortly before his death in 1968 and launched Mercer Pharmaceuticals onto the international stage. Mercer subsequently caught the attention of Cranium's MD, Carl Hermolin, who in 1970 paid an undisclosed sum to the remaining founder, Charles James, to take over the company.

Philip Stone. Hadn't the letter referring Ivy to a psychiatric hospital been written by a Richard Stone? And Sam was sure the same name had come up on Kitty's phone in the car. Stone was a common enough surname, but somehow this didn't feel like a coincidence.

She googled Richard Stone and Mercer Pharmaceuticals and waited for a result. Nothing, except one article on a website called *Psychology Today*. It was an interview in which Richard Stone, a renowned psychiatrist, mentioned a falling-out he had had with his father, Philip Stone, in the 1960s. The article didn't give details, but mentioned that the two did not speak again until just before the older man's death.

Sam felt a rush of panic and dialled Kitty's number, which went straight to answerphone. 'Kitty, it's Sam. I'm with Ivy's mother now. This might be a coincidence, but I think you may be meeting with a man called Richard Stone this morning. I was wondering if it was the same Richard Stone whose father founded a company called Mercer Pharmaceuticals. There may be a link between him and St Margaret's, but I have no idea what. Just a bit worried about you; please call me back.'

Chapter Thirty-Four

Monday 6 February 2017

Richard Stone finished his breakfast, as he did every morning, by gulping down a large tumbler full of orange juice, then made his way into the bathroom. His morning bath was ready, and after taking off his dressing gown and easing himself into the steaming water, he let out a groan of pleasure. It was his favourite indulgence to leave the tap running slightly, ensuring the bath stayed piping hot so that he was constantly engulfed in steam.

Richard lay back and listened to the silence as the room morphed into a sauna. He tried to relax, but his mind kept wandering back to his session with Kitty the day before. The revelations about St Margaret's had been a huge shock and brought back old memories he had worked hard to forget. He was not looking forward to going over it all again in her session later today. His grief was taking a huge emotional toll and he didn't know if he had the strength Kitty needed from him. He would see how today went and then perhaps they could discuss the possibility of referring her. His son James was right: it was time to retire completely.

He tried to relax but his head throbbed and his back ached mercilessly. In his younger years there would have been a reason for his body to feel so bruised and broken: a fall from his bike or a pummelling from his brother. Now it was just the daily grind of old age. He closed his eyes as condensed water from the fogged-up mirror began to drip into the sink below it, echoing through the room in high-pitched clinks.

As he listened to the hissing of the slowly running tap, goose bumps started to slowly trickle over his skull, then down his back. He shifted in the water, rearranging the pillow at his head to try and get comfortable. The bath oil, which normally soothed him instantly, was irritating his skin; like an itchy woollen blanket on a hot summer's day. As he tried to ignore the displeasure in the back of his mind, he slowly became aware of a feeling of nausea rising in his stomach.

He slowly opened his eyes again, running them around the room and trying to work out what it was that was making him feel ill at ease. The room was so thick with steam, he couldn't even see his toes at the end of the bath, and the familiar sound of the extractor fan was strangely absent. The realisation that he was starting to feel disoriented made him sit up and take several deep breaths. He felt an overwhelming need to get out and let this strange feeling pass. Perhaps he was too old to be wallowing in steaming hot baths; maybe they were yet another one of life's remaining pleasures he would be denied.

As he sat forward in the water, contemplating getting out, the doorbell rang. Who could that be? It was nine in the morning; Kitty wasn't due until noon. After a few moments, he was startled to hear a woman's voice in the hall. Had his son and daughter-in-law popped in for a surprise visit? No, there was no chance of that; they would have called ahead.

As he tried to convince himself he must have imagined the voice, he suddenly heard a door slam, making him jump.

He placed his hands on either side of the bath to push himself up, but he had no strength in his arms and fell back into the water.

'James? Is that you?'

Alarmed now, he attempted to push himself up out of the bath again, but lost his grip on the slippery sides, this time falling back into the water with a violent thud. The world was suddenly a blur as he went under, his panicked breathing sounding loud in his ears. He let out a scream under the surface, inhaling water, which he coughed up frantically as he managed to push himself back upright.

'James!' he spluttered, finally finding his breath. 'James! Help me!'

As he clung to the side of the bath, retching up water and gulping for air, a pair of dirty, bloodied feet appeared on the bathmat next to him. Slowly he looked up. A girl of roughly eight was standing over him. Her head had been badly shaved, so that stray clumps of hair stuck out like continents on a map. Her neck was so swollen that her head was tipped back and her skin was burning with a fever. She was filthy, the sweat from her forehead leaving tracks through the grime on her face.

'I don't feel well,' she said as she clutched her shivering body. Richard could see that she had a lesion halfway up her arm. She was scratching at it, scabs of skin coming away under her fingernails. 'My throat hurts,' she rasped, putting her hand up to her swollen neck and rubbing it.

Richard could hardly bear to look at her. He said nothing,

263

too terrified to speak. She leant in further, her breath rancid, blood from the lesion dripping into his bathwater.

'Mother Carlin gets angry when I cry, but it hurts so much I can't stop. Please, you have to help me.' Slowly she reached out for Richard's hand; he pulled it away.

'Please don't,' he said.

The girl ignored him, tugging at his arm, causing him to lose his grip again on the side of the bath. He grabbed at it with the other hand, clinging on as if he were hanging from the edge of a cliff.

As the child stared down at him, he heard the bathroom door handle turn and the hinges creak. Footsteps clicked across the tiled floor, and he squinted to see who was walking towards him through the steam.

'Hello?' he said. 'James, is that you?'

No reply.

'For God's sake, help me. I can't move!'

His hands began to shake violently, and as the last of his strength drained away, he fell back into the water. Struggling to keep his head above the surface, he stopped thrashing and tried to calm himself.

Slowly he managed to ease the shower head off its cradle with his toe. It sank to the bottom of the bath with a clunk and he pushed it down the bath and under his buttocks, propping him up so that he could keep his nose and mouth above the surface of the water. Then he pulled out the plug with a sharp tug.

He began to count: one, two, three, breathe. Stay calm, don't panic, you can stay like this until the water drains out and you get your strength back. You're not going to die here. But as he stared up at the ceiling, he felt the presence of the girl in overalls next to the bath again. Slowly he turned his head towards her.

She was not alone any more. Next to her stood Kitty Cannon.

Her long grey hair was pinned back, her head was bowed, her chin close to her chest. Her brown eyes were fixed on him and she stood silently staring at him for several seconds. She was holding a box, which she slowly lowered to the bathroom floor.

'Kitty, thank God. Help me.' His mind was a fog now; sounds were muffled, and when he moved his head, he was overwhelmed with nausea.

Kitty said nothing; instead she began taking things out of the box. Heels clicking on the porcelain tiles, she left and returned with another box, repeating the process as the little girl watched her quietly, smiling. Richard twisted his neck and peered over the edge of the bath. The floor was scattered with files, some with photographs attached to them, some without. So many files that by the time she had finished, they covered the entire floor.

'Kitty? What are you doing? Please, Kitty, get me out of here, for God's sake!'

'My name is Elvira,' she said calmly, reaching out her hand.

Richard took it instinctively, thinking she was going to help him, then let out a cry of pain as she sank a kitchen knife into his wrist, making a deep cut along the inside of his forearm. Blood gushed out through the open wound. So much blood that within a minute the bath was red. He tried desperately to pull away from her, to find some strength in his body, but there was none.

'I see the cocynaranol is working,' she said as his wrist screamed out in agony. 'You remember that drug, don't you, Richard? I certainly do; it had some nasty side effects when you and your father tested it on us. I was surprised how easy it was to get hold of with a letter to Cranium Pharmaceuticals on a sheet of your headed paper. It appears your signature still holds a lot of weight.'

He watched in horror as she walked round to the other side of the bath, then lifted the knife again. His mind raced. Elvira. This was Kitty's sister, Elvira. It was Kitty who had died that night, and this woman in his house had been part of his father's trials at St Margaret's.

'You were one of the children!' he said, letting out another cry as she dug the sharp blade into his other wrist. The pain was unbearable; like being branded with burning-hot irons. 'Kitty, please don't do this. I fell out with my father over those trials; I didn't speak to him for forty years because of what he did.'

'And you did nothing wrong?' said Kitty. 'Are you sure about that? You didn't refer Ivy Jenkins to a psychiatric hospital because your father told you to? Because they were worried about her friendship with an eight-year-old girl called Elvira? An innocent little girl who told her about how she and the other children at St Margaret's were being used in your father's drugs trials?'

Richard closed his eyes as he thought back to that day, back to the meeting his father had ordered him to attend.

They had all been there to decide Ivy Jenkins' fate. Sitting round a table in the back room of Preston church: Father Benjamin, Mother Carlin, Dr Jacobson and Helena Cannon. He had arrived late, after getting lost. As he had made his way through the church into the small, stuffy room, Father Benjamin was escorting out a young man with blond hair and blue eyes. Richard later learnt that his name was Alistair Henderson, and that he was the father of Ivy's baby.

The priest had made the introductions, and then proceeded to take control of the meeting.

'Thank you, everyone, for coming,' he said slowly and confidently, as if he were conducting a service. 'As you all know, we have a number of children here at St Margaret's who for various reasons, mostly problems at birth, are unsuitable for adoption. Rather than turning them out on the street, we have utilised an opportunity offered to us by Mercer Pharmaceuticals that has enabled us to continue with our good work at the home.'

Richard had felt the heat rush to his head at the harsh reminder of the horrific situation at St Margaret's. He knew his father was using the children at St Margaret's to fast-track a new drug he was desperate to get the green light on. When Richard had first heard about it, he had made his disapproval known, but since then had not spoken of it and did his best to stay away.

Father Benjamin had then turned to him. 'However, a situation has arisen that I need your help and discretion with. A girl we have here, Ivy Jenkins, has befriended one of the children taking part in the trials, and we believe she may be aware of what is going on. Obviously, she is not admitting as such, but she is due to leave St Margaret's soon, and should word get out, the work your father's firm is conducting would be in jeopardy.'

Richard had said nothing, ashamed to be a representative of his father's company in this matter.

'A second issue has come to light,' Father Benjamin had continued, 'which is that the father of Ivy's child, Alistair Henderson, has received a number of letters from her of a very distressing and obviously fabricated nature, which he has returned to me today. Mr Henderson has a promising sporting career and is very nervous about Ivy making life difficult for him. He would be willing to help us with any costs incurred in keeping her with us for the next few years.'

Dr Jacobson had finally spoken. 'A few years? How are you going to manage that?' His arms were crossed defensively, his body turned away as far as it could be from the conversation.

Father Benjamin had ignored him and looked at Richard. 'Dr Stone, I understand you are recently qualified as a psychiatrist.'

Richard had said nothing; it was quite obvious where this conversation was going. He had known immediately why his father had sent him to this meeting. To punish him for speaking out against the trials in front of his colleagues. To remind him who was in charge.

'Your father seems to think that you may be able to help us with our problem with Ivy Jenkins. Since having her baby, she has been experiencing violent episodes, delusions; she has even been on hunger strikes. And it occurs to me that she may not be entirely safe either to herself or the wider community if she leaves St Margaret's at this time.'

'I really don't see the need for me to be at this meeting,' Dr Jacobson had snapped, at which point Mother Carlin, who until now had said nothing, turned to him.

'We think it is important that we are all fully aware of the situation with regards to Ivy Jenkins, Dr Jacobson. We all need to be involved in this decision. I don't see why you should be enjoying the large payments given to you by us for referring these girls while allowing yourself to believe you are not privy to our decision-making. God is watching. Indeed, the very hairs on your head are all numbered. If you want this to stop, to go back to your GP salary, with that large house you and your family have just moved into, please let us know now.'

The nun had not looked away once during her little speech, as Dr Jacobson's face had turned every shade of red. Though it was quite obvious what he wanted to say, he had remained silent until she had finished, then he stood up and stormed out.

Father Benjamin had then stood up and walked over to Richard. 'Here are the letters Alistair Henderson gave me. Please study them, but I trust that you will come to the same conclusion as I have. That Ivy Jenkins is unstable and would be best placed in an institution for the foreseeable future. Obviously the important work we are doing here will come to a natural conclusion, and when the trials are finished, we can review her situation.'

Richard had looked down at the five envelopes that Father Benjamin had placed on the table in front of him. 'When do you want her assessed?'

'Now. Obviously we want her to speak to you, so we have told her that she is having a medical because she is going home.'

'Isn't that rather unnecessarily cruel?' he'd said, unable to stop himself.

'Your father has cleared your schedule for the day. Once you find there are grounds to admit her, I think it best if she goes immediately. Shall we?' Father Benjamin had stretched out his hand towards the door, and with that one simple gesture, Ivy Jenkins' fate was sealed.

Richard slowly looked down at his frail body in the empty bath; he was shaking now with cold and fear. 'Please, Kitty, I was young and stupid. Call me an ambulance, I beg you, then we can talk about this.'

'I'm tired of talking to you, Richard. I gave you a chance. More of a chance than I ever gave any of the others. I don't mean to offend, I know psychiatry is your life's work, but I have to say, you're not terribly good at it. You've been seeing me for how many months, and you didn't see this coming, did you?'

As he watched her face, perspiration dripping from her forehead, the light in the room began to fade.

'I told you about the night my father died, didn't I?' she said. 'Didn't you sense there was so much more I needed to say?'

A black outline grew slowly around her as she held up the bloodied knife and surveyed her work.

'I didn't mean to cause him to crash; it wasn't my intention for him to die. I woke up from a nightmare, dreaming of Kitty. I was haunted by her. I couldn't stand it any more; I decided I had to tell him the truth. That it was his beloved Kitty who was buried at St Margaret's; that I was an impostor.'

She wiped the beads of sweat away from her forehead with the back of her gloved hand.

'I went out in the blizzard to get the bus to the hospital, desperate by that time to tell him and Helena together, whatever the consequences. Then when there was no bus to the hospital, I just kept going. I knew the way so well, we went nearly every day to visit her. For an hour, I pushed on through the snow.

'Then suddenly his car was there. He swerved to avoid hitting me and came skidding off the road at such speed that when I ran over to him I knew immediately he was dead. I had seen so much death at St Margaret's; I knew he was gone.

'I don't know how long I stood there, but a man came and startled me, so I ran all the way home. I waited for the police to come and arrest me and take me back to St Margaret's. But when they finally arrived, they told me that there had been a terrible accident. They didn't know I'd been there, that I had caused it. After the shock wore off and I realised I had got away with being responsible for my father's death, I developed a whole new perspective about it and it became rather inspiring.'

Suddenly there was a clatter as the knife fell onto the bathroom floor, and then with a click, the bathroom door closed.

'Please don't leave me,' said Richard weakly, praying for some comfort in his final moments.

But no bright light appeared, and slowly the blackness grew. Utterly alone, he lay in the cold, empty bath and watched his blood trickling down the plughole. It will be over soon, he told himself, beginning to cry. He missed his wife; he prayed she would come and meet him now.

'Evelyn,' he said over and over as the blackness took hold, 'I'm sorry.'

Chapter Thirty-Five

Thursday 12 February 1959

Ivy woke with a start to the sound of a child crying. She hadn't meant to doze off, but exhaustion had overwhelmed her and she cursed herself for being so stupid. She had heard the children crying many times before, been told by Elvira about the injections which made them all so poorly that all the children in the attic had to look after one another. But until tonight she had been utterly powerless to do anything to help them.

She sat up and looked around the room, watching for any signs of movement from the other beds. All the girls were asleep, the only sounds the murmurs accompanying the nightmares from which they all suffered.

She still couldn't believe she was going home. It had all happened so suddenly. Mother Carlin had approached her at breakfast and told her that her mother was coming for her the following day. All girls had an appointment with a doctor before they left; it was routine, and she must cooperate with him fully.

He was a young man, almost as young as her, she thought, with floppy chestnut hair, a smart blue blazer, and an accent that suggested a privileged upbringing. He had been nice to her, asking her how she was feeling about her baby and her stay at St Margaret's. She knew better than to trust him, however, and had given very little away. As he took notes, she had told him that she was grateful for her time there, that she was happy Rose had gone to a good, loving home and that she was looking forward to putting the whole episode behind her. He had commented on her weight and brought up the hunger strike, but she said she had just been desperately homesick and that obviously Mother Carlin and Father Benjamin had noticed it and kindly decided to let her go. He had smiled at her answers, nodding gently as the nib of his pen scratched the paper which lay on the desk between them.

Ivy pushed back her covers and the cold rushed up her legs and down her back. Shuddering, she pulled the blanket from her bed and carefully wrapped it around her, then started tiptoeing across the room, the creaking of the boards beneath her feet slicing into the silence. She knew Sister Faith would be waiting on the other side of the door, dozing in her rocking chair as she did night after night. She had never tried to pass her before; never had the courage or thought her chances of success were high enough. But now that she was leaving, she knew she had no choice. She had to talk to Elvira. There would be no other opportunity.

Barely breathing, she approached the door and looked down at the brass handle. She knew it would make a noise, and that when it did, Sister Faith would stir, but still she found her shaking hand reaching out for it. It turned with a click, and she took a deep breath, pulling the heavy oak door slowly towards her, her chest starting to hurt from the pain of her heart throbbing inside it.

In the silent hallway outside the dormitory sat an empty rocking chair, gently moving as if its occupant had only recently left it, a tartan blanket thrown onto it in haste. Ivy stood staring at it, paralysed with indecision. Her head prickled with goose bumps as the sound of running water suddenly came from the lavatory next to where she stood. She glanced at the long corridor to the left of her, at the end of which was another door. A door she knew led up to the attic and Elvira's dormitory.

Her heart lurched as she quickly closed the dormitory door behind her and began to run, her bare feet silent as they fell on the glistening floorboards. Sprinting for the darkness at the end of the corridor, she could hear the bathroom door latch lifting, the sound of footsteps, and as she grabbed the handle and turned it, Sister Faith let out a loud cough, which jolted through her like an electric shock.

She stood on the steps up to the attic and slowly pulled the door to behind her until eventually it gave a tiny click. She waited, trying to make herself breathe, and when she felt sure Sister Faith wasn't coming, she began to climb the steep steps up to the attic, two by two.

Standing at the end of Elvira's dormitory, looking round at the rows of cots lining both sides of the narrow, window-less room, she pushed away the tears she hadn't allowed to fall for so long. Each cot contained two children, aged between one and seven, tied by their ankles to the bars at either end. Most were sleeping on their filthy mattresses, the thumbs in their mouths their only comfort. But some lay awake, their eyes open and staring in the moonlight, rocking backwards and forwards like animals in cages. Some of the children were dark-skinned, with long, matted hair; some she knew to be mongoloid; others were so physically disabled they never moved from their cots.

274

In the corner of the room, a filthy ceramic basin protruded from the wall, a single bar of soap lying on the floor beneath it.

'Ivy?' Elvira's little voice was so distinctive, and Ivy turned to see the beautiful little girl she had fallen in love with staring over at her. 'What are you doing here?'

Ivy ran over, knowing her time was short. Elvira's hair was tangled, her face dirty; her mattress stank of urine. Ivy wanted desperately to pick her up there and then and carry her out of that godforsaken place.

'Elvi, listen to me. I can't stay long, but I've come to tell you I'm leaving.'

'When?' Tears immediately sprang to the little girl's eyes. 'Please don't leave me.'

'It's all right, Elvi, I'm coming back for you. I'm going to the police tomorrow to tell them about what is happening to you and all the other children here, and after we get you out of here, I'm taking you home to live with me.' She had pulled Elvira into her chest and squeezed her tight.

'To live with you?' The little girl's eyes sparkled as she looked up at her, and Ivy felt so sad for Elvira, and the life she had lived until that moment, that it gave her a physical pain in her chest.

'Yes, would you like that?' she said, still holding Elvira tight.

'I'd love it more than anything in the world.'

'Then it's done. But listen, Elvi, you must not say a word of this to anyone. Do you understand? My mother is coming to pick me up tomorrow, and then I'll be back.'

Elvira nodded. 'Will it be before the doctors come again?'

'Yes, I promise. I had to come and tell you not to worry.

I knew you'd be upset when you realised I was leaving, and I couldn't do that to you. You've been through enough.' Ivy pulled away and took her hands.

Elvira started to cry, the tears causing streaks to form in the black grime on her face. 'Something will happen to you before you come back. Something bad will happen because *I'm* bad.'

'Elvira, look at me. That's not how it is. You are not bad, you are an angel. Nothing the sisters say about you is true. Listen, God knows the truth, he sees everything, he sees the bad things they do to you and knows how you suffer. He knows that you are good down to the strands of hair on your head. Luke, chapter twelve, verse seven says, "Even the hairs on your head are all numbered." Don't be afraid.' She took Elvira's face in her hands.

The little girl was sobbing now, her body shaking as she lost control of her emotions. 'I'm not an angel. They said I did something bad to their baby, that I tried to push him under the bathwater. But we were just playing and he slipped.'

'Elvira, you were a baby yourself. You do not deserve this. You are not the reason why you are here, they are. *They* are the ones who are bad, not you. And I am going to get you out.'

'Don't leave me.' Elvira clung to Ivy so hard that her fingernails scratched her skin.

'Elvira, please stop,' said Ivy, looking anxiously over at the other children, who were starting to stir. 'Please, Elvi, please stop crying. You have to trust me, darling.'

She held the little girl until her cries began to slow and then eventually stopped. 'I have to go now. I'll see you in the morning in the laundry, but you're to say nothing, do you understand? Promise me, Elvi.'

'I promise.'

'I love you, Elvira,' Ivy whispered.

'You love me?' said Elvira, wiping the tears away.

'Yes, I love you. Now go to sleep, we've got a big day tomorrow.' Ivy smiled and blew the little girl a little kiss before creeping back across the dormitory floor. Wide eyes followed her, children too full of fear to make a sound. She wanted to scoop them all up and run, but she couldn't. Not until tomorrow.

All she needed now was Rose's file. There was no way she could get downstairs and break into Mother Carlin's office without being seen. She would have to find a way to get out of breakfast and go then.

As she reached the bottom of the stairs, she could hear Sister Faith's snores from the other side of the door, but still her whole body throbbed with fear as she passed her in the corridor with only inches to spare. She could see her top lip twitching, feel the heat of her breath on her hand as she passed, and as soon as she was clear, she crept back to the safety of her bed.

Staring up at the dark wood ceiling, her brain began to form a plan. Adrenaline was racing through her; there was no way she would be able to sleep. A flutter of something she hadn't felt for many months entered her heart, an emotion she could barely recall, but as the sun slowly began to come up, she realised what it was that she was feeling.

Hope.

Chapter Thirty-Six

Monday 6 February 2017

'Are you all right in there, dear?' asked Maude from the other side of the door.

'Fine, thank you,' said Sam, flushing the toilet and running the tap. As she stepped out into the hall, her eye was caught by a framed tapestry she hadn't noticed on her way past.

Maude followed her gaze. 'Ivy made that when she was fourteen. Isn't it beautiful? She tried to show me how, but it was too hard. She had such patience teaching the children at Sunday school.'

Sam studied the beautifully hand-stitched material, with the words *The very hairs on your head are all numbered; do not be afraid.*

'She used to say that all that time. "Don't worry, Mummy, God sees everything you do, he knows how good you are." She used to look at her Uncle Frank and whisper, "And he knows who is not good too."'

Sam smiled gently, taking Maude's hand. Her skin was as thin as paper. Sam could feel the unhappiness radiating from her; it was as though any part of her, including her heart, could snap in two at any minute.

'You look so like her,' said Maude, looking at Sam intently.

'Who?' said Sam.

'Ivy,' said Maude, pointing to a photograph on the wall. 'She must have been about seventeen there.'

Sam stared. With her long red hair, Ivy was the image of her.

'When I first saw you, it was like seeing a ghost,' said Maude.

Sam started to feel uneasy. What was the old lady trying to say? Scanning her trusting, kind face for clues, Sam tried to untangle Maude's words in her sleep-deprived brain.

'I have to say, I was a little disappointed when I saw you coming down the path on your own,' said Maude. 'I'd rather hoped that you turning up like that meant Rose had forgiven me.'

'What do you mean?' said Sam, starting to feel panic rising in her without understanding why. 'Rose who?'

Maude let out a slightly nervous laugh. 'Your grand-mother, of course.'

'Nana? She's got nothing to do with this. She just found those letters in my grandfather's papers when he died. He was an antiques dealer; he often found letters and personal documents in the furniture he sold.' Sam could hear the words coming out, wanting desperately for them to be true but knowing already that they weren't.

'But I gave the letters to your grandmother myself, nearly fifty years ago,' said Maude, a look of total bewilderment on her face. 'When she and her friend came to see me.'

The words hung in the air. Sam couldn't take them in. 'My grandmother, Annabel Creed, was here? Fifty years ago?'

'Yes, when she was twelve. I thought that's why you were

here. I thought she'd given you the letters and explained what happened between us.'

Sam suddenly felt very faint and sat down on the floor, putting her head in her hands. 'But how did you get them?'

'They arrived in the post a few days after Ivy died,' Maude said, looking up at the picture of her daughter. 'They broke my heart. I'd had no idea what she had been through. I went back to St Margaret's with them, but Mother Carlin told me that what Ivy had written was all part of the psychosis she was suffering. That was when she gave me the letter from the psychiatrist confirming that Ivy was not in her right mind and that what she'd written was pure fabrication.'

'But Nana never said a thing to me about meeting you,' Sam said. 'I don't understand. Are you sure it was her? Annabel Creed?'

'Annabel Rose Creed, yes. Samantha, she's Ivy's daughter. She's the Rose Ivy talks about in the letters.'

Sam turned and rushed into the bathroom, throwing up into the toilet. Slowly she pulled herself up, steadying herself at the sink. She splashed water on her face, then looked at herself in the mirror before walking back out into the hall.

'I'm so sorry, Samantha, I really thought you would have known all this. I was so happy when I read your note this morning. I thought your grandmother had finally forgiven me.'

'Forgiven you? What for?' said Sam, staring again at the picture of Ivy.

'It was her friend who did most of the talking that day – she was a little bit older than Annabel,' said Maude. 'Annabel just sat very quietly. The adoption laws had recently changed and adopted children were allowed to contact their birth parents. The council wrote to me to say that Annabel wanted to get in touch. They set up the meeting.'

Sam listened, shaking her head. She couldn't take it in, that Nana had known where her grandmother was, who her mother was. Why had she never talked to her about it? Why?

'And this friend of my grandmother's, what did she say?' said Sam.

'It was terrible. I had been overwhelmed at the thought of meeting Annabel Rose, counting down the minutes until I saw her for the first time. She was so beautiful, the picture of Ivy, when she let me hold her I had to stop myself smothering the poor girl.

'I hadn't wanted to give her Ivy's letters then, because they were so upsetting, but I got the box of Ivy's things out to show her a picture, and her friend found them and sat in the corner reading them while I chatted with Annabel. That half an hour was wonderful – she was such a lovely girl, she reminded me so much of Ivy. But then her friend finished reading the letters and became very angry. She was shouting and said I should be ashamed of myself for not rescuing Ivy, that it was my fault she died. That I might as well have killed her myself.'

'Oh my goodness, that's horrendous. I'm so sorry, Maude.' The old lady looked so pale, Sam thought she might faint. She grabbed a chair from along the hall for Maude to sit on.

'Thank you,' said Maude, as Sam helped her into it. 'She was the one who tore Richard Stone's letter up, and threw it at me; she was in a terrible rage. She told me the letter was all lies, that Ivy wasn't mad. It was stupid of me to tape it back together. But I have so little to remember Ivy by, I have to cling onto anything.'

Sam took Maude's hand in hers. 'Who was she, this so-called friend?' she asked.

'Her name was Kitty. I remember, because years later I saw her on television. I couldn't believe it,' said Maude, as she wiped away a stream of tears with the back of her hand. 'She told me to never contact Annabel again, and that if I did, she'd kill me.' Sam fetched Maude a tissue.

'Jesus Christ,' whispered Sam, shaking her head. 'Kitty called me Ivy when I first found her at St Margaret's. She denied it, but when I showed her Ivy's picture, she was visibly upset.'

'You know Kitty?' said Maude, crushing the tissue in her hands.

'I met her for the first time today,' Sam said quietly, lost in thought.

'When she was here that day with Rose, she talked about Ivy like she knew her, but how can she have?' Maude said quietly.

'She couldn't have,' said Sam slowly, 'but her twin sister could.'

'Her twin sister?' said Maude.

'Kitty told me this morning that she and her twin, Elvira, were born at St Margaret's to her father's mistress who died in childbirth. Kitty was raised by her father but Elvira was adopted by a couple who sent her back to St Margaret's. She would have been there at the same time as Ivy.'

Sam looked up at the picture of Ivy again, then at her own reflection in an antique mirror on the wall. 'I think

282

the reason she called me Ivy was because she recognised me like an old friend would. She was disoriented and forgot herself; she didn't know what she was saying.'

'Forgot herself?' said Maude. 'What do you mean?'

'Kitty can't have known Ivy, but Elvira did.' Sam's eye caught the tapestry on the wall. 'Kitty has one of those tapestries in her flat. I think Ivy taught her that psalm when they were together at St Margaret's.' She looked back at Maude.

'When Kitty and Ivy were together at St Margaret's? I thought you said it was Elvira?' said Maude.

'When I was with Kitty she told me about the day she met Elvira for the first time. They were eight and Elvira had escaped from St Margaret's and managed to find Kitty. They hid in an outhouse by St Margaret's and when it was dark Kitty said she went to find help. But she fell and woke up three days later in hospital to her father telling her Elvira was dead.'

'How utterly dreadful. The poor little thing,' said Maude, her eyes filling with tears.

'What if it was Kitty that died that night,' said Sam, 'and Elvira took her place for fear of being sent back to St Margaret's?'

'I don't understand what you're saying. How can she just have taken her sister's place – it's impossible.' Maude's blue eyes were troubled.

'Is it?' said Sam. 'They were twins.'

'But they would have looked different, surely?' Maude was leaning towards her. 'Elvira lived at St Margaret's, she would have been neglected, whereas Kitty came from a loving home. Elvira's hair, nails, teeth would have been filthy and she would have been much thinner than Kitty, wouldn't she?'

'Not necessarily. Kitty said she woke up in hospital three days after she met Elvira. She said she spent the night in a ditch. So she would have been caked in mud by the time she got to hospital anyway, and they would have cleaned her up.'

'But her mother and father would have known; a mother knows,' said Maude, staring at Sam.

'Their birth mother was dead. If you're talking about Helena Cannon, she was very ill in hospital at the time and George would have been stressed and distracted.' Sam paused. 'It's possible that Elvira, knowing Kitty was dead, took her sister's place and has spent her life getting revenge for what happened to her.'

'Revenge? What do you mean?' Maude looked confused, tugging at the tissue in her hands.

'Everyone that Ivy mentions in her letters is dead. And I think they were killed by Elvira.'

'Good heavens,' said Maude, pausing for a moment to take it in. 'Well, everyone except Rose.'

Sam stared at Maude, her eyes wide with horror, 'Oh my God. Nana.'

'What is it?' said Maude. 'What's wrong?'

Sam raced to the front door, grabbing her bag and pulling on her shoes as she shouted out to Maude, 'Call the police, tell them an elderly lady has been attacked at Flat 117 on the Whitehawk Estate.'

Chapter Thirty-Seven

Monday 6 February 2017

It didn't take Fred long to find the detached Victorian house the lady at the post office had directed him to. He didn't hold out much hope that the Jacobson family would still be living there, so his heart fluttered when an attractive elderly woman in a pink cashmere cardigan came to the door. She propped her glasses on top of her perfectly blow-dried hair and examined him closely.

'Mrs Jacobson?' said Fred with a warm smile. He had read in Dr Jacobson's obituary that he had died in 1976 and that he and his wife had been married for twenty years prior to that so Mrs Jacobson had to be in her eighties. Still, she clearly took pride in her appearance, thought Fred, and looked well for her age.

'Yes?' she replied nervously.

'I don't know if you remember me. I used to live in the area as a boy. I'm Fred Cartwright; your husband was my father's GP for years,' he lied, feeling guilty about it but pushing on for Sam's sake.

The woman frowned, trying to make sense of her unexpected visitor.

'Dad always spoke very highly of him. I believe he wrote when your husband died. He was very upset,' said Fred.

'I see. How can I help?' the woman replied.

Fred paused. 'I'd like to ask you a question or two about your late husband if you have the time.'

'Well, I don't know, I was just catching up on Saturday's episode of *Casualty*,' said the woman, looking over her shoulder.

'I was sorry to hear of Dr Jacobson's death. You and your daughters must miss him dreadfully – Sarah and Jane I think Dad said their names were, is that right?' Fred had memorised the names in the cuttings he'd pored over earlier.

'Thank you. Yes, that's right.'

'It really won't take more than five minutes. We could talk out here on the bench, perhaps?'

'Oh no, it's terribly cold. Forgive me, I'm an old lady on my own, so I get a little nervous. It's always lovely to talk about Edward – do come in.' He followed her down the hallway. 'Would you like some tea?'

'Thank you, Mrs Jacobson,' said Fred, nodding.

'Call me Sally. Please come through and have a seat while I make a fresh pot.'

She led him into a large sitting room with a plethora of soft furnishings, family photographs and flowers. The room was immaculate, not a cushion out of place, and the huge house had obviously been recently decorated. There was no way a frail old lady such as Mrs Jacobson could tend to a house this size on her own. Edward Jacobson had obviously made sure his wife was well provided for long after he was gone.

As Mrs Jacobson busied herself in the kitchen, Fred studied the selection of photographs on a polished antique table. He picked up a picture of Dr Jacobson with his arm round a honey-coloured spaniel.

'We all loved that dog,' said Mrs Jacobson, who had appeared behind him with a tray of tea and biscuits. 'I think I cried more when Honey died than when Edward did. She was such wonderful company after he went. It was the final straw losing her.'

'I can imagine. So how are Jane and Sarah doing?' said Fred.

'Gosh, so grown up now, I can hardly believe it. Sarah is a doctor like her father, and Jane is an architect,' she said, setting the contents of the tray on the table. 'They try to come and see me as much as they can, but they're very busy. You know how it is.'

Fred smiled. 'You must be so proud of them.'

'Yes, it just makes me sad that Edward didn't get to see how well they've turned out.' Sally handed him a cup of tea. 'So what are you doing with yourself these days, Fred?'

Fred smiled. 'Well, Sally, actually I'm a historian, and I'm trying to find out about a place called St Margaret's in Preston. I don't know if you've heard of it?' He took a biscuit from the plate offered to him and put it on his saucer.

'Of course, the mother-and-baby home. It's been derelict for years, but they're tearing it down soon, I think.'

'Yes, that's right,' said Fred, pausing to find the right words. 'I was just wondering if you knew whether your husband had any dealings with St Margaret's?' He watched Mrs Jacobson's face, waiting for any sign of defensiveness, but there was none.

'Well, yes, they took in unmarried pregnant girls, didn't they? Edward used to go up there sometimes to help with difficult births, but he didn't like to speak of it much.'

Fred nodded. 'It would have been typical of him to want to help,' he said, taking a gulp of tea.

The elderly lady sat back on the plump sofa cushions as she sipped from her bone-china cup. Fred immediately pictured the scene: Sally tucked up in silk sheets, barely stirring as the front door clicked shut and Dr Jacobson crept in, his hands still covered in blood from fighting to save a poor young girl's life. She would have stirred and lifted her head as he stood in the bedroom doorway and whispered, 'I'm just going to have a bath, darling, I'll sleep in the spare room so I don't disturb you.'

A Persian cat appeared at the French windows and made them both jump.

'What are you doing there, Jess?' said Sally, getting up to let it in.

'Your garden is beautiful,' said Fred, looking beyond the French windows as Sally closed them quickly and wrapped her cardigan tightly around her. 'It can't be easy to run a house this size on your own.'

'Well, I'm lucky that I can afford help. The girls keep trying to get me to leave, but I can't. It's all very well them thinking they know what's best, but how is it good for me to move somewhere I don't know, to live on my own and leave Edward behind? I'd be letting him down.' She put her cup on the table. 'He died here, you know.'

'I didn't know. I'm sorry, that must be very hard.' He waited for her to go on, but she remained lost in thought. 'Had he been ill?'

'No, not at all. He drowned in the pool house. We still don't know quite what happened, but somehow he got trapped under the cover. The autopsy showed he'd dislocated his

288

shoulder. We think Honey got stuck under there and he was trying to get her out and fell in.'

'How dreadful. Were you here at the time?' said Fred.

'No, I was out Christmas shopping. My car got a puncture, so I was gone for a while . . .' Sally's voice tailed off as she played with her hands in her lap. 'We'd bought the strongest make of pool cover so that the children couldn't fall in; it should have held him, but he hit his head when he fell, so he was unconscious when he slipped into the water.'

'That's terrible. Were the police helpful?' said Fred, watching Sally's face carefully.

'They were. I kept telling them that something wasn't right. Honey hated that pool house; she feared water and would never have gone in there. And Edward broke a pane of glass trying to get in – his fingerprints were on a rock he used. He knew where the key was; why would he break into his own pool house? I don't blame the police for not listening to me. I was in such a state after his death, I had to be sedated for several days. I couldn't attend the inquest. I knew the verdict would be accidental death. Why wouldn't it be? There was no reason for anyone to want to hurt Edward.'

'No,' said Fred, looking at Dr Jacobson's photograph on the wall, surrounded by his girls.

'I'll never forgive myself for not being here.'

'I'm sorry, Sally,' said Fred. 'He was always very kind to our family. Life's really not fair sometimes.'

Sally wiped away a tear with the back of her hand. 'It's selfish of me, I know – we had twenty incredibly happy years – but I sometimes still see friends bickering with their husbands and I want to scream, "You don't know how lucky you are to have someone to get cross with!"'

Fred waited for her to go on, sad that she was so lonely she would share so much with a stranger.

'He wanted to come shopping with me, but I made some excuse. He was a bit of a hindrance to shop with, you see. If only I'd had more patience with him, he'd still be here with me now.'

'As my father says, every man is guilty of all the good he did not do,' said Fred.

Sally looked up and smiled, her eyes still full of tears. 'I'm sorry, I'm sure you didn't come here to listen to me talking about Edward. How can I help you?'

'Well, I was just wondering if you'd kept any of Dr Jacobson's paperwork? I thought he might have information on some of the girls he helped to save at St Margaret's so I could interview them. It would make a lovely tribute to him in my dissertation.'

'Oh, I'm not sure,' said Sally, frowning suddenly. 'I've never really had the heart to go through his paperwork properly. I just want to leave everything as it was.'

'I completely understand,' said Fred, pausing for effect. 'Perhaps if you were to just see whether he had any files for St Margaret's, then you could maybe have a think and talk to your daughters. I could come back another time if you felt comfortable. No pressure.'

Slowly Sally digested his proposal. 'Well, that sounds fine. But I have to say, I don't think there will be much. It was very strange: just before he died, he was sorting through four or five boxes of files that had been delivered to him that week by Father Benjamin. I presumed they were to do with St Margaret's.'

Sally thought back to that day in mid December 1976, a

week before Edward had died, when Father Benjamin had turned up on the doorstep.

'Hello, Sally, is Edward in?' he had said, standing on the doorstep, walking stick in hand.

'Um, yes. Is he expecting you, Father?' She had known he wasn't; that he had been looking forward to a quiet evening at home. But obviously she couldn't turn Father Benjamin away.

'What on earth does he want? Can't you tell him I'm ill or something?' Edward had snapped when she went to find him, a look of alarm in his tired eyes.

Sally had been slightly taken aback by her husband's tone. 'Well, I can't tell him that now, Edward, it's too late.'

'Oh for goodness' sake. Well, you'd better let him in then,' he had hissed at her, huffing and puffing as he moved paperwork off his desk.

After showing Father Benjamin up to Edward's study, she had stood nervously on the landing, listening to their raised voices from inside.

'Well, I can hardly see what you want me to do about it all now, Father,' Edward had said. 'I warned you at the time that you needed to keep proper records for those poor children, God rest their souls.'

'Those children were fed and sheltered by us; we had no other way of paying for their upkeep. I take offence at the moral high ground you have taken over this, Edward. You have always known this went on, and yet you have continued to benefit extremely well from the girls you send to us.'

'Sent, Father, sent. I haven't referred a girl to you for nearly six years.'

Sally had heard Father Benjamin laugh at this, a harsh,

empty laugh that made her feel sick to her stomach. 'I think your part was well played out before then, Doctor. I don't want this to turn acrimonious, but I have records in my car, records the council is now legally entitled to see. If I refuse, I could be in contempt of court if it were to go to trial.'

'You should have thought of that before you spent all the money Mercer Pharmaceuticals gave you.'

'Listen to me, Edward Jacobson,' Father Benjamin had roared so loudly that Sally had scuttled back down the stairs. 'If I have to answer questions over this, I am taking you down with me. You and you alone are able to go through these files and find explanations for what is in their pages. We have one week, and I suggest you get started tonight.'

Sally had heard the study door open and had rushed into the kitchen as the priest marched downstairs and out of the front door, leaving it wide open. She had watched him fling open the boot of his car, pull out four large box files and lug them into the house, leaving them in the hallway. He had said nothing as he had caught Sally staring at him; simply turned and slammed the front door behind him.

Fred looked up at her now, his ears pricking up. 'Well, if they were St Margaret's files, I'd certainly be very interested to see them,' he said, trying to hide his eagerness.

'I'm not sure what he did with them. I never saw them again; they certainly aren't in his study. To this day I don't know where they went. Would you like to wait here and I'll go and see if I can find anything useful?' said Sally, smiling cheerfully.

Fred nodded. As soon as he heard footsteps above him, he looked at his shaking hands and went over to the drinks cabinet. He opened it, poured himself a small whisky and downed it. After a few minutes, he heard Sally's voice; quite obviously she was on a phone call. Someone had called her, he thought, or she had begun to worry and called them.

'Well, I presume so, I don't know, darling!' she was saying, her voice slightly raised in agitation. She walked back into the room with the phone to her ear.

'I'm afraid you're out of luck,' she said to Fred, her warm body language and tone changed entirely. 'There are no such files and my daughter, who lives in the next village, is due any moment. I think it might be an idea if you left now.'

'Of course,' said Fred, trying to hide his panic. 'Thank you for the tea. Could I possibly use the lavatory quickly before I go? I've got a long drive back to London ahead of me.'

Sally's lips pursed. It was obvious that since checking in with her daughter, she'd been utterly spooked. 'Yes, all right, it's just along there on the left.'

Fred walked down the hall, glancing into the other rooms as he passed. As he went to close the door to the bathroom, he spotted an open door on the landing at the top of the stairs opposite him. He didn't hesitate. Checking that the coast was clear, he closed the bathroom door and quietly went up the stairs, walking into a large study furnished with a mahogany desk, leather chair and two filing cabinets, one of which had a set of keys in its lock.

Knowing he had only minutes before he was discovered, he twisted the key urgently and pulled open the first row of hanging files on their runners. Finding nothing under 'S' for 'St Margaret's', he looked at 'M', but that only held a file entitled 'Mercer Pharmaceuticals'. He pulled it out. The file contained a single piece of paper, what seemed to be a contract, on headed paper, the words *Private and confidential* at the top. At the bottom were two signatures, Dr Jacobson's and that of the president of Mercer Pharmaceuticals, Philip Stone. Fred pushed on, and under 'F' he found a bulging file with Father Benjamin's name on it. With trembling hands, he pulled it out and opened it.

The first documents were Father Benjamin's medical records – various references to minor ailments – but behind them were accounts of around forty deliveries Dr Jacobson had attended, most of which appeared to have ended in stillbirths, and all of which had taken place at St Margaret's.

Desperate as he was to give the documents the attention they deserved, his thumping heart reminded Fred that he didn't have the luxury of time. As he sped through as many as he could, he came to a small file at the back held together with a flimsy paper clip. From Dr Jacobson's scribbled notes, it seemed that he had attended children as young as three or four at St Margaret's with fever, neck pain, stiffness, spasms, vomiting, listlessness and seizures. Who were these children? As far as Fred knew, St Margaret's was a mother-and-baby home where mothers gave birth to babies who were then adopted.

Sally Jacobson's voice came echoing up the stairs. 'Fred?' Smashing his knee against the desk, Fred rushed to the doorway and saw her hammering on the bathroom door below.

Hands shaking, he removed the letter from the Mercer file, folded it in half and pushed it down the back of his trousers. Then he closed the main file and returned it to the cabinet as fast as he could. Checking that all was as he had found it, he snuck out of the study and ran down the stairs.

'Thanks so much, Sally, it's been lovely to meet you,' he said airily, heading for the front door.

'What were you doing up there?' she asked, flushed with anger.

'Using the bathroom,' said Fred hastily, desperate now to escape. 'Bye, Sally, give my regards to your daughters.' He turned the front door handle, relieved that it wasn't locked, let himself out and hurried down the path to the road.

Once he was safely back in his car, he pulled out his phone. He was about to call Sam and update her on his chat with Sally Jacobson when a black Jaguar passed him. A woman with long grey hair was at the wheel. Fred recognised her immediately, but it was several seconds before it sank in: Kitty Cannon. He knew from reading the cuttings on George Cannon's accident that the road he was parked on, Preston Road, led to St Margaret's.

Fred swung his car around and began to follow her.

As he drove away, he looked in his rear-view mirror to see Sally Jacobson glaring at him stony-faced from her open front door.

Chapter Thirty-Eight

Saturday 18 December 1976

Dr Edward Jacobson woke with a jolt at the sound of the doorbell.

For a moment he sat motionless in the dark, trying to orientate himself as the outside light triggered by the visitor at the door shone onto the sea of archive boxes carpeting the floor. The carriage clock on his desk told him it was past six. Sally hadn't mentioned anyone coming over; who would turn up unannounced?

He shivered. The room felt cold. Condensation had built up on the window while he was asleep, and for some reason the heating hadn't clicked on. He had no idea what time he'd fallen asleep or why his wife hadn't woken him. He held his breath and listened for her, but the house was completely silent.

Bang, bang, bang. Whoever it was had moved on from the bell and was trying the door knocker. They weren't giving up; he'd need to go down himself and answer it. He eased his stiff frame forward and pushed himself up from his chair, letting out a groan of discomfort as he did so. His neck ached from sleeping awkwardly and his joints had seized up from sitting still for so long. He went over to the window and looked down onto a row of bobble hats and song sheets waiting at his front door. Carol singers. He could hear them talking amongst themselves: 'The lights aren't on . . . Sally said they'd be here . . . give it one last try.' One of them stepped back to look up at the window and Edward pulled back out of sight. He didn't want to stand on the doorstep in the freezing cold and listen to the local choir warble at him. He had to put up with enough of that at church.

Bang. One last try, then eventually the crunch of icy gravel underfoot and they were gone.

He sighed heavily and lifted his spectacles to rub his eyes. It had been an unrelenting week. A winter flu epidemic in the village had meant sixteen-hour days at the surgery, after which he'd come home every night to increasingly urgent messages from Father Benjamin. He'd managed to avoid him for the first few days, but when the priest had resorted to calling in the middle of the night, Edward had picked up the phone in case it was one of his daughters.

'I hope you are managing to get through the files I left for you last week.' His voice was curt.

'Yes, I'm doing my best, but I could go to prison for tampering with these. They're harrowing reading to say the least.'

Father Benjamin let out a heavy sigh. 'Well, hopefully you will see to it that they become more digestible,' he said menacingly. 'So that we can all sleep easier in our beds.'

'I warned you about these records at the time, Father, that they could be open to scrutiny in the future.' Edward's chest had tightened with anxiety.

'The parish had no obligation to show any of its records before now,' Father Benjamin had snapped. 'We couldn't have foreseen the adoption laws changing to allow those women access to them – so now you need to provide more palatable explanations of what happened to their children.'

'How?' He had recalled the contents of some of the faded death certificates Father Benjamin had unloaded from his car. 'How do you expect me to paint a better picture of . . . psychotic episodes, seizures and chronic neglect?'

'I don't know, Edward, you wrote them,' the priest had replied. 'Destroy the worst of them, and come up with plausible explanations for the rest. You've done very well out of St Margaret's, so I suggest you find us a way out of this. As I said, if any of it comes out, I'll see to it that your involvement does not go unnoticed.'

After Father Benjamin had hung up on him, Edward hadn't slept. He had desperately wanted to wake his wife to share his concerns, but any mention of St Margaret's was always met with silent disapproval. Despite the fact that the money Father Benjamin gave him for referring pregnant single girls paid for their daughters' education, her mother's care home and their large and comfortable house, Sally chose not to dent her clear conscience with thoughts of the place.

Edward was suddenly jolted back to the present by the faint sound of a dog yelping outside, and saw that Honey's bed was empty. He had no idea where his constant companion had got to; he couldn't remember a time she hadn't come up to see him after her dinner. Perhaps Sally had taken her for a walk to see a friend in the village. But he would have heard her returning from her Christmas shopping earlier in the day; the familiar sounds of keys clattering, cupboards banging and the dog barking for her dinner would have woken him. Even if Sally was still sulking over Father Benjamin's visit, she'd have let him know where she was going. Maybe something had happened to her, or to one of the girls, and she'd left the house in a panic.

'Sally?' he called out as he made his way down the corridor towards the stairs. 'Where are you?'

After walking stiffly down the stairs he reached the hallway. The slate floor was uncomfortably cold as he walked barefoot across it to the kitchen, grumbling to himself as he went. Where in heaven's name were they? As he reached the back door, he heard the dog yelping again. He spun his head around in response. Was that Honey?

Concern began to drown out the irritation that had been brewing inside him. He sat down on a kitchen chair and pulled his wellington boots over his bare feet. Perhaps his wife had fallen in the garden somewhere and Honey was trying to get his attention. He opened the hall cupboard and scrabbled through the pile of coats for his Barbour, sending a basket of umbrellas clattering to the floor. Then he wrenched open the back door, gasping at the shock of the freezing-cold wind, and ventured into the garden.

The gravel beneath his feet crackled and crunched and the sound of the carol singers in the grounds of the neighbouring house drifted over to him.

'Honey?' he shouted as he headed for the fence. The winter sunlight had faded completely and the picturesque whiteout from the morning had disappeared entirely so that Edward found himself drowning in blackness. The ground underfoot had turned to a murky sludge and dark clouds threatened more snow. He ploughed on, using the fence to steady him through the rockery, hedgerow and conifers. As he went past the rose bushes, he pricked his hand on the thorns of a fat stem.

'Sally? Are you out here?' he shouted, wincing as a warm trickle of blood slid down the back of his hand. 'Honey!'

The numbness in his feet began to travel up his legs, making it increasingly hard to walk on the uneven ground. He stumbled at every other step, shouting and whistling for Honey until he came to his favourite oak tree. He stopped for a moment to lean on it and unsettled a barn owl above him, which let out a long, harsh scream. Edward craned his neck, looking up through the bare, claw-like branches to see a pair of black eyes blinking down at him. They stared at each other briefly, then the owl let out another piercing scream before taking off, dislodging a clump of snow from its perch. Edward startled at the noise and took a step back to avoid the falling snow, catching his foot on a root. Once he had lost his balance, it was impossible to right himself. He grabbed at the air but his feet were frozen and slow to respond, and as he went down, he instinctively put out a hand to break his fall.

As soon as his palm hit the ground, a shooting pain splintered up his arm into his shoulder. He let out a roar and rolled over onto his side, clutching his arm and sucking in gulps of air to try and cope with the pain. He'd dislocated his shoulder as a teenager and he knew instinctively that he'd done it again. He reached under his jacket and felt his shoulder: the ball joint had come out of its socket and was protruding from his arm.

He didn't dare to move: the pain would be too much to bear if he did. But he was soaking wet now from rolling on the ground, and snow had seeped into the neck of his coat and down his back. He was shaking with the cold and the shock. He had to get up; if he didn't, he'd freeze to death within minutes.

'Hello? Can anyone hear me?!' he called out. He knew he was alone, that the carol singers would be long gone, but the thought that no one would come to help was unbearable.

He lay in the cold for another minute, panting through the pain. He needed to move; he couldn't stay here. He tried to gather his thoughts and calm himself. He had no choice: he had to ignore the pain and pull himself up. He was not far from the house: the porch light had come on and he could see it from where he lay. If he could make it back there, he could call an ambulance.

He was a bloody fool. He was tired and upset from his week; he shouldn't have come outside. That yelp couldn't have been Honey. It must have been another dog, or even his imagination. She wasn't out here; nobody was. When he got to the hospital, they would track down his wife. She and Honey would be together somewhere. He just needed to pull himself up using the tree roots and get back to the house quickly.

As he rolled himself over, teeth gritted, he suddenly heard the distinctive sound of Honey whining nearby. Panic gripped him. He had been right after all. She was out here in the freezing cold and she was trapped. He fumbled at the roots around him for one big enough to pull himself up with. Nothing. Using his heels, he pushed himself through the slush, grabbing in the dark until he found the fat root he had tripped over. Letting out a sob, he eased himself over, clutching it in his freezing hands, and heaved himself up onto one knee, then the other, until eventually he was standing.

He took a moment to steady himself, then, trying to ignore the intense lure of the house, headed in the direction of Honey's cry. He couldn't just leave her out here; she could freeze to death. Clutching his arm, dizzy from the pain, he began to shout her name again, desperate for her to let him know where she was. His eyes fell on the pool house. Walking as fast as his trembling legs would allow, he eventually reached it, and cupped his hand to the steamed-up window. For a moment there was nothing – the garden had fallen completely silent – then finally he heard a faint whimper coming from inside.

'Honey?' He rushed towards the door. The pain from his shoulder shot through his arm so violently that tears filled his eyes. But the image of his beloved spaniel in distress spurred him on. 'Honey, hang on, I'm coming.'

He pushed the handle down hard but the door remained steadfastly shut. He rattled at it in frustration, kicking at it frantically, but it was locked. They keys were back at the house; it would take for ever to get back there in his state. Honey let out another faint yelp and he slammed at the door with his good hand. If she was in the pool, she could be drowning. He looked around for something that might help, and picked up a rock. Lifting his arm as high as he could, he hurled it at the door, shattering one of the panes of glass, then pushed his hand through the jagged hole and reached inside to turn the lock. *Click.* He was into the warm room.

'Honey? Honey, are you in here?' he shouted, turning on the light and pacing round the pool in his clumsy boots, clinging to his injured arm.

A panicked yelp came from under the pool cover, and Edward saw something moving.

'Hang on, Honey, I'm coming.' He staggered towards her, slipping twice on his way. He could see her wet paws clawing desperately at the side of the pool. The cover was tied down tight and he struggled with one arm to undo it and pull it back. Eventually a small, sodden brown face appeared, the dog's eyes bulging and terrified. He let out a choked cry. 'Honey! What the hell are you doing in there?'

The dog was clearly in a state of utter exhaustion, scrabbling at the side of the pool as Edward leant in to pull her out.

It was then that he heard footsteps behind him, but before he could even turn his head, he had been pushed with such force that he had no chance of keeping his balance and toppled into the pool.

Water filled his ears and eyes and mouth as he went under. With only one arm, it was a huge struggle to kick his body to the surface again, every movement like a knife twisting in his shoulder. When finally he reached the surface, coughing and choking, he grabbed for the side, looking around desperately for whoever had pushed him. Feet appeared at ground level in front of his eyes, flat black leather boots, soaked through from the water, but when he looked up, the pool cover was being lowered over his head, and though he tried to push it up again, he had no strength.

'Please . . . no,' he spluttered. 'Stop, what are you doing?'

He tried to go on kicking, but the pain in his arm made any movement excruciating and he had no energy left after his fall. Honey was still in the water with him, clawing at his bad arm, and soon her panic began to rub off on him as he tried to keep his head above the surface. But the cover continued to press down on him, and now only one corner was open. He tried to grip the side of the pool with his numb fingers.

'Hang on, Honey,' he said. 'We'll get out of here. Just

'hang on.' He was retching water as Honey clambered onto his dislocated shoulder, scrambling up and slipping down his arm. He'd never known pain like it in his life.

Suddenly a hand plunged into the water, dragging the panicked spaniel out, then in one final movement the last corner of the pool cover was pulled over Edward's head.

He began to beat at the vinyl. He couldn't control the panic now and began to sob uncontrollably. It was Christmas in a week; images of his girls running down the stairs on Christmas morning filled his mind. Now this Christmas, and every one after it, would be ruined for his wife and his daughters. He cried out their names, screaming for Sally with all the strength he had left in him, clawing at the cover until his fingers started to bleed, turning the water red.

He slipped under, fighting it at first: up and down, sink and swim, sink and swim. Sink. Sink and swim. Sink . . . hold your breath, fight for your girls, fight.

Don't do this to them, hold your breath, go back up for more air.

Sink.

Sink.

His lungs began to take in water, sheer terror forcing him back up to the surface to be faced again with the thick, impenetrable cover as he prayed and prayed that Sally would come and find him.

And then the lights went out.

Terror like nothing he had ever experienced in his life engulfed him. No one would know he was here, for hours, days maybe. They would find his swollen body eventually, floating in the water.

His mind raced to the records on the floor of his study.

That was what Sally would find when she got home and came looking for him. She would call out for him and then head up to his study, and find the boxes and boxes of death records. The last one he had read forever etched in his mind: *24 years of age, two-day protracted labour. Breech birth, episiotomy. Haemorrhage. Mother deceased. Twin infants survived.*

As he sank under the water again, he could hear Mother Carlin's voice: 'Their pain is part of the punishment, Doctor. If they don't suffer, they don't learn. We'll call you if we need you.'

He had tried to help. It wasn't his fault; there was nothing he could have done. As he sucked in his last breaths, Dr Jacobson listened to his beloved spaniel scratching at the pool-house door. He struggled for a few seconds more, coughing out Sally's name as their wedding song began to play over and over in his head . . . *Dream a little dream of me.*

Chapter Thirty-Nine

Monday 6 February 2017

Kitty Cannon looked at the out-of-order sign on the lifts of the Whitehawk Estate, then craned her neck up to the tenth floor.

As she started her climb in the aromatic stairwell, she remembered the first day she had set eyes on the eleven-year-old Annabel at Brighton Grammar School. It was the first day of the autumn term of her upper-sixth year and she had heard a commotion in the playground and looked over. A group of first years were in a circle, around what or whom she did not know. Normally she wouldn't have cared, but something about the intensity of it had made her take notice. The jeers were particularly loud, the group unusually large.

So she had jumped down from the wall on which she was sitting, and slowly walked over to the noisy scene. As she got closer, the chanting became audible: 'Ginger nut, ginger nut, get back in the biscuit tin.'

As soon as Kitty came near them, a few of them looked round and stopped what they were doing. Most of the sixth-form girls would cause a first year to stop and take notice, but Kitty was a particularly imposing sight: tall, with poker-straight raven-black hair, Mediterranean skin and dark-brown eyes that glared at the unfolding scene.

A first-year girl was in the middle of the circle, curled up into a ball with her hands over her head as if she had long since given up trying to escape and was protecting herself as best she could against whatever was coming next. Her hair was indeed a sight to behold, long, curly and fiery red. Most of those in the circle fell silent one by one as Kitty stood over them, but a scrawny, mean-faced boy with dirty fingernails and scuffed trousers was too high on the adrenaline of pursuing his prey to have noticed her. He suddenly pulled back his leg, as if he were about to kick the girl like a football on a pitch. As he started to swing it forward, Kitty stepped closer and pushed him hard.

He had not seen her coming, so was caught off balance and didn't have time to put his arms out to save himself. Just before he hit the ground, he managed to get his hand between himself and the concrete, and his entire weight crashed onto his wrist resulting in a strange cracking sound. The group went completely silent, the whole mood entirely changed with that one gesture: the hunter become the hunted. Then the boy looked up at Kitty with a look of bewilderment in his eyes and started to scream.

Kitty had ignored him, walking over to his victim and holding out her hand to pull her up. As the eleven-year-old girl uncurled herself and looked up at her, Kitty's blood had run cold. She knew instinctively that this was Rose, Ivy's baby. She couldn't have looked more like her. As Kitty stood in stunned silence, the girl had smiled shyly, wiped her nose with the back of her hand and run off in the direction of the bell for lessons.

In the weeks that followed, Kitty discovered that her gut instinct – that the red-headed, blue-eyed girl was Ivy's daughter – was right. She was adopted, she told Kitty, and not only that, she was miserable. As they walked side by side on their way home, Kitty taking a huge detour every day in order to be with her, Annabel Rose slowly revealed her unhappiness. She tried so hard to be a good daughter, but nothing was ever good enough for her parents, and she felt constantly like a square peg trying to force herself into a round hole.

She had reminded Kitty of Ivy so much, the memories that now returned felt so vivid, it was as if Ivy had found a way back to her. When Annabel smiled in the same way that Ivy had, all in her eyes with her mouth closed; when she played with her hair when she was unsure of herself; when she turned her head and her long red corkscrew curls fell in front of her eyes. It could have been Ivy herself.

Of course, none of this she could share with Annabel. She had never been able to admit the truth to anyone, and it ate away at her. But what she did share was something they both felt. Loneliness, and an overwhelming grief they carried with them every day for the people they loved and had never known. Kitty for her twin sister and Annabel for her birth mother.

Over the weeks and months that followed, Kitty showed Annabel a side of her character that she had never revealed to anyone. Slowly and carefully at first, she had tested the water. Waiting for Annabel to reject her as everyone in her life had done up until that point, she told her the story she had told her father: that she had seen Elvira behind a gravestone, that Elvira had taken her to an outhouse, that she had been too scared to leave. That Elvira had died because Kitty had got lost finding help.

Annabel had listened and comforted her, and confessed

that she pined for the woman who had given birth to her. She thought of her birth mother often. She craved knowing who she truly was and why she had chosen to give her up. And so together they had found Maude. And that was when it had all begun to unravel.

Kitty had expected to sit in the background at Maude Jenkins' house, to be there for Annabel as she met her grandmother for the first time, but instead she had felt herself shaking with hatred as soon as the old lady answered the door.

In the box of Ivy's things had been a bundle of letters, and despite the old lady's protests, she had sat in the corner and read them.

She remembered very little after that, other than telling Ivy's mother that it was her fault her daughter was dead. She had blurred memories of dragging Annabel out into the street, giving her Ivy's letters and telling her to read them. Maude should have rescued Ivy, Kitty remembered telling Annabel Rose as she clutched her by the shoulders, and that if Annabel ever saw Maude again, she'd kill her. She didn't recall getting home that night, but when she woke in the morning, it was with a feeling of overwhelming panic.

She waited for Annabel at the school gates as usual the following morning, but she wasn't there. In the weeks that followed, Kitty tried to talk to her, but Annabel shut her out. There was a coldness behind her eyes, an emptiness in her smile, and Kitty felt as if she had lost Ivy all over again.

She tried to stay away, but she felt as if her heart were breaking in two, and her nightmares, from which she had experienced some respite since meeting Annabel, returned with a vengeance.

At two o'clock one morning, she had walked round to Annabel's house and knocked on the door. Annabel's adoptive father had answered in a highly agitated state.

'I'm sorry to wake you, Mr Creed, but I need to see Annabel.' Kitty had tried to smile at the man, to soften the dislike radiating from him.

'This is getting out of hand. I'm not sure why a girl so much older than my daughter would take such an interest in her, but Annabel hasn't stopped crying for a week and I suspect it is something to do with you.'

'Please, I just need to talk to her, and explain.' Kitty had felt the tears coming, and angrily brushed them away.

'Get away from here, and if I find out you've been bothering my daughter again, I shall call the police.' He was flushed red with fury but his skin was white as he had stood with his boney fingers pressed into his hips, his narrow ankles sticking out from the bottom of his silk pyjamas.

'She's not your daughter,' Kitty spat. 'You stole her. And she hates you for it.'

As she had walked away from the house, she had turned and looked up to Annabel's bedroom, where the young girl stood at the window looking so much like Ivy it was as if she had come back to life.

Over the following weeks, the rejection began to take hold of Kitty. She felt as if she was losing her mind. The letters haunted her; a desire to hurt those responsible for Ivy's death became overwhelming. Violent images ran repeatedly through her mind, following her around day and night like a silent film. No words, only pictures, of her taking revenge for Ivy's life.

Visits to her mother in hospital, once a part of her daily

routine, became an unbearable grind and one that she started to dread from the second she woke up. The smell of death in the corridors, the weak smiles of the nurses, Helena lying in her bed, swollen and useless. She was tired of the ugliness of it, the tubes, the pain, the never-ending, drawn-out death of the woman who was ultimately responsible for her being abandoned at St Margaret's.

She had spoken to her so many times about Elvira, but it was obvious from Helena's clipped, short answers, from the way she turned her head away and changed the subject, that she felt no remorse.

Kitty was tired of being beholden to a woman who didn't care for her.

She was tired of waiting for her mother to die.

She needed to be free to focus.

Chapter Forty

Wednesday 3 July 1968

Helena Cannon came to with a start. Her small hospital room was dark, save for the narrow beam her bedside lamp cast onto her sweat-soaked pillow. It was unusually hot for July, and the room was stifling, even though the sun had recently set. The thick humidity from the day lingered in the air. She could hear the faint sound of babies crying on the maternity ward below, but other than that, all was silent.

Helena's dialysis machine had apparently long since finished its work. Its dials were still and in the dim light the machine had the appearance of a robot whose eyes were watching her. The night nurse had been very slack of late: rarely there to unhook her from the tubes when they finished and wheel her back to the ward. Her nightie and bed sheets were soaked with sweat, in stark contrast to her mouth, which was dry as a desert storm.

A wave of nausea hit her as she turned her head to the window, but it remained steadfastly shut despite her repeated pleas to the nurses to open it. Though her body was being assessed, cannulated, catheterised and injected seemingly without respite, her mind did not appear to be of interest to any of the doctors having endless conversations over her head. She tried to be patient, knowing there were others more in need than her, but she was desperate to feel heard to keep herself from going insane. She dreaded her daily visits to the dialysis room. Chained to the churning machine day after day, she felt the walls closing in. Before long, all four walls would be pressed up against her swollen limbs, the ceiling of her coffin lowered and its catches shut into place: *click, clunk*.

She looked at the alarm clock on the bedside table to find out how long she had been asleep, but its face was turned away. It was impossible to reach while she was still hooked up to the machine, as was the red call button, which she stared at longingly. Her crawling skin and increasing need to vomit led her to believe she had slept more than the allotted hour between blood-pressure checks. Either that or she had been too exhausted to stir from her increasingly harrowing dreams. Dreams of George that were so real, she could touch him, smell him. Their life before all the pain and the hospital appointments and the endless needles, when they were happy and madly in love. Dreams so vivid that when she woke, she felt as if she had lost him all over again.

As she lay in her bed on the ward, trying to shake the fresh grief from her groggy head, she would watch with gut-wrenching jealousy as husbands came and went, collecting their mended wives, happy that their one-off visit to the hospital was behind them and all was well with the world again.

She wanted to scream at them: 'That should be George and me, we should be growing old together.'

He had been dead for over seven years, and they had lied: it didn't get easier. All that the passing of time meant was that friends stopped asking, stopped mentioning George for fear her tears would start again. She knew everyone expected her to have moved on. Moved on to what? Time hadn't healed; her grief had just slowly evolved into a rage that had stayed trapped in the pit of her stomach like an unexploded bomb.

Her eyes scanned the room for anything that could help her reach the call button, and fell on a fan on the counter that Kitty had brought to cool her down during the long dialysis sessions. It had only been a few hours, but she missed her daughter desperately. If Kitty were there, she would have gone to find someone, chastised the nurses, made sure they returned her mother safely to her bed on the ward.

Helena lay in the dimly lit room, thinking about Kitty. She had been subdued of late, asking her about Elvira again. Helena was so tired of the subject, so tired of being made to feel bad. It had taken an enormous amount of forgiveness to allow George to bring even one of the twins home from St Margaret's, and the choice of which it should be was obvious. Elvira had struggled to breathe when she was born, Father Benjamin had said himself that she had needed special care as a baby which George wouldn't have been able to give her. It was hard enough to bring up one baby on his own.

'Did you ever think about Elvira when I was growing up?' Kitty had asked that morning, her eyes stony as they always were when she talked about her sister. 'I just need to know if you cared about her at all.'

The room spun and Helena found herself swallowing the vomit rising in her throat. At that moment she had just wanted Kitty to leave, but now that she had gone, she was desperate for her to come back.

'Nurse,' she croaked. Her liquids were being kept as low

as her body could endure to stop further build-up of fluid in her lungs and legs, but cutting back day after day on the water she was allowed, so that her mouth was so dry she could hardly speak, was having little effect. She was still barely able to catch her breath, and her legs continued to swell so that now they were impossible to move and no longer looked like hers, the skin so stretched and raw it felt as if it would tear at the slightest pressure.

Helena's ears throbbed with the silence, and the slightest movement made her nausea return in forceful waves. Soon she would vomit, she wouldn't be able to stop it, and when she did, her dehydration levels would become desperately low. *Stay calm, someone will come soon.* She was thirsty, so thirsty: they hadn't given her any water since the small cup at breakfast, and she was sweating profusely. The itching on her skin had escalated to a new level; she felt as if the insects crawling on it had burrowed down to her bones. However much she tore at her skin, there was no way for her to reach them.

Suddenly, and without warning, liquid filled her mouth and she began to vomit, letting out a sob as it poured down her front, the acid burning her throat.

Barely able to lift her hand to wipe her mouth, she prayed for the sound of anyone in the corridor. But there was nothing; just her own heart throbbing in her chest. She looked down at the thick needle lodged in her arm. She couldn't remove it herself; she was completely trapped.

As she lay fighting the second wave of nausea, she heard the faint cries of the babies again on the maternity ward below. She often heard them crying in the night. Some nights the screams of a woman in the throes of labour would travel up through the floor, louder and louder as the hours went on. Then finally silence, followed by the sound of a newborn's cry.

To most it was the sweetest of sounds, but to Helena it was like sharp nails down a blackboard. An unwanted reminder of the hundreds of ashen-faced girls who had knocked on Mother Carlin's office door. Girls who had sat in silence watching her pen scratch the surface of the contract that would seal the final details of their baby's fate. And then she would give her speech about it being for the best, and the sensible ones would sign. Others put up more of a fight, but they all gave in eventually, thanks to Mother Carlin's powers of persuasion.

Helena couldn't begin to imagine the agony of giving up a child; the pain of not being able to bear one of her own was excruciating enough. And the girls just kept on coming, younger and younger, paler and thinner. She had tried so many times to stop, to hand the job over to someone else, but Father Benjamin had insisted she continue. She had a knack with the girls, he said; they trusted her. She was a young trainee solicitor in a man's world, and she didn't want to get fired from her first job.

Suddenly she heard the sound of a key turning. She had no idea why the door was locked: perhaps she'd been forgotten and this was one of the cleaning staff. It didn't matter why she'd been left; for now, all that mattered was that she had been found. She felt a flood of overwhelming relief as the door creaked open and the light from the corridor momentarily lit up the room. The head of her bed had its back to the door, so she couldn't see who it was that had entered, but she could hear them moving around behind her.

'Hello?' she croaked, dried vomit cracking at the sides of her lips.

The person didn't say a word. Helena listened to their shoes on the floor, waiting for them to appear by her bed and comfort her.

'Hello?' She strained her voice, but only a whisper came out. 'Please answer me. For God's sake help me.'

Still nothing as the person stood completely still somewhere behind her.

'What are you doing?' Helena pleaded. 'I can't move. Please help me.'

As she twisted her head, desperately trying to see who was in the room with her, she felt warm breath on her neck and looked down to see a hand reach out for the light next to her bed and switch it off. Immediately the room was plunged into darkness.

She felt a sudden tug at the needle in her arm and a shooting pain soared up her hand. She gasped with the shock of it, trying to lift her other arm to feel what had happened. Tears stung her eyes as her fingers fell upon the torn tape around the needle to her fistula, which was now dislodged.

As her swollen fingers fumbled clumsily in a panic, she tried her best to push the needle back in but only managed to dislodge it still further. She let out a silent scream from the agony of her bruised skin tearing around it. Shoes clicked across the floor, the door quickly opened and then closed again. Helena felt liquid running down her hand and over her swollen fingers, forming in a pool underneath her palm.

Blood: suddenly so much blood. She pushed as hard as

she could on the hole where her fistula had been, but she knew it had been fitted directly to an artery and she was haemorrhaging uncontrollably.

As the pool of blood became bigger and bigger, it poured over the edge of the bed and dripped onto the floor below. Helena started to sob, pleading for someone to help but knowing that her fading voice would never be heard at the end of the long corridor. Weak and disoriented, she reached out for the call button, but her arm was so heavy it barely responded. Desperately she pushed the bedside lamp over, hoping it would smash to the floor and raise the alarm, but it just tipped onto its side, rolling backwards and forwards out of her reach. Nausea built up in waves and she was sick again, this time over the side of the bed as she slumped over, unable to support herself any longer.

As the seconds ticked by, the room began to spin, and images of George flashed in her mind's eye. The night of their first date, her yellow dress, dancing on the beach under the stars, sun-kissed from the sweet summer sunshine, melting into him. She could still smell the salt in the sea air.

She tried to roll over, knowing the fall from her bed might kill her, yet thinking perhaps the noise of it would bring someone running. But her swollen legs were too heavy: she heaved and sobbed and begged, but soon she was too dizzy and weak to continue. The room started to spin out of control, over and over, round and round so that she felt it would never stop.

'Help me, George,' she cried as she clung to her soaking sheets, praying that he would be on the other side waiting for her.

A heavy pain began to move down one side of her body: her leg, her arm, and then her face, a creeping paralysis. Then she could no longer move at all.

And as she closed her eyes and cried pitifully, waiting for the end, she prayed to God over and over to forgive her.

Forgive me, please, dear Lord.

Forgive me for my sins.

Chapter Forty-One

Monday 6 February 2017

Kitty walked slowly along the graffiti-covered hallway towards Annabel Rose's flat, the sound of televisions blaring and babies crying coming from under the front doors she passed. Eventually she reached number 117 and looked up and down the corridor before pressing the bell.

No answer. Immediately she felt a rush of irritation. She tugged her jacket straight and took a breath. She had made a promise to herself to stay calm. She didn't know Annabel's side of the story and she needed to hear it before she got herself in a state. She hadn't slept, it had already been a very difficult morning, and she needed to stay composed. She reached out her finger, and pressed the bell again. This time she heard movement from inside. 'Hold on a minute,' said a familiar voice. Kitty clasped her hands in front of her and waited.

When the door opened, Annabel had a smile on her face. Almost immediately, recognition dawned in her eyes and her expression changed. Kitty waited patiently for the fake niceties to kick in, her foot already slightly across the threshold in case Annabel tried to slam the door shut.

'My goodness, Kitty, I didn't know . . . I mean, I didn't expect to see you here,' said Annabel, slowly wiping what looked like flour from her hands onto her apron and turning a deep shade of red. 'It's been such a long time.'

She looked dreadful, thought Kitty. Her skin was pale and her enormous clothes hugged the fat bloating from every crease of her skin. Despite the fact that Kitty was six years her senior, Annabel looked ten years older than her. She must have put on forty pounds since Kitty had last seen her, almost fifty years ago. Her hair was greasy and scraped back from her round, lined face, and she stood awkwardly as if her hip or leg was hurting her. Kitty stared at her, anger simmering at the thought of her lazy, ineffectual life. Why did Annabel care so little about what had happened to her own mother? Why had it been up to Kitty to make it right? She felt a knot of rage in her stomach, pulsing, ready to explode.

'Well, are you going to invite me in?'

Annabel glanced along the corridor, then down to Kitty's foot positioned just across the doorway. Kitty waited, her hands clenched in front of her. Her chest tightened as the anger intensified. Annabel's dithering indecision was as infuriating as ever. Kitty wanted to slap her. Although she had suspected that Annabel wouldn't be pleased to see her, there had still been the tiniest flame of hope that despite everything that had happened between them, there was still love there. That after all they had shared, and all Kitty had done for her, their friendship would prevail. Clearly not.

As Annabel continued to dither, Kitty heard voices coming along the corridor and stepped forward so that she was over the threshold. 'Let me in, Annabel, for God's sake,' she hissed.

Nana stepped back, wincing as her hip jarred. Kitty wafted past, the distinctive smell of Chanel No. 5 catching in the back of Nana's throat and making her gag. She closed her eyes, praying Emma wouldn't appear; as she hobbled past the little girl's room, she pulled the door closed quietly, her hands shaking on the handle as she did so.

When Kitty reached the lounge, she stopped and scanned the room, a look of disdain on her face. The television was on, the daytime television presenters carrying on in their usual sycophantic fashion. The gas fire was ablaze, but the room was cold, and newspapers, blankets and children's toys littered the floor. Nana stood in the doorway behind her in silence, her mind racing, too overwhelmed to manage fake niceties. She had to get Kitty out before Emma woke up.

'How can I help you, Kitty?' she asked, moving from one foot to the other. Her hip was throbbing mercilessly. She looked at the clock on the mantelpiece. Sam had phoned at six, and said she would be home by eleven; it was now past midday. Surely she couldn't be much longer. It was a miracle Emma was having a nap – she rarely did any more – but she was poorly and had been up in the night. *Sleep, my angel, please sleep.*

'I see you've fulfilled your potential,' said Kitty, looking around at the array of newspaper cuttings and photographs.

'It's home and I like it,' said Nana. 'What do you want, Kitty?' Her voice shook slightly, but as Kitty turned back to her, she looked her firmly in the eye.

Kitty flicked her head and crossed her arms. 'Why have you been talking to your granddaughter about me?'

'I haven't,' said Nana, looking over at the phone by her rocking chair. 'I haven't spoken a word to her about any of it. She found Ivy's letters.'

'Because you left them somewhere for her to find,' said Kitty, moving closer. 'Have you been back to see Maude?'

'No. I have moved on, and you should too,' said Nana, leaning against the chair next to her.

'I don't have that luxury. One of us had to do something, and you deserted me.'

'I didn't desert you, Kitty. We were kids, we grew apart.'

'You turned your back on me when it mattered most. They're tearing St Margaret's down tomorrow; if it wasn't for me, they would all have got away with what they did.'

'What do you mean, Kitty?'

'You've always been a coward. They killed your mother, they killed my sister. Why should they die warm and contented in their beds?'

Nana started to feel frightened. 'Kitty, please, Sam will be back in a minute, we can all talk about this. You're right, I'm a coward. I've always been too afraid, but now that you're here, we can tell her, we can help you.'

'You don't care about me. You abandoned me like they all did. I looked after you, I loved you.'

'I loved you too, Kitty. But you made it so hard. I didn't want to live my life full of hate.'

Nana walked around the chair and sat on it. She was short of breath, and struggling. She looked over to Kitty, tears in her eyes. 'I'm not well, Kitty, my heart isn't strong.'

'Your heart is weak because you are weak.'

Emma appeared in the doorway behind Kitty, and the room started to spin. Nana felt a pain in her arm. 'Don't hurt her, Kitty, please don't hurt her.'

'Ah, so now you care,' said Kitty, standing over her.

323

Nana was slumped in her chair, the colour in her cheeks completely gone. Emma rushed to put her arms around her.

'Nana's just tired.' Kitty smiled at the little girl. 'Shall we go out and let her sleep? We can play hide-and-seek. Would you like that?'

Emma nodded. Kitty took her hand and the two of them left the apartment, closing the door behind them.

Chapter Forty-Two

Monday 6 February 2017

Elvira Cannon pulled up outside St Margaret's, switched off the engine and turned to the little girl sitting in the back seat.

'Do you want to see where Nana was born?' she said.

Emma pulled the lollipop from her mouth and nodded. Elvira climbed out of the car and opened the little girl's door, then walked round to the boot and took out a petrol can and a torch, before locking the car and taking Emma's hand.

It was two o'clock and the light was already fading as they pushed their way through the hole in the fence. Elvira could see two men chatting over by the house.

'Shall we play hide-and-seek?' she said to the little girl by her side.

Emma nodded, looking up at her with her big blue eyes. Her hair was strawberry blond, much less red than Sam's and Ivy's. Ivy was fading, her light was going out. Soon she would be completely forgotten. They all would.

'I'll count to ten and you hide behind one of those big stones,' whispered Elvira, looking over to the men, who were still deep in conversation. 'One, two, three . . .'

The little girl ran towards the biggest gravestone, giggling, as Elvira lugged the can of petrol along, looking for the trapdoor that led to the house. Eventually she found it, kicking away the undergrowth and placing the heavy canister beside it. She pulled the key from her pocket and fitted it into the lock. It was stiff at first, full of earth and debris, which she had to pull at with her fingers. But eventually it turned – *clunk* – and she pulled up the trap door that hadn't been opened in decades. The smell emitting from the tunnel below her made her turn her head away. When she looked back she saw Emma, sticking her head out from behind a gravestone, waving to get her attention.

The image of her chilled her blood; it was a freezing cold afternoon, the fading light just as it had been on that day in 1959 when she had first caught Kitty's attention.

Sixty years later and she was still trapped in that moment. She felt just as desperate, just as lonely, just the same. Nothing she did was ever going to change the wretchedness.

Chapter Forty-Three

Sunday 15 February 1959

Elvira Cannon crouched behind the headstone in the graveyard of Preston church and watched the girl in the red duffel coat with the same face as hers.

She knew she didn't have long, that soon the girl would leave again on the bus and then her chance would be gone. She had been waiting in the snow all day, after hiding in the outhouse for two nights; she knew she couldn't last much longer. She couldn't feel her feet or hands and she was so hungry that her belly had stopped begging her for food.

Her body shaking from the freezing cold taking hold of every part of her, she waited until the little girl was looking over in her direction, then poked her head out from behind the headstone and beckoned her over.

At first she didn't know if she had seen her. She darted back into her hiding place, unable to control her panicked breathing, terrified that she would be spotted by someone other than her twin. Then through the silence she heard the crunch of snow, footsteps coming closer and closer and eventually stopping in the space next to her.

Her instinct had been to grab her. Grab her and run, fast, behind the church and across the fields beyond it, to the outhouse that backed onto the grounds of St Margaret's.

When they were safely inside, they had stopped. Still holding hands, they had stared at each other, panting and trying to catch their breath.

'Who are you?' said Kitty, smiling gently as if she already knew.

'I'm Elvira, I'm your twin,' Elvira had said, returning Kitty's smile though every part of her hurt.

'I don't understand,' said Kitty. 'How can that be?'

'We were born at St Margaret's. Our father took you home and I was adopted but they sent me back. Do you have any food?' Elvira asked.

Kitty reached into the pocket of her red coat, and pulled out the shiny green apple she had been saving for the bus home. 'Here.'

'Thank you,' said Elvira, her eyes lighting up as if it were a table full of food. She snatched it and sat on the floor to eat it hungrily.

Kitty looked down at her sister's shaking, grime-covered body. Her feet, in open-toed sandals, were white from the cold. She was dressed in brown overalls, and her arms looked as if the blood inside them had turned to ice.

Kitty took off her coat. 'Here, put this on.'

Elvira finished the apple and took the coat, sliding her arms into the sleeves and tying up the toggles. 'It's beautiful,' she said.

Kitty instantly felt the absence of her coat and hugged her arms around her body. She peered out through a crack in the outhouse. The light was going; it was nearly dark. For the first time, she started to feel nervous. The bus would have left by now and she would be stuck out in the countryside at night. She hadn't left her father a note; she

328

hadn't seen the point. She had thought she would be home before he got back from the hospital.

'Does my father know about you?' she said, crouching down next to Elvira and beginning to tremble slightly herself from the cold.

'I don't know,' said Elvira.

'We have to get home,' said Kitty, standing up and taking her twin's hand. 'It's nearly dark.'

'I can't go out there again, they'll kill me.' Elvira pulled her hand away from Kitty's and pushed herself backwards as if her sister was going to drag her out against her will.

'Kill you? What do you mean?' Kitty stood staring down at the sister she'd had no idea existed without a clue what to do next. She couldn't process what was happening; she felt scared and overwhelmed. 'I know, I'll go and get my father and we'll come back for you,' she said, stepping back towards the door they'd come in through.

'No! Please don't leave me,' Elvira begged.

'I need to go now, before it gets too late. My father will be worrying,' said Kitty. 'It will be fine, he will help you.'

Elvira pulled herself up on her knees and grabbed Kitty's hand. 'Something bad will happen to you and you won't come back.'

'Nothing bad will happen to me,' said Kitty, her voice shaking.

'It will, something bad will happen because *I'm* bad.' She had started to cry then, collapsed on the floor, and Kitty had sat down next to her and put her arms around her.

Eventually, after an hour or two had passed, Elvira had let Kitty go. She was too weak to fight any more. She had made Kitty promise that if she wasn't there when she came back with her father, she would use the key to the tunnels in the graveyard at St Margaret's and come and find her.

'Don't cry out, promise me you won't cry out.'

'I promise,' Kitty had said, so cold she couldn't feel her hands when Elvira took them.

Elvira waited all night for Kitty to return, and then finally, knowing something was wrong, she had left the shelter of the outhouse and ventured out into the breaking dawn in Kitty's red coat.

She could still remember the fear flooding her veins, her blood on fire with adrenaline. She had run as fast as her frozen feet would take her towards the church – the direction Kitty would have gone in to catch a bus back home and get help. Something had happened to her, she knew it. She would have been back by now if she had made it home.

She could picture the moment she saw it: Kitty's black patent shoe lying abandoned on the frozen ground. She had stood staring at it, fearing that her sister had fallen, that she was hurt somewhere, unable to move. She had looked around desperately for any sign of her, and as she looked up towards St Margaret's she saw Kitty's second shoe, reflecting the light of the rising sun. It was then that it hit her.

It hadn't crossed her mind before that moment. But since Kitty had left her, no one had called her name. No one had come looking in the outhouse. No one had come because they thought they had found her. They had found Kitty in the night, wandering in the direction of St Margaret's by mistake, and thought she was Elvira. Kitty had got lost, cried out in desperation for help and they had come running.

Her body convulsing now, Elvira looked up at St Margaret's in the morning light. If she went to the house now, Father Benjamin and Mother Carlin would realise their mistake and kill her to keep her quiet. She had to do what Kitty had set out to do. It was their only hope. She had to find their father and return with him to save her sister.

Her feet numb and cracked, she put on Kitty's shoes and began to run. Several times she slipped on the icy ground as she tried to get to the church. The last thing she remembered was seeing the cross on its roof through the mist. Not twenty feet away; she was nearly there. She was going to make it.

And then she fell.

Two days later, she had woken in hospital, the father she had never met asleep on the chair next to her bed, holding her hand.

Chapter Forty-Four

Monday 6 February 2017

The rear doors of the ambulance were open as Sam pulled up next to it in the car park of Nana's estate. Nana was on a trolley, with a mask over her mouth.

'Oh my God, Nana!' Sam screamed, rushing to hold her hand as they lifted her into the ambulance. 'What's happened to her? Is she going to be okay?'

'She's suffered a small heart attack. She's going to need surgery. Are you the lady that called the police?' said the paramedic, hooking Nana up to the monitor inside the ambulance.

'I'm her granddaughter. Where is the little girl who was with her? Is she up in the flat still?' said Sam, trying not to panic.

'I don't know about that, you'd have to go up there. We need to leave now. If you're not coming in the ambulance, can you step away, please.'

Sam leapt from the ambulance and hurtled towards the stairs, taking them two at a time. She raced along the corridor towards the apartment she knew so well, where a policeman was standing at the door.

'Emma!' Sam yelled, dashing past him.

'Hold on a minute, miss!' said the man, as two police officers in the front room turned to look at her.

'Where is she? Emma!' Sam screamed, darting from room to room. 'Where's my daughter?'

'Miss, I need you to calm down,' said a policewoman, walking towards her. 'Who are you?'

'I'm the granddaughter of the woman who lives here; she was looking after my daughter this morning. She must have been with her when she had her heart attack. Where is she?' Sam rushed into the bedroom again, looking under the bed. 'Emma?'

'Okay, please can you tell me how old your daughter is?' said the policewoman.

'She's four. Oh God, please let Ben have her. Please, God, please,' said Sam, pulling her phone from her bag and dialling Ben's number. She paced back and forth as the phone rang out.

'Ben, it's me, please can you call me back immediately. I need to know if you've got Emma. Nana's had a heart attack in her flat and Emma's not here. Call me.'

'Is there a neighbour, anyone you know who might have your daughter?' said the policewoman, watching Sam as she paced.

'No, I don't think so. Oh God,' said Sam as the phone inside her pocket began to ring. She answered it frantically. 'Ben?'

'Sam, it's Fred, I'm at St Margaret's. Kitty's here and I think she's got Emma. They've just gone through some kind of trapdoor in the graveyard, I'm going after them.'

Chapter Forty-Five

Monday 6 February 2017

Fred put his phone away and switched on his torch. He was standing at the top of a flight of stone steps that disappeared down into the darkness. He had lifted the trapdoor as carefully as possible, easing his fingers under the heavy wrought-iron plate and pulling it up and over until it finally fell onto the undergrowth covering the graveyard floor. He had waited, listening hard for any sign of life other than his own panicked breathing, but could hear only dripping water and the trickle of a stream. He had leant forward, attempting to ascertain how far down the steps went, but was hit with a sharp, putrid smell that made him retch and stumble back.

After spotting Kitty Cannon driving past Dr Jacobson's house, Fred had followed her car at a distance to the building site entrance. She had turned onto the bumpy track and in the fading winter daylight he had pulled up on the main road and watched her car slowly move alongside St Margaret's. With his engine still running, he had waited for her to get out before turning in and parking up behind her.

With darkness quickly descending, he had stepped out into the cold and seen a hole in the fence next to where Kitty had parked her car. At first there had been no sign of any workmen, but as he got closer to the house, he heard a car door slam and stopped in his tracks.

'Bye, Andy. Last day tomorrow, see you at dawn,' said a male voice.

'Later, Stan,' replied a second man, and Fred heard footsteps moving off in the direction of the house.

A car engine started, then the crackle of gravel was followed by silence. Fred had ducked down and waited as the man who had been left behind walked past the house and towards a Portakabin on the far side of the site. Last day tomorrow. He could already imagine the team standing around as the wrecking ball hit the house; slapping each other on the back as the external walls finally came crashing down. The preparations were finally in place; they were all set for demolition day.

Pausing for a moment to calm his breathing, he had stared up at the house. In the fading light it was hard to make out its features, but it struck him as a tragic sight: the ivy-covered Victorian mansion, which should have been a beautiful home full of happiness, now reflecting on its pitiful purpose in life and surrounded by a sea of machinery waiting to tear it limb from limb. The pointed turrets sticking up from its roof made its silhouette look jagged and harsh and it seemed to Fred like a giant creature unable to give up the fight even in its last moments, like a dying bull impaled in the ring.

A dog had barked in the distance then and Fred had turned to see a flash of light in the heart of the graveyard. He had made his way through the gap in the fence by Kitty's parked car and over towards its source. At the edge of the graveyard he had seen her, and realised she wasn't alone but holding hands with a child who was too small for him to have spotted before. Kitty had started down the steps, and the little girl had stopped at the entrance. Fred could see Kitty pulling her arm. As he got closer, he had heard the little girl crying, then for the first time he had got a good look at her and, just before the two of them had disappeared, realised with horror that it was Emma, Sam's daughter.

Now he stepped down onto the first step, shining his torch onto the green slime covering it and feeling his way along the wet stone wall before continuing onto the next. Pausing occasionally to listen for signs of life, he eventually reached the bottom, where he found himself standing in a head-height tunnel, a stagnant pool of rancid-smelling water at his feet.

Though he had left the trapdoor open, the smell was overpowering, and he tugged a handkerchief from his pocket and held it over his mouth. In his other hand he held the torch in front of him as he walked along the dark, saturated tunnel, his shallow breathing his only companion.

Every few steps, he stopped and looked back, terrified that someone would come across the trapdoor and slam it shut. Though the darkness was blinding, his steamed-up glasses disoriented him further as his breath quickened in his makeshift mask. He began to feel dizzy. With no idea where he was going, he reached out to touch the tunnel walls that were his only guide. It felt as if they were closing in on him.

'Fuck,' he muttered to himself as he bent over, coughing from the fumes.

As he paused to catch his breath, a child's cry rang out through the tunnel, suddenly followed by a loud bang like a heavy door slamming shut. Fred jumped. Distance was hard to judge, but the noise he had heard was in the opposite direction to the trapdoor and could not have been more than ten feet away.

'Where are you going?' Fred whispered to Kitty in the darkness.

Sam's face flashed into his mind as he picked up his pace and headed in the direction of the child's scream, the stagnant water soaking through his suede shoes.

At last he reached it. A brick wall at the end of the tunnel, and in the centre of it, a steel-framed wooden door. His mind was starting to blur as he felt for the handle and turned it. With a slow, moaning creak the door opened and a wall of smoke hit him.

Chapter Forty-Six

Monday 6 February 2017

With the policeman's shouts ringing in her ears as he tried to catch up with her, Sam ran through the graveyard desperately searching for the trapdoor. The police had driven her with their blues and twos screaming all the way from Nana's flat to St Margaret's, but when they had got there, the gates had been locked. She had opened the car door and made a run for it, rushing around the perimeter fence until she found the hole.

When she finally found the open trapdoor in the graveyard, smoke was pouring from the empty space below her. 'Oh my God, call the fire brigade!' she shouted over to the policeman, as she put her scarf over her mouth and started down the slippery steps in front of her.

'Stop, don't go down there!' shouted the policeman as she disappeared into the darkness.

Sam coughed through the thick weave of her scarf as she blundered through the stagnant water. The tunnel felt like hell on earth: dark and damp despite the smoke billowing around her. She lifted the scarf away from her face. 'Fred, where are you?' she shouted as loudly as she could.

'Sam!' came a voice from the blackness. As she ran towards it, she pictured Emma in the tunnel, alone and terrified without her.

'Fred!' she called again as she staggered through the thick smoke. 'Emma!'

Suddenly Fred lurched into view, coughing and retching.

Sam launched herself at him. 'Where's Emma?'

'She's with Kitty, they went through a door at the end of the tunnel, but you can't get through it now, she's started a fire,' said Fred.

Sam tried to keep going, but the thick wall of black smoke was poisoning her eyes and throat. The entire tunnel was engulfed and she could barely see.

'We can't leave her,' she said desperately. 'She could be trapped the other side of that door.'

'We'll find another way. Go back.'

Sam held her breath as she turned back, feeling her way through the smoke-filled tunnel. When she reached the trapdoor, she sucked in huge gulps of cold air as she and Fred helped each other up the steps. Outside, they stood, doubled over, as they coughed the smoke out of their lungs, then staggered through the graveyard towards the house.

'How has Kitty got Emma?' said Fred as they ran.

'It's not Kitty, it's her twin sister Elvira. She knows Nana, they went to school together; she must have been with them when Nana had her heart attack. The tunnel leads to the house. I have to get in there,' said Sam, stumbling in her desperation to reach her daughter.

As soon as the house came into sight, they both stopped dead in their tracks.

The whole of the ground floor was on fire. Smoke was billowing from the front door, and as Sam ran along the front of the house, every room was filled with leaping flames. Suddenly there was a huge explosion, and sparks and smoke poured from broken windows. Sam let out a primal scream, then ran to the front door and started trying to kick it in.

As Fred held her back, two policewomen came rushing over.

'My daughter's in there!' Sam cried. 'Emma!'

'You need to stay back, miss, the fire brigade will be here very soon,' said one of the officers.

Sam ignored them and ran around to the side of the house, desperate to find a way in. But the heat from the fire was making it impossible.

Suddenly she screamed, and Fred looked up in the direction of her horrified stare. On the roof, the figure of a woman was visible through the smoke, standing right at the edge. Sam ran towards the house again, the police-woman catching her and pulling her back. 'I can't let you go in there, miss.'

'We can't wait for the fire brigade! My daughter's up there!' As Sam thrashed and pulled, two more police cars pulled up outside the burning house, their sirens blaring.

Fred looked up at Kitty on the roof, then over at his car, which was parked less than a hundred metres away. The decision took no time at all. He ducked through the hole in the fence and opened the boot of the vehicle, scrabbling through the paraphernalia for his climbing shoes and head torch. In seconds he had pulled them on and was running towards the back of the house.

When he reached it, he looked up, assessing the texture of the bricks, through which he could feel the furnace from the fire. As he hesitated for a moment, Sam's screams for Emma and the fire brigade's sirens, still miles in the distance, pierced the descending night. He looked up and stepped back five paces, planning his route up the crumbling mortar, then took a breath and ran for the house, launching himself off the ground. Just as he grabbed the first-floor windowsill and began pulling his legs up, a policeman appeared on the grass below him.

'Hey! Get down from there!' The man ran over to him, grabbing at Fred's ankles, just as the heat from the window from which he hung hit him. Fred hooked his heel onto the windowsill and pulled himself up but the fire inside the house was overwhelming.

'Get down on the ground now!' the policeman shouted again, as Fred curled his legs up and away from his grasp.

Gripping the windowsill, he felt for an edge with his right foot, then found another with his left and carefully placed it on. His feet firm in their holds, he gripped the mantel tight and began swinging right to left, down and up, gathering momentum before launching himself up at a windowsill diagonal to him on the next floor up. For a second he was in mid-air, with nothing stopping him from falling twenty feet to the ground, then he grabbed the ledge, clutching on as gravity pulled his body down. He scrabbled at the wall for a hold for his feet and pushed them in as deep as he could, then hung still for a moment, his fingers cold, the ledge slippery, and looked around him for anything to help.

He hooked his heel up to the window ledge and pulled himself up onto it. He could see the roof now, but he still had two floors to climb. The ledge directly above him was two feet from his reach. He crouched down as low as he could and bounced twice before launching himself up onto it, clinging on before pulling himself up once more.

He looked up to where thick black smoke was billowing into the sky. He was nearly at the top, but the next window was a small attic one and too far away for him to reach. He caught sight of a wrought-iron lamp hanging from the wall and reached out, pushing against it with his right foot to check it was strong enough to take his weight. It held firm. He braced his foot on the light, stretching his arms up and feeling for more holes in the wall with his fingers.

The sound of fire engines arriving below was a comfort as he pushed himself up, listening to his own heavy breathing. Momentarily putting all his weight on the light, he moved methodically across the wall of the house like a spider, using the chipped-away brickwork as holds.

As the attic window appeared above him, he reached up to it, pulling himself up and pushing his foot into the bracket of a storm drain that ran around its perimeter. He paused for a moment, glancing down at the fire engines below him. They looked like wooden toys, the men rushing round them pulling out hoses, turning the ladders towards the house, just like the characters he'd imagined as a child in his own little worlds. He could no longer hear Sam, or anyone; just the rushing of the wind as it whipped the fire below him into an insurmountable frenzy.

The fire brigade were aiming water at the house from every angle as Fred carefully scrambled up the tiles that overhung the attic window, then ducked down to look across the roof. There, less than ten feet away, stood Kitty, with her back to him. Sitting slightly behind her was Emma. She was crying and begging for her mother. Kitty was ignoring her, leaning forward and looking down at the commotion below.

'They're all here for you,' she said, turning to the little girl, 'because you're loved.'

As Kitty turned away again, Fred crept silently towards them over the roof, terrified that one of the tiles would slip and make a noise. He could see one of the firefighters extending a ladder up towards them, closing the gap between them and the ground.

'Step back from the edge,' a loudhailer belted out from below them. 'There is a ladder on its way up to you and a member of the fire brigade will be coming up to help you.'

Fred looked around. A turret stood on the other side of the attic roof, and he slowly climbed up and over to it, keeping his eyes on Emma, who was curled up in a ball, crying. A whirring of machinery rang out as the top of the ladder appeared next to where Kitty was standing. Emma screamed, and Kitty grabbed her arm and pulled her in Fred's direction, her feet dislodging a tile and sending it smashing to the ground below.

'Stay back!' Kitty screamed to the fireman climbing up the ladder towards them.

'Mummy!' Emma cried out.

'Please, let us help you both down. We know you don't want any harm to come to the child,' said the fireman, attempting to climb onto the roof with them.

'Stay back, or I'll jump,' said Kitty, dragging Emma further away from the ladder. Emma let out a desperate cry.

Fred squatted down, his heart pounding mercilessly, his hands shaking. He tried to think straight, desperate for some idea of what his next move should be. He suddenly felt an overwhelming rush of panic. What if he only made things worse? He had been so arrogant, rushing to climb, to get to Emma, for one reason and one reason only. Because he loved Sam. And now he was here, there was a chance he could make a fatal mistake and get her daughter killed.

The thick smoke continued to billow past. Fred could hear the smashing of glass below them and feel the heat of the fire.

'Please, you need to come with me.' The fireman reached out his hand. 'We have to get you and the child down now, the house isn't stable.'

'Where were you when she needed you?' said Kitty, as Emma screamed in panic.

'Who?' said the fireman.

'Ivy. I saw her jump from the dormitory window. I was in the fields and I turned back and saw her on the roof. She had her arms outstretched like a bird. She wanted to fly. I wanted to be with her. I want to be with her now.'

'We care about you both and we want to help you, but we need to get you down from here now. Just let me come onto the roof and I can help.'

'No, stay back!' shouted Kitty.

Fred stared desperately at the space between him and Emma. Kitty had the little girl held tightly by the top of her arm. If he tried to grab her, Kitty could wrench her back from him and lose her balance in the process, sending them both falling to their deaths. He could see another ladder trying to get close to the back of the house, but being pushed back by the heat.

'Please just give me your hand. I can't stay up here much longer.' The fireman reached out with both hands, and Kitty took one more step away from him and closer to Fred.

An explosion rang out, and the fireman's radio crackled into life. As Kitty loosened her grip on Emma, Fred saw his chance and shot to his feet, running towards them across the pitched tiled roof.

'We can't put the fire out,' a voice said over the radio. 'We're pulling you back from the house, John.'

'There's a little girl up here, I can't leave her. For God's sake, please, give me the child,' shouted the fireman as the ladder began to pull away.

As Fred reached Emma, the ladder was already five feet away from the building. A second explosion went off below them, shaking the building to its core. Kitty stumbled, loosening her grip on the little girl.

'Jump, for God's sake, jump now!' shouted the fireman to Fred as he spotted him for the first time.

Fred felt a surge of adrenaline as he reached out his arms to Emma, who instinctively launched herself at him. He snatched Emma up from the roof and holding her tightly in his arms ran towards the ladder.

As the world stopped turning for a second, everything went silent, and Fred jumped.

Epilogue

Sam shifted in her seat and massaged her temples as she paused to read over what she'd just typed.

The Times *today reveals the incredible birth story of broadcaster Kitty Cannon, who died in an apparent suicide last month.*

Famous for prising the truth from her guests, much-loved host 'the Cannonball' hid a secret of her own, more explosive than anyone could have imagined.

She was born Elvira Cannon, but stole her dead twin sister's identity. Aged just eight, she was forced to impersonate Kitty in order to survive herself.

Today, writing for this newspaper, the great-granddaughter of the woman who made Elvira's survival possible lays bare a saga spanning six decades and four generations. Journalist Samantha Harper stumbled upon a story in her own background more shocking than any she has ever covered.

Some might say Kitty Cannon's life was a web of lies. But I have discovered that some lies are necessary. This is the case for Elvira and my grandmother. Both were so traumatised by the start of their lives that lying became the only option.

Elvira's life ended at St Margaret's and so did her sister Kitty's – the real Kitty, sixty years earlier.

It was where my grandmother Rose's life began.

The twins – born at St Margaret's Mother-and-Baby Home in Preston, East Sussex, in 1950 to their father's mistress – were dealt very different hands from the day they came into the world. While Kitty came out strong and fighting, Elvira struggled to breathe and was left for dead until she was later found to be alive and taken off to the infirmary. With his wife gravely ill in hospital, the twins' father, George Cannon, took home only the stronger sister, and left Elvira in the hands of the cruel nuns at St Margaret's.

While Kitty grew up in a life full of love and warmth, unaware of her birth mother, Elvira's tragic story continued when she was adopted by a young couple, only to be returned to St Margaret's at the age of six. There she stayed for two terrible years, working in the laundry as a child slave, and where, in a cruel twist of fate, she met my great-grandmother, Ivy Jenkins.

Sam paused from typing the article and looked down at Ivy's letters on the desk next to her. Letters she had pounced on like an addict, missing the signs from Nana that all was not well. So desperate to escape her job and living in Nana's cramped flat with Emma that she found herself walking into a trap of her own making, where her search for the holy grail of a story meant that she had to shine a floodlight on her own life. A tale that started with a young, innocent girl falling pregnant in 1956 and ended with her own car crash of a life: a single mother and soon to be a divorcee at the grand age of twenty-five.

'So is there going to be an inquiry?' After three unreturned phone calls to the Medicines and Healthcare Regulatory Authority in the weeks following the fire at

St Margaret's, Sam had finally got hold of one of their inspectors.

'You'll have to speak to the press office,' said the man, his voice flustered.

'I'm not press, I'm related to one of the children involved in the trials,' Sam lied. 'I just want to know if this is happening or not.'

Eventually she had got Scotland Yard's press office to confirm there would be an inquiry into the drugs trials that had taken place at St Margaret's.

'But it will be years before any kind of conclusion is reached, and we can't mention the trials in the meantime,' she said, looking up at Miles, the news editor, who was perched on the edge of her desk.

'And what about the deaths of everyone in these letters?' he said, looking down at the list of names in her notebook.

Sam thought about all the people whose deaths she was sure Elvira had been responsible for. From being at the scene of her father, George Cannon's, fatal car crash in the winter of 1961, through to Father Benjamin, whom she had probably lured into the tunnels underneath St Margaret's nearly fifty years later.

'They're saying there isn't enough evidence to reopen the inquests. Too much time has passed, I guess.'

'None of them?' Sam shook her head and Miles looked away. 'What about the psychiatrist?'

Sam scanned the press cuttings on her desk and lifted the one showing a portrait photograph of Richard Stone under the headline: *Psychiatrist found dead in apparent suicide.*

'I think Elvira had a part to play, but she did a pretty good job of covering her tracks – as always.' Sam smiled

349

weakly, thinking back to the morning she had spent in the coroner's court, listening to Richard Stone's son talk about how his mother's death had affected his father deeply.

'Did you know that Kitty Cannon was a client of your father's?' the coroner had asked the middle-aged man in a grey suit, white shirt and narrow black tie. His skin was pale, the dark circles under his eyes highlighting his bright blue eyes.

'No, but I knew he had one client he refused to stop working with, despite being well into his eighties. Mother was always trying to get him to retire completely, but he said he owed it to this woman to do his best. Now I guess we know why,' James Stone had mumbled into the small microphone in front of him.

'And did you know of his history with the drugs trials at St Margaret's?' The coroner had stared over his half-moon glasses, waiting patiently for Mr Stone's reply.

'Not really.' James coughed, and paused for a moment. 'I knew there was something unspoken about his past – and his relationship with my grandfather deeply troubled him. I know they didn't speak. Father used to descend into these periods of depression, which my mother called his black days. Looking back, I think she knew what was troubling him, but she protected us.'

'Do you think it is fair to assume that your father committed suicide, Mr Stone?' The coroner had removed his glasses, placed them on the desk in front of him and scribbled something on his notepad.

James Stone cleared his throat before speaking. 'The papers are saying that this woman Kitty Cannon was born at St Margaret's. Could she have been part of the trials and blamed him in some way? I mean, was there any evidence that she was there when he died?'

'Not that we are aware of, Mr Stone. Her fingerprints are in his consulting room, but that is to be expected.'

'So he took a sedative, then cut his wrists in the bath?' James Stone had said, his voice breaking.

The coroner nodded, then put his glasses back on and looked down at his notes. 'It appears that way. And not just any sedative: your father wrote to Cranium Pharmaceuticals a fortnight before his death to request a sample of cocynaranol for research purposes. Cocynaranol was the drug used in the trials at St Margaret's.' He looked up again. 'It would seem that the part he played tortured him more than anyone realised and in the wake of his wife's death overwhelmed him.'

'Well, we know there was a mass grave under that house,' said the news editor, snapping Sam back into the present. 'We can say there is going to be an inquiry into the drugs trials. We've got confirmation that the swap happened, and that the skeleton of an eight-year-old girl was found in the septic tank with the others. Is that right?'

Sam nodded, biting down on her lip at the thought of what little Kitty must have been through that night at the hands of Mother Carlin. Her remains had been found in the tank along with hundreds of others who were still being identified with the help of the records surrounding Richard Stone's body.

'It's still an incredible story, even without the deaths,' Miles continued. 'We want a first-person piece on this, Sam: you and your grandmother telling us how a baby taken from its mother affects generations of women.'

'But I don't want to be the story; Kitty's the story,' said Sam.

'Of course, but Kitty Cannon's dead, and you and your grandmother can bring it all back to life. You represent all the hundreds of women out there still affected by the evil of that place. I think you should open with the reunion between your grandmother and Ivy's mother. Do your best, Sam, I need it by tomorrow,' he added, as a colleague called him over and Sam watched him walk away.

Sam stared at the blinking cursor in front of her and felt the weight of responsibility for those hundreds of women who had given babies up at St Margaret's bearing down on her. Women in their sixties, seventies and eighties, picking up their copy of *The Times* as they ate their breakfasts, sitting alongside their husbands, who possibly knew nothing of their pain and suffering.

She let out a heavy sigh and lifted the page on top of the pile – the first of Ivy's letters, which had started it all.

12 September 1956

My love,

I am fearful that I have not heard from you. All my anxieties have been confirmed. I am three months pregnant. It is too late for anything to be done; it is God's will that our baby be born.

Nana: that baby was Nana. She still struggled to get her head around it and still felt angry with Nana for not telling her the truth about the letters right at the beginning.

She knew Nana hadn't planned for her to find Ivy's letter in the way she did; it was an accident that she had fallen asleep reading it. But to then lie to her about finding the

352

second letter, then the third; to not try to warn Sam when she was running headlong into a cataclysm that would affect them both so deeply – it was still hard to accept. She was her grandmother after all. Sam knew it would have been incredibly hard for her to find the words to explain, but she should have tried, for Sam's sake and Emma's.

'Why on earth won't they discharge me?' Nana had still been in hospital several days after the fire. 'I feel fine, and they are so short of beds.'

'Nana, you had a heart attack,' said Sam quietly.

'A mild one,' Nana snapped. 'And I'll have another one if I have to eat any more of this disgusting hospital food.'

'I'm sorry, but I really need to understand what happened with Ivy's letters.' Sam had looked at Nana, who was still staring at her uneaten lunch. 'Why didn't you just tell me?'

'*Just* tell you?' Nana had glared at her in a way that was unfamiliar to Sam. 'Which part? The letters? Kitty preying on me? I never even told Grandad about it. Once it all started, it was impossible to find the words. I knew you would have so many questions.'

'But I had a right to know.' Sam felt her voice shake; she had never argued with Nana before. Just another beautiful thing to have been infected by the toxins of St Margaret's.

'Of course you did, and I'm sorry. I hadn't read those letters in thirty years. I only got them out because it was my birthday and I wanted to think about the woman who brought me into the world, have a little cry. And for the first time, Grandad wasn't there to ask questions.'

'But I was,' she had said quietly.

'I wasn't prepared for you to find them or for you to react

the way you did . . . Nurse!' Nana had called across the room to the stressed woman, who hadn't heard her as she bustled past.

'It's unfair to try and blame me, Nana. You lied to me – you've never done that before.' Sam had wiped a tear away with the back of her hand.

'I'm not trying to blame you, but those letters made me feel sick. The way you reacted to them – it was overwhelming; you were like a hungry shark. Could you get the nurse, darling? I need to get home, I can't sleep with all this racket, I can't eat, this place is making me ill.' Nana had tried to adjust the pillows behind her head, tugging and pulling at them in between heavy sighs.

'Okay, Nana. Do you still want to see Maude? I thought I might bring her in tomorrow.'

'Well, I'll be gone by then, God willing, so she'll have to come to the flat.'

'You do want to see her, though, don't you?' Sam said gently. 'She's your biological grandmother after all.'

'For goodness' sake, yes, but I don't owe that woman anything.' Nana pulled her crossword puzzle book onto her lap and opened it as if signalling the end of the conversation.

Sam had left it then and gone to find the nurse, her mind preoccupied with how much she still didn't know about her grandmother. About her life before they had found each other. About Nana having a daughter of her own who was taken into care, became a mother in her teens and then died an alcoholic. About the pain of being adopted and discovering her birth mother had suffered unimaginable unhappiness before taking her own life. She could hardly begin to take it all in.

Now she took a deep breath, turned back to the letters that had lit a fire inside her and tried to gather her thoughts.

The letters my great-grandmother wrote speak of a world of heartache and backbreaking work unimaginable for any woman, but intolerable for someone eight months pregnant.

'The nuns are beyond cruel,' she wrote in December 1956. 'They beat us with canes or anything they can get their hands on if we so much as talk. A girl burnt herself so badly on the red-hot steel sheets that she developed a blister up her arm that is now infected. Sister Mary Francis just came over and scolded her for wasting time. The only time we are allowed to speak is to say our prayers, or to say 'Yes, Sister.' There are prayers before breakfast, mass after breakfast, prayers before bed. And then black emptiness before the bell at the end of the dormitory wakes us again at 6 a.m. We live by the bell; there are no clocks, no calendars, no mirrors, no sense of time. No one talks to me about what will happen when my baby comes, but I know there are babies here because I hear them crying at night.'

After the terrifying birth of her baby, Ivy's daughter – my grandmother – was taken from her against her will. Ivy slowly spiralled into a pit of depression that left her unable to sleep or eat. Her only joy was meeting a little girl called Elvira.

'So tell me once again why you broke into St Margaret's on two separate occasions.' Sam let out a sigh and thought back to the detective who had taken her and Fred into custody after the fire. She remembered him sitting back in his chair, his arms crossed over his bulging stomach. She had tried to answer his questions, attempted to stay calm, and be cooperative, but a childhood spent in police stations with her own mother haunted her.

'I told you, my grandmother gave me some letters from a girl who had a baby at St Margaret's.'

The police hadn't shown much interest in Ivy's letters or the fact that every person mentioned in them was dead. Their obsession began and ended with charging Fred for climbing up the side of St Margaret's while they stood doing nothing. Despite saving Emma's life, he was questioned relentlessly as to whether he'd had a part to play in starting the fire, and about how he came to be there in the first place.

'Yes, so you keep saying,' said the detective, looking up at the clock, 'but I don't see what right that gave you to trespass on private property.'

By the time they let her and Fred go with a warning, she understood why Elvira had killed all those people. She had known that if she didn't, they would never truly pay for what they had done; they would have died peacefully in their warm beds, their consciences clear. And she had got away with it by being patient.

It was only because of the fire she had started that they'd found the children's bodies at all.

'It was clever what she did,' said the detective as he walked Sam out. 'A rotting corpse isn't dead at all, it's teeming with life. Dead bodies release methane. Over decades it would have built up and become like a bomb waiting to go off. It was as if they were all working together to tell us where they were.'

Sam looked up at the three clocks on the wall in the *Times* newsroom. It was already midday. Four hours until she needed to leave with the first draft of her piece written.

On the morning she was to be admitted to a mental institution, Ivy took her own life, but not before making sure that her death would provide the distraction Elvira needed to escape and get a chance at life.

Elvira waited for two days in the freezing February cold, her feet in sandals, brown overalls her only clothing, until Kitty, smartly dressed in her warm red coat, turned up at church. The two girls instantly recognised one another, and ran away together to hide, but that night, when Kitty went to get help, in a cruel twist of fate the nuns captured her and, thinking she was Elvira, beat her so severely that they killed her. They threw her body into the septic tank at St Margaret's, where it lay hidden until the fire exposed it and that of hundreds of other babies and young children who had suffered a similar and terrible fate.

Waking up in hospital with the father she had never met holding her hand, Elvira was told that her sister was dead. For fear of being sent back, the terrified little girl said nothing, but over the years, her soul remained trapped at St Margaret's.

Sam's fingers shook as they hovered over the keys. All around her, the rows of monitors glowed like the lights of a runway leading across the floor to the huge black letters on the white wall: *The Times*, centred with the Hanoverian coat of arms.

Everyone had been friendly enough at the start of her first shift, as Miles had walked her round and introduced her to the team milling about. She had smiled politely at each new face, her overwhelming nerves meaning she forgot everyone's names as soon as they were told to her.

Now she sighed and looked around at all the unfamiliar

357

faces, some glaring at their screens, others chatting animatedly with one another, and ached for Fred to be sitting next to her. Taking the piss out of her, comforting her, bringing her endless cups of watery coffee. She missed him so much more than she missed Ben, whom she had barely spoken to for the past month, other than to discuss their ongoing arrangements for Emma. She'd tried to call Fred a couple of times, but he'd quit Southern News and disappeared.

She had never felt so alone, the gulf of St Margaret's eating away at her relationship with Nana like a cancer. They never really spoke about it now, but still it sat there, the elephant in the room.

She hadn't even really broached the subject of the piece with her – which was set to be a four-page spread in the *The Times* that Saturday. She'd had no idea her new boss would want to make her and Nana such a prominent part of the story, and the phrase 'sell your own grandmother down the river' was buzzing round in her brain like a trapped wasp.

She suddenly felt sick. She couldn't do it; she might as well be sitting in the office stark naked given how utterly exposed she felt writing this story the way Miles wanted it. It wasn't right. She'd just have to tell him – even if it meant losing the job she had fought so hard for.

She slowly highlighted the words she had spent the last two hours writing, and was about to hit delete when her mobile rang. Nana's name flashed up on the screen. Sam picked it up.

'Hi, Nana,' said Sam.

'Are you all right, darling? You sound tired.' Sam could hear classical music playing loudly in the background.

'I'm okay, bit of a rough day at work. How are you?'

'I'm fine. Guess who has invited us all to Sunday lunch?' said Nana. 'Maude Jenkins, isn't that lovely?'

'That is lovely.' Sam felt her voice breaking as she pushed back her chair and headed towards a quiet spot on the far side of the newsroom.

'Her neighbour is going to host, as Maude says it's too much for her to cook. Apparently you met her, Mrs Connors. You were very kind to her when her father died,' Nana continued cheerfully. 'Do you think Ben might want to come?'

Sam shook her head, her eyes filling with tears before she could stop them. 'No,' she managed. 'No, I don't think he'll come. We're barely speaking, Nana. He blames me for Emma being in that fire.'

'Well, that's nonsense. It wasn't your fault; none of it was your fault. If it was anyone's fault, it was mine.'

They both fell silent then. Sam could hear Nana's breathing on the other end of the phone.

'Nana, I need to talk to you about something. My new boss at *The Times* wants me to include us in this piece about Kitty. You and me. Write about how St Margaret's has affected us all.'

There was a long silence as Sam stood looking down at her shoes. A tear dripped onto them and she wiped her face with the back of her hand.

'Well, how do you feel about that idea?' Nana's voice was faint.

'I don't know, Nana. I'm scared, I guess, but I'm also tired of hiding away. I kind of feel as though in some way I need to do it. But I can't do it without you with me.' Sam bit her lip as tears streamed down her face.

359

'Then I think we should.' Nana's voice was soft. 'We owe it to those girls to be brave. We owe it to Ivy.'

'Really, Nana, are you sure?' Sam could barely get the words out.

'Yes, my darling, I'm sure.'

Author's Note

Whilst St Margaret's is totally fictional, it is an amalgamation of lots of homes and stories I have read about in my research, and the workhouse conditions portrayed within in it are, tragically, real. Admittedly they were reserved mostly for the Irish mother-and-baby homes, but some of the homes known to have existed in the United Kingdom embraced similar abuse.

Indeed, in her book *The Baby Laundry for Unmarried Mothers*, Angela Patrick speaks of being sent to a convent in Essex in 1963 that was 'run like a Victorian workhouse' and where, after eight weeks, she was 'forced to give up her son'. I believe there are still thousands of women in the UK who gave up babies and have kept that secret locked inside them – away from their husbands, subsequent children, and closest friends – because the sense of shame that these highly profitable institutions relied upon to function stays with them to this day.

Babies being taken from their mothers against their will first came to my attention when I read an interview with Steven O'Riordan, who has campaigned for many years for justice for the hundreds of thousands of women incarcerated in Ireland's Magdalene laundries.

After reading of the 'harrowing physical and psychological abuse' that the Magdalene women endured for decades, I wondered whether an apology made on 19 February 2013 by the then Irish Taoiseach (prime minister) to the Magdalene women went far enough. Not one of the nuns or priests who inflicted terrible suffering has been made to apologise; they remain tucked away safely out of the media glare. And it also occurred to me that those abusers who have subsequently died would have done so warm in their beds, their consciences utterly untroubled.

But what really resonated was that it was not 'evil nuns' that enabled the systematic abuse of thousands of women and children to take place. Nuns were the face of the institutions, but it was the wider communities in which these young girls lived that really allowed these atrocities to occur: the parents, the uncles, the doctors, the local government solicitors and adoption agencies – everyone who turned a blind eye.

And whilst the Magdalene stories have started to receive their rightful attention, most people are unaware that these institutions also existed in the UK.

Mother-and-baby homes first appeared in England in 1891. By 1968, there were a total of 172 known homes for unmarried mothers, the majority run by religious bodies. Many young women were pressured by their parents or social workers into giving up their babies against their will, with an all-time peak in 1968 of adoption orders granted in England: 16,164 in all.

Indeed, whilst the abuse that was so prevalent in Ireland was less common (although not unheard of) in the UK, what was undeniable was the pressure that was put upon young unmarried mothers to have their babies adopted. Information about welfare services, housing and financial help that could have enabled them to keep the babies was intentionally withheld from them so that they felt they had no choice. The experience traumatised many of these women to such a degree that they have suffered years of mental and/or physical ill health ever since, and many were unable to have more children.

In reference to the drugs trials, there is no evidence that these ever took place in the UK, but trials in Ireland are widely reported – see Sources below. As with the abuse at the homes, I suspect no one has ever really been brought to account for these drugs trials, and it is that lack of accountability that provided the inspiration for *The Girl in the Letter*.

Sources

Books

Sue Elliott, *Love Child*. Vermilion, London, 2005

Angela Patrick with Lynne Barrett-Lee, *The Baby Laundry for Unmarried Mothers*. Simon & Schuster, London, 2012

Nancy Costello, Kathleen Legg, Diane Croghan, Marie Slattery and Marina Gambold with Steven O'Riordan, *Whispering Hope: The True Story of the Magdalene Women*. Orion, London, 2015

Ann Fessler, *The Girls Who Went Away: The Hidden History of Women Who Surrendered Children for Adoption in the Decades Before Roe v Wade*. The Penguin Press, New York, 2006

Nancy Newton Verrier, *The Primal Wound: Understanding the Adopted Child*. Gateway Press, Baltimore, 1993

Sheila Tofield, *The Unmarried Mother*. Penguin Books, London, 2013

Films

The Magdalene Sisters, Momentum Pictures, 2002

The Forgotten Maggies Documentary, Steven O'Riordan Productions, 2009

Philomena, 20th Century Fox, 2013

Websites

www.motherandbabyhomes.com

News articles

'Irish care home scandal grows amid allegations of vaccine testing on children', *Telegraph*, 9 June 2014

'Thousands of children in Irish care homes at centre of "baby graves scandal" were used in secret vaccine trials in the 1930s', *Daily Mail*, 6 June 2014

'Special Investigation – vaccine trials on children worse than first thought', *Irish Examiner*, 1 December 2014

'Nun admits children involved in medical trials', *Independent*, 9 June 2014

Acknowledgements

As Ivy wrote, I do not know where to begin.

Firstly, I would like to thank my mother for making up stories for my little sister Claudia and me at bedtime. She would invariably fall asleep halfway through – due to the exhaustion of being a working mother – then, much to our amusement, wake up with a startle and continue with a totally different story. Now, more than ever, I treasure those memories. Thank you also to Mr Thomas of St Lawrence Junior School, who introduced me to my first page-turner, reading a chapter of Roald Dahl's *Boy* to St Lawrence Junior school every Monday morning.

Thank you to my husband, Steve, who I told about an idea I'd had for a novel one fateful evening. Fast-forward several years (and two babies, one dog, two house moves) to me crying down the phone that I'd been offered a two book deal. Thank you for your unfaltering belief in me, for taking the girls out every weekend so I could write, for endlessly talking plots, keeping me focused, dusting me down after every draft. I could not have done it without you, baby, baby, baby. I love you.

Huge thanks also to Helen Corner-Bryant at Cornerstones Literary Consultancy who saw some potential in my first ramblings and put me in touch with the brilliant Benjamin Evans. Thank you Ben for caring so much about the book and going above and beyond to teach me the art of storytelling. Thanks also to the gorgeous Suzanne Lindfors who spent days copywriting an early draft in the hope it might catch an agent's eye. It worked, I hit the jackpot when Kate Barker took me on, working on the book with me for a year, with no guarantee of a deal. Kate, you changed my life that day, you are my fierce protector and you have become a true friend, so thank you.

Thanks also to Sherise Hobbs at Headline, for making the wait so short, for being so thoughtful yet determined to always get the right result and, of course, for being the best editor a girl could wish for. Thank you also to Georgina Moore, Emily Gowers, Phoebe Swinburn, Viviane Basset and Helena Fouracre at Headline. So many books to look after, yet you always make me feel that mine's got your undivided attention. Thank you also to Caroline Young for my beautiful book cover.

Thank you to Polly Harding for always understanding me, to Sophie Cornish for teaching me true grit and for holding my hand through everything for as long as I can remember. Also to Claudia Vincenzi for having my back for all time and making me laugh till I sneeze. Thank you to my lovely brother-in-laws Mike Harding, Simon Cornish and Stuart Greaney for putting us all back together and to Penny & Paul Vincenzi for showing us all what it is to be brave.

Thank you Claire Quy, Sophie Earnshaw, Sophy Lamond and Laura Batten for being all the therapy I ever need and also to Clodagh Higginson/Bridget for your incredible help with all things reporting and for loving me just the way I am. Thanks to Sue Kerry for being researcher extraordinaire, for the childcare and for sharing your experience of working in Sussex Police. Thank you to Chris Searle at Chimera Climbing for all your technical input. Thanks to Rebecca Cootes for thrashing out the plot with me over endless cups of tea and for screaming in the playground when I sold my book. Thanks to Esra Erdem and Emily Kos for all your invaluable help with my babies and to the lovely Laura Morris for all of Merlin's walks. Thank you to Rachel Miles, Kate Osbaldeston, Sophie Cornish, Steve Gunnis and Honor Cornish for reading the early drafts and for your extremely helpful feedback. Thank you to Nicole Healing for all your social media expertise and friendship.

And last but not least, to Grace and Eleanor – as JG Ballard so beautifully put it, 'The pram in the hall is the greatest motivator of all'. I love you beyond words, you are my loves, my life, my inspiration.

Keep in touch with

EMILY GUNNIS

Join the community on Facebook
f @EmilyGunnisAuthor

Connect on Twitter
🐦 @EmilyGunnis

Follow on Instagram
📷 @emilygunnis